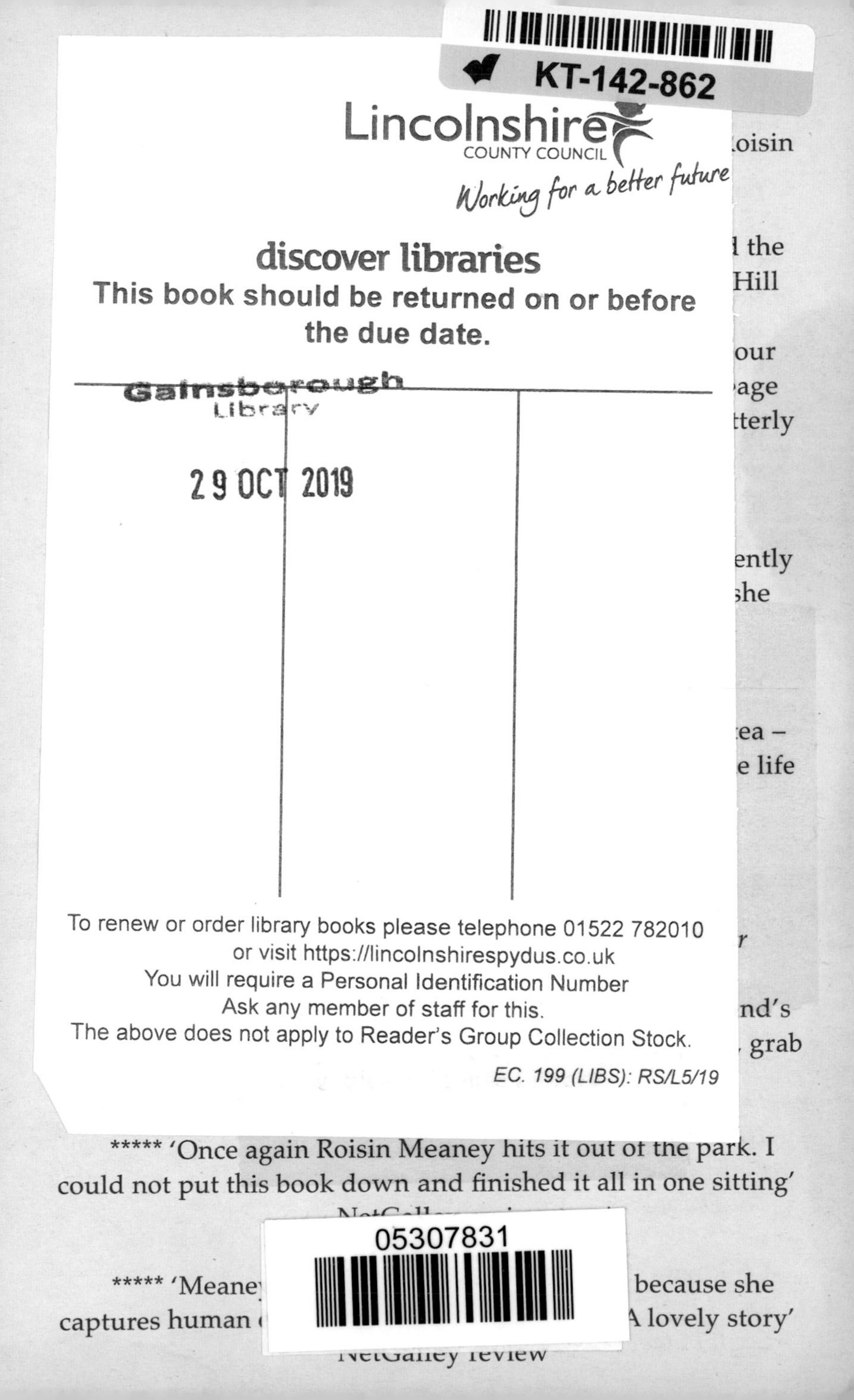

...oisin

...l the
...Hill

...our
...age
...tterly

...ently
...she

...ea –
...e life

...r

...nd's
..., grab

***** 'Once again Roisin Meaney hits it out of the park. I could not put this book down and finished it all in one sitting'
NetGalley review

***** 'Meane... because she captures human ... A lovely story'
NetGalley review

Roisin Meaney was born in Listowel, County Kerry. She has lived in the US, Canada, Africa and Europe but is now based in Limerick city. She is the author of numerous bestselling novels, including *The Reunion, Love in the Making, One Summer* and *Something in Common,* and has also written several children's books, two of which have been published so far. On the first Saturday of each month, she tells stories to toddlers and their teddies in her local library.

Her motto is 'Have laptop, will travel', and she regularly packs her bags and relocates somewhere new in search of writing inspiration. She is also a fan of the random acts of kindness movement: 'they make me feel as good as the person on the receiving end'.

www.roisinmeaney.com
@roisinmeaney
www.facebook.com/roisinmeaney

Also by Roisin Meaney
The Reunion
I'll Be Home for Christmas
Two Fridays in April
After the Wedding
Something in Common
One Summer
The Things We Do For Love
Love in the Making
Half Seven on a Thursday
The People Next Door
The Last Week of May
Putting Out the Stars
The Daisy Picker

Children's Books
Don't Even Think About It
See If I Care

Roisin MEANEY

The Street Where You Live

HACHETTE
BOOKS
IRELAND

First published in Ireland in 2017 by
HACHETTE BOOKS IRELAND
First published in paperback in 2018

1

All characters in this publication are fictitious and any resemblance to real persons, living or dead, is purely coincidental.

Cataloguing in Publication Data is available from the British Library

B format paperback ISBN 9781473642997
Ebook ISBN 9781473643017

Typeset in Palatino by redrattledesign.com

Printed and bound in Great Britain by
Clays Ltd, St Ives plc

Hachette Books Ireland policy is to use papers that are natural, renewable and recyclable products and made from wood grown in sustainable forests. The logging and manufacturing processes are expected to conform to the environmental regulations of the country of origin.

Hachette Books Ireland
8 Castlecourt Centre
Castleknock
Dublin 15, Ireland

A division of Hachette UK Ltd
Carmelite House, 50 Victoria Embankment, EC4Y 0DZ
www.hachettebooksireland.ie

To readers everywhere, heartfelt thanks.
I'd be nothing without you.

Saturday, 6 August

'Who took my lip balm? I left it right here. Right *here*. Ultan, did you take it?'

'I most certainly did *not*. I wouldn't *dream* of using someone else's lip balm: *God*.'

'Have we a full house, did anyone see?'

'Rita, your lip balm is on the floor, over there . . . No, there, under that chair.'

'Has someone got a comb I could borrow?'

'There's no paper in the loo, just letting everyone know.'

'I'm going to be sick.'

'You're not. Deep breaths, you'll be fine.'

'George, your shirt tail is sticking out.'

'Who's got the right time?'

'I've lost my phone. Has anyone seen my phone?'

' . . . Are you alright?'

'I'm fine.'

But Emily didn't look fine. She looked far from fine. She was paler than usual, and blinking too rapidly, and worrying at her bottom lip with her teeth. She looked, Molly thought, as if she was just waiting for the nod from someone to burst into tears, to fall apart completely.

In the tiny gaps between the chatter in the dressing room, rain could be heard pelting against the windows. Molly caught her daughter's hand and squeezed it. 'It'll be OK, love. You always get this way before a performance. You'll be grand as soon as we start, wait and see.'

The door opened and Christopher appeared. You could almost smell the tension from him. Dark hair rumpled, jaw clenched tight, red dicky bow askew. 'Anyone seen Jane? Anyone heard from her?'

No one had seen Jane. No one had heard from her.

It was ten minutes to performance.

Six weeks earlier

For the fifth day in a row the country had sweltered. Temperatures climbing into the early thirties, tar turning to goo on roads, ice-cream vans chiming around housing estates from early morning. Since the start of the unaccustomed heatwave, the weather had taken precedence over all other happenings. Sunburnt splashing beachgoers featured on the front pages of newspapers each day, politicians and scientists held earnest discussions on global warming, water safety messages were broadcast regularly across the airwaves.

In chemists and supermarkets, supplies of sun protection cream and hair depilatory products disappeared as quickly as they were produced. Meteorologists smiled with relief, if not downright smugness, on television screens each evening as they predicted more uninterrupted sunshine, more unblemished blue skies.

But now it was heading towards eight in the evening, and while the fierce burn of the day had loosened its grip, the air was still warm and heavy. Walking to the primary school that lent the choir one of its classrooms to sing in, shirt sleeves rolled to his elbows, Christopher Jackson was aware of a fresh layer of sweat on his skin, despite the cool shower he'd stood under for a good ten minutes after getting home from work. His armpits felt damp and ticklish; moisture crawled lazily down his spine. The palm that was curled around the handle of his briefcase felt unpleasantly clammy.

Notwithstanding this mild physical discomfort, his mood was buoyant. Tonight, after eight weeks of polishing already-learnt songs and numerous voice training exercises and general honing of its melodic skills, the choir was beginning to rehearse for its next performance. The concert theme, a tribute to the popular musicals of the twentieth century, was one particularly close to his heart: as a boy, those splendid old films had inspired and nurtured his love of music, and the playlist he'd devised was made up of all his favourite numbers. It boded well, and he was quietly hopeful.

This time his group of singers might finally make him proud. This time they might manage to avoid the errors he'd noticed in previous performances. He was pretty sure most listeners would have missed those millisecond miscalculations in timing, those tiny variations in timbre, those minute errors in tone or rhythm, but *he'd* heard them, and they'd stung.

In fairness though, they hadn't done too badly in the eighteen months or so since he'd brought the choir into being, and selected the eighteen male and female voices that comprised it. They'd picked up a couple of minor festival awards and earned some positive reviews in the local press, and recently they'd received an invitation to participate, albeit in a very minor way, in a prestigious choral event in Wales next year. People were beginning to take notice of Lift Up Your Voices, which was gratifying.

He must try to hold his patience during this set of rehearsals.

He must try to coax rather than demand results from them. It wouldn't be easy – he'd never been good at counting to ten – but he'd do his best. A new member had joined them lately, a replacement for Grace, whose arthritic hip had forced her to bow out. The new arrival – Jane something or other – had a richly rounded voice that sat nicely in the altos. Yes, he was definitely hopeful this evening.

When he arrived at the school he found a few choir members already waiting by the side door. Conversations petered out as he approached; one or two said hello, others simply nodded at him. He opened the door and stood back to allow them entry, tapped in the alarm code as they walked ahead of him towards the classroom.

They weren't his friends. He was well aware of it, and not at all put out. He had a professional relationship with them, which was precisely what was needed. He hadn't founded the choir to make friends.

In the room he opened his briefcase and lifted out the sheaves of stapled pages as the remaining members showed up in ones and twos and took up their usual positions. 'Fifteen songs,' he told them, distributing the pages, 'most of which I assume will not be new to you. I shall expect you to be word perfect within three weeks.' Looking pointedly here at Ultan, who had the sense to blush.

Ultan McCormack's beautifully modulated tenor voice – he claimed, possibly truthfully, to be directly descended from John – was all that stood between him and ejection from the choir. Always last to learn the lyrics, always casting sneaky glances at his pages as they sang, long after Christopher had banned them – how hard could it be, for God's sake? – but the voice saved him, just about.

Halfway through the warm-up exercises, the door to the hall was flung open. 'Sorry, sorry!' She hurried in, peeling off a diaphanous outer layer. 'Traffic was murder. Hello, everyone.'

Christopher regarded her with irritation, aware of the ripple of amusement her entrance had caused. The scales practice interrupted now, they'd have to return to the start. 'I don't tolerate lateness,' he told her, whisking the final bunch of pages from the table behind him. 'Leave home earlier next time.'

'I will,' she promised, reaching for the sheaf, the movement causing a waft of her scent, fingertips brushing his. 'I definitely will, Christopher.'

She was good-looking: he wasn't blind to it. Light brown hair cut to frame her face in choppy layers, shot through with gold and caramel streaks. Enormous dark-fringed eyes of a startling blue, skin without a blemish, unless you counted the mole – beauty spot? – to the left of her generous mouth. She had a face you didn't ignore, and she knew it. Well turned out too, clothes cut to accentuate her curves. Money there, clearly. A gold ring on the usual finger, thick and wide. Somebody had snapped her up.

Three weeks she'd been with them. Long enough for her to have made her mark, with breezy comments thrown into the pauses between songs, usually earning her a titter from the others. Plenty of sidelong glances too, from the male choir members. Even Ultan, who definitely looked in another direction for his amusement, seemed taken with her: Christopher had heard them giggling together at the break.

Jane, who was most certainly not plain. But pretty or not, good voice or not, if she kept up her nonsense he'd have no qualms about sending her packing. Ultan might be slow to learn his words, but during rehearsals he had focus, like the rest of them.

At nine thirty on the dot Christopher called a halt. He waited while the room emptied out, checking his phone for emails. When he looked up, only Jane was left.

'Looks like we've missed the crowd,' she said, drawing on her gossamer thin jacket, or wrap, or whatever it was. 'You do know they've gone to the pub to complain about you, don't you? At least, that's what they did last week.'

Smiling at him, waiting for his reaction. He was in two minds about her, torn between annoyance at her refusal to treat him like her director, and his reluctant physical attraction.

'I'm sure you'll catch them up,' he said, 'if you hurry. I'd hate you to miss the entertainment.' Holding the door open for her.

She walked towards him, taking her time. 'You know, I'm not really in the mood for them tonight. Why don't we find another pub and you can buy me a drink?'

Again he felt a dichotomy within him, part exasperation, part flattery. 'I don't mix business with pleasure,' he said, letting his gaze fall deliberately to her wedding ring.

If she noticed, she gave no sign. 'Oh, come on, Christopher – the choir isn't business, it's fun. Don't you enjoy it?'

He frowned. Here was his chance to tell her that she needed to treat the rehearsals with a little more respect, show up on time, cut out the silly remarks – but for some reason he said none of this. For some reason he remained silent.

She laid her palm on his chest, pressed lightly with the tips of her fingers. 'Come on,' she said softly, 'loosen up a little,

Christopher. I'm just looking for a different kind of fun, that's all. No strings – and I can be very discreet.'

She was propositioning him. It was outrageous. He was her choir director: entering into any kind of relationship with her would be most inappropriate, totally unprofessional.

But he hadn't had that kind of fun in months – and if nobody found out about it, where was the harm? The fact that she was more than likely married was her problem, not his.

'We're both consenting adults,' she went on, slipping two fingers between his shirt buttons. 'What do you say?'

Her touch on his bare skin, light as it was, sent a bolt of desire through him. 'It can't get out. No one can know – and I mean no one.'

Her eyes widened. 'I'm like the grave, Christopher.'

Outside the coast was clear, the others gone. He sat into her red car and directed her to his house. Once there, she ignored the glass of wine he poured for her.

'I have a better idea,' she said, slipping off her outer layer, letting it drop onto his carpet. 'This way,' she said, making for the stairs. Knowing he would follow.

* * *

Molly Griffin loved the heat. She basked in it like a seal. True, the muggy nights made sleep a challenge, had her tossing and turning in sweaty sheets, but a shower in the morning perked her right up – and wasn't it worth anything to be able to pull out the bright, summery clothes that usually lived at the back of her wardrobe? Wasn't it lovely to witness happy faces everywhere she looked – well, apart from the ones who complained about the heat – to see winter-pale faces freckling and blooming, to feel the sun warm on her own skin?

And this morning was particularly uplifting. This morning, as she cycled towards the house of a woman she had yet to meet, Molly's heart pattered joyfully at the thought of no more Websters. No more working her way through Bella Webster's laminated list for a hundred and twenty minutes every Wednesday: two apricot bathrooms to be cleaned, five pale blue work shirts to be ironed, the insides of all the windows to be washed, the wooden floors to be mopped, the houseplants that had long since taken over the smaller living room to be misted – not watered, *misted* – and so on, all the while taking no notice whatsoever of Polonius, or Patagonia, or whatever daft name they'd given the bony Siamese cat that sprawled in his special chair, hissing softly at her if she came within six feet of him. And never a single window opened in case he did a runner, cloying cat smell fighting eternally with her furniture polish, no matter how much of it she used.

No more of that, ever – because last week Carl Webster had gathered up his lump sum and his gold watch and his pension and taken himself, Bella and the Siamese off to France, to live out their days in a village somewhere high in the mountains, where Bella would undoubtedly hunt down some unfortunate French equivalent to Molly, and subject her to the laminated list.

In fairness though, she hadn't left Molly stranded. *My niece Linda is looking for someone,* she'd said, and so Wednesday mornings had been passed on to Linda, who'd sounded normal enough on the phone. *Our house is third from the end, the one with the mailbox at the gate. If you get lost give a shout.* She didn't sound like someone who was in the habit of laminating. She didn't sound like Siamese cats were her thing.

Molly pedalled along, legs pumping as she whizzed past parked cars, relishing the breeze on her hot cheeks. *You go too fast on that bike*, Emily told her, more like her mother than her daughter. Emily would never speed: it wasn't in her nature. Emily kept within the limits in everything she did – which of course wasn't a bad thing.

As she cycled, Molly sang. She sang about a beautiful morning, with the corn as high as an elephant's eye. The August concert would be a breeze: she already knew each song inside out; all she'd have to learn were her alto parts. She'd grown up with the soundtracks of the old musicals: her father had had the whole collection on vinyl. For as long as she could remember she'd sung along to *My Fair Lady*, *Oklahoma!*, *South Pacific*, *West Side Story* and the rest – and singing them now evoked the innocent happiness that her early childhood memories were drenched in.

She loved being in the choir, she adored it. To think it might never have happened if Christopher hadn't come home that day and heard her singing as she'd thumped the dust from his mats. The idea of joining a choir would never in a million years have occurred to her – choirs were for serious singers, polished singers – but when he'd told her he was starting one, and suggested she come along to the auditions, she'd gone in a flash, and dragged Emily with her, and he'd accepted both of them.

He certainly took his role as choir director seriously. She wondered how he didn't pop a blood vessel sometimes, he got so fired up when they went wrong. She'd been surprised to see that tempestuous side of him: there'd been no sign of it in the little interaction she'd had with him up to then, and Emily said he was quite distant anytime *she* encountered him at work – but there was nothing distant about him at the choir practices.

Molly didn't take too much notice of his outbursts though. He wasn't really mad at them, he was just trying to knock them into shape, get the best out of them – it showed that he cared, didn't it, when he got so het up? Poor man, he didn't deserve the things some of the members said about him in the pub afterwards – but she had to admit that Ultan was hilarious whenever he took him off.

She reached the road where Linda lived – and there was the promised mailbox by the gate of the third from last house. A silver car was parked in the driveway, next to a well-tended lawn. A small yellow tricycle sat by the red front door, as if waiting to gain entrance. Good: she liked houses with little children in them, even if it meant more mess, which it usually did.

The house was detached, like the others on the road. Fair bit of money here, by the look of it – which would make sense for a relative of the Websters. Stone walls, bay windows to either side of the door. Three or four bedrooms; at least one en suite, more than likely.

She propped her bike by the door and rang the bell, feeling the familiar pleasant tremble in her legs after the vigorous pumping she'd given them. Her dress was sticking to her – she pulled it free and shook out the damp creases. The sun was hot on the back of her neck as she stood dabbing at her face with a tissue and listening for a sound from within.

And here it came, the soft pat of approaching footsteps. The door was opened: she saw blonde hair, navy top, white shorts, tanned legs.

'You must be Molly.' A hand outstretched. 'Linda. Thanks for coming.'

Despite the heat, her hand was cool. 'Where should I leave my bike?' Molly enquired.

'You can wheel it around the side. It'll be fine.' She emerged and lifted in the yellow tricycle. 'Isn't it hot?'

The tiled hallway was blessedly shady. Molly smelt lemons – maybe from Linda herself – and the strong dark scent of real coffee.

'Let me get you some water.' Linda led the way into the kitchen, a light-filled room that ran the width of the house, with a dining area at the far end and a pair of patio doors that opened onto the back garden. Through them Molly saw a small curly-headed child seated cross-legged on the grass outside, surrounded by an assortment of soft toys. A little tea party maybe, like Emily used to have with her dolls at that age.

Linda held a glass beneath a spout in the door of her giant fridge and pressed a button, and a slush of water and ice tumbled out. 'Whatever you normally do will be fine,' she said, handing the glass to Molly. 'The usual cleaning, nothing out of the ordinary. You come highly recommended by Aunt Bella. We'll try to stay out of your way.'

All very promising. Molly gulped the water as Linda indicated a door to the left of the fridge. 'That's the utility room: all the stuff you should need is there. Let me know if there's anything else you want me to get. My office is the room at the foot of the stairs – just give a clean to the floor and leave the rest; it looks messy but I know where everything is.'

'I usually start with the upstairs, and work my way down.'

'Fine, whatever you prefer. I'll leave you to it then.' She crossed the room and went out through the patio doors, sliding them half closed after her.

Molly drained her glass and rinsed it. In the neat utility room she found bucket and mop, vacuum cleaner, a bundle of fresh cloths and dusters and a collection of cleaning fluids and sprays. Over the following hour she worked steadily through the upstairs rooms, pulling out beds to get at the dust behind, going down on hands and knees to wipe skirting boards. Shining mirrors, wiping fingermarks from door handles and window catches. Polishing wooden floors, mopping the bathroom tiles, running the vacuum cleaner over the landing carpet.

In one of the bedrooms that overlooked the back garden – the child's room, full of toys and picture books – she glanced out and saw her playing at a sandpit by the fence. Blue T-shirt, green shorts, a pair of yellow sandals on the small feet. An only child, she must be, just two of the four bedrooms in use. Linda looked to be in her mid-thirties: time enough for brothers and sisters, if they were in the plans.

In the master bedroom a photo in a silver frame on the dressing table caught her eye. Linda held her little girl in her arms, each gazing into the other's face, noses practically touching. A beach scene, sand dunes climbing up behind them. A year or two earlier, Molly thought, given the more babyish look of the child, who wore only a little pair of orange swimming trunks. The big curly mop of her.

The child's father, maybe, had taken the photo. Funny there was no snap of him around the place. Odd that she saw no man's slippers by the bed, no pyjamas beneath a pillow, no tie or jacket slung across a chair. No evidence of a man's presence in the bathroom either. No shaving foam, no aftershave or men's cologne.

Maybe they were living apart, for whatever reason – or

maybe he was dead. None of her business: if Linda wanted to tell her, she'd tell her.

The house was silent on her return downstairs. She dealt with the remaining rooms, leaving the kitchen till last. In the small office she ran the vacuum over the floor and left the rest alone as instructed. Nothing she could see offered a clue as to what work Linda did – a laptop computer and a printer sat on the desk, along with a stack of manila folders, a mug of pens and a little dish of paperclips; hard-backed notebooks and box files filled the trio of shelves behind. Linda had called it messy, but Molly had seen far worse.

As she re-entered the kitchen she saw Linda and her little girl sitting now at the wrought-iron table on the patio, a jug of cloudy liquid between them. She cleaned the worktops and the sink, wiped down the table, emptied the dishwasher and discovered homes for the crockery and cutlery.

As she worked she listened to the high-pitched chatter of the child, audible through the half-open patio door. She seemed to be outlining to her mother in great detail the plot of a film she'd seen, or maybe a story someone had told her: '. . . an' then the pig jumped into the car and drived away really fast, an' the duck runned after him but he was too slow to catch up, an' then he falled into a puddle an' his clothes got all wet an' he got mad. It was *so* funny, Mummy.'

Nice to hear it. A long time since small children had featured in her own house. She slid the patio door closed to polish its glass. Linda looked up at the sound and smiled at Molly, but the child didn't turn her head. Shy in front of strangers maybe.

She pulled the door open again before sweeping and mopping the floor. In the utility room she rinsed her various cloths and draped them over the waiting clothes horse. She undid her pinafore and put it into her rucksack. The clock on the kitchen wall read ten past twelve.

She returned to the patio. 'All done,' she said.

Linda got to her feet. 'Thanks, Molly – let me get your money.' She entered the room and crossed the floor, Molly following. The child remained seated at the table.

'What's your little girl's name?'

Pulling open a drawer, Linda smiled. 'A lot of people make that mistake. It's Paddy, and he's a he.'

'Oh, sorry – I thought, with the hair . . .'

'Not at all. It's my own fault – I can't bring myself to cut those gorgeous curls. He's starting school in September; I suppose I'll have to do it then, or he'll be teased to death.' She handed Molly the envelope. 'Thanks so much: can I get you some more water, or a glass of lemonade, before you go?'

'Mummy.'

They turned. The child stood at the patio door. 'Can I have a ice-cream?' Gaze directed towards his mother, ignoring Molly but presenting her with her first proper look at him.

Jesus God almighty.

She was instantly thrown back twenty-five years. He was the image, the absolute image. The same little face, look, see the dark-fringed grey eyes, the full mouth, the sharp nose, the small cleft in the pointed chin. Take away the curls and everything else, everything, was the same.

He was Philip. He was her son. She was looking at four-year-old Philip.

'Molly?'

She dragged her eyes away from him.

'Water? Or lemonade?'

'No, thank you . . .'

'Are you alright?'

'I'm fine . . . It's just the heat. I'm grand.'

She wasn't fine, and the heat had nothing to do with it. Her face was cold, her mouth dry. Her mind was spinning. She stowed the envelope at the bottom of her rucksack, watching as Linda peeled the wrapper from an ice-lolly and gave it to him, as he turned and trotted out through the patio doors, again not paying Molly a blind bit of notice.

It was a coincidence, it had to be. Just a coincidence. People resembled other people all the time, didn't they? Look at that magazine Emily brought home from the supermarket: they had a page of photos each week, ordinary people who looked like celebrities. You'd swear some of them had to be related. It happened.

But cycling home she couldn't let it go, kept turning what she knew around in her head. There was no sign of a father on the scene. Philip would be gone five years in March: he'd left the day after Molly's fifty-second birthday. This boy was starting school in September, so presumably he was four. It fitted, everything fitted – and it would make sense of so much if it was true.

Could it possibly be true? Could this curly-headed child be Philip's son, her grandson?

It could. It could. She might be a grandmother. Granny Molly.

Out of nowhere, a dog darted out suddenly through a gateway and ran right in front of her bicycle. She pulled sharply on the brakes, causing her front wheel to skew sideways and collide with the kerb. The impact sent her flying over the handlebars: she landed hard on the path, the breath knocked out of her. As she lay sprawled and shocked, afraid to try to move in case she couldn't, waiting for the pain to kick in, she heard someone's hurried approach.

'Don't move. Stay still.'

A female voice. A woman crouched beside her. 'I'm a doctor, I live right across the street. I saw what happened. That dog is a menace. Don't try to move just yet. Where does it hurt?'

Molly did a lightning mental check. Her palms were starting to sting, her knees to burn. 'My hands,' she said, her voice wobbling, 'and my knees.' A painful smarting began in the cheek that rested on the road. 'My face.'

'Can you wriggle your toes?'

She tried. 'Yes.'

'That's good.' She felt the woman's hands coming to cradle her neck. 'Now I want you to roll slowly onto your side. Stop if anything hurts too much. Take your time.'

Molly obeyed, moving in little cautious jerks, trying to keep the weight off her sore palms. Everything, it seemed now, was stinging.

'You OK?'

'I . . . think so.' She began to feel immensely foolish. Her cheek continued to throb painfully. She wondered what it looked like.

'Can you sit up? I'm afraid I can't bear your weight in my condition—' and only then did Molly see the enormous mound that strained against the light cottony top.

'I can manage,' she said, and little by little she made her shaky way to sitting, the doctor's hands still braced around her neck. Her palms and forearms and elbows were grazed and bleeding, her knees the same. 'You have a cut on your face,' the doctor told her. 'It's not deep, but it needs cleaning.

We can do it in my house. Is there anyone you can call to come and get you?'

'I can cycle,' Molly said. 'I'll be OK in a while to cycle.'

Her companion shook her head. 'Not a hope. Look at your bike for starters' – and Molly's heart sank as she took in the badly buckled front wheel of the bike that lay sprawled by the kerb. No way would it get her home – but who could she phone? Not Emily, at work till six. Not Dervla, on holiday in Portugal until the middle of July. Not Tracy next door, hands full with her grandchildren. She could think of nobody.

'We can call you a taxi from my house. Come on, let's get you on your feet. Can you use the wall to pull yourself up?'

But a taxi would be a tenner at least, and what taxi driver would take a bicycle? And she still had to pay Clem for the job he'd done last—

Clem. She could call Clem. He mightn't be too far away. She got to her feet, wincing at the stabs of pain from her various injuries, as her Good Samaritan retrieved the rucksack that had toppled from the bike's basket. They made their way slowly across the road, the doctor – 'I'm Patsy' – manoeuvring the damaged bicycle, Molly hobbling along beside her.

'There's a friend I can try,' she said. 'He works out and about – he might be in the area.'

'Give him a go so.'

In the house she scrolled through her list of contacts and found him under H for Handyman. He kept her waiting, as he always did, until the seventh ring.

'Hello.'

'Clem, it's Molly.'

'Hello, you – what's up?'

She explained her predicament.

'You OK? You hurt?'

'Not badly, just a few cuts and bruises – but the bike is out of action. Are you in the middle of something?'

'Nothing that can't be interrupted. Where are you?'

Where was she? She suddenly couldn't remember the name of the road. 'Hang on,' she said, and passed him over to Patsy. He could be anywhere – people were always calling on him. A blocked drain, a door that was sticking, a fence that needed mending, a leaky roof. Turn his hand to anything, that man.

'He's across town, take him half an hour,' Patsy said, passing the phone back. 'Would you drink tea?'

Out of a rusty bucket. 'I'd love a cup. You're very kind, thank you so much.'

'Not at all – wouldn't anyone do the same? I'm glad I was able to help.' While the kettle boiled she added antiseptic to a basin of warm water and cleaned and dressed Molly's various injuries. 'You'll be stiff and sore for a bit, but you'll live. Take it easy tomorrow, stay in bed if you can. Have a bath in the evening, let the plasters come off in the water. No need to put more on, I'd say, just a small dab of Sudocrem, or whatever you have. Looks like your bike might need a new front wheel.'

A new wheel – God, how much would that cost? To take her mind off it, Molly asked when the baby was due.

Patsy grimaced. 'Last week. I'm being induced tomorrow, thank God. The heat makes it feel like I'm carting a small elephant around.'

'Is it your first?'

She shook her head. 'Third, and definitely last. You have children?'

Molly nodded. 'Two. Grown up now.' The familiar pang whenever she talked of Philip, however briefly.

'Any grandkids?'

Maybe. 'No. Not yet.'

They chatted on, drank more tea. A sandwich was offered that Molly refused, not wanting to impose any more than she had to. Eventually the doorbell rang.

'There's your chauffeur now.' Patsy lumbered to her feet. Molly attempted to follow and found that her knees had already stiffened up, so she stayed put until Clem appeared.

He whistled when he saw her. 'Been in the war.'

'Feels like it,' she said.

The state of him. Ancient grey Thin Lizzy T-shirt, fabric stretched taut across the rise of his belly, dark patches under the arms. Baggy blue cargo pants, more pockets in them than anyone could possibly need. Clumpy boots spotted with paint. Chin dark with stubble, hair awry, a distinct whiff of sweat.

She caught herself. Who cared what he looked like – hadn't he dropped everything to come to her rescue? 'Thanks so much for this,' she said. 'Sorry for asking – I had nobody else.'

'No problem. Can you walk?'

'I can, if you let me hang on to you.' He offered his arm and she grabbed it, and began to limp-hop her way towards the hall, leaning heavily against him.

'Ah, here,' he said, and whisked her up into his arms as if she weighed nothing at all. She tried to protest but he took no notice. She was pressed against the damp, pungent bulk of him, forced to put an arm around his neck as he carried her through the hall and outside.

The blazing sunshine, after the shady house, made her feel as if she was being thrust into an oven. Clem negotiated the cobble-lock driveway carefully, breathing out coffee. All she needed was for him to keel over with a heart attack and send her flying. They must look ludicrous, like a parody bride and groom. She imagined Patsy's neighbours smirking out at them.

When she'd been installed in the front seat of his yellow van – God, the van, *wash me* spelt out in the dirt of the side door, *say please* scrawled underneath – Patsy passed Molly's rucksack in through the open window. 'I hope you feel better soon.'

'Thank you again,' Molly said. 'Best of luck with the baby.'

'Fear of me,' she replied, smiling. 'No harm to get yourself a bicycle helmet too, by the way.'

'I know. I should.' Emily kept telling her the same: she had no intention. Helmets cost money.

Patsy waited on the path while Clem loaded the bicycle into the rear of the van. She stood, a hand draped across her bump, while he slid into the seat beside Molly and gunned the engine. 'Bye,' she called, waving them off. Molly watched in the wing mirror as she lumbered back to the house.

'She's a doctor,' she told Clem.

'That right? About to pop, by the look of her.' He turned at the end of the road, not bothering to indicate, whistling something that Molly didn't recognise.

Her seatbelt was broken. The van smelt of turpentine. She was grateful for the breeze on her hot face. Her stomach rumbled, reminding her that lunchtime had come and gone.

Lunchtime. Kathleen. She sat up, saw no dashboard clock. 'What time is it?'

He lifted a shoulder. 'Half one maybe.'

She'd have to ring Kathleen the minute she got home. The thought didn't appeal in the least. She sank back, closed her eyes.

'You're not going to faint on me, are you?'

'Haven't a notion of it. I've never fainted in my life.'

'Glad to hear it – I'm fresh out of smelling salts.'

Coming up on four years it must be since they'd met. She'd found him in the *Golden Pages* when she'd noticed water trailing in a thin stream from a pipe that poked out beneath the roof at the rear of the house. Might be nothing, might be something.

Handyman, his ad had said. *No job too small.* She could only hope this job fell into the small category. His address was local, a mile or so from her. She dialled the number and he answered on the seventh ring, as she was about to hang up.

Water, she said, *coming from the attic, I think. You're not too dear, are you?*

I'm not. Where are you?

She told him.

Be there at seven – and at ten to, a dirty yellow van pulled up to the path. From the landing window she watched him clamber out. Heavy-set, clean-shaven, scruffy clothes, small bald patch at the crown of his head. He stood by the van to allow a woman with a buggy to pass before advancing to Molly's front door: that was a point in his favour right off.

You rang about the attic, he said. Somehow he squeezed himself through the trapdoor, and within two minutes he was back. *Stopcock got jammed,* he said. *That was your overflow pipe, just letting you know something was up. If it happens again you might need to think about replacing the stopcock, but for now I'd leave it alone.*

That's a relief. What do I owe?

Forget it, he said. *Couldn't charge you for that,* so instead she gave him half of the caraway seed cake Emily had made the day before to take home with him, although cake was the last thing he needed. Before he left he promised to drop back with a new washer for the kitchen tap that had dripped steadily as she'd cut the cake. *I have them usually,* he said, *but I'm out of them just now.*

Handyman Clem was how he'd gone into her phone, Clem Handyman was what he'd ended up as in her head. Every couple of months, it seemed, she found something else he was needed for: a new lock on the back door, a split floorboard, a clogged gutter. Nothing major, all little things, the kind she'd been inclined to neglect before he'd come on the scene. After a while she wondered how on earth she'd managed without him.

On every visit he turned up within ten minutes of when he'd said he would, and charged so little she always felt obliged to throw in whatever she could find in the cake tin. She knew virtually nothing about his personal life, only that he'd moved to London after school and lived there for a number of years – *a while* was how he'd put it – before returning to Ireland to move back in with his father Doug after the death of his mother.

And now she knew Doug too.

Would you come and clean for us? Clem had asked about two years earlier, packing up his tools after replacing a broken window catch. *Whatever day would suit.*

All my days are gone, she'd told him, *but I'll put you on a waiting list* – and as luck would have it, poor Mrs Green had been moved to a nursing home the very next month, and Molly's Tuesday mornings were freed up.

Their house – roughly the same small size as hers – was as sorely in need of a good scrub as she'd anticipated. Every horizontal surface was covered with dusty clutter, windows were grimy, dirt was ingrained between floor and wall tiles, bathroom fittings buried under limescale – but, far from being daunted, she thrived on the challenge, and Doug, pale, frail, smiling Doug, was a delight.

We're a disgrace, he said. *We're useless at keeping the place clean. Clem hasn't the time, he's working all hours, and I haven't the energy. You're an angel from Heaven, Molly. We're blessed to have you.*

He never complained, with plenty of cause to. *He's rotten with arthritis,* Clem told her. *It's everywhere. He's on a cartload of pills, and still it kills him. His heart is too feeble for an operation. They won't risk it.*

Clem was generally out and about when Molly arrived each Tuesday, but invariably she'd find Doug reading his newspaper by the sitting-room fire in an armchair that was grimy with use, and moulded to his shape. *I'm grand,* he'd say, when she asked how he was. *Grand altogether.*

But his fingers were so horribly gnarled she didn't know how he held onto the paper, and his hands shook terribly so when they lifted a cup to his lips. And when he rose to make his way to the toilet her heart was in her mouth as she watched him shuffle unsteadily across the room, praying he wouldn't stumble and lose his balance.

'Here we are.'

She opened her eyes as Clem pulled up outside her house. 'I'll have a go at the bike this evening,' he said. 'I should be able to sort it out.'

'Clem, I can't ask you to do that.'

'You didn't ask me.'

'Well, but – only if you'll let me pay. I owe you anyway for cleaning the chimney. You can add it on.'

'Don't be daft. I'm doing you a favour, it's not a job.'

'Come to dinner so,' she said. 'Some night next week.' The idea jumping into her head, completely unplanned – but why not?

He shook his head. 'Will you stop, woman? There's no need for that.'

'It's either dinner or money,' she told him. 'Emily will cook something nice.' He'd met Emily a few times. 'Come on, I really want to thank you for collecting me – and for fixing the bike.'

'Haven't fixed it yet.'

'But you will. I'll see what night Emily is free next week, and let you know.' Emily was free most nights, apart from Monday with the choir and Friday for a film with Charlotte. 'Alright?'

He shrugged. 'Alright, if you insist.'

'I do.'

Now that she'd thought of it, she found the idea appealed to her. She never had anyone apart from Dervla around for a meal, and Dervla didn't count because she brought dinner with her when she came.

He helped her from the van and let her lean on him as far as her door. Thankfully he didn't attempt another Officer and a Gentleman.

'Give me your keys,' he said, and she handed them over. He unlocked the door, offered her his arm again.

'I can manage from here,' she said, but he insisted on linking her into the kitchen. 'Wouldn't be much good,' he said, 'bringing you to the door and having you collapse as soon as my back is turned.'

'I have no intention of collapsing' – but to keep him quiet she took a seat at the table and let him open the window for a bit of air.

'You want to sit outside?' he enquired, looking onto the yard.

'I don't think so, too hot.' She'd fry like a kipper, even under the shade of the swing seat.

'Would I make you tea? Or a sandwich?'

Lord, the sandwich he'd make. 'Not at all, I'm grand. I had tea in the doctor's house, and Emily will be home in a while.' Emily wouldn't be home for several hours, but he wasn't to know that.

'I'll give a shout later so, let you know about the bike.'

'Do that. Thanks again.'

She listened to him stomping out, heard the front door pulled after him, the muffled sound of his van as he drove away. He was a good man, make someone a fine husband if he smartened himself up a bit.

A thought struck her: would he suit Emily? Granted, he was a bit older. Emily wouldn't be thirty for another month, and Clem must be well into the forties – but did age matter really? And it was true that Emily had shown scant interest in him so far – well, they barely knew one another – but sometimes people just needed a little nudge in the right direction, didn't they?

Emily was terribly shy, not inclined to make new friends easily – and Molly couldn't see Clem, despite his heart of gold, catching the eye of a woman anytime soon. Wouldn't she only be smoothing the way a bit for both of them?

Wasn't it worth a try at least? Emily would be at ease in her own surroundings, and Clem would definitely be impressed with the dinner she'd dish up to him. Yes, the more she thought about it, the more promising it seemed.

She pulled her phone from her rucksack and found Kathleen's number: better get it over with.

'Kathleen? It's Molly Griffin.'

'*Who?*'

'Molly, the one who reads the paper to you.' Over four years she'd been doing it, every afternoon from Monday to Friday.

'Yes? What is it?'

'I'm afraid I can't come today – I've been in—'

'You *what*? Speak up!'

Eventually the message was conveyed, and met with precisely the reaction Molly had been expecting.

'You're not in hospital, are you?'

'No, but I'm stiff and sore, and my bike—'

'So you'll be back tomorrow?'

'I will, or the day after. I'll let you know.'

'The day *after*? You're going to miss *two* days?'

'I'll have to see how I feel tomorrow. I'll do my best,' she said, through gritted teeth. 'I'll give you a ring in the morning. Bye now.'

She hung up before Kathleen could say any more, torn as usual between sympathy and irritation. She should ring Martin, let him know she had to miss his mother's session: as the person who paid for them, he had a right to know. Or maybe she'd leave it till the morning, wait till she knew if she was going to be out of action for a second day. Yes, that made more sense.

Despite the open window the kitchen felt stuffy: maybe she'd go out after all. She planted her palms on the table and got gingerly to her feet. She should make herself a bit of lunch but she didn't have the energy. She hobbled to the fridge and poured a glass of Emily's lemonade and brought it out to the tiny courtyard that served as their back garden, grabbing a banana from the fruit bowl as she passed it.

She lowered herself into the swing seat and set it swaying gently with a foot, and went back to thinking about the child with the curly hair she'd met that morning, and the man who might have fathered him, the man who'd broken her heart into smithereens.

Could it possibly be that she'd stumbled on her own grandson? Had Philip run away after Linda had broken the news of her pregnancy to him? These days, men often did a runner if a woman told them they'd fathered a child – but would any man go all the way to New Zealand, without a word to his own family? And would he still be there five years later?

On the face of it, it seemed highly unlikely – but there was no getting away from the similarity. There was no denying the land she'd got when she'd looked for the first time at Paddy's small face, and seen her own son looking back at her.

One way or another, she had to find out. She had to know the truth – and with Philip out of reach, she'd have to hear it from Linda, however she was to manage it.

She'd say nothing to Emily, not a word. Emily would think she'd lost her reason. Molly wouldn't tell a soul, not even Dervla. She didn't want anyone, however well-intentioned, telling her she was wrong – or worse, looking at her as if she was to be pitied. They hadn't seen him. They couldn't possibly understand.

The minutes ticked by. She ate the banana slowly and folded the empty skin into a parcel. It must be after two: she should be at Kathleen's now. Her face, the injured side, felt hot and tight. When she lifted her glass the cuts beneath the doctor's gauze coverings on her forearm twinged in protest. She drank lemonade, listening to the chirp of invisible birds, watching a lone honeybee bob his way around the nasturtiums in the hanging basket. The sun blazed steadily, but the seat's canopy protected her from its bite.

A cat from a few doors away leapt suddenly onto the brick wall that bordered the courtyard on three sides. 'Hello,' she said, but he ignored her as he padded around the wall and hopped down on the far side. Off on his travels.

Her eyelids grew heavy. Hard to sleep these nights with the heat; it caught up with her in the afternoons. She set her empty glass on the short wooden bench she'd found on a skip that served as their outdoor table. She rested her head against the seat's cushiony back, giving another little push with her foot. She floated off to sleep, rocking gently.

* * *

If she didn't drink something in the next minute she'd collapse. She dropped her bags on the table and looked for the jug of lemonade in the fridge, and didn't find it. She closed the door and saw it sitting empty on the draining board. She held a glass under the cold tap and gulped the entire contents standing by the sink. She refilled the glass and brought it out to the yard – and stopped dead.

Her mother stirred, woke, saw her. 'Hello, love. You're home.'

'What happened you?'

'I took a tumble off the bike. It looks worse than it is, nothing's broken. I had to miss Kathleen's, though. She wasn't too happy.'

Emily took in the bandages on her cheek, her hands and arms, her knees. 'Did you go to hospital?'

'I didn't have to go near a hospital, a woman in a house across the road saw what happened – and guess what? She was a doctor! How lucky was that?'

Trust Mam, finding the positive.

'She was lovely, cleaned all the cuts and made me tea. She's pregnant, going to be induced tomorrow.'

Emily sank onto the swing seat, trying to picture a heavily pregnant woman rushing to Mam's aid. She pressed her glass in turn to her cheeks, trying to cool them. 'And of course you had no helmet.'

Her mother smiled. 'I knew you'd bring that up again.'

'Mam, it's not a joke. It's serious.'

'I know, love, you're right. I should get one. I had a great sleep just now.' Changing the subject like she always did. 'It's so hard to sleep these nights, isn't it?'

Emily made no response. She'd be killed off that bike for want of a helmet, racing around like she was in the Tour de France.

'Clem brought me home. He's so good.'

Clem. The name rang a bell, but Emily couldn't— Oh, wait. The odd-job man, wasn't it? She'd met him a couple of times, vaguely recalled someone short and heavyset. 'Why didn't you ring me? I could have come and got you.'

'Ah, no, I couldn't drag you away from work. I knew Clem wouldn't mind, he's very obliging. He dropped everything when I rang, came straight over. And he's going to try and fix the bike too – the front wheel is all bent.'

Clem was beginning to sound like a proper knight in shining armour. Maybe he had his eye on Mam.

'I asked him to come to dinner some night. I hope you don't mind.'

Emily looked at her in surprise. 'Did you?' They never had anyone to dinner. Dervla didn't count: she was like family. 'Why?'

'I just felt I should, after him going out of his way for me like that. You don't mind, do you?'

'No, of course I don't.'

It seemed a bit over the top all the same. Wouldn't he have been just as happy with a fiver? She finished the water and got to her feet, fighting weariness. 'Have you eaten?'

'Just a banana at lunchtime.'

'Stay where you are. I'll do a salad and bring it out.'

'Thanks, love.'

Her calf muscles protested as she crossed the kitchen floor to wash her hands and fill the kettle. So tired this evening, the heat sapping every ounce of energy from her. She craved a cool shower but food was a more pressing need – she'd had nothing since a limp tuna sandwich at one, nearly six hours ago.

'So what exactly happened?' she asked, taking cooked chicken and green olives from the fridge. She listened to her mother's voice floating in from the yard as she shredded lettuce and chopped tomatoes and celery and made a honey and garlic and lemon dressing. A dog bounding out – Mam could have been killed if she'd fallen in the path of a car, her unprotected head crushed under a tyre in an instant.

Tipping everything into a bowl, tossing the dressing through it, she thought how quickly things could change. Look at their father, taken abruptly from them when Emily and Philip were three. Look at a customer at the supermarket a few months back, keeling over in the fruit and veg, sending a display of pineapples crashing with him to the ground.

She remembered the gawkers who had quickly gathered, the nurse who'd materialised and made frantic efforts to revive him until the paramedics arrived. No good: dead before he reached the hospital. His black golf umbrella propped forgotten by a display of oranges, and then sitting for weeks on a shelf in the locker room, nobody knowing what to do with it, until it finally disappeared.

Look at her only brother, her twin, here one day and vanished the next. On a plane halfway around the world before they realised he was gone, before they found his note stuck into the mug of keys beside the television. Mam wanting to call the guards right away, wanting them to start tearing the place apart looking for him. Emily persuading her to hang on, telling her that he was an adult, that the guards would do nothing for forty-eight hours.

She divided the salad between two plates. She could still see Mam's devastated face when she'd made the discovery of the missing money later that evening. Kept it in an old handbag under the sink, behind the washing soda and the bleach and the scouring pads, despite Emily's urging to open a post office savings account. The bag still there, the money gone, the nest egg she'd been building for her old age. No more mention of the guards after that.

I'm sure he had his reasons, she'd said. *He wouldn't just go off like that unless he felt he had to. And he'll pay me back, I'm certain of it*. Still making allowances for him even then, even with his treachery staring her in the face. Still confident now, five years later, that there was a rational explanation, that the money had been borrowed, not stolen. Still believing in him, despite the fact that not once in five years had he bothered to pick up the phone and make sure they were still alive.

The kettle came to the boil and clicked off. She snapped her mind back to the present and made a pot of strong tea: Mam drank it like tar. She put everything on a tray and brought it out, and laid it carefully on the rickety little bench.

'Isn't this lovely?' Mam said. 'You have me spoilt. I love those olives.'

'You want some bread? I brought home rolls.'

'No, this is just grand. Sit down and relax now.'

Emily poured tea. 'So how was your new lady?'

'Oh, she's lovely, very easy. Much less fussy than Bella.'

'That's good. I hope you're not thinking of working tomorrow. You should rest up.'

'I'll see how I feel in the morning. You never know, I might be fine after a night's sleep.'

Even though she couldn't sleep in the heat. 'But you have no bike: how will you travel?'

'Clem might have it back. And even if it's not fixed I could get the bus. Tomorrow is Paula's day and she's on a bus route. If I'm OK to walk to the stop I'll be grand.'

No talking to her. Money was what she was thinking of, of course. She'd become so much more anxious about it since her savings had legged it to New Zealand. They had no reason to worry: they'd manage on Emily's salary no bother for a week or two, longer if they had to – but Mam hated being beholden to anyone, even her own daughter.

'And Kathleen wouldn't be pleased if I missed two days in a row.'

'Pity about Kathleen. If you can't go you can't go.'

'Ah, you don't know her, love. She can be very cranky.'

Emily was well used to cranky. She got it all the time in the supermarket – mothers harried by their yelling babies, stressed business people, everyone too wrapped up in their own lives to be civil to the checkout person. Her smile ignored, no *thank you* when she helped them to pack, often no eye contact made as they paid. She hardly noticed it any more. What she noticed were the nice ones, the ones who smiled back, who actually looked at her as they took their change.

She'd met a nice one last Saturday morning. Patting his jacket pockets with growing dismay as he stood at her cash desk, face reddening, the queue silent behind him. *I must have left my wallet at home,* he'd said finally – and before she could think about it she'd rummaged a fiver from her bag and told him she'd cover it: he could pay her back when he was in next. Something she'd never thought of doing before, but anyone could see he was honest – and anyway, it was only a couple of bags of peppermint creams.

Thanks so much, Emily, he'd said, reading her name badge. *I'll drop that in to you* – and sure enough he was back a couple of hours later with the cash, and a small box of Roses for her. *Thanks again,* he'd said, and she'd wished everyone was like him.

'More salad?' she asked, but even eating took more energy than either of them had in the heat, so they drank a second cup of tea instead as the sun finally decided to leave them alone.

Later, standing under the shower, letting the wonderful cool water wash the muggy day away, she found herself humming the song that had been playing on a loop in her head all day as she'd scanned tubs of ice-cream and slabs of beer and barbecue-ready meats. She'd seen the film plenty of times – Mam rooted out the DVD at least once a year – but she'd never really paid heed to the words of this particular song before, never realised just how lovely they were.

Tony it was who sang it, right after meeting Maria at the

dance and falling instantly in love. Her name, when she said it, was transformed for him into all the beautiful sounds of the world in a single word. Imagine how it must feel to have that effect on a man, to be loved so powerfully, so profoundly, that your name becomes that special for him.

Imagine anyone loving *her* like that. She couldn't see it happening – and yet, it wasn't impossible, was it? She might meet someone next week: he might walk into the supermarket and end up at her checkout desk and fall instantly in love with her as she rang up his sausages and garden peas. He might ask her out on the spot, invite her to dinner. *It was love at first sight*, he'd tell her later, weeks later, when they knew everything there was to know about one another. *I knew the minute I laid eyes on you*.

It could happen. It wasn't a complete impossibility.

She'd fallen in love once. She'd been sixteen going on seventeen, like Liesl in *The Sound of Music*. He looked a few years older, maybe early twenties. He was part of a team of builders involved in widening a stretch of road by the river: she and Charlotte walked past the site each day as they made their way to and from school.

He was red-haired – dark red, that glorious russet shade of a horse chestnut leaf in autumn – and wiry, and not very tall. He lifted his head every day to watch them approach, and to smile at them.

No, not at them, at her. Only at her.

Orange Day-glo jacket, denim jeans coated with dust, workman's heavy yellow boots. Blue eyes he had, and a face full of freckles, and small teeth, and his smile was the most wondrous thing she had ever seen. It crept into her heart and set off fireworks there.

Don't look, Charlotte would whisper, *don't encourage him* – but Emily looked every time, and felt her cheeks getting hot as she returned his smile with one of her own, and walked on with a pattering heartbeat, already looking forward to the afternoon, when she'd see him again.

His face was there whenever she closed her eyes. His narrow frame, his freckled hands gripping the shovel or pickaxe. She imagined sitting in a darkened cinema with his arm draped across her shoulders, or walking hand in hand in the moonlight, or lying close together under blue skies on a beach of white sand that had nobody else at all on it.

And then, after several weeks, after a few months it must have been, she and Charlotte had walked past one day and the barriers were gone, and the road was wider, and the team had vanished, and she never saw him again.

She could still recall the pain of it. For weeks she'd mourned him silently, the trip to school tainted by his absence. She wished she'd known his name; she sensed the sound of it would somehow put a shape on her feeling of loss, her deep sadness. It would be the most beautiful and the saddest sound she'd ever heard.

No man in the dozen or so years since then had smiled at her the way he had. Not a single one had looked at her with anything approaching interest, unless you counted Tony at work, who didn't count. No invitations to dinner or the cinema, no Valentine cards, no flowers or chocolates on her birthday. No boyfriends, no kisses.

And maybe, after all, it had meant nothing to him. Maybe she'd imagined his interest, and the only attraction had been on her side. Maybe he'd forgotten her as soon as she was out of sight.

But maybe he hadn't. Maybe she still crossed his mind, even now.

She dried herself and got into the vest and shorts that had replaced her usual pyjamas since the start of the heatwave. The lines of the song were still running through her head, making her melancholy. She climbed into bed, relishing the cool sheets against her skin, and set her alarm for half six. She switched off her lamp and curled onto her side and listened to the radio drifting faintly as usual from Mam's room. For the past few years, Mam hadn't been able to fall asleep without the radio. Not that she'd get much sleep tonight, with her cuts and scratches on top of the heat.

Emily's tongue probed gingerly at a tooth that had been stabbing at her off and on all day. She'd eventually quietened it with a couple of extra-strength painkillers, but now it was awake again. She should probably get it looked at, but since childhood she'd been terrified of the dentist. She remembered sitting with her mother in the waiting room, stomach clenched tight, palms damp and cold with dread. She'd give it a few days, hope the pain would go away.

Drifting towards sleep she found her brother wandering into her thoughts again. She wondered what he was doing right then, right at that moment. It was morning already in New Zealand: was he still in bed, or gone to work? Did he even have a job – or a bed to sleep in, come to that? Nothing, they knew nothing about his life now. All they knew was that he was still alive.

He was her twin, her womb companion, but they couldn't have turned out more different if they'd been born into separate families on opposite sides of the world. They'd grown up together, shared a cot and then a bedroom for the first five years of their lives. They must have been so close at the start, must have chuckled and gabbled at one another as babies, played together with bricks and Lego and plasticine after that. Hard to imagine it now, with such a gulf having opened up between them over the years that followed.

Philip was the devilish charmer, the handsome one, the glint-in-his-eye one. Emily was like a washed-out version of him, the paler, quieter, more diluted edition. He was the star of every situation; she was in a minor role that nobody paid much heed to.

All through school he'd got away with murder. While Emily struggled to produce barely average work that was received with noncommittal nods, teachers overlooked her brother's slipshod homework, his bullying tendencies, his pilfering of others' lunch treats, so bewitched were they by his dancing eyes, his adorably dimpled smile, his pathetic but amusing excuses, his earnest lying promises not to offend again.

And it was the same at home. Mam always went easier on him, made allowances time and again for his various crimes. As he moved into his teens nothing changed except that girls came onto the scene. They flocked around him like doomed moths bewitched by a flame, and he took complete advantage of their fascination for him. He used them and dropped them as he felt like it, and Emily became a reluctant shoulder to cry on for his heartbroken victims. And Mam, when Emily complained to her of his callousness, made little of it, saying boys would be boys, and he'd grow out of it.

To be perfectly frank about it, to be completely honest about it, Mam loved him more. Emily had no idea when she had become aware of this, but by her mid-teens it was an inescapable fact, like her own insipid eye colour – not quite blue, not quite grey – or the blush that suffused her face whenever anyone looked properly at her, or the hair that wasn't curly enough to be curly, or straight enough to behave itself. She taught herself to live with it, just like she lived with the other things she couldn't change, and she vowed not to let the unfairness of it ruin what she and Mam had.

She liked to imagine that she'd been her father's pet. In baby photos she was always in his arms, while Mam held Philip. She told herself it had been Dad's choice as much as Mam's: it was better to think that way, better to believe that she *had* been loved like Philip, once upon a time.

But Dad had died so long ago, too long for her to have any but the very faintest snapshot memories of him – a pair of white hairy legs in rolled-up trousers on a forgotten beach, her hand in his at the water's edge; or perched on his shoulders, arms wrapped around the prickly skin of his neck, looking down from a terrifying, wonderful height at Philip.

And now Philip was gone too, and it was just her and Mam. And in her lowest, loneliest moments, the knowledge, the cruel reality, would rise up and taunt her: if Mam could have chosen which child would leave her, it wouldn't have been Philip.

Emily didn't give space to it. When it came nudging at her she pushed it away – but it was there, it was there. When another of his callous, empty postcards would drop onto the hall floor, Emily would see the renewed sorrow blooming in Mam's face, and she would hate him for causing it.

They never talked about him now. They'd tried to, at the start, but both of them quickly realised that they couldn't, so wildly differing were their opinions of him, with Emily raging at his thoughtlessness, his treachery, and Mam determined to defend him – *Don't be so hard on him, we don't know what was in his mind* – and each time Emily would retreat, baffled and hurt, and eventually his name was dropped altogether from their conversations.

In private, Emily imagined all sorts of dark causes for his departure. It must have been something bad – the lack of contact information on his postcards only bore that out. If they didn't know where he was, they couldn't tell anyone who might come looking for him.

Eventually, about a month after he'd left, Emily finally went to the library and spent an afternoon on one of the computers there. She scoured newspapers from the day of his departure, and those immediately preceding it, searching for anything that might enlighten her. Hoping, of course, to find nothing. Hoping her fears would prove unfounded, and that he'd simply left because he was sick of his bartending job, or bored with his life.

But tucked away on an inside page of one of the papers, taking up less than three inches of text, she read something that made her suspicions come tumbling back to lodge uncomfortably in her head.

Five years later they were still there. She might never know the truth, he might never come back to them – and hopefully she was wrong anyway. But maybe she wasn't.

Another throb from her tooth. Her clock radio showed nearly midnight: less than seven hours before the alarm would go off. She pushed back the sheet, found the Tylenol in her bag and swallowed two more.

Eventually she fell asleep, and dreamt about Maria and her

doomed Tony jiving across the floor of a high school gym, eyes only for one another.

* * *

He saw his mother's name on his phone, and turned down the Mahler symphony that was flooding the kitchen.

'Chris, it's me.'

She was the only one who called him Chris, the only one allowed to call him Chris. 'How are you, Mother?'

'Well, I'm hot, and not moving very fast, but otherwise I'm fine. Any news?'

'Not a lot.'

They'd spoken at the weekend. He took her out to lunch every Sunday, but she always rang him at least once during the week. He tried to come up with anything that would be of interest to her. Not Jane's home visit two nights earlier, obviously. Jane would hardly have his mother nodding in approval.

'Have your new neighbours moved in yet?' she asked.

'I think they might have, last week.' He should never have told her the house next to him had been sold: bad mistake.

'You think they might have? You're not sure? They're right next door, for goodness' sake.'

'And I'm out at work five days a week. There was some activity – a truck of some sort, or a van. I wasn't paying too much attention.'

Her sigh sped down the line to him. 'Chris, you're a disaster. You need to call around and welcome them to the neighbourhood, it's only mannerly. You could bring them a cake.'

A cake? He nearly laughed out loud. Did she know him at all? 'I might wait a while, let them settle in.'

Another sigh. He often made her sigh. 'Darling, it wouldn't kill you to be sociable. Do you even know how many are there? Is it a family, or a single person, or what?'

'Not sure. Sorry.'

A downright lie: he'd spotted a woman and a small girl coming and going a couple of times, but he had no intention of passing on that information – she'd have him married off before he'd finished the sentence.

He thought of a new topic. 'We've started rehearsals for the next concert.'

'What concert?'

'The songs from the musicals. I told you about it on Sunday.' She only remembered the stuff she wanted to remember.

'Oh yes, that sounds lovely. I'm so glad you have your little choir.'

He hated the way she called it that. His little choir, as if it was something he kept in a box and took out now and again to amuse himself. As if it didn't really matter. The truth of it was that the choir was what got him up in the mornings. He loved it, even while rehearsals were driving him quietly berserk, even though he knew that most of the members were fit to throttle him at times. Music of every kind – or nearly every kind – was his passion, his escape from the soul-shrinking monotony of his day job, and the choir, for all its faults, was all about the music.

'What date is the concert again?'

'Sixth of August. It's a Saturday.'

'I'll be there.'

She was supportive, he had to give her that. She'd turned

up for every performance, making the journey from Dublin each time and staying overnight in his spare room.

'Chris,' she said then, in a different voice, 'I have some news from England.'

He tensed. News from England was never welcome.

'Heather is pregnant again,' she said, in the same careful tone. As if the words would break if she said them too quickly, or too loudly.

He felt the small tightening of his ribcage that the mention of her name always evoked, the swoop within him that she could still cause.

'I'm just telling you so you'll know.'

He had a nephew and a niece he'd never laid eyes on, not even in a photo. Their names had been made known to him – his mother, determined to ignore the fact that her sons had no communication with one another, passed on all information to Christopher – but he'd deliberately and promptly forgotten them. Now there was a new child on the way, another addition to the family. With any luck, it would keep its parents from sleeping through the night for at least two years.

'I've got to go,' he said. 'There's someone at the door. I'll see you on Sunday.'

He cut her off while she was still saying goodbye. He shouldn't take it out on her: it wasn't her fault. She was doing the best she could with the impossible situation she'd been landed in. The situation he'd landed her in.

He dropped the phone on the bed and yanked off his tie. He unbuttoned his damp shirt and peeled it off. God, the stink of him after the day, even though he'd spent most of it sitting behind a desk. Imagine if he'd been on a building site in this weather. He prised off his shoes, undid his trousers and let them drop to the floor. He walked in boxers and socks to the window. He shoved it open and stuck out his top half – but no breath of wind obliged. Dead heat, even now at six in the evening, nothing at all moving. As hot as Lanzarote in July, and minus the sea breeze.

In the garden he spotted the dog's head poking out from beneath a shrub. Water bowl more than likely empty. He whistled softly and the head bobbed up: not dead from dehydration then.

In the bathroom he turned the shower on full blast and stood under the cold jet, tilting his head this way and that. Trying to empty his mind of the memories his mother's news had stirred, Heather and Robert and the way that had gone, all the grief and ugliness he'd been running from ever since.

Afterwards he pulled on shorts and a washed-out blue T-shirt with a giant banana on it that must have amused him once upon a time. Downstairs he propped open the back door with a chair and set Mahler to play again. He sat at the kitchen table and took from his briefcase the spiral-bound report that was the company's half-yearly returns. He opened the first page and began to read.

In less than a minute he heard the dog's claws clattering across the tiles behind him. 'What,' he said, without looking around. But he knew what. He set down the report and got to his feet and went outside for the water bowl – and stopped short at the sight of a barefoot little girl standing in the middle of the lawn. His new neighbour, one of them.

'How did you get in?'

She didn't look too put out at being discovered. 'There's a hole,' she said, pointing towards the hedge.

She appeared to have an American accent – acquired, he

guessed, from too much rubbish TV. He regularly cringed at the overheard conversations of young people, all *my bad* and *whatever* and *awesome*, every sentence tipped up at the end as if it were a question. And don't get him started on *like*.

'Show me where,' he commanded, and she trotted ahead of him down the garden and stopped at a gap in the hedge, just about large enough to accommodate her.

'Does your mother know you're here?' he asked.

She shook her head. 'She's at work.'

At work? Had the child been left home alone? She couldn't be more than three or four. Her pale reddish hair was gathered into two messy bunches secured with mismatching clips – and dotted, he now saw, with privet leaves. Blue trousers rolled to her knees, grubby white vest top. Filthy toes.

'You got a big banana on your T-shirt.'

He looked down. 'So I have.'

'Do you *like* bananas?'

'As it happens, I do.'

'Me too, but they gotta have no *spots*.' She pointed at the blue plastic basin on the grass. 'What's *that* for?'

'It's the dog's water bowl.'

She bent and picked it up. 'It's empty.' She looked accusingly at Christopher.

'That's because he drank it all.'

'You gonna give him more?'

Ridiculous. He was being interrogated by a toddler. 'Look, I think you should—'

'What's your dog's name?' She made it sound like dawg.

He frowned at her. 'What?'

'What's his *name*?'

'He doesn't have one.' Were all small children this curious? He had no idea.

Her face filled with scorn. 'Course he has a *name*. Everyone has a *name*.'

'Well, he doesn't.'

'So how d'you call him then?'

This was getting out of hand. 'Listen,' he said, 'you need to get home. You can't just come into other people's gardens whenever you feel like it.'

'I just wanted to see the dawg.'

'Well, you've seen him now.' The dog stood at the back door, tongue lolling as he regarded them. 'Go back to your own house.' She wasn't his responsibility. If her mother was happy to leave her unattended, what business was it of his? 'Go,' he repeated, pointing to the gap. 'Shoo.' She threw him a baleful look before squeezing back through it. The soles of her feet were even blacker than the rest of them.

She wasn't his concern, she had nothing to do with him. He cast about for the blue basin but it had vanished along with the intruder: great. He returned to the house and filled a cereal bowl with water and set it on the patio. Immediately the dog began to lap enthusiastically, sending droplets flying.

He returned to his report. He made his way through a page, but nothing went in. He read it again, trying to concentrate. At length he raised his head and listened, and heard only the chirrupy sound of his garden's bird population. He sighed as he abandoned the document once more. He went outside and listened, and heard nothing at all from the adjoining garden.

'Hello?'

No response.

'Are you there?'

Nobody, it would appear, was there.

Damn it.

He went back inside, stepping over the dog, which had decided to have a nap in the doorway. He took a bottle of water from the fridge and slugged from it. He stood at the sink and folded his arms and stared at the shrubs some previous owner had planted once upon a time, shrubs he'd ignored since he'd taken possession of them.

She was what – three? Four? He thought of all the hazards in a house for a small child. Electrical sockets just begging to be poked with a fork. Curtain cords she could wind around her neck. Heavy things that could be pulled off shelves to come crashing down on her head. A bath waiting to be filled with enough water to drown herself in.

And if she killed herself, if she died in one of the many, many ways she had right now at her disposal, if the mother came home from work and found her child dead, at some stage someone would say, 'Where did that blue plastic basin come from?' and eventually it would be traced back to him, and he'd have to come clean about encountering her in his garden, and sending her back to play with all the lethal weapons in her house. And however guilty by negligence the mother was deemed to be, he'd have to take some responsibility too.

Damn it to Hell.

He shoved his feet into sandals and left the house and made his way next door. Immediately after ringing the doorbell he realised that she wouldn't be tall enough to open it. He dropped to a crouch and pushed open the letterbox flap and peered inside, waiting for his eyes to adjust to the dimness. 'Hello?' he called.

The door swung inwards with a rush, pulling him with it. He was propelled forwards and sent sprawling onto the tiles.

'What the hell—' A loud female voice, sounding none too pleased. Bare toes with red painted nails whisked hastily out of his way. He scrambled to his feet and found himself face to face with a scowl.

'What's going on?' she demanded. 'What *are* you – some kinda peeping Tom?'

American or Canadian, he could never tell. He scrambled to his feet, gathering what dignity he could muster.

'I was looking,' he said, 'for your child. She told me she was home alone.'

No trace of guilt on her face. If anything, her suspicious expression deepened. 'You were looking in through a mail slot for a little girl you thought was alone? And can I ask what precisely you were planning to do when you found her?'

He felt his temper rising. Here he was, coming to the rescue of an abandoned child, and he was being treated like some kind of criminal. 'She *told* me,' he said stiffly, 'that you were out at work. If you must know, I was concerned about her.'

Her eyebrows lifted a fraction at that. She wore some ridiculous kimono-type thing full of peacocks that was belted at the waist. She smelt of peaches or apricots or something; her hair was wrapped in a blue towel. She didn't look like someone who'd just got home. 'You're the guy from next door,' she said.

'Yes. My name—'

'The one who plays the loud music.'

'Yes,' he said tightly. 'That one.' If she wanted him to turn it down, she could bloody well ask.

'And may I ask just when you were talking to my daughter?'

Again he felt a surge of anger: how dare she make it sound like he was the one who needed to explain his actions? 'For your information, I found her trespassing in my garden. She *said* you weren't here.'

She scrutinised him for a few seconds. He saw her gaze flicking for an instant to the giant banana. Her eyes were cat-green, and outlined heavily in black; in contrast her skin was so pale it was almost translucent. A trio of tiny gold studs, barely bigger than pinheads, clustered in an earlobe; a minuscule green gemstone blinked at the side of her nose. 'Trespassing, huh?'

'Yes. She came through a gap in the hedge.'

She half turned into the house and yelled, *'Laurie!'* so stridently he winced. The movement caused the top of her garment to gape slightly – he averted his eyes from the curves and hollows it exposed.

'Yeah?' An answering shout, through the closed door at the end of the hall that must lead to the kitchen.

'Get out here *now*!'

The door opened a crack. 'What?'

'Come out here, lady.'

She emerged from the kitchen, dragged her way up the hall. *'What?'* Not meeting anyone's eye.

'Did you go into this guy's garden?' her mother demanded.

This guy made his hackles rise again. Couldn't care less what his name was.

'I just wanted to see his *dawg*. He had no water.'

'Look,' Christopher said, 'it doesn't matter.' Wanting to be shot of them now, thinking of the report waiting for his scrutiny. 'I would appreciate it if you made sure it doesn't happen again.'

The mother eyed him critically. 'You left a dawg with no water in this weather?'

'*What?*' His irritation climbed up a new notch: preposterous woman. 'Listen, I came over here because I was *concerned* about your child – she told me you were at work, and now you're trying to shift the—'

'You honestly think I'd go out and leave a small kid by herself?'

'I have no idea what you'd do,' he shot back. 'And if you *were* at home, you didn't do a very good job of looking after her, did you? I could have been a—' He broke off, glancing at the child who was now regarding him curiously. 'For all you knew,' he hissed, 'she could have put herself in danger, wandering into my garden.'

Again the mother slitted her eyes at him. 'Are you saying you're a child molester now?'

'*What?* No, of course not! Don't be—'

'So she wasn't in any danger then, was she?'

'Well, you can hardly afford to take *my*—'

'Not like your dawg, who by the sound of it coulda died of thirst.'

She was infuriating. More worried, it seemed, about a dog she'd never met than her own child. He switched his attention to the little girl. 'Where's the basin?' he demanded.

'What?'

'The blue basin, for the dog's water. You took it.'

'It's a *bowl*, not a basin.'

'Where is it?' he repeated, stifling an impulse to throttle either her or Mommy. Or both. Yes, preferably both.

'It's in the hedge.'

'I'm guessing you don't have kids,' the mother put in. Folding her arms across her chest. Sounding, to his increasing rage, faintly amused at this stage.

'Oh, for *God*'s sake!' He turned and marched away, fuming. Feeling, for some reason, that she'd got the upper hand in their exchange. Absurd woman, in her absurd get-up. Trust him to end up with weird neighbours. And noses were never meant to be pierced.

And he only had her word that she'd been in the house all along – what reason would the child have had for telling him her mother was at work if she wasn't? She might have got home two minutes before Christopher's arrival, might have hopped straight into the shower. And not surprisingly, there was no sign of a father – some poor sucker probably paying her a truckload of alimony or child support now. Glad to be shot of her, more than likely.

Back home he shoved his arm into the gap in the hedge and yanked out the basin. He took the lead from its drawer in the kitchen and clipped it to the dog's collar; he was in no state to do more reading. The dog's walking days were pretty much behind him, so they crawled the quarter mile to the riverbank and plopped down under the shade of an ancient oak.

Christopher leant back against the trunk and closed his eyes, hearing the soft wheeze in the dog's panted breaths, the sound of various footfalls as people passed him on the nearby path, the low wash of the river as it made its sluggish way to the sea, the various calls of birds in the branches overhead.

I'm guessing you don't have kids.

He was thirty-seven, with no wife and no children, and no plans to acquire either anytime soon. As far as women were concerned, he took what was offered to him along the way – every so often someone like Jane would offer – but he made it clear that he had nothing lasting to give them in return. If anyone showed signs of becoming attached he brought things to a close as swiftly as he could, and moved on.

Even the dog wasn't really his. It had appeared in his front garden five or six years earlier, coat matted, looking half starved. He'd chucked out the bone from his chop and thought no more of it. Next day it was sitting patiently by the front door when he'd got home from work. He'd brought it around to the back and washed the worst of the dirt off with the hose, and fed it bread mashed in milk, and that was that.

He didn't regard it as his dog. It was a dog that lived in his garden – and in very wet or cold weather, in his shed. He fed it because someone had to, and he'd walked it in its younger days because dogs needed walks, and it was no skin off his nose if it slept on the old duvet he'd thrown into a corner of the shed.

He looked after it, but he wasn't attached. He didn't get attached.

For the past twelve years he'd been assistant manager, and then manager, of a large supermarket on the far side of town. It was his second job: after leaving college with his business degree he'd endured a bleak three years of trying to manage a run-down little hotel in one of Dublin's less salubrious areas. His salary was laughable, his staff mostly incompetent, and resentful of the inexperienced young manager who'd been brought in over their heads.

All his spare time was spent applying for other work, but his applications went largely ignored. By the time the supermarket offer had come along, in a town that was an hour from Dublin, a town he barely knew, he'd lost count of how many CVs he'd sent off.

He did a good enough job, he thought – the supermarket had held its own through the worst of the recession – but in all his time there he'd forged no connection with the rest of the management staff beyond what was necessary, and he doubted that he instilled in them any great devotion, to him or to the supermarket.

He concentrated on the administrative end of things, rarely interacting with the people who worked on the shop floor, the shelf-stackers, the checkout operators, the ones who manned the various counters. They were mostly anonymous entities to him, with names he seldom remembered; his strengths lay behind the scenes, keeping the official wheels in motion.

Of course he knew Emily, who worked on one of the checkouts. She'd turned up to audition for the choir with her mother Molly, who'd been his cleaner for a few years. *I brought my daughter Emily along,* Molly had told him, saving him the embarrassment of having to ask her name. Thankfully her voice, while not as strong as Molly's, was sweet enough to merit inclusion – bit awkward if he'd had to turn her down. Quiet creature, but learnt her stuff and didn't cause him any grief. Must have been surprised to see him there – nobody at work knew of his musical leanings. Come to that, nobody at work knew anything at all about his life outside the supermarket.

The previous manager had retired some years earlier. Terry Johnston, jovial man, universally popular throughout the store. Terry didn't believe in working behind the scenes. He knew every staff member by name, and many of their spouses too. As a going-away gift, the entire staff had come together and got him an air ticket to visit his sons in Australia. Christopher couldn't see them making a similar fuss when the time came for *him* to leave.

The idea of founding a choir had come about after a particularly non-eventful Christmas last year. His mother was spending the festive season with Robert and his happy family in England, so Christopher, impervious to the usual pleas to accompany her, to bury the hatchet, had been left alone. It didn't bother him in the least: Christmas was for other people, significant only for the time off work it afforded him.

On the day itself he cooked a fillet steak, and found a documentary on TV afterwards about dolphins that kept him mildly entertained while he opened his mother's present of another blue scarf and drank a few too many fingers of Jameson.

After the dolphins he flicked around the channels and came across a choral concert in some cathedral. He listened to 'O Holy Night' and 'Joy to the World' and 'For Unto Us A Child Is Born', and he watched the rapt faces of the singers, and he thought, *I could start a choir.*

He could do it. He had the musical background, and the management skills to steer it in the right direction. He could start a community choir, keep it small, audition people so he got the right voice combinations – but by the time the Jameson had worn off, so had his enthusiasm. Why bring the work on himself, for little or no reward?

And then, a week or so later, when Molly Griffin was doing her first clean of the new year in his house, he'd come home early after a cancelled meeting with head office and overheard her singing – and he'd stood and listened, and thought, *With a bit of training that voice would be something*. And there and then, before he could change his mind, he'd invited her to audition, and she'd been surprised and delighted, and had agreed immediately. Within a week he'd placed an ad in the local paper looking for singers.

He had no close friends. He'd lost touch with most of the people he used to hang out with in school. By the time he graduated from college, anyone he'd known was married (or as good as) or had emigrated; either way, they'd left him behind.

He put in the hours at work, and kept his soul alive with music and the choir, and the rest of the time he and the dog muddled along together.

He was damaged, he knew that. He was emotionally closed for business. He was well aware that his mother worried about him – more so, he thought, since his father's death five years earlier. He hated that she was caught in the middle of the mess that was his relationship – his non-relationship – with his only sibling, but his guilt about that wasn't as strong as his reluctance to reconcile.

He and Robert had hardly spoken in over seventeen years. Their last proper encounter at their parents' house, when Robert had called in to announce his engagement to Heather, had ended with Christopher expressing his fervent desire that Robert and Heather would both end up in Hell, right before landing a not very effective punch on his brother's jaw.

They'd come face to face again, of course, at their father's funeral. Stiff handshakes had been exchanged, along with subdued greetings. Heather had come too, with the only child they had at that stage, a tow-headed toddler. She was plumper than he remembered, and her hair was shorter. The plumpness, it turned out, was another child coming into being in her womb, but he'd heard no talk of it that day. *How are you?* she'd asked, and he'd told her fine, and hadn't enquired about her, or made any move to engage with the child in her arms, and eventually she'd got the message and turned away.

And still. The sight of her could still. He still.

He sat up, put a hand on the dog's warm belly to rouse him. 'Come on,' he said, and the animal struggled to his feet, and they walked slowly home together in the sunshine.

* * *

My dear Philip,

I hope this finds you well. We've been baking in the heat here for a week or so – today is the first day of July – and it's set to continue for at least another week. Well, that's what the forecast says anyway. Of course you'll be well used to the heat in New Zealand.

Stop talking about the weather. Give him some news.

Dervla and Gar are on holidays in Portugal, they've one week down and two more to go. I'll be looking forward to their news when they get back.

Move on. He wouldn't be interested in Dervla or Gar.

Remember the choir I told you about, the one Emily and I are in? The director is Christopher, the man I clean for on Mondays. Well, we've just started rehearsing for a new concert, it'll be on at the beginning of August. Songs from the musicals, My Fair Lady and Oklahoma! and others. You wouldn't know them, they're all before your time.

He'd never been into music: Emily was the one who'd got

that gene. Emily had a beautiful voice, and so many CDs you couldn't count them.

Emily is fine, she sends her ~~love~~ best wishes.

Emily wouldn't send him her love. They might be twins, but you'd be hard put to find two people less alike, or less close. Philip had always been the confident one – a bit too confident at times, in and out of every sort of mischief growing up, but no real badness in him. Emily was altogether quieter, happier out of the limelight, just like her father. And Philip had done a lot better in the looks department too – poor Emily would never turn heads like he used to, like he probably still did.

Emily hadn't forgiven him for his abrupt departure – that much was plain. She'd never said it in so many words; she didn't need to. She barely looked at his postcards when they arrived – and anytime Molly tried to defend him, Emily got annoyed. She said nothing, but you could see it. Of course Emily was cross about him taking the money, which was understandable, but it wasn't just that. She'd always been harder on him than Molly had. Maybe you had to be a mother to understand, and to make allowances.

Back to the letter. Where was she? Oh yes, Emily.

Charlotte and herself saw the new Ryan Gosling film last weekend. Emily enjoyed it, but Charlotte didn't think it was as good as his other stuff.

She was prattling. She needed to get to the point, or this letter would go on forever.

Philip, there's something I have to tell you. I met a little boy two days ago – he's the son of a woman I've just started cleaning for, and he looks so like you I can't believe it. He's got curly hair, which I know you never had, but his face is the very same as yours was at that age. Philip, I don't know if I'm right, but I think he might be your child.

Was that putting it too bluntly?

How else could she put it?

I'm not angry if he's yours. I don't want you to think that. Everyone makes mistakes – I've made plenty of them. If this is why you went away, I understand. You got a shock, you weren't expecting it, and you couldn't see a way out so you left. But if that child is yours then he's my grandchild – and now that I've met him, I need to find out if he is, even if it's not what you'd want me to do. I wish I could talk to you about it, but I can't, so I have to do what I think is right.

She paused, searching for the right words. It didn't matter, he'd never read them, but she still wanted them right. She started again, her pen scratching across the page.

If I'm right about this, if that's what's keeping you away, you should come home. We can work something out with the child's mother – we can contribute to the boy's upbringing. I love you so much, and I miss you every day. The place is too quiet without you. I'd love it if you came home, we both would. I'm counting the days till we see you again, and I'm sure one day we will, when you're ready.

She wasn't sure, not one bit. How could she be? But she needed to keep telling herself that some fine day she'd open the door and there he'd be. She had to keep believing that, or she'd never get out of bed again.

I know I've said it before, but I want to repeat that no mention will be made of the money you took when you left. We all do foolish things when we're young, and I'm sure you'll make it up to me in your own way when you can.

Nearly eight thousand euro he'd taken, fifteen years of a

tenner a week she'd been putting aside. The thought of him being that cruel, taking away the comfort of her savings, was hardest to understand. She doubted that he'd ever make it up either, even if he could. He'd never been one to save – money spilt through his hands like dry sand – so she didn't hold out much hope that she'd ever see a penny of it again. But what harm, if he only came home to her?

Day to day they managed though. Emily insisted on paying the electricity and gas bills when they came, and brought home food from the supermarket every few days. And Molly had begun again, shortly after his departure, to put a little aside each week – in a post office book this time. They'd survive, they'd be fine, if only he came back to her.

I hope you're happy in New Zealand. I hope you've made some friends and maybe got yourself a nice girlfriend.

All my love,

Mam xx

She read it over. It sounded feeble and stilted, it hadn't come out the way she'd wanted, but no matter. Nobody but herself was ever going to read it.

His last postcard had arrived two weeks ago. *Fine here,* it read in his spidery hand. *Hope all OK at home.* He'd signed it *P* like he always did, with no kiss. It was addressed, like all the others, to *Mrs M. Griffin*. So formal, so wrong that sounded. Why couldn't he at least have put 'Molly'? No return address for him, no way of writing back. No way of him knowing if all was OK at home. The two of them could be dead and buried for all he knew.

New Zealand he'd gone to. She knew nothing about the place, except that it was on the other side of the world. When the first postcard had arrived, a month after he'd disappeared, she'd gone to the library and taken an atlas from the shelves and looked it up. Two islands, North and South, floating in the Tasman Sea, below and to the right of Australia. On the far side of Australia.

Just about as far from her as he could get.

She'd been out of Ireland once in her life. She'd travelled to the Isle of Man, the morning after she and Danny had promised, in front of a clutch of relatives, to love one another till death separated them. She was twenty-five, he was two years older. Most of their lives still ahead of them, years of happiness to be enjoyed together.

For four solid days of their honeymoon it rained. Each day they sat on the veranda of their boarding-house and played gin rummy and forty-five with fellow holidaymakers, and told them the kinds of things you tell people you'll never meet again, like Molly's aunt who'd married a widower with seven children in her forties, and given him three more in as many years, and Danny's grandfather who'd joined the British Army just before the Second World War, only to be shunned by his entire village on his return, crippled and shell-shocked. In the evenings they walked to different restaurants under a borrowed umbrella.

On the fifth day, their last, they woke to blue skies and a sea that dazzled in the sunshine. After breakfast they pulled the suitcase from under the bed and found their swimsuits and headed straight for the beach. They ran into the chilly water, holding hands like a couple of teenagers.

What would Danny think of this child she'd found? Would he see his son in him, as Molly had? Philip had been three when Danny died, he and Emily still asking where Daddy was weeks after the funeral, and Molly not knowing what to say to them that would make sense. How did you explain 'never' to a three year old? How did you make death less incomprehensible, less terrifying? She'd done what she could: she'd talked about Heaven and angels, and other things she didn't believe in, and by the time their fourth birthday came around they'd stopped asking.

She scanned the letter once more. She folded it and brought it upstairs and put it away with the rest. Five years' worth of words, five years of letters he'd never read, and still she went on writing them. It was all she could think of to do, her only way to feel in any way connected to him.

But now she had a new way, or she might have. She closed her eyes and conjured up the little face beneath the curls, and felt again the conviction that he belonged to them. Maybe she could offer to babysit: apart from Mondays and Fridays her evenings were free. Yes, that might be an idea. It might not help her get to the truth but it would give her more time with him.

Downstairs she pressed a squeezed-out facecloth to the burning skin of her cheeks and neck and throat. Friday, the first day of July, and still no end in sight for the heatwave. *Scorchio* the main headline on yesterday's newspaper; seventy-five years, according to last night's weather forecaster, since they'd had such a prolonged hot spell – and now with the schools closed for the summer holidays the children could take full advantage of it. Paddling pools all round.

Two days after her mishap her cuts were mending, her bruises fading, everything returning to normal. She'd had to cancel her cleaning slot with Paula the previous morning, still too stiff and sore to face it, but by the afternoon she'd felt loosened up enough to make her slow and careful way to Kathleen's on her mended bike.

It'll do for now, Clem had told her, *but you'll have to think about a new wheel at some stage. And take it handy, no speeding.*

She'd repeated her invitation to dinner. *Next Wednesday,* she'd said. *Come around seven.* She'd asked if there was anything he didn't eat and he'd thought a bit and said he wasn't too mad about snails or octopus. She'd get a nice bit of fish: Emily had a way with fish.

She hoped he and Emily would get on. She'd do what she could, find ways to let him know what a kind, thoughtful daughter she had – and maybe she could invent a headache and go to bed early, give them a chance to get to know one another a bit better. Yes, she'd do that. She'd be forgiven the lie.

She looked at the pile of clothes in the laundry basket: much too hot for ironing. She brought a magazine out to the yard and flicked through the pages as she waited for Emily to come home from work.

* * *

'What's that you're humming? I know it but I can't think in the heat.'

'It's from *My Fair Lady*, I was listening to it in bed last night. It's stuck in my head now.'

'Oh yes, that's the posh fellow when he's on the street where she lives. Is that one of the concert songs?'

'It is.'

The fourth of July already, the concert just a month away: her stomach flipped at the thought. If it had been left up to her she'd never have joined the choir. She'd always loved music – Mam had taught her how to play the little piano that Dervla and her husband had given her and Dad as a wedding present, and she'd often sing along to the radio, but that was as far as it went. And then Mam had come home one day from one of her houses, full of excitement.

Christopher is starting a choir. He asked me would I like to audition. I'd be mortified to go on my own though – will you come? You've a lovely voice, you'd be great in a choir, but Emily was already shaking her head. Singing with the radio was one thing, but in public, in front of strangers? No way.

Get Dervla to go with you.

Dervla? She hasn't a note in her head. Don't tell her I said that.

Of course Emily had seen what Mam was doing. Mam would have no problem turning up to the auditions on her own: singing in front of anyone wouldn't knock a feather out of her. No, this was for Emily, to 'bring her out of herself'. She knew that was how Mam saw it, how she thought of it in her head. Emily needed to meet new people, broaden her horizons. Emily needed to be brought out of herself.

Mam, I can't.

Emily, you can, you really can. You'd be wonderful, and I know you'd love it. Please come, just for me. Please.

And in the end she'd worn her down, and a horribly nervous Emily had gone along – and nearly died when she discovered that Mam's Christopher was also her manager, Mr Jackson.

I can't, she'd hissed, *I just can't, I'll wait in the car* – but it was too late, he'd already seen them, and Mam was introducing her, and there was no avoiding it.

You're working on the checkouts, he'd said, not looking too put out to have one of his employees turn up at the auditions. So after Mam had marvelled at the smallness of the world – *I can't believe you're Emily's boss!* – and belted out 'You Do

Something To Me', a horribly embarrassed Emily – she was singing in front of *Mr Jackson!* – had managed a shaky first verse of 'Mystic Lipstick', and both of them had made the cut. Whatever about accepting Mam, who had actually been invited to audition, he'd probably felt obliged to take Emily, knowing their paths would cross at work.

On their first night coming together as a choir they'd been placed according to their voices and made to sing endless scales and sequences before being taught a simple four-line round that had come alive when they'd sung it in parts – and to her amazement, Emily had found herself charmed and uplifted by the harmonies they created. Since then the choir had grown steadily on her, and before long she was looking forward to Monday nights.

Her boss in his new role was another surprise. Even though everyone else called him Christopher, he remained Mr Jackson in her head. She was astonished at how volatile he was as their director: at work she'd got the impression of someone distant, not given to outbursts, but at rehearsals his temper was never far from the boil. *No, no no!* he would yell, flailing his arms to stop them. *You're not* listening *to me! Your timing is ridiculous!*

He would fuss over a single line – *Again! Again!* – getting them to repeat it endlessly until he was satisfied. His scowl would deepen ominously if their delivery dragged – once he'd flung a notebook over their heads, narrowly missing Ultan, who'd had plenty to say about it in the pub afterwards but who perhaps wisely had held his tongue at the time.

But to Emily, one thing was obvious: Mr Jackson loved the choir. The supermarket might pay his bills, but his heart was with the group of singers he'd brought together – or rather, it was with what they represented for him. She would watch his face as they sang: when they got it right she could see everything soften and relax in it. The music they made moved him – and moved her too.

She still dreaded their public performances though. She knew she'd be OK in the upcoming concert as soon as she managed to lose herself in the music: she just had to get past the angst of the days that preceded it, and the first few terrifying minutes on the stage.

'I don't know why I keep drinking this crap.' Charlotte regarded the dregs of her paper cup in disgust.

'Probably because it's free.'

'That must be it.' She crumpled the cup and flung it in the general direction of the row of bins lined up to their left. 'This weather,' she said, fanning her face with her hand.

'I know.'

'I don't want to give out – but the nights kill me.'

'Mam is the same. She can't sleep.'

'How is she, after her tumble?'

'She's fine. Back to normal.'

'That's good. Poor Molly.'

Silence fell. Emily's tooth began to throb again, the painkillers she'd taken after breakfast wearing off. She'd have to do something, or take pills every day for the rest of her life.

Charlotte and Emily were on their morning break. They'd abandoned the canteen – far too hot – and were sitting on an opened-out cardboard box with their backs against the pebbledash wall in the rear yard of the supermarket, trying not to inhale the stink that wafted every so often from the bins. They'd kicked off their shoes and hitched up their navy uniform skirts.

Charlotte's legs were the colour of butterscotch: once a fortnight, more frequently in the summer, she got a discounted spray tan at the salon where her sister-in-law worked. Beside her Emily was pink and freckled, and covered with factor thirty.

'Nearly forgot,' Charlotte said. '*Casablanca* is on telly on Wednesday night. Want to come round to mine? We could get a pizza.'

'Can't – Mam's invited our handyman to dinner. I'm on cooking duty.'

'Your handyman?'

'The man who does odd jobs for us. Mam owes him a favour – he drove her home after her fall, and he fixed her bike.'

'Did he now? And Molly has asked him to dinner.'

'Just to say thank you.'

'Maybe she fancies him. Maybe she's been waiting for her chance.'

Emily smiled. 'Ah, no.'

'Why not? Is he available?'

'I don't know, maybe – but he's younger than her.'

She had no idea how old he was, hard to be sure with the weight he was carrying, but hardly more than fifty. Pleasant enough though, as far as she remembered.

'What harm if he's a bit younger? All the more reason for her to be giving him the glad eye.'

'Charlotte, she definitely doesn't fancy him. He's not exactly—' She broke off. Not exactly what? She wasn't exactly herself, and still she harboured secret hopes of finding someone some day. 'I just can't see them as a couple.'

However pleasant he was, she couldn't imagine any woman going for him. It didn't work like that. People didn't fall for the pleasant ones, or the kind ones: they fell for the good-looking ones, or the ones with the quick jokes, or the healthy bank balance. That was the way it worked, as far as she could see.

'Pity. Your mam deserves someone nice.'

'Don't we all?'

Charlotte threw her a look. 'I don't know what you're complaining about. You could have Tony in the morning if you wanted.'

Emily groaned. 'Don't start.'

'I'm just saying. He's dying to take you out.'

'Stop. He doesn't mean a word of it.'

Tony worked behind the meat counter. Beneath his striped hat his dark hair was cut so close to his scalp it looked like someone had used a pen with a very thin nib to cover his head with tiny black dots. His neck was wide, his cheeks round and pink. For some reason, he put her in mind of a bulldog. When he rolled up his sleeves you could see his tattoos, arms covered with them. He had to keep them hidden at work, but every now and again he'd whip up a sleeve and give customers a flash, just to get a laugh.

He was loud and brash, and always in good humour: his booming guffaw carried as far as her checkout desk. Emmy, he called her. *We're two awards*, he'd say, *a Tony and an Emmy. We're made for each other. C'mon, what do you say to a drink after work, just you and me?* Everyone within earshot laughing and sniggering, knowing he was making fun of her. She wished he wouldn't. It was cruel to tease her like that – but she said nothing, lacking the courage or the know-how to make him stop. All she could do was ignore him, and hope he grew tired of it, and switched his attention to someone else.

'So what are you serving the handyman for the big dinner? Lobster and Champagne?'

'Hardly. Mam is going to get some fish, and I'll do a salad.'

She couldn't remember the last time she'd cooked a meal for anyone other than herself and Mam. Even when Philip was still around he'd been out more often than not, eating in friends' houses, or grabbing a takeaway with his girlfriend of the moment.

Maybe Mam enjoyed the thought of having someone new to entertain, even if it was only the man who fixed the toilet when it blocked up. Or maybe Charlotte was right, maybe Mam did fancy him – why shouldn't she? They seemed to get on well, and Mam of all people would see beyond someone's appearance.

Maybe Emily should try to make it a bit special. She could bring home some candles – and didn't they have an offer on rib-eye this week? Steaks instead of fish, push the boat out. She'd have to get them from Tony, but no matter. And she could do that raspberry and custard pie for dessert that Mam loved.

'Any word from the bad boy lately?' Charlotte asked.

'Not for a while.'

Every so often she'd mention him. Still wanting to talk about him, still eager to hear news of him despite his casual, cruel dismissal of her each time they'd met. Emily watched Charlotte's crumpled cup skittering across the tarmac, caught up in a sudden little breeze.

From the moment she'd laid eyes on him, Charlotte had had a thing for Philip. Philip would drop in to the supermarket about twice a week to get Emily's discount on the cigarettes he'd begun smoking at fourteen, and it wasn't long before half the female staff were keeping an eye out for him.

He dated a few of them – and inevitably two-timed them, or dropped them altogether as soon as he got bored – but Charlotte, with her lanky frame and gap-toothed smile and frizzy curls, didn't interest him. Emily could have killed him when she saw how offhandedly he treated her friend, making no secret of the fact that she wasn't worth bothering about.

Two weeks since the arrival of his last postcard. As devoid of information as all the rest, giving them no indication as to his precise whereabouts or current situation, and sending Mam into her usual melancholic tailspin.

'Back to the madhouse.' Charlotte got to her feet, brushed down her skirt. 'Roll on lunchtime.'

They were going shopping, spending their precious forty-five minutes running around in search of shoes for an upcoming family wedding of Charlotte's. She'd asked Ian, a newly appointed assistant manager, to accompany her, partly on the basis of his smart suits – he wouldn't disgrace her – and partly because he didn't drink, so she'd be safe with him as her driver. He was shorter than her by an inch or so: the shoes would have to be flat.

Emily splashed the last of her coffee onto the tarmac. She retrieved Charlotte's cup and threw both of them into the bin. Her tooth gave another stab: she ignored it as she made her way through the supermarket and back to her checkout desk, taking the long way around to avoid the meat counter.

For the rest of the morning, in an effort to divert her attention from the pain in her mouth, she filled her head with songs from the concert. As she scanned groceries and made change and gave cashback she washed that man right out of her hair, and wondered how to solve a problem like Maria, and dreamt a dream in times gone by.

Mr Jackson would have been proud of her.

* * *

He was eighteen. It was the summer after he'd finished school, and he was spending it in Lanzarote, busking on the prom in the afternoons, gigging in the bars at night. He'd come over with his friend Jack, who spent his evenings behind the counter of a sports bar and his days on the beach, checking out the talent.

Christopher was too busy to check out the talent. He was on a mission to prove to his parents that he could make a living from his music. They'd agreed to stop insisting he went to college like his brother Robert for as long as he could support himself financially as a singer-songwriter. His plan was to start in Lanzarote, where a friend of a friend had got him a couple of regular gigs for the summer, and take it from there.

So far, the going had been tough. Despite playing music for hours every day, he made barely enough to live on. He sang from three to seven under the blistering sun, midway between the resort's two main beaches, with a straw hat on his head and another on the ground in front of him. At seven he'd pocket his takings – they rarely amounted to very much – and grab a shower and a bite to eat, and sometimes a nap. After that he'd head to whichever bar had agreed to have him that evening, and play there until midnight or so.

Afterwards he'd drink a bottle or two of beer, usually part of his payment, before making his way back to the shabby little room above a restaurant that he and Jack rented for far more than it was worth. Most of the time he had it to himself, with Jack regularly finding another bed to spend the night in.

When he wasn't singing or sleeping he was writing new songs, hunched over his guitar in the room, tweaking words and melodies, playing with rhythms and structures until they made sense. He wrote, of course, about love: first love, enduring love, unrequited love, doomed love. He wrote about lives torn apart by love and lives redeemed by love, and everything in between – all the while aware, as he strummed and scribbled and revised, of the irony.

He'd never been in love. Not from lack of opportunity: looking like he did – more than once he'd been likened to Kevin Costner – there was always plenty of interest from the opposite sex. From his early teens, girls had bypassed his older brother and gravitated towards him, clamouring for his attention. And while he'd had fun discovering what there was to be discovered, and while a few of them had made his blood race for a while, none of them had claimed his heart.

And then he'd met Heather.

Almost three years his senior at twenty-one, newly qualified as a teacher. In Lanzarote for a few weeks with a group of friends, soaking up the sun before beginning their careers. Dark-haired and petite, the polar opposite of the leggy blondes he'd veered towards in the past.

Their first encounter was on the prom. He was covering Neil Young, having learnt that people were more inclined to throw you a coin if you played something they recognised. He watched the girl in the red sundress as she approached alone, hair hidden beneath a white hat, beach bag slung over a shoulder, green plastic water bottle in her hand.

She drew level with him and stopped, and stood silently until the song was over, oblivious to the other holidaymakers who walked around her. He felt self-conscious, although he was used to people stopping for a bit if he was playing something they liked. This was different. For one thing, she was on her own. For another, she seemed to be really listening, really focused, swaying a little as he sang. Not quite facing him, so he could take her in covertly.

Her nose was tipped with pink, her shoulders peeling. The sun had caused the skin of her lips to chap. One cheek was dotted with freckles; a single dark mole sat high on the other. Her eyes were hidden behind tiny round purple-framed sunglasses.

The red dress stopped at mid-thigh. Her legs were solid. She wore a little silver chain around one ankle. Her toenails were painted turquoise, an exact match for the flip-flops she wore.

I love that song, she said when it was over. *You made a great job of it.*

Thanks.

She pulled off her hat then, and dark hair fell down her back. *Phew,* she said, raking her fingers through it. *So hot today. You must be roasting. Here, take this.* She thrust the water bottle at him. *You probably need it more than I do. Sorry I've got no cash on me.*

He took the bottle, thanked her. It was half empty.

It's just water, she said, *in case you were hoping for gin.* Her sudden smile pushed the mole upwards. A pink strap strayed from beneath the dress: a swimsuit, or a bikini. Her breasts were small, hardly disturbing the fall of the dress. She smelt of coconuts.

Water is fine, he said. He unscrewed the top and drained the bottle in a few swigs, conscious of the dark sweaty patch on the underarm of his T-shirt that she couldn't miss. The water was warm but he didn't care.

She twirled her hair into a knot and shoved the hat on again. *Time for a swim,* she said. *See you around.* She began to walk off.

I'm singing in the Terrace Bar tonight, he called after her. *Across from the church, up the stairs.*

She wheeled around and walked backwards for a few steps. *I know where it is.* She flashed him another smile, lifted a hand and turned away again.

He watched her until she passed a bend in the prom and vanished. Her calves were firm: a runner, he decided. He mentally lifted the red dress and saw a tiny pink bikini underneath.

She left something behind, a charged feeling in the air she'd displaced. He sang for another hour and went home to shower and nap before his gig. He lay sleepless under the sheet, listening to the cicadas whirring outside the window. They sounded louder than he remembered. Everything seemed somehow heightened as he replayed their short conversation, trying to recall it word for word.

He'd given up on her by the time she showed up in the bar. It was close to eleven, and he'd just come back after his break. *Requests,* he said, and someone called up *Neil Young* and it was her, in a group of four. Long white dress, hair loose. She flashed him a smile and he grinned back, feeling ridiculously happy at the sight of her. *Just for you,* he said, and sang the same song as before.

He kept her in his sights for the rest of his shift, willing her not to leave. She and her friends were drinking cocktails, and in high good humour: every so often peals of laughter would erupt from their table. At one stage she got up to dance with one of the others. He watched her shimmy and gyrate with abandon, her hair flying about with every toss of her head. He wondered if she was aware of his eyes on her, and if she was enjoying it and playing up to it. Or maybe she was just happy, with a few cocktails inside her.

It was the fourth of July. Eighteen years ago to the day.

They were still there when he finished his gig; she left her friends and came to join him at the bar. *Thought you looked lonely*, she said, leaning into the counter, letting a hand rest lightly on his arm. He bought her a cocktail, trying to hide his delight. He learnt that her name was Heather, and that she had two younger brothers and no sisters. She lived in Limerick but was moving to Galway in September to take up her first teaching job.

He walked her home, her friends maintaining a discreet distance ahead. *I'm drunk*, she told him, giggling. *Those cocktails are lethal. No taking advantage of me*. The evening air was heady and warm. He was sweaty after his performance but she didn't seem to mind, leaning into him as they walked. She was tiny – he was a foot taller than her. He felt protective, almost wished for some kind of attack so he could defend her.

This is me, she said, and he realised that her friends had disappeared into an apartment complex. He put his hands on her waist and swung her easily onto the thigh-high wall that surrounded the building, causing her to give a small shriek as her feet left the ground. He placed his palms on the sides of her head and brought his face close to hers.

Heather, he said quietly.

Christopher, she replied, in a half-whisper.

She crossed her ankles behind his thighs, wrapping him in the folds of her dress, trapping him. She touched his mouth with a finger: he grabbed it lightly between his teeth. She laughed and pulled it away. *Kiss me,* she said, cupping the back of his head with her hand, so he did. As he ran his tongue along her chapped lips, nudging them open, she gave a little moan that inflamed him instantly. Their kiss was long and deep and hungry. He ached to tear off the white dress, and whatever else was underneath it. He wanted to devour her, inhabit her, drown in her. He was oblivious to everything but the rush of her exhalations and the small moist sounds of their kiss and his burning, pulsing body.

Eventually she pulled away. *Better go,* she whispered. In the moonlight her eyes were black, her lips shining and slightly parted. He'd never seen anything as beautiful as her face. He couldn't bear to let her leave.

He ran the back of his hand along her cheek. *When can I see you?*

Her smile was wonderful. *Whenever you want.*

I'll be on the prom tomorrow from three, same place as today.

Catch you there then. She eased out of his embrace and jumped down from the wall, stumbling a little, falling against him. *Oops,* she said. He grabbed her and pulled her close again, pressing his face into her hair, smelling cigarette smoke from the bar. She pushed him away, laughing softly. *Down, boy*. She caught his hand and squeezed it briefly – *God, I'm so drunk* – then turned and walked a little unsteadily through the entrance and into the building.

He made his way back to his room, every cell in him humming with desire, trying to hold onto the warm soft feel of her, the sweetish alcoholic taste of her mouth, the wonderful music of her laugh.

For once Jack was home, and snoring beneath his sheet. Christopher pulled off his clothes and lay down, bone weary – but for the second time that day sleep eluded him. Instead, the questions crawled one after another into his head, banishing his feeling of well-being.

Why hadn't he arranged to meet her for breakfast, or lunch, or anything specific? Why had he said three on the prom? It was too loose an arrangement, and three was twelve hours away, a lifetime.

A fresh and disturbing thought struck him: who was to say she'd even remember him in the morning? The cocktails might well wipe out the memory of the person who'd walked her home and tried to eat her face for ten minutes.

And even if she remembered him, what if she decided she wasn't all that bothered with him in the cold light of day? What if she laughed with her friends about the busker she'd managed to pull?

And even if they didn't laugh, even if she turned up on the prom like she'd promised, he had practically no money. It hadn't been a problem up to now – he could get by with very little – but how was he to take her out, buy her dinner, buy her anything at all, on his meagre earnings?

And worst of all, he had no idea how long she was staying: what if she had just two more days on the island, or was even going home that very day? What if she came to the prom simply to say goodbye?

He lay tortured and tormented, his mind spinning with unanswerable questions until he finally lost consciousness as the restaurant below began pulling up shutters – only to be woken again almost immediately, it felt, by Jack's clattering of the frying pan in the tiny kitchenette at the far end of the room. He watched, bleary-eyed, as his mind replayed the previous evening's events.

I met a girl, he said eventually, through a mouthful of sleep.

Jack looked across. *The dead arose. You want eggs?*

Yeah. He was suddenly ravenous. He sat up, yawning, stretching, rubbing sleep from his eyes. He checked his watch and saw that it was after eleven. In four hours he'd be on the prom, waiting for her. *She's a teacher*, he said. He had to talk about her. *Heather.* Her name conjured her up: white dress, tumble of dark hair. He felt a lance of desire.

Good for you. Jack cracked eggs into the pan. *You want bread?*

Yeah. He could eat a house of bread, a country of bread.

We're out – you need to get some.

He pulled on shorts and a T-shirt, found coins in his jeans pocket. His eyes felt gritty. At the bakery on the corner he bought two long warm crusty rolls, keeping a lookout for her on the street outside. After breakfast he might walk in the direction of her apartment block—

No: crazy stalker behaviour. He'd survive till three.

The time crawled. After Jack left for work he tried to write a song about her. He sang the first verse through once, crumpled it up and wrote another, threw that away too. He couldn't do her justice, couldn't capture how she made him feel in words and music, how she lit him up inside. Every love song he'd written seemed trite to him now; hollow words, hackneyed clichés that meant nothing. He finally gave up and paced the floor, unable to sit still.

At half past two he took up his usual position on the prom

and began to sing, watching the approaching faces, praying she'd appear, frightened by the intensity of his feeling for her. Twenty-four hours earlier he hadn't known of her existence: now it felt like his life would be over if she failed to show up.

Three o'clock came and went.

Four o'clock.

Five.

Coins clinked into his hat. A few people stopped now and again to listen for a while. A couple asked if he could play Dylan. *'Make You Feel My Love' was our first-dance song at our wedding,* they told him, so he sang it for them, the words sour as vinegar in his mouth. They gave him a fiver and he thanked them. He watched them walk off arm in arm, and he knew he'd met and lost the only woman he would ever want to be with.

He'd go back home, he decided. He'd apply for college, like his parents wanted. He'd study whatever course he was accepted for – because what did it matter which path he took now? What did any of it matter?

I was afraid you'd be gone.

He swung around. She stood there, out of breath. *I was asleep,* she said, *until ten minutes ago. I look like crap, but I was afraid I'd miss you.*

Her hair was tousled. Her face was bare of make-up. She wore pink shorts and a white lacy top. Her chin was covered with tiny red spots that he knew his unshaven jaw had caused the night before.

You look beautiful, he said. He swung his guitar sideways and opened his arms and she laughed and stepped into his embrace.

And that was how they began.

A week later they waved off her friends and she moved her

things into the room above the restaurant, Jack having agreed to relocate to an even smaller one on the next level. She found a waitressing job and worked from noon until ten, and made more in tips than in salary, and smuggled food home.

She told her parents she'd decided to stay on until the end of the summer. *They're not happy about me being here without the girls*, she told Christopher. *They're afraid I'll meet a sex maniac who'll rob me of my innocence.*

Too late.

In those first glorious weeks nothing mattered but the two of them. They spent every spare minute together. She came to his gigs when she finished work; his evenings brimmed with anticipation until she walked in. His joy bubbled over at the sight of her. He couldn't believe she was his.

On rare mutual days off they rose early and packed swimsuits and towels, and trekked to a string of sandy coves a mile or so outside the resort, and spent the day in and out of the clear sparkling water, and watched the sun go down from a little hilltop beach bar.

Lying on the sand they made plans. They'd travel home at the beginning of September. He'd move into the rented house in Galway that she and her friends had organised until they'd saved enough to afford a place for just the two of them. He'd busk by day, like he was doing in Lanzarote, and look for gigs in the bars at night – it had to be easy in Galway, with its multitude of live music venues.

He said nothing about her to his parents. In his occasional call home from the phone box at the end of the prom he told them he was doing fine, but was thinking of returning home at the end of the summer to look for better-paid work. *I'm considering Galway*, he said. *I've heard good things about the music scene there.*

You could always go to college in Galway, his mother replied, *and play your music by night. We'd be happy to fund your studies, you know that.*

Still wanting him to be like Robert, six years his senior. Robert, who'd bagged himself a job with a firm of architects in Dublin within five minutes of graduating. Robert, who was still in the two-year probationary period he had to complete before being declared fully fledged, but whose work was already in the running for a big award. Robert, who played by the rules. Robert, who was everything his younger brother wasn't.

We'll see, he said. *How's the weather there?* Waving to Heather who was looking out from her nearby restaurant.

His every waking thought was of her. When he closed his eyes his dreams were full of her. He tried repeatedly to write a song for her but each time he was defeated. He simply couldn't encompass in two verses, a bridge and a chorus what she meant to him, how profoundly she had changed him.

The days flew by, hurtling towards autumn. On a sultry cloudy morning in early September they flew home, emerging to the rain at Dublin airport. He watched her in the arrivals hall being embraced by her parents – they'd agreed not to go public on their relationship until it could be seen to be more than a holiday romance. He took the bus home, already counting the days (four) until they were to meet again in Galway.

And in Galway, it all fell apart.

Oh, not right away. Right away it was fine, apart from the coolness of her friends, who didn't appreciate gaining an extra housemate. But otherwise it was fine, apart from the rain that fell steadily as he strummed his guitar on the streets, giving him a cold that drifted to his chest and forced him to bed, coughing and feverish, on antibiotics for most of a week. But the rest of it was fine, apart from not being able to find a bar that was looking for a new musician, nobody at all willing to employ a singer-songwriter they hadn't heard of.

He earned barely enough from the busking to contribute to the weekly food bill in the house. Nothing was left over for rent, or for going out. *Doesn't matter*, Heather said, *I can pay* – but letting her pay for nights out made him uncomfortable, so most evenings they stayed at home and watched rubbish television. Eventually he gave in and got a job as a barman, and his guitar lay propped against the bedroom wall gathering dust as he pulled pints and collected glasses and wiped tables with a damp dishcloth.

On his days off he'd sit in their room and try to write new songs, but nothing happened, nothing came out right, and eventually he gave up the struggle. It would come back to him, if he just stopped trying to force it.

But they were still OK. Up to Christmas they were OK. Their relationship had come through the first all-consuming phase – inevitable that the fierce passion would eventually burn itself out. They moved into a quieter, steadier rhythm, which was fine by him. They were still good together, she still meant everything to him.

And then they decided the time had come to be introduced to one another's families. *You first*, she said, so they got the bus to Dublin the week before Christmas, and she met his parents. She also met Robert, who was by then living in a city centre apartment. Everyone took to her. He watched her laughing with Robert about something and marvelled at how well she was fitting in.

Her family, just before the end of the year, was a different story. Her brothers were friendly enough, but her parents left him in little doubt as to their opinion of him. A penniless would-be musician earning his living as a barman was clearly not what they'd had in mind for their only daughter. He did his best to charm them, but their stiff conversation over the dinner table made it plain that he wasn't what they were looking for.

They'll come round, she promised, *when they see we're serious* – but he heard, or imagined he heard, uncertainty in her voice. She was a teacher, a professional: what could he offer her but a dead-end job, a handful of not very good tunes, and his undying devotion?

In January he came to a decision: he would go to college. He'd enrol in an arts course, and then find work as a music teacher. If he had to repeat some Leaving Cert exams to gain enough points, so be it. He imagined his parents' delight when he told them he'd decided on third level study after all. But he was doing this for himself and Heather, not for anyone else. He was doing it for their future.

Teaching had never featured in his plans. He had no idea how good or bad he'd prove to be – but it needn't be forever. He could still pursue the real dream, could get back into songwriting once he was immersed again in the world of music – and this time he'd have the security of a degree, and a salary to keep him solvent until he achieved his ultimate goal. The more he thought about it, the more sense it made, and the more determined he became.

January was the coldest he ever remembered. Temperatures dropped to minus fifteen. Leafless trees became magical white sculptures; cars skidded and twirled on unsalted roads; water froze and swelled in copper pipes. Coal supplies ran low in fuel merchant yards; consignments of shoe grips that gave pedestrians added protection on icy paths sold out within hours of landing on shop shelves.

He called to the university when Heather was out at work and got the information he needed, and discovered to his relief that his Leaving Cert points were enough for what he wanted. He sent in his application for an arts-degree course and waited for a response.

If he got accepted, he'd take her out to dinner. He'd wait until they were on dessert before telling her his news. He'd say he was planning to keep on the bar work; he'd get a schedule to suit his college hours so he could still earn some money. He'd point out that they could live in the accommodation his parents would be happy to help pay for once he was doing what they wanted. She'd see how carefully he'd thought it all through.

And before they left the table, he'd ask her to marry him.

Why wait? They were soulmates, destined for one another: why not make it official? Granted they were young, him not twenty till November, her not twenty-three till Christmas – but if he was certain, and he was, why wait? His parents might be iffy at first but he'd talk them round. They liked Heather, and he was carrying out their wishes by going to uni. And her parents' resistance would thaw too, he was sure, when they heard of his plans for an academic future.

A week passed, and another. January ended and February began, and the first signs of spring could finally be seen. Snowdrops and crocuses pushed up in window boxes, daylight stretched to teatime, a pair of thrushes set up home in the hedge that separated them from the neighbouring garden.

And then, while he was still waiting to hear from the university, when they were alone in the house one evening, Heather dropped the bomb.

It's not you, she said. *You're still wonderful. It's me. There's something wrong with me. It happens every time I go out with someone – it's fine for a while and then . . . I just . . . I don't know, I have to move on.*

He couldn't believe it. *You're breaking up with me?* It was a joke; it had to be.

I'm sorry, she said. *I really am. It's not you, Christopher, honestly.*

But of course it was him. *I'm going to go to college,* he said. *I've been checking out courses, I've applied to do arts. I'm going to teach music.* To hell with his plan to wait: he had to tell her now. He had to change the look on her face, whatever it took.

But it didn't work. It made no difference. *This has nothing to do with you and college,* she said. *It's not that.*

What is it then? Tell me what you want me to do, he begged. For her he would have slithered naked over broken glass – but she shook her head and told him again how sorry she was.

Is there someone else? he asked, straight away wishing it unsaid, terrified to hear her answer – but she said no, nobody else.

It was over, and he hadn't seen it coming. He'd had no idea. He felt as if she'd ripped out his heart and trampled it to pulp. *Don't do this,* he said. *Don't leave me. Please don't leave.*

But she left – or rather, he did. The following morning, after a sleepless, endless night on the living-room couch, after she and the others had gone to work – the careful voices in the kitchen, saying things he couldn't hear – he packed his things and moved out. Before leaving he phoned the bar and told his boss he wasn't coming back, and hung up while the boss was still telling him what he thought of him. He left his keys on the bedside locker and closed the front door behind him and took the first bus home, drowning, suffocating in grief.

For a week he stayed in bed, getting up to eat purely to avoid his mother force-feeding him from a tray. *You're as well off*, she told him. *Better that it happened now than later. You're still young, you have years to find the right person.* Every word was like a fork digging deep, twisting in his flesh. He hated her for not understanding, hated everyone who couldn't see that his world had ended. He thought about his plan to propose, and saw how close he'd come to making a complete fool of himself.

One morning, when he dragged himself downstairs for breakfast, his mother handed him an envelope. He saw the university logo in the corner, and his forwarded address in Heather's looped handwriting. He ripped it open and read that he'd been accepted on an arts-degree course for the following academic year.

His initial reaction was to tear it into pieces – what did he want with college now? What did anything matter any more? He looked up and regarded the silent hope in his mother's face. He dropped the letter onto the table and left the room without a word, ignoring the egg she'd scrambled for him.

For the rest of the day he walked, unwashed, unshaven, hands thrust into the pockets of the jacket Heather had given him for Christmas. He turned everything over in his head, trying to find a way out of his misery, trying to crawl out of the hell he'd been plunged into. Trying to find a shape for the rest of his life.

College, no college. Eeny meeny miny mo. His mind turned

endless corners as he trudged along, averting his gaze from approaching pedestrians, praying he wouldn't meet anyone he knew. He'd submitted his college application for all the wrong reasons; he could see that now. Trying to change for her, trying to be someone he wasn't – but maybe the time had come to change who he was.

He hadn't written a song in months, hadn't picked up the guitar in nearly as long. He'd failed to find work as a musician in Galway, hadn't managed to get a single paid gig: what hope did he ever have of making his living from it?

Maybe it was time to face up to the fact that he simply wasn't good enough.

He could give college a go. He could try it for a year, or even a term. It wouldn't kill him. And if he made it all the way to graduation, a degree still didn't bind him to anything. It just gave him more options.

He wouldn't study music though. He was finished with music: it held too many painful associations now. He'd choose something a million miles away from music.

When he returned home at dusk, frozen and weary and starving, his mind was made up. 'I'll start college in the autumn,' he told his parents, 'but I'm going back to Lanzarote until then' – suddenly craving blue skies, and more distance between him and Heather. His parents made no objection, no doubt relieved that he was finally doing what they wanted. His father even paid for his return air ticket.

In Lanzarote he chose a different resort. He found work behind the counter of an English bar, and worked as many hours as they'd give him. In his free time, just for the hell of it, he played his guitar on an unfamiliar prom, and people threw coins into his hat like before. After work he slept on a sofa-bed in the apartment of another barman, in return for a quarter of his nightly wage.

He got close to no one. He told girls who asked – and they did ask – that he had a girlfriend at home. If that didn't put them off he gave them what they wanted – and took what they were offering – but he kept his heart out of it. From time to time he was reminded of Heather: he'd hear a similar laugh, catch a whiff of her scent, see someone who dressed in the same style, or who walked with feet turned inward, like she had. Each time he'd banish the churned-up sadness with too much beer.

He flew back to Ireland with a hangover on a chilly morning towards the end of September. His mother met him at the airport, and in the car on the way home she told him, in the gentle manner of someone announcing a death, that Heather and Robert had been seeing one another for a while.

Before Christopher had finished his first year in college they were married. The wedding was in Rome: he tore up his invitation.

In the years that followed his graduation, music crept back into his life and became his solace. He didn't compose, and rarely played any more, and never to an audience, but he listened. He listened to virtually everything – classical, jazz, folk, bluegrass – and now and again he attended concerts. And of course he had the choir. Music could still speak to him: he'd just stopped speaking back.

And now the happy couple had two children, with a third on the way, and he was an emotional train wreck, determined never to let anyone hurt him again.

'Mr Jackson.'

He turned from the window and saw his secretary standing

in the office doorway in her usual tailored suit and crisp white shirt. So precise she always looked. He wondered if she was married, or had children. Despite having taken her on over four months earlier, he knew next to nothing about her.

'You have a meeting with the Oxfam people in five minutes,' she said.

'Thank you, Dawn.' He pushed away the useless memories and readied himself for whatever appeal was on the way.

* * *

He didn't possess a single decent pair of shoes. He had four pairs of work boots in various states of disrepair, and one pair of ancient runners from the time when running more than a hundred yards didn't leave him on the point of collapse, and brown leather sandals he'd had for almost as long, which he wore winter and summer around the house when he came home from work. It would have to be the sandals.

He rubbed them with a damp cloth. They still looked terrible. Why hadn't he bought a new pair in the past few days? He showered and shaved and clipped his toenails. He patted on aftershave – Lidl's best; they all smelt the same to him. He pulled on the loose cotton trousers he wore when he wasn't working, and the most respectable of his T-shirts.

Mary used to dress him; she did it without thinking. She'd come home from town with a shirt or a pair of trousers, and he rarely had to bring something back because it didn't fit, or didn't suit. She had an instinct for what looked good on him; he'd never had a clue what suited him or what didn't.

He regarded himself in the spotty wardrobe mirror. When had he got so fat? He attempted to pull in his stomach; nothing much moved. He should shove on the runners again, force himself out in the evenings. He might, when the heatwave passed. Running in this weather was looking for a heart attack.

'You're not going in a T-shirt?' his father asked.

'What's wrong with it?'

'You'd be smarter in a shirt and tie.'

Upstairs again, he found the white shirt he'd bought for his mother's funeral and hardly worn since. It barely closed across his belly – no way would he be able to eat a bite without popping a button. A denim shirt he'd completely forgotten about was even worse; no closing it at all. He took it off and got back into the T-shirt.

'It's this or nothing. My shirts are too tight, and it's too hot for a jumper.'

His father's gaze flicked to his midsection. 'You could do worse than drop a few pounds, I'd say.'

'I could, I suppose.'

'What are you bringing them?'

'A bottle of wine.' He waited for the comment, but none came. He'd gone for a red he and Mary used to like, trying not to think about how long it had been since he'd had a glass of it.

'You could pick up a few flowers on the way. They'd go down well, I'd say.'

'I could.' But flowers were tricky. Flowers might say things you weren't sure anyone wanted to hear.

Her dinner invitation had thrown him: he'd been on edge since she'd mentioned it. He knew there was nothing behind it, she was only saying thank you – but the evening loomed ahead of him like an exam. Normally he was fine to pass the time of day with people, but dinner was a whole different ball game. He was out of practice with proper dinner-table talk, that was the trouble. He couldn't remember the last time he'd been invited to someone's house for a meal.

When had he turned into this person, this man who worked and ate and slept, and did little else? He thought back to the days with Mary, and then with her and Lucy: they seemed to have happened in another lifetime, to another man. He remembered dinners then, lots of them, with friends around the table, and wine, and laughter. He shook the images away – too sad, too painful to recall, even after all these years. All these empty, lost years.

His bald patch was coming along nicely. He should give in and get the head shaved, beat it at its own game. Would it make him look worse though, to have a big round dome on top of his big round belly? Like a snowman in work boots.

'Should I shave my head?' he asked his father.

'Might be no harm.' At eighty-four, his father still had a shock of pure white hair; Clem had been unlucky enough to inherit the early hair-loss pattern of his maternal uncles. 'You could always wear a cap if it got cold. Have you no better shoes?'

'No. They're bad, are they?'

'They're not the best. But Molly won't mind, I suppose.'

Clem checked the clock, ten to seven already. 'I'll be off so. You don't need anything else?'

'I do not. Enjoy yourself, son.'

Clem had fried a couple of sausages and opened a small can of beans for him half an hour earlier, pushing down his own hunger pangs. His father's appetite wasn't the best; after a boiled egg every morning with a thick cut of bread he ate little or nothing until Clem came home in the evenings. Despite frequent reminders to get himself something at lunchtime he tended to ignore the fruit, the tomatoes and cheese, the cream crackers and biscuits that were always in stock.

The only day he had a proper lunch was on Tuesdays. Before leaving, Molly would make up a plate of whatever she could find without even asking him. He had great time for Molly – she was like a daughter to him. He'd do better with a woman around the place to look after him: Clem should see about getting a public health nurse to call now and again, or some class of a home help.

'You have the remote control?'

'I have. Go on away, you'll be late.'

He stopped at a garage on the way to her house. They had bunches of pink carnations that were half wilted in the heat. He selected the best of them and took his place in the queue. Just before his turn came he changed his mind and returned them to the bucket. Getting back into the car he had another change of heart and retrieved them. The young fellow behind the counter gave him a wink when he took his money. Clem pretended not to see it.

Two hours, three at the most. He'd survive.

* * *

He brought flowers, a bunch of pink carnations that had seen better days – never mind, it was the thought that counted – and a bottle of red wine with a Spanish-sounding name. He wore a blue T-shirt over navy trousers that bagged everywhere, and the kind of awful brown sandals that monks and saints wore in paintings. But he'd made an effort, you could see that. He'd shaved – and cut himself twice, twin red scratches on his chin – and his thinning brown hair was combed, and he smelt . . . tangy.

Molly had been like a cat on a griddle before his arrival. They'd eat outside in the yard – no, they'd eat indoors: the yard was much too small, and the flies would drive them mad. They'd have drinks in the yard first and then move in – yes, that should work.

She didn't know if he took a drink, hadn't thought to ask, so there were two cans of beer sitting in the fridge, and she'd got Emily to make a jug of lemonade, just in case. Pity she hadn't thought to get nibbles to have with the drinks – maybe she should run to the shop and pick up a few packs of peanuts.

Calm down, she'd told herself, *it's not the President of Ireland paying a state visit* – but the jitters refused to budge. She had to get this right. She had to make sure the evening went well enough for him and Emily to want to meet again.

There are olives, Emily had said, *they'll do to have with the drinks* – but Molly didn't think he was an olive kind of person. In the end Emily had made a quick batch of cheese straws while the dessert pie was baking, and Molly had changed into the orange sundress that was a small bit roomy on her, but at a fiver in the Simon shop you didn't let the wrong size stand in your way, and everyone said the colour suited her.

What are you going to wear? she'd asked Emily. *He'll be here soon.*

Emily, transferring the cheese straws to a wire rack, had looked at her in surprise. *What's wrong with what I've on?*

What she had on was a washed-out pink dress she'd had forever. It did her no favours; Clem would hardly notice her in it. *I just think your lovely green top and those loose black pants would be nicer* – so Emily had shrugged and gone upstairs, and come down looking a whole lot better. And now Clem was here, and Molly was exclaiming over the flowers and pretending they had a vase she couldn't locate.

'How's the bike?' he asked, as Emily found an old cracked jug and arranged the carnations in it.

'Fine, fine, good as new. Emily, bring Clem out to the yard and I'll follow with the drinks. Clem, would you fancy a beer?'

'I won't,' he said, after a tiny pause.

'Wine, so?'

'Actually,' he said, 'I don't take a drink.'

'Neither does Emily. Will you try some of her homemade lemonade?'

Two non-drinkers: there was something they had in common right off. Molly poured two glasses of lemonade and opened the wine for herself. Seemed impolite to ignore it, and she quite liked the odd glass.

Clem demolished the cheese straws practically single-handedly. 'Now they're very tasty,' he said.

Better and better. 'Emily made them. I don't know what I'd do without her.'

'They're easy,' Emily murmured.

'For you, maybe. She's a born cook.'

'Very tasty.'

Was she imagining it, or did he seem a little ill at ease this evening, not as chatty as he normally was with her? When the lemonade made him belch he looked embarrassed. 'Pardon me,' he said, in the awkward way that let you know he wasn't used to having to apologise for his gassy emissions.

Emily didn't have a whole lot to say either – but she had the rosy little flush in her cheeks that she always got when she cooked, and she'd clipped up her hair with a couple of sparkly butterflies. A bit of lipstick would make such a difference, a nice deep pink would be lovely on her, but she'd never been one for make-up.

In between trying to keep the conversation moving along Molly sipped the wine, which was really very pleasant. There was a peppery kick to it, and a kind of woody aftertaste. She should treat herself to a bottle more often, only a few euro in Lidl – and she wouldn't know the difference between the cheap and the dear.

The sun was dipping slightly but still putting out plenty of heat, although the little yard was by now in shadow. The three of them pretty much filled all the space, Molly and Emily on the swing seat, Clem in a faded canvas chair that had seen many a summer. Thank God it held him up.

'I wonder how long this weather will last,' Molly remarked.

'I'm not much of a one for the heat myself,' Clem admitted. 'Hard to work outdoors in it.'

'It's nice here in the shade though.'

'It is.'

'And isn't this seat lovely? Emily treated me for my birthday a few years ago, didn't you, love?'

'Very generous,' he replied, darting a smile in Emily's direction.

She made no response. The flush deepened a little in her cheeks as she dipped her head to her glass. Molly was going to have her work cut out if she hoped to arouse Clem's interest.

In due course they moved inside, leaving the door open to catch any breeze, and as Emily served up the rib-eye steaks she'd arrived home with on Monday, Molly refilled her glass. Wine didn't keep long, did it, once it was opened? Shame to have to throw it out.

'This is good,' Clem said, attacking his steak. 'A real treat. Don't know when I had a decent steak.'

Molly had seen inside their kitchen presses: packets of soup, cans of beans and spaghetti, tins of steak and kidney pie that she thought had gone out with the ark. Sausages and rashers and black pudding in the fridge, fish fingers and frozen chips and ice-cream in the freezer. No herbs or spices, no pasta or rice or fresh vegetables, no evidence of any real cooking.

'I'm spoilt with Emily,' Molly told him. 'She could easily make her living from cooking.'

'Mam.'

'I'm only telling the truth.'

The more Molly thought about it, the more perfect the idea of him and Emily became. If they were married he'd be well fed – maybe too well fed – and he'd keep everything in their house ticking over. Might be a bit quiet around the dinner table though – but only until the children arrived. Emily turning thirty in a few weeks, plenty of time for three or four babies at least.

She sipped wine – it really was delicious – and wondered if Clem had ever been married, or had children. Maybe a marriage hadn't worked out; maybe that was why he'd moved home from England. He'd never mentioned a wife – Doug hadn't either – but that wasn't to say one hadn't existed, once upon a time. Maybe she'd blotted her copybook, run off with someone else. That would explain why neither of them talked about her.

The meal passed off. Molly enquired about Clem's work, and learnt that he was currently putting a new roof on a house. She asked if he had any interest in hurling and was told that he did, but he hadn't much time for rugby. She told him the steaks were half-price till Sunday – 'just in case you want to pick up a couple for you and Doug' – and made Emily tell him how she'd cooked them.

And with every sip of wine, she found more to talk about. Had he heard of the plans for a new shopping centre on the far side of town? A rumour going around that Marks & Spencer would be part of it – she'd believe it when she saw it.

Would he by any chance like a kitten? The cat from three doors down had had five of them a couple of months ago, lovely cute little things, although to tell the truth Molly wasn't all that much into cats, give her a dog any day. They'd had a succession of terriers at home when she was growing up, great dogs to kill mice and rats, as good as any cat.

Had she ever told him about the blind woman she read the paper for every afternoon? God help her, poor woman hadn't a good word to say about anyone or anything. Lots of money there, a beautiful garden that she never ventured into; what Molly wouldn't give to have a garden of her own.

Finally she stopped for breath. When she reached for her wine glass she found it empty again. Going down a bit too easily.

'Dessert,' Emily said, getting to her feet and beginning to gather plates.

'I hope you have a sweet tooth,' Molly said to Clem. 'This one is my favourite. What do you call it again, love?'

'Raspberry and custard pie.'

'Wait till you taste it, Clem. And she's musical too, did I mention? She plays the piano, and sings beautifully.'

'*Mam.*'

'What – am I not allowed boast about my only daughter? She's in a choir, you know, Clem.'

'We both are,' Emily said. 'It was Mam's idea. Her voice is much better than mine.'

'Is that right?' He seemed more relaxed now. When you looked at him properly, he actually wasn't a bad-looking man. He smiled his thanks at Emily as she set his dessert bowl before him. Getting used to her, not minding maybe that she was quiet.

'Put the kettle on, love,' she said. Nearly time to make her exit. 'Now, Clem, what do you think of that dessert?'

'Delicious.'

'Isn't it? And you should taste her summer pudding. She can make that for you another time.'

Another time – why not? In fact, why not make it a regular thing altogether, once a fortnight or so? He wouldn't say no to a good meal, and it would give Emily a chance to get to know him properly.

She wondered what sort of living arrangements they'd organise, if things went the way she hoped. He could always move in here with them, if he didn't mind having his mother-in-law on the scene. Then again, they couldn't leave Doug on his own, so Emily would probably move there. The house could be spruced up, given a lick of paint, new curtains, fresh carpets.

Doug would want to hang on to the armchair. Maybe they could get it covered.

The kettle boiled. 'Tea or coffee, Clem?'

'Coffee, thanks.'

But before Molly could move, Emily got swiftly to her feet. 'Would you mind if I went to bed? I have a toothache.'

Molly stared at her. 'A toothache? You never said.'

But she was already shaking hands with Clem, telling

Molly to leave the dishes, they could do them tomorrow. And with that she was gone.

A beat passed. Molly became aware that the Dean Martin CD she'd chosen as background music had finished some time ago. 'Sorry about that,' she said. 'You might have noticed she's a bit shy with new people. Once she gets to know you she'll be grand.'

A toothache, out of nowhere.

'No big deal,' he replied, stacking dessert bowls, bringing them to the sink. 'Where d'you keep the cups?'

They loaded up a tray and moved back out to the yard, where the sun was finally leaving a sky that blazed with streaks of red and orange and violet. Shepherd's delight, another beautiful day tomorrow.

The wine had left Molly feeling a bit feathery around the edges, a bit soft and sentimental. Was it her fault that Emily had vanished so abruptly? Had she made her feel self-conscious, gone on about her a bit too much in front of Clem? Her motives had been good, but with Philip gone, the last thing she wanted to do was alienate her remaining child.

The thought of Philip brought its usual wash of emotion. She blinked hard, took a breath in. Steady now, you have a visitor.

'Will I pour?' he asked.

'Do.' She watched as he lifted the coffee pot and filled the cups. 'I have a son,' she said. 'I don't think I told you about him.' The words coming out unbidden, making their way into the air between them without asking permission.

He looked at her in surprise. 'You didn't. I thought you only had Emily.'

'He's her twin. Philip.' His name halted her tongue for a

few seconds. *Philip*, she heard, echoing in the still evening air. 'He . . . took off five years ago, out of the blue. We haven't seen him since.' Another stop. She kept her face turned to the sky and blinked hard again. She shouldn't have mentioned him.

'Does he keep in touch?'

'Oh, he does.' She collected herself and reached for her cup. 'He sends us postcards. He's in New Zealand.' Might as well tell it all while she was at it. 'We have no address for him, though. He never puts an address.'

He made no response. Silence, even when it stretched out like it was doing now, didn't seem to bother him.

'We didn't have a row, nothing like that. He just . . . went off.' Watching the little jiggle on the surface of her coffee, putting her other hand on the cup to steady it. 'I write letters to him, but I have nowhere to send them – isn't that daft?' She bit her lip hard, waited for the tremble in her chin to go away. 'Sorry,' she said. 'I don't know where all that came from.'

'No bother. Sometimes it helps to say things out.'

'I think the wine might have loosened my tongue.'

'It can do that, for sure.'

'Mind you, I'm an awful talker at the best of times.'

He gave a small laugh. 'Nothing wrong with that.'

She sipped coffee. 'Emily is quiet. More like her father.'

'Nothing wrong with that either.'

'No . . . I might have embarrassed her a bit tonight though. I can't help boasting about her. To be honest, I don't know what I'd do without her.'

'I'm sure she sees that,' he said. 'I wouldn't worry about it.'

His words comforted her. She turned to regard him. 'You know something, Clem? I can't imagine what I'd do without you either. For the jobs,' she added, when she heard how it sounded.

He smiled. 'I could say the same about you – with you cleaning for us, I mean. We were in a right state before you started coming.'

They fell silent again. The colour was beginning now to leach from the sky. She touched her foot to the ground and made the seat sway gently, her composure restored. Room enough for two: he and Emily might sit here eventually, exchanging dreams, making plans.

'Thanks for this,' he said eventually. 'It was very pleasant.'

'For us too,' she told him. 'We hardly ever have people to dinner, and it's as easy cook for three as for two. Well, for Emily it is. I can't boil an egg.'

'Me neither.'

His features were becoming indistinct in the twilight. 'You should try those steaks. Get a couple tomorrow in the supermarket.'

'I might do that.'

'Will you have more coffee?'

He shook his head, hauled his bulk upwards. 'I'll be off now, let you get to your bed.'

She stood on the path and waved until the yellow van pulled away. Her head buzzed softly. She couldn't believe she'd told him about Philip; she so rarely brought him up in conversation. Blame the wine, definitely – but at least she'd kept quiet about Paddy.

She'd seen him again today, a week since their first encounter – and for the second time the resemblance to Philip had halted her in her tracks. He couldn't be someone else's child; he just couldn't.

She'd made her offer of babysitting, trying not to sound too eager. *I'm free every evening except Monday*, she said, having decided that she'd sacrifice Fridays if she had to: Dervla would understand – but Linda told her she already had a local girl who babysat. *I will need someone when he starts school though*, she said, *to collect him two afternoons a week and hang on to him for a bit while I meet clients* – but Molly's afternoons were taken up with Kathleen, so that was that. Disappointing, but nothing to be done.

Closing and bolting the front door after Clem's departure she thought, *Tomorrow is Thursday*, and her spirits lifted. Thursday was Paula's day. Paula, who paid Molly thirty euro for two hours of cleaning her little one-bedroom apartment. Paula, whose only instruction, eight years ago, was that Molly should help herself from the biscuit tin whenever she felt like it.

Paula, who left out a sweater or a top every now and again that looked as if it had hardly been worn. *Please hand in to a charity shop if you're passing one*, the accompanying note would say, only Molly knew that was her way of saying, *Help yourself to this if it's any good*. Paula, who always gave Molly an extra twenty euro on the last Thursday before Christmas.

Back in the kitchen she regarded the dishes piled on the draining board. Not that much, wouldn't take more than a few minutes. She started Dean Martin off again and turned on the taps. She got to work on the glasses as the kitchen filled softly with *amore*.

* * *

It hurt. It wouldn't stop hurting, even with painkillers. Her whole face was a mass of pain, waves of it emanating from the back of her mouth, where the gum had gone an angry red, and the tooth, if tapped with a cautious fingernail, sent a spear of agony shooting through her head.

At rehearsal on Monday night it had begun to take hold in earnest, making it hard to concentrate on the songs, earning her a look of irritation from Christopher when she'd missed an entrance. Since then it had been steadily worsening, growing to a deeper, more insistent pulse that eventually shoved everything else to the background and made her feel dragged-down and miserable.

You OK? Charlotte had asked yesterday at break. Emily had told her toothache and Charlotte had said, *Go to the dentist*, and Emily knew she should but she still couldn't face the thought. She was still holding out, still hoping for a miracle.

What's up, Emmy? Tony had asked, as she'd passed by the meat counter later. *Have you run out of smiles?* She'd snapped at him to leave her alone and had felt bad afterwards, but not bad enough to tell him she was sorry, in case she drew him on her again.

The dinner with the handyman last night had been torture: she'd thought she'd never get through it. She could see Mam had been put out when she'd made an early exit, but she just hadn't been able to sit there any longer listening to Mam prattle on, hadn't been able to keep smiling and giving out recipes and pretending everything was alright.

This morning she'd finally given in. Before Mam was up she'd crept downstairs and phoned the dental surgery and asked for an emergency appointment, and here she was half an hour later, having rung the supermarket to say she wouldn't be in to work. Here she was at the surgery, locking her car and approaching the building with a quaking heart, telling herself that it would all be over soon.

Three or four years at least since her last visit here. A filling in an upper back tooth, she thought, replacing one that had attached itself to a toffee or something and been yanked out. Several check-up reminders ignored since then, living in hope that she'd never have to come back.

The whole business of the dentist terrified her. She particularly hated the initial injection, the surge of whatever it was that smelt like oranges but stung like mad as it was administered, making her eyes water, her toes curl with the pain. And then there was the drill, the awful shriek of it, her hands gripping one another, everything clenched as she endured it, waiting in terror for it to hit a nerve – and then the different ache of keeping her mouth wide open, and the saliva that pooled under her tongue—

Stop. Stop it.

She took a deep breath and crossed the lobby and made for the stairwell, steering clear of the lift as she always did: another fear, another thing to be avoided at all costs. She grasped the handle of the door that led to the stairs – but suddenly the thought of dragging herself up four flights was too much. She couldn't face it, not after a night of no sleep. She'd take the lift just this once.

The lobby was quiet. A couple stood waiting by the lift doors. Emily took up her position a few feet behind them, trying to empty her mind, trying to think of nothing at all. Out of nowhere, one of the concert songs came floating into her head. She played it through silently, grateful for the small distraction of top hat and white tie and tails.

There was a soft ping. A red light blinked on above the left-hand door. The three of them moved towards it in unison as it slid open and two occupants emerged. Emily, last to enter, didn't look at her companions as the doors slid shut.

'Which floor do you want?'

She started at the man's voice: in her preoccupation she'd forgotten the buttons. 'Fourth,' she said, giving him the briefest of glances, and he obliged. She thought there was something familiar about him but couldn't figure out where they might have met.

The lift gave a small judder, then bore them upwards with a muted whirr. She closed her hands into tight fists and kept her eyes on the numbers above the door. She ordered herself not to panic, forced herself to breathe, breathe. For as long as she could remember, she'd hated being shut up in a lift, or in any small space. Trapped, no control. No defence, no escape if the walls began to close in, if the ceiling came sliding down—

Stop.

In her head she sang about putting in her shirt studs, polishing her nails. She sang about breathing in an atmosphere that simply reeked with class as her tooth throbbed, as her skin crawled with fear.

Number one lit up, then two. Nearly there, soon be over.

The lift stopped at the second floor: the doors parted smoothly. The woman stepped past Emily and exited alone. Not a couple then, as Emily had assumed. She and the man stood in silence for the handful of seconds it took to get moving again. He was positioned to the left of her and slightly behind, out of her view.

The doors swept closed and off they went again. Number three lit up – and directly afterwards the lift gave a peculiar wobble, and jerked to a halt. The light blinked out, leaving them in almost total darkness. Emily gave a little involuntary scream, terror instantly seizing her.

'It's OK,' the man said, a disembodied voice. 'It's just stalled, that's all. Happens at least once a week.'

His words hardly registered, so distraught was she. 'I'm – I'm—' she stuttered, unable to speak, forgetting to breathe, hands going to her chest, scrabbling at the neckline of her dress.

'Are you claustrophobic?'

'Y-yes, yes, yes.' The word jumping out again and again in frightened little gasps. Her throat was closing – she couldn't get air in. 'I – I – I – I—'

'Breathe,' he commanded, 'you must breathe,' showing her how, inhaling slowly. 'Come on, breathe in, take your time . . .' She drew in a shuddering, jerky breath, and let it tumble out again. 'Good,' he said, 'that's good. Come on, another one, keep going, you're doing fine. Here, hang on to me . . .' and she felt his hand reaching for hers in the dimness, and she clutched it with both of hers and held on to it as if it was the only thing stopping her drowning. 'Breathe,' he repeated, and somehow she breathed.

As her eyes grew accustomed to the darkness she could make out the blurred shape of him, his shoulders and his head, the lighter blob of his face. She began to cry then, great loud gulping messy sobs, overwhelmed by pain and terror and shame. 'I'm s-suh-suh-sorry, I'm – I'm—'

'Don't talk,' he said, 'just breathe,' and again she heard him inhaling – and out of nowhere she was reminded of Christopher at the last rehearsal, warming them up with breathing exercises, raising his arms on their inhalations, letting them drift down on the exhalations, and this image managed to steady her a little as she drew in ragged breaths and let them out again, and tried not to fall apart.

'Won't be long,' her companion said. 'I've pressed the help button, right here – ' but her eyes swam with too many tears to make it out. 'Honestly, you're in no danger,' he went on. 'It's just a mechanical thing. I work in this building so I'm used to it. It'll be fixed before you know it, and we'll get going again.'

His words were something else to hang on to, she drank them in and continued to grip his hand tightly as her legs trembled and wobbled and threatened to buckle under her. *Please don't let me collapse. Please keep me upright.*

'You're OK,' he said, his hand strong and warm in hers. 'You're completely fine. You're in absolutely no danger. I've got you. Just keep breathing, OK? Just keep breathing. You're doing wonderfully, well done. Soon be out . . . They won't be long. They're never long.'

His voice was like balm. She willed him to keep talking while she concentrated all her efforts on drawing air into her lungs, letting it out again. In, out, her face ice-cold despite the scalding tears, in, out, her nose running, her armpits soaked, in, out, rivulets of sweat running down her back.

'Thuh-thuh-thank you . . .'

'Ssh,' he said, 'no talking, just breathing,' and she held on to his hand and managed not to go to pieces, and his voice went on comforting her and encouraging her, and she went on breathing, and after a hundred lifetimes the lights snapped on, and the lift gave a jerk and began its upward climb again. She dropped his hand instantly, mortified at the show she'd made of herself.

'See?' he said. 'All over.'

She swiped at her eyes, at her wet burning cheeks. God, she must look a complete mess.

'You OK?'

She lifted her head and dared to look at him – and immediately she recalled where they'd met.

And so did he. 'It's . . . Emily, isn't it? You work in the supermarket.'

She gave a shaky nod.

Again he offered her his hand. 'Martin Fitzgibbon. I don't know if you remember me.'

'You forgot your wallet,' she murmured.

'And you were very kind.' His smile was wide. 'I'm glad I was able to do something in return.'

'Thank you,' she said. It seemed so inadequate. She'd have had a full-blown panic attack without him. Given herself a coronary, most likely. Fainted at the very least.

The lift came to a stop again. For a second she felt a rush of fresh fear – and then the doors slid apart. A sign on the opposite wall pointed her towards the dental surgery.

'Goodbye,' she said. As she stepped out she stumbled slightly, bumping her shoulder against the door – and instantly she felt his hand on her elbow, steadying her.

'OK?' he asked. 'You want me to walk with you?'

'No . . . I'm fine.'

She didn't feel fine, she felt far from fine. Her dress clung to her back, her throat was tight from crying, her tooth was still killing her – funny how she'd almost forgotten it with the terror of the stalled lift – but she'd imposed enough on him.

'Thank you,' she repeated. It was all she had to give him.

His smile returned. 'Not at all. Nice to see you again.' As

he lifted a hand in farewell the doors slid closed and he was gone, climbing higher. Climbing to the fifth floor, which was the top floor. Working on the top floor, he must be.

Martin Fitzgibbon.

He'd remembered her name.

* * *

'You're such a *bully* at rehearsal.' Tracing a line with one crimson nail, going all the way from his chin down to the top of his boxers. '*Bossing* us all around, do this, do that.' Pulling out the waistband, letting it snap back. Teasing him, like she always did.

'You love it,' he replied, unzipping her skirt, pushing it down past her hips. 'Always egging me on, trying to make me lose my cool. "Christopher,"' throwing his voice into falsetto, '"oh please, give us one more week to learn our words, pretty please."'

Her palm landed hard against his cheek, so fast he didn't see it coming. 'Beast!' she said, laughing.

He grabbed her arms and pushed her onto the bed, pinning her beneath him. 'You want beast?' he breathed. 'I'll show you beast.' Bending to nip her shoulder with his teeth, grabbing a fistful of her hair as she pretended to struggle while she goaded him on. This was the way she liked it, rough and fast – and he made no objection.

She was narcissistic and shallow and vain: nothing about her personality appealed to him. He was using her, pure and simple. She was accomplished in bed – she was like a drug he'd become addicted to. In the two weeks since she'd propositioned him she'd been to his house half a dozen times, pulling up in her red car within ten minutes of his own arrival home from work. Giving him just enough time to shower.

She was married. From the start she'd made no secret of it. Christopher felt an occasional qualm of conscience whenever he considered the husband they were making a fool of, but Jane had no such misgivings.

He's boring, she'd said, their first time together. *He's soooooo dull*. She'd lain with her head on Christopher's stomach, their appetites temporarily sated. *His idea of excitement is having an extra scoop of ice-cream in his cone*. Extending her bare foot to regard her perfectly painted toenails.

So why did you marry him?

Why do you think? Draping an arm along his thigh. *He was my boss. He owns his own company, inherited from Daddy – which means he has a nice big wallet*. Running the back of her hand along his leg, causing the skin to rise in tiny bumps. *I'm afraid love didn't come into it – not on my part anyway, although of course he was head over heels.*

Christopher could imagine some poor bastard falling for her – particularly someone who maybe hadn't had much experience with women up to then. Unable to believe his luck when his glamorous secretary, or PA, or whatever she'd been, seemed to feel the same about him.

His mother saw through me, of course. Old bat did her best to turn him against me, but I managed to persuade him that I was worth a few of her hissy fits. Turning her head, smiling her wicked smile. *I can be very persuasive*. Reaching up to tug on his chest hair. *Don't you think?*

He wondered if she'd kept her word about not telling the rest of the choir what they were up to. He thought of people like Molly Griffin finding out that he was in a relationship with a married woman. Molly wouldn't like it; she'd think less of him. He hoped she didn't know.

But that was the way the world worked, wasn't it? Decent people like Molly were the exceptions. People were fundamentally selfish, doing as they wanted, regardless of who got hurt in the process. Lives were ruined, hearts broken without a second thought. If Jane wasn't being unfaithful with him, he was pretty sure she'd have found someone else. He wondered how long they'd last, how long before she got bored with him, or he'd had all he could take of her shallowness.

Later he watched her getting dressed. She wore suspenders and sheer black stockings with seams up the back, even in the heat. All her underclothes were black or red, and very flimsy and lacy. She was a caricature of a mistress.

'There's a small child in your garden,' she said, looking out the window as she pulled on her top.

'She lives next door. She's taken a shine to the dog.'

'How does she get in?'

'There's a hole in the hedge.'

'So she just lets herself in. Her folks are alright with that?'

'Seem to be.'

The mother hadn't made any effort to block up the gap, and neither had Christopher. The little girl appeared most days, but she wasn't bothering him. He'd look out when he got home from work and see her sitting on the grass next to the dog, holding an earnest one-sided conversation, or feeding him whatever she'd brought with her; after her visits he'd find a scatter of raisins, a half-eaten banana, fragments of biscuits.

He had no idea if she was left alone in the house by day, but after his encounter with the mother he had no intention of probing further. He'd caught glimpses of the two of them a few times since then – coming and going from their house, emerging from the library once as he'd driven past, getting into a small white car outside the supermarket – but thankfully he'd managed to avoid another face-to-face meeting.

'See you on Monday,' Jane said, bending to kiss him. 'If you behave at rehearsal I'll drive you home afterwards.'

He listened to her footsteps on the stairs, the click of the front door opening, the slam of it closing. In the bathroom he showered in cool water, washing away the feel of her, the smell of her. Until the next time.

As he rubbed a towel through his damp hair his phone rang.

'Chris, is that you?'

'It's me, Mother. Is everything OK?'

'Everything's fine. How are you?'

'All good, no complaints.'

She still lived in the house in Dublin where Christopher had spent his entire childhood and adolescence. For the first twelve years of her marriage she'd shared a kitchen with her mother-in-law, whose home she had invaded. Christopher barely remembered his paternal grandmother, who had died when he was five – his grandfather gone before her, long dead by then – but when he was older, old enough to have an adult conversation with his mother, he learnt that the two women had endured an uneasy alliance.

She never let me cook, his mother told him, *and she was terrible at it. If it wasn't underdone it was burnt. And she always gave you and Robert far too many sweets, even when I asked her not to.*

Every Sunday since his father's death Christopher had taken the motorway home and brought his mother out to lunch at the local pub. She'd have the lamb shank and he'd have the roast chicken or fish, and afterwards they'd share a dessert. She was partial to a fruit crumble, and a single cigarette in the smoking area afterwards. Her sin, she called it. *Come out with me till I have my sin.*

The weekly lunch was his way of saying sorry. Sorry that he persisted in having nothing to do with Robert and his family – even when she'd begged him to reconcile before his father died. Sorry for depriving her year after year of the pleasure of a proper family Christmas, with everyone gathered around the same table. Sorry that he'd given her no grandchildren, no daughter-in-law who might make a fuss of her. Sorry that he'd turned into a failed musician and a reluctant businessman, that he'd been a disappointment to her in pretty much every way.

'See you Sunday,' he said. 'I'll be there around noon.'

'Take your time, Chris. No hurry.' As if his time was precious. As if he didn't have the world of it to waste once he clocked off work.

After hanging up he stood at the window, looking down at the child who was still in the garden. She lay on her front, her head hidden beneath a shrub, under which presumably the dog was hiding from the sun. She wore some kind of flowery dungarees, and again her feet were bare. Even from this distance he could see how black her soles were: did the mother never bathe her? And it was past eight o'clock – surely a child of her age should be in bed.

He made his way downstairs and out to the garden. At the sound of his approach her head swung around. 'I'm just talking to Billy.' Defensive; her little body poised to spring up and make a swift exit.

Billy: she'd given him a name. Christopher tried to remember hers, and failed. 'You want to feed him?'

Her face lit up – it literally transformed. *'Yeah!'* Her teeth were small and very white. She had a smudge of something blue across her nose.

She hopped after him into the kitchen. 'Your house is *clean*,' she said, watching as he poured kibble into a mug.

'Yours isn't?'

She shook her head. 'Mommy says messy houses are happy houses.'

He bet she did. 'Where's Mommy now?'

'At work.'

Left alone again, at this hour of the evening: he had a good mind to report the woman. He handed the child the mug. 'His dish is outside – try not to make a mess. So is nobody at home with you?' But she'd vanished. He followed and watched her casting about for the dog's bowl.

'It's over there, under the tap.'

'What's a *tap*?'

He pointed.

'That's a *faucet*.'

'If you say so.' He watched her transfer the food. 'Here, Billy,' she called – and the dog shuffled out from under the shrub and trotted towards them.

They stood by as he crunched. She looked up at Christopher. 'What's your name?'

'Christopher. What's yours?'

'Laurie. And he's Billy.'

'Is he now?'

'When I get a brother, I'm gonna call him Billy,' she said.

'You're getting a brother?'

'Yeah, Mommy said.' So a man on the scene after all. Didn't live with them; mustn't be into messy, happy houses.

'I'm four,' she told him. 'My birthday was in Easter. I got a chocolate cake with four candles, an' I only didn't blow out one.'

'Very interesting.' He refilled the dog's water basin at the tap.

'Billy likes soda, not water.'

'How do you know?'

'He *told* me. He talks to me.'

'Is that right?' Christopher placed the basin next to the food. 'Soda's bad for you. It's full of sugar.'

'Not *diet* soda.'

Diet soda, at four years of age. 'That's worse,' he told her. 'It's full of stuff that's worse than sugar.'

'Well, my mommy drinks it a *lot*.'

'Do *you* drink it?'

She gave him a pitying look. 'Soda's not for kids, only grown-ups. Kids drink *milk*, and sometimes water. But milk is more better for dunking cookies.'

At least the woman had some sense. 'So who's looking after you today?'

'Mommy.'

'You told me she's out.'

'She's not *out*, she's at work. In her office.'

'Her office?'

'Yeah. I have to be quiet when she's at work, or she gets mad.'

So she worked from home: he was marginally relieved. Still sounded like the child was left to her own devices a fair bit though. 'What time do you go to bed?'

'I don't know. When Mommy tells me.'

'Aren't you sleepy? It's very late.'

'Is not. It's only late when it's *dark*.'

He let it go. 'Will you be starting school soon?'

'I'm *already* in school. My teacher is Kate.'

Playschool, it must be. A few hours in the morning. At least she wasn't expected to amuse herself all day. 'So what work does your mommy do?'

'Laurie!'

An ear-splitting screech sounded from alarmingly close – she must be standing at the back door. He wondered if she'd overheard their conversation, and decided he didn't much care. 'Off you go,' he said.

She scampered down the garden and disappeared. He listened to the rustle in the hedge, the soft little pit-pat of her feet on the grass as she hurried up the other side. He wouldn't have minded having a daughter – as long as she was well behaved and not at all whiny. That one didn't seem too bad.

He glanced at his watch: almost eight thirty and nothing at all to do until bedtime. Not in the mood for simply listening to music: Jane's visit had energised him. He needed to move.

He regarded the dog, sprawled again on the ground. 'Fancy a walk?'

It lifted its head and regarded him wearily.

'Just around the block. I'll go slow.'

Its tail gave a limp wag.

'Good enough.' He went in to get the lead.

* * *

Monday morning, the start of their third week of sunshine. No sign of a break – if anything, it was getting hotter. The nasturtiums in the hanging basket were limp and tired, despite her dousing them with a jug of water whenever she thought of it. Sleep was continuing to be a challenge, half the night spent trying to find a cool place on the sheet. Even the radio, the only thing that had put her to sleep since Philip's departure, wasn't really working any more.

After lunch she showered and changed into a pair of wonderfully baggy khaki shorts – well, khaki once upon a time, more like a dirty cream now – and an ancient blue shirt of Philip's, equally roomy and cool, sleeves rolled above her elbows. Hardly the height of fashion, even without the frayed shirt collar, the scorch mark on the shorts' right buttock – but who'd see her?

Kathleen's house was across town, not too far from the supermarket where Emily worked. At busy times the journey from Molly's by bus, or rather buses, could take up to forty-five minutes; on the bike it was twenty at most.

Today she wasn't going straight to Kathleen's though. Today she was giving herself an extra fifteen minutes for a detour, because Linda's house was sort of on the way to Kathleen's. She just wanted to cycle past, see if there was any sign of him. Just a glimpse would do, just a look at his face to keep her going till Wednesday.

It was shocking how much she thought about him. He had taken up residence in her head, right next to Philip. He was her connection: that was the truth of it. He made her feel closer to her son.

She cycled slowly past the house. Linda's car was in the driveway but there was no sign of the little yellow tricycle, or the boy who owned it. At the end of the road she doubled back to pass the house again. It occurred to her that Linda might look out a window and see her – but so what? There was no law against cycling on a public road.

Still no sign of him – and she had to get moving or she'd be late for Kathleen. She swallowed her disappointment and cycled on. Shortly before two she dismounted outside a large detached house and wheeled her bicycle around to the back. Before she had a chance to rap on the door it was opened.

'Am I glad to see you.' Jenny's fringe looked as if it had been glued to her forehead. Beads of sweat clustered on her upper lip. 'She's like a bear today. Nothing is right.'

'Lovely.' Molly dropped her house keys on the table and glanced at the front-page headlines of the newspaper that sat waiting for her. A threatened transport strike, another gangland killing, more bombs falling in Syria, a rise in the number of homeless. Plenty of ammo if Kathleen was in the form for a rant.

Jenny shucked off her white cotton mules and threw them into her bag. She pushed her bare feet into blue flip-flops that waited by the door: 'Oh God, that feels so good.' She slung her bag onto her shoulder, swiped hair off her face. 'See you at four. Good luck, Molly.'

She pulled the door shut behind her, leaving a waft of something sharp in her wake – window cleaner? Furniture polish? Molly listened to the receding *slup slup* of her steps, the distant slam of the car door, the burst of sound that was the engine coming to life, the silence it left behind after its departure. The air in the room, once it settled again, was close and heavy. The window was tightly closed, like all the windows in the house.

Time to face the music and dance. Molly stepped out of her sandals and left them where Jenny's flip-flops had lain. She took her slippers from her bag – but today the feel of the cool tiles on her bare feet was too lovely to pass up. She shoved the slippers back and tucked the newspaper under her arm and walked through to the sitting room.

'Here I am!' She heard the hearty voice that always materialised for Kathleen. 'Another beautiful day – aren't we getting a great run of it?'

'It's too *hot*.' Peevish. Sitting at the end of the sofa where she always sat, directly facing the window even though the view beyond it was lost to her. 'How can you *move* in this weather?' Hands lying limply in her lap, mouth a narrow discontented line, pale cheeks blotched with pink. 'I'm worn out from it. Did you take off your shoes?'

'I did. I'm in the bare feet today.'

'Well, there's no need for *that*.'

'No, I like it. And I just had a shower, so they're perfectly clean.'

Kathleen had a thing about outdoor shoes in the house. Kathleen had lots of things about lots of things. The hunched shoulders were covered today with a knobbly blue cardigan that was buttoned to the neck. A pair of navy trousers underneath, bony left leg doing its usual series of little toe-heel hops – a legacy of the stroke – causing the loose fabric to bounce lightly about her calves.

'Maybe if you had a lighter top – that cardi looks a bit warm for this weather. Would I go upstairs and see if I can find something?' Knowing even as the words were coming out that she was wasting her time: Jenny would surely have tried to steer her towards something more appropriate, and had clearly failed.

'I *like* this cardigan. I suppose *you*'re as cool as a cucumber.' Tilting her head a few inches in Molly's direction, unblinking gaze falling several feet short of her to land somewhere on the wall behind.

'Indeed I'm not. That's why I'm leaving my indoor shoes off, to try and cool down. You should see my face – it's like a beetroot!'

But of course Kathleen couldn't see her face, and neither could Molly. No mirrors in the room, no mirrors anywhere in the house according to Jenny, who got to see it all.

Molly took her usual seat, a wing chair covered with faded pink chintz, whose arms supported hers as she held the paper. 'I must say the garden's looking really lovely these days.'

To tell the truth, it was a touch too orderly for her taste – if she had a garden she'd fill it with more splashes of colour, more variations in height and style – but you had to admire the neat beds of flame-red geraniums and orange begonias, the clipped line of shrubs whose names Molly didn't know, running alongside the sweep of lawn all the way to the graceful tree at the far end – beech, she thought – that was casting dappled shade today on the wrought-iron seat beneath it. All down to Tim, who tended the garden on Tuesdays and Fridays, another member of the small army of people employed to look after Kathleen.

'I cannot imagine how any garden could look lovely in this weather.'

A heavy sigh, a brief closing of the eyes, as if the conversation was wearing her out even more. Just three years older than Molly at sixty, but it often felt like they were a generation apart. If she'd only try to be more cheerful, focus on the positive. She could be sitting out today in the shade of that beautiful tree, enjoying the fresh air and the birdsong instead of being stuck inside in a house far too big for her, surrounded by musty old furniture and mildewed books she refused to let anyone touch.

She could be getting on with life instead of pandering to the stroke four years earlier that had robbed her of her sight and weakened her left side. It must be horrible to be blind, of course it must – but she wasn't *dead*, for goodness' sake.

Two hours each weekday afternoon Molly spent here. Ten hours a week for the past three years and nine months, reading to a woman who never gave the smallest sign that she appreciated it. Molly was here because of Kathleen's son, who had appeared on her doorstep out of the blue.

Do you remember me? he'd asked, and she'd had to tell him she didn't. And then he'd said his name, and she'd recalled the boy whose father had owned the company where her husband Danny had worked, the boy who would meet Danny every day when he called in after school to get a lift home from his father. The boy who'd stood between his parents at Danny's funeral, who'd shaken Molly's hand along with all the other mourners, even though he was only eight or nine at the time.

I took over the business after Dad died, he'd told her, and she'd said yes, she'd heard that. She'd gone to his father's funeral. She would have shaken the son's hand then, but she couldn't recall it. Must be ten years ago, or a bit longer. Cathal Fitzgibbon had been good to Danny – and good to her after Danny's death, calling around with a cheque that had made things a lot easier in the first few awful months, while she was still coming to terms with her changed circumstances.

I hope you don't mind my calling around, the son had said. *I thought it might be better to meet you in person. I got your address from my neighbour*. His neighbour, who happened to be the daughter of a woman Molly had cleaned for some years earlier. Small world.

You need a cleaner? she'd asked, and he'd said no, it was for his mother. *She had a stroke just over a month ago. It's left her blind.*

I'm sorry to hear that. Molly had searched her memory for his mother, and had dimly recalled a quiet, rather stiff woman. *She's looking for someone to clean for her?*

No, I have all that sorted. This is something a bit different.

He'd wanted Molly to read the newspaper to her. *She misses it a lot. She always read the paper. If you could do an hour or two a day – and it would be just during the week. I'd cover the weekends.*

It wasn't something Molly had ever done before. She'd read bedtime stories to the children when they were small, but this would be entirely different. She didn't bother with the daily paper herself, only on Sunday when it was more gossipy than newsy, and she liked the magazine that came with it. Sometimes she and Emily tried the quizword while they were waiting for the chicken to roast, but they never got far. Emily was good at the films and who won what Academy Award, and Molly could usually manage the music questions, but neither of them had much of a clue about politics or history or sports.

I know it's not the kind of thing you normally do, he'd said. *So if you'd rather not, I'll understand.*

It would have to be afternoons, she'd replied. *My mornings are all taken up*. Already having decided that she would do it for him because he'd shaken her hand when she'd lost her husband. She'd do it because he loved his mother, and hadn't run off with her savings. Kathleen turned out to be impossible but Molly kept going for his sake; every day she turned up for him.

And whenever his mother talked about him, it was with contempt.

That fellow, she called him. *Can't change a light bulb*, she'd say. *Useless around the house. And gardening? Disaster, wouldn't know a weed from a flower. Only thing he's good at is making money.*

That fellow, who'd organised everything she needed. That fellow, who called over every Saturday and Sunday to do what Molly did during the week. It was at times like these that Molly found it hardest to hold her tongue. Count your blessings, she felt like saying. You have a son who cares about you, who makes sure you're looked after. Not every mother is as lucky. So what if he's not into DIY? What does it matter if he can't tell a dandelion from a daffodil? But she said nothing, knowing it wouldn't change a thing.

'Would I open the window a little?' she asked now. The room was as stuffy as a tomb. No air-conditioning, although Kathleen could well afford it.

'And let the flies in? You'll do no such thing.'

'What about getting a fan, Kathleen?'

'A *fan*?' The word heavy with incredulity, as if Molly had suggested she install a home cinema, or replace the bath with a swimming pool.

'A ceiling fan. It would make a bit of a breeze. Or you could get one you plug in that stands on the floor.'

Kathleen gave an irritated toss to her head. 'I have no intention of getting a fan. I don't *want* a fan. I want you to read me my newspaper like you're *paid* to do.'

'Right.' Molly gave up and scanned the headlines again, and wished, as she often wished, that she could change some of them, put a better spin on things. Why didn't reporters hunt down the happy stuff? Why didn't they celebrate the communities that worked together to achieve the impossible, the small local businesses that didn't end in bankruptcy? Why didn't they seek out all the tiny acts of kindness that were carried out every day by people whose names nobody recognised? 'There's not much good news on today's front page, I'm afraid.'

Kathleen gave another sigh, her empty gaze directed outwards once more, towards the beautiful garden that she would never see again. 'Go on.'

* * *

'You poor thing. It must have been terrible.'

'It was, awful.'

'I mean, you were bad enough when you just had the dentist to cope with, but then to get stuck in the lift as well.'

'I know. What were the chances?'

'You were lucky that man was there.'

'I was.'

They were at the cinema. It was Tuesday, not their usual Friday. The bruising on the lower part of Emily's cheek had still been too visible on Friday for her to venture out. Her face hadn't returned to normal, not completely, until yesterday, a full four days after her visit to the dentist.

An extraction she'd had. *It's that or a root canal treatmen*t, the dentist had said – and when he'd explained that treating the root canal would involve at least two visits, Emily had opted for the tooth to be taken out.

The injection had been bad enough, every bit as painful

as she'd anticipated – but the actual procedure, though over relatively quickly, had been brutal in its execution. And while the anaesthetic had protected her from the physical pain of the dentist's tugging – how he had tugged! – and his further poking and prodding at the crater left behind, she'd still cringed and clenched and winced her way through it, praying for him to finish and release her.

If you bruise easily you'll be a bit black and blue for a few days, he'd said, peeling off his latex gloves while she'd rinsed and dribbled and dabbed, *and you'll need painkillers when the numbness wears off, but you'll be right as rain before you know it. Good job it's a back tooth: nobody will even notice it's gone.*

She'd driven home, feeling battered and tender and a long way from right as rain. The house had been blessedly quiet, with Mam gone to work. Emily had made tea before remembering that she wasn't to eat or drink for several hours. Despite the heat she'd run a warm bath and peeled off her crumpled clothes. She'd lain silently in it, listening to the water that rushed through the pipes to refill the tank in the attic above.

The lower left side of her face had had a curious pulled-sideways feel to it. When she'd pressed cautious fingers to her chin, her cheek, her mouth, it had felt weirdly like she was touching someone else's skin. Her eyelids had scraped across her eyes when she'd blinked: a legacy of the scalding, terrified tears she'd been powerless to stop in the darkness of the lift.

She'd cringed at the memory. Such a gibbering wreck she'd become: what must he have thought of her? Never, never again would she set foot in a lift, even if it meant climbing an eternity of stairs.

After the bath she'd scribbled a note to let Mam know she

was in bed, and left it on the kitchen table. The following morning her face in the bathroom mirror had looked like she'd done a dozen rounds in the ring with someone far bigger and stronger, the affected side of her jaw a mass of black and purple and yellow blotches. *No way can you go to work,* Mam had said. *I'll phone and tell them.* Out for a second day, the first time in eleven years that she'd been off sick. She'd dozed in bed till lunchtime and pottered about the house for the rest of the day, and put a salad together to go with the pizza that Dervla always brought around on Friday nights.

Saturday was her day off, allowing the bruising another day to heal. By Sunday it had faded enough to be hidden by a few dabs of Mam's concealer. She was surprised at the number of people at work who'd asked how she was: she'd imagined most of them wouldn't even have noticed her absence.

Tony, for once, had said nothing. He'd raised a hand in greeting when she passed by the meat counter, but that was it. Finally leaving her alone. She'd smothered a stab of guilt, remembering how she'd snapped at him. He'd get over it.

Cinema Tuesday night? Charlotte had asked, so here they were. The ticket queue was short, the place not as full as it was at weekends. They'd plumped for a low-budget Ukrainian film that had made it into the mainstream cinemas after a surprising win at Cannes.

Charlotte fanned herself with a leaflet she'd found on the way in. 'This is the hottest summer on record, apparently.'

'I believe it.' So enormous the new crater in her mouth felt; her tongue insisted on probing it.

'Hotter than Athens today, I heard on the radio.'

'Really?'

Neither of them had ever been to Athens. The furthest

they'd got was Majorca three summers ago, when Emily's pale skin had been covered in mosquito bites within hours of their arrival, and Charlotte had eaten shellfish halfway through the week that had made her violently ill for two days, and the occupants of a neighbouring apartment had partied till sunrise every night. They hadn't ventured out of Ireland since.

'I'm just waiting for someone to die from heatstroke – can't believe it hasn't happened already. I mean, we're not equipped for this kind of heat, are we? Most places don't have air-conditioning, and half the time people don't bother using sun cream. It's like when it snows here, and everything grinds to a halt.'

Emily thought longingly of snow, and frosty air that caught in her throat and put a different kind of fire into her cheeks. She imagined an autumn day with its crisp pale light and sweet smoky scent of bonfires: this muggy heat would be hard to conjure up then.

Charlotte paused in her fanning to frown at a fingernail. 'That varnish doesn't last two minutes. Did I tell you Ian got a new suit for the wedding?'

'Did he really? There's commitment.'

The wedding was only ten days away. Ian's name had been dropping more and more into Charlotte's conversations. Emily had seen the two of them chatting on the shop floor, Charlotte laughing in a different way with him.

'Something tells me you might be starting to fancy him,' Emily said, tamping down the tiny selfish niggle of jealousy the mention of his name always seemed to create in her.

Charlotte smiled. 'Maybe I am, a little bit. He's really nice. We'll see how the wedding goes.'

'I'll be dying to hear all about it.'

'Shame you're not coming.'

Emily was vastly relieved not to be going. The few family weddings she'd attended had been exercises in endurance, with relatives invariably asking, the pity evident in their tones, when she would be giving them a day out.

They reached the ticket desk and paid. 'Give me a minute,' Charlotte said. 'I need the loo.'

As she waited, Emily scanned the posters for coming attractions. A period drama, another *Bourne*, a couple of thrillers that looked promising, a comedy that didn't, a science fiction they'd definitely be avoiding.

She heard a familiar booming laugh and glanced over her shoulder – and there was Tony from work in the ticket queue, an arm slung about the shoulders of a dark-haired woman, both of them chortling about something. His tattooed arms were on show tonight, emerging from the sleeves of a black T-shirt.

So he had a girlfriend, or maybe a wife: so much for Charlotte's notion that he fancied Emily. She was pretty too, much prettier than Emily. She watched them covertly, ready to duck if he turned in her direction. She had to acknowledge that he wasn't unattractive: the shaven head actually suited him. And Emily mightn't be a fan of tattoos, but she knew some people regarded them as art. It was just that he was always . . . turned up to full volume.

She did regret snapping at him that time: he might genuinely have been concerned. And maybe his earlier teasing hadn't had any badness in it either; maybe it just was his idea of banter. Laughing with her, not at her.

She spotted Charlotte approaching from the opposite direction: hopefully she wouldn't spot him. Knowing Charlotte, she'd want to go over and say hello, find out who his companion was – and even if Emily had misjudged him, she'd prefer to limit him to working hours.

They made their way to screen four, and the other two didn't appear. As the lights dimmed Emily found her thoughts returning to her Good Samaritan in the lift. So kind he'd been, and she'd hardly thanked him.

Martin Fitzgibbon, working on the floor above her dentist. Working in Fitzgibbon Office Supplies, whose logo she'd found on a list in the lobby after her treatment. She wanted to show her appreciation for his kindness, do something to thank him properly. She'd get him a small thank-you, nothing fancy. Maybe a box of sweets like he'd got her. She'd leave it in Reception for him, no need to present it face to face. She'd do it soon, before he forgot about the lift episode. She was on shifts that started at eleven next week: she'd call in some morning on her way to work.

The trailers ended. The opening credits began to roll. She put him from her mind.

* * *

Paula O'Brien threw a punnet of Wexford strawberries into her trolley. She'd forgotten to put cream on the list: she made a mental note to pick it up when she got to the dairy section. Couldn't have strawberries without cream. Harry at work put black pepper on his: Paula couldn't imagine anything less appealing. *Try it before you condemn it*, he'd said, but some things you just knew. Strawberries without cream made as little sense as a brown bag of chips without lashings of salt and a small lake of vinegar.

She moved along the aisles, adding cereal and toilet rolls and tea and sardines and custard creams to the trolley. She had a terrible weakness for custard creams, got actual withdrawal symptoms if she went more than three days without one. At the meat counter she waited while Tony sliced ham on the bone for an elderly customer.

'Nice little bit of marbling in that, love,' he said, holding up the slices for her attention. 'Good for what ails you.'

'I like the bit of fat, and so does my Gerard.'

'And you're dead right. Too many turning up their noses at it these days.'

'All I know is it never did us any harm, never sick a day in our lives. How much are your pork chops?'

'Three for a euro to you, love.'

Paula listened to the exchange. He could talk to anyone, he was nice to them all. She bet his customers loved him. She bet some people shopped in this supermarket just because of him.

Thank God she'd had the sense not to marry him.

Eventually Gerard's wife moved off and he turned to Paula. 'Yes, madam – what can I help you with today?'

She regarded the displayed meats. 'Any special offers?'

'Cheapskate. Chicken breasts are half-price.'

'What are you doing for dinner tomorrow night?'

'Going to yours, by the sound of it.'

'I'll take two chicken breasts so, and half a pound of sausages.'

'How're things?' he asked, assembling her order. 'Haven't seen you in a while.'

'You saw me on Tuesday. We went to the cinema.'

'Lot can happen in three days.' He slapped the sausages onto waxed paper. 'God made half the world in three days.'

'So they say. I'm afraid I have nothing as dramatic to report. I did buy a new kettle yesterday though. Blue.'

'Well, that's something.' He handed her the package. 'Would we chance the movies again after dinner? My treat.'

'Only if it's something I want to see. I haven't forgiven you for that spy thing.'

'Right, this time you choose – as long as it's not mush. See you around six.'

They'd grown up together: he was literally the boy next door. Their birthdays were a fortnight apart. She couldn't remember a time when they hadn't been friends. Not inseparable: once they'd hit their teens, different schools and different interests steered them in new directions – sometimes days would go by without them meeting up – but they remained friends, always perfectly comfortable in each other's company.

He wasn't the first boy she'd kissed: that honour fell to Seamus Harvey, on the back seat of a bus when she was fifteen. She didn't get together with Tony for another two years; he didn't propose for another five.

They were both twenty-two. They were young, but he was her best friend. It was the right thing to do, she told herself. You didn't have to be head over heels, you just had to be right together, and they were as right together as any couple could be. Everyone said so. Tony and Paula, as well matched as strawberries and cream.

They booked the church and the hotel and the honeymoon. She'd always wanted to see Venice. They sent out the invitations and organised the cake and the flowers and the photographer. She went shopping with her mother and her bridesmaid for a dress.

And every time the doubts surfaced, she pushed them

down. Every time her gut instinct railed, she stifled it. Every time she cried silent, private tears, she washed her face and blotted it dry and covered the puffy skin around her eyes with concealer.

And then, a week before she married him, she finally gathered her courage together and told him why she couldn't. And because he loved her their friendship, although badly battered, eventually endured. And in time everyone else stopped talking about her behind their hands and accepted that Paula O'Brien preferred women to men.

It was a lot harder for her parents, she knew that. Her mother had eventually come to uneasy terms with it; her father still didn't know how to look at her properly, how to talk to her like he used to – but she and Tony survived.

And now they were in their mid-thirties, and so far neither of them had found anyone else. She'd had her moments, and so had he, but nothing had come of them. She told herself she was happier alone, and sometimes she believed it. She was sorry he hadn't met someone though. She hoped she hadn't scared him off women for life: under the tattoos and the ebullient exterior beat a kind and generous heart that deserved to be loved deeply.

She was at the checkout when she thought of the cream. 'I'll get it,' the assistant said, rising from her stool. 'Which one do you want?'

'Just a small tub, the normal stuff.'

'Is own brand OK?'

'Fine . . . thank you.'

She was one of the obliging ones: she helped you pack too, if she wasn't busy. They weren't all like that. As Paula waited for her cream, pretending not to hear the shuffling in the queue behind her, she caught a flash of red outside the window and saw a shiny BMW pulling into a mother and toddler parking space. She watched the female driver emerge with no toddler or baby in tow and approach the supermarket entrance; she saw the two male customers on their way out who both turned to follow her progress. Good haircut, expensive clothes. You could tell by looking at her that she was used to being stared at, and that she liked it.

'I got the longest date I could find.'

'Thanks so much.' Paula turned her attention back to the job in hand. She paid for her groceries and packed them into her canvas bag. She scanned what she could see of the shop floor as she made her way towards the exit, but the BMW driver had disappeared. Outside, she walked past the red car, parked where it had no right to be.

Typical of the driver to park wherever the hell she liked. Ironic that she'd chosen a mother and child space, given that she and her husband had produced no child in eight years of marriage.

Eight years since she and Paula had met, eight years since Paula had taken over her job. Receptionist marrying the boss – wasn't the first time it had happened. The wife worked part-time in a small art gallery now – in the kind of job, Paula imagined, that required you to look good, and little else. She rarely appeared at her husband's workplace, and when she did she pretty much ignored everyone on her way to his office.

For the hour or so she put in at the Christmas party each year she looked bored to tears. She'd married him for his money; that much was patently obvious to all of them. He was wrong for her in every possible way. Paula could imagine how easily she'd seduced him, how skilfully she'd charmed him until she had his wedding ring on her finger, his gold credit card in her purse.

She was probably playing around: a woman like that wouldn't think twice. Plenty of pickings at the art gallery, or wherever she spent her time when she wasn't looking pretty there. It was none of Paula's business – but her heart bled for him. He was a good man who'd been horribly used, who was still being used. It was nothing to do with her, but in unguarded moments she glimpsed the sadness in him, the weary resignation of a man who'd made a wrong choice, and who didn't have the courage, or the know-how, to effect a change.

Paula very much doubted that the wife would ever leave him: why would she, when she had it so good? Was he to spend the rest of his life shackled to her, letting her bleed him dry, watching her spend the company's profits as soon as they were made?

Not her problem. Not within her gift to help him, much as she wished to. She loaded her groceries into the boot of her little blue Fiat. She climbed in and drove out of the car park and turned for home.

* * *

Putting on the new roof wasn't the problem: he'd been putting on roofs for twenty odd years. The problem was the bending, the crouched position he was forced to adopt while he fitted the tiles. His lower back and calves ached on the way home, his body reminding him that he was just two months away from fifty candles on the cake. Not that he was planning a cake, or anything remotely resembling a party.

But fifty wasn't old. Look at all the well-known people who were still going strong on the wrong side of it. Granted, more than a few had shuffled off their mortal coils lately – David Bowie, Alan Rickman, Muhammad Ali – but there were still a fair few hale and hearty over-fifties doing the rounds.

Look at Molly Griffin. She was his own age, or thereabouts. Energy enough for two that woman had, their house never so clean since she'd started giving it the treatment every Tuesday. And today was Tuesday: fresh sheets on his bed tonight. Never in his life had he had his sheets changed every week.

Molly on her own a long time, like himself. The news of a son had come as a surprise, the night he'd gone to dinner. Can't have been easy for Molly, the boy upping and leaving like that. A row maybe, despite her saying there hadn't been one. Something anyway must have triggered it. Bit cruel all the same, not to let them have an address for him. Five years a long time to hold a grudge.

I can't imagine what I'd do without you, she'd said in the yard, her features dimmed by the fading light. For the jobs, she meant – she'd said that too, right afterwards – but it was still nice to hear. *I can't imagine what I'd do without you*.

Tnx for enjoyable night, he'd texted the following day. *Next time my treat*. Sent off to her before he could change his mind, not even sure what he'd meant by it. He could take her out maybe, buy her a meal to return the favour – except that *her* dinner had been in return for fixing the bike. It would be like thanking her for thanking him.

Did there have to be a reason though? Could you not just take someone out, treat them to dinner because you enjoyed their company?

He'd done nothing about it since, nearly two weeks ago now. She'd probably forgotten it. Maybe he should forget it too, leave well enough alone. She might get the wrong idea.

Would it be the wrong idea though?

He got home and pulled up to the path, laying the subject aside. He sat looking out at the modest red-brick frontage, the door and single window downstairs, the two smaller windows above. The house sandwiched between two identical others, ten altogether in the row. Like a line of Lego blocks, except not as colourful. Molly's house wasn't dissimilar, roughly the same size, in the middle of a terrace too, except her layout was a bit different inside.

He remembered how cramped, how shabby his boyhood home had appeared to him when he'd moved back from London to live in it again. Two bedrooms upstairs, kitchen and sitting room and bathroom below, all huddled together under the slate roof.

But shabby or not, he still felt great affection for the little house. It was where he and Paul had grown up, where they'd been fed and clothed and nurtured until they were old enough to do it for themselves – and in those days it had always seemed plenty big enough for the four of them.

Coming home to live with his father had never been on the cards. To keep things simple, he generally told people – new people like Molly, who hadn't known him before – that he'd moved back after his mother's death, implied without saying that it was to look after his father. The truth was a bit more complicated than that. The truth was that his mother had died several years before he'd left London. The truth was that *he*'d been the one in need, not his father.

Things had shifted since those days, of course: now Clem

was the one doing the looking after. He did it willingly, remembering how close he'd come to self-destructing before his father had come to his rescue, and the scant gratitude he'd shown him at the time.

There was never a question of Paul being involved in the care of their father. Paul had a wife and family; he had a life in the States. Paul, it would appear, harboured little sentimentality for the house he'd come from.

Seventeen years Clem had been away from it. Twenty-two when he'd first headed off, Paul already settled in America by then. But Clem had chosen to go in the other direction, preferring to stay closer to Ireland. And in London it had all gone right for him – until it had all gone wrong, over a decade ago.

He swiped an arm across his damp forehead as he got out. He slid open the van's rear door and hauled his toolbox from the floor, prompting another twinge in his back. He locked the van: couldn't be too careful, even if it was on its last legs, threatening to give up on him any day. A miracle it had passed the last test – he doubted it would survive another. Face that when he came to it in November.

Middle of July already, past it. Where was the summer going? And how long was this heat to last? He'd never known anything like it. Plenty of hot weeks in London during the summers, but nothing that had gone on for as long as this. Wouldn't be sorry to see the back of it – easier to roof in the cold, easier to do a lot of things in the cold.

His stomach rumbled as he let himself into the house – and abruptly he remembered the shopping list he'd made out that morning, the one that was still sitting in his overall pocket. No matter: he'd have a shower and go out for a takeaway, chipper only down the road. Cod for him, battered sausage for Dad, large chips between the two of them. Never varied, pair of sticks-in-the-mud.

Silence met him in the tiny hallway, and the fresh smell of the lemon polish Molly always used. 'Hello?' He pushed open the sitting-room door and saw the single bed in the corner, and nobody sitting in his father's chair. The fire Dad liked to see even in the heat had gone out, not a hint of red in the small pile of ash. Molly would have kept it up till noon – looked like it hadn't lasted much beyond that.

He went into the kitchen, to find it equally deserted. A mug sat upside down on the draining board, a plate in the sink. He turned off a dribbling tap. The door to the back was open: he stepped out.

His father sat on the cast-iron seat, hands folded in his lap, head bowed, his walker on the ground beside him. 'There you are,' Clem said. 'I was going to send out the search party.'

No response. No movement, no lift of the head.

'Dad?'

Still nothing. Was he asleep? He crossed to the seat.

'Dad?' He reached out and touched the wrinkled skin on the back of his father's unmoving hand. 'Ah, Dad,' he said softly. He turned the hand over and pressed his fingers to the wrist, felt about for a pulse that he knew he wouldn't find. 'Ah, Dad.'

He sat next to him, close to him. He put an arm about the stiff shoulders and tipped his head to rest it against his father's. 'Dad,' he said, stroking the cold, gnarled fingers. No more pain now, gone to search about in Heaven and find Mum.

Eventually he phoned his father's doctor, who was tied up in surgery but promised to summon an ambulance. While he waited for that to arrive he phoned his brother, who had to be called out of a meeting. After hanging up he phoned Molly Griffin, needing to hear a concerned voice, but there was no response from her mobile, and he thought it wasn't the kind of voice message she'd want to get, so he left none.

And hours later, after the ambulance and the paramedics, after the neighbours with their fruit cakes and sympathy, after the hand-patting and the tea-drinking and the head-shaking, he stood under the shower he'd been planning to have six hours earlier, his father's toothbrush in its mug on the shelf bringing the release of tears at last. He lifted up his face to let them be washed away, along with the grime and sweat of the day.

When he climbed into bed and closed his eyes, his body was crying out for sleep but his mind was far from ready to shut down. He knew precisely what lay ahead: he'd had his share of funerals to organise. He didn't look forward to it: the hushed tones and the handshakes, the yawning grave and the meal afterwards that nobody wanted. The whole palaver of saying a final goodbye to someone.

Eventually, towards morning, just after remembering that he'd meant to try ringing Molly again, he slept.

* * *

'I turn my back for a few weeks and you nearly kill yourself.'

'I didn't nearly kill myself, I just got a few cuts and bruises.'

'Close your eyes.' Dervla snipped at the front of Molly's hair. 'You could have gone under a bus. I could have been buying a hat for your funeral.'

'If I'd gone under a bus I'd have been buried long before you got home.'

'Wouldn't we have cut the holiday short? I'd hate to miss a good funeral. I suppose the choir would have sung you out.'

'I suppose they would. Maybe I should prepare my playlist, just in case. I might suggest it to Christopher at the next rehearsal.'

'Poor man, leave him alone – he has enough on his plate with the concert. How's that going anyway?'

'Fine, we're nearly there. I'm really loving the songs, all my old favourites.'

'Well, we're looking forward to it. Keep your eyes closed. Can you believe this weather? It's as good as Portugal.'

'I know.'

'My tan is wasted; everyone will think I got it here. So have you anything else to report?'

'I got a new woman, did I mention?'

'You did not. Who's gone?'

'The Websters. Remember, the ones with the Siamese cat.'

'Did they have the list?'

'They did. He retired, they moved to France. She passed me on to her niece.'

'Well? Any improvement?'

'Much better. She's nothing like Bella. I've been there three times now . . . She has a little boy, Paddy. He's very cute.'

She said nothing more. Dervla was the one person apart from Emily who knew about the savings Philip had taken when he'd left. The less said about him in her presence, the better.

It was the only time they'd fallen out. In the weeks following his departure Molly had been torn up with loneliness for him, unable to be angry about the money, so lost, so deserted she felt, unable to stop wondering aloud if somehow she'd been to blame for his leaving. And Dervla had held her tongue for as long as she could until one morning she'd finally had enough.

Ungrateful, she'd said, and thoughtless, and self-centred, and selfish, all the words Molly hadn't wanted to hear about him. *He stole from you,* she'd said. *He took your life savings – how can that be your fault? How are you not angry with him? I'd want to kill him if he was mine.*

You don't understand, Molly had countered, trying still to defend him. *You can't possibly know what it's like, you don't have children—* and as soon as the words were out of her mouth she'd wished them unsaid, but of course it was too late, and her stuttered attempt at retraction, her stumbling apology had only added to the awful atmosphere that was suddenly there between them.

No children for Dervla and Gar, despite years of trying, despite countless tests and remedies – medical and otherwise – and repeated rounds of fertility treatments. Every month a fresh kick in the teeth, more dashing of their hopes, until they'd finally given up waiting for Fate to smile on them and decided to opt for adoption – to be told that at forty-six and fifty-one, their ages would most likely work against them. In the end they hadn't applied, unable to face the possibility of more dead ends, more failure.

You don't have children: the cruellest thing Molly could have said to her friend. *I'm sorry,* she'd repeated, and again, *I'm so sorry,* and Dervla had nodded and finished her coffee and gathered her things and left.

Thankfully the rift had lasted only three days – on the third evening Molly's doorbell had rung and Dervla had stood on the doorstep. *I'm not going to let him come between us,* she'd said, and Molly had apologised again, and they'd hugged and made up and never looked back – but since then each of them had skirted around the subject of Philip when it felt like the conversation was headed in that direction.

'There,' Dervla said, setting aside her scissors. 'Go and have a look.'

The perks of having a best friend who was a hairdresser: you didn't have to go all the way to the salon for a cut. Molly regarded herself in Dervla's bathroom mirror. 'Lovely,' she called, but the face looking back at her wasn't what anyone would call lovely. It was fine if you weren't expecting beauty, or a classic bone structure. It was pleasant and given to smiling, and she'd minded her teeth, and that was about it. Danny used to call her his beautiful Irish Molly, but everyone knew that love was blind.

She was grateful, after he died, that he'd lived long enough to be a father, to hold his children in his arms, to see them safely through their first years of life. She always suspected he'd had a soft spot for Emily – the look on his face when he'd gazed at her, the fierce adoration shining out of it. What was that Paul Simon song, something about there never having been a father who loved a daughter as much as he loved his? She thought Danny would have given him a run for his money.

Over the years that followed his death, when Philip was proving a handful, she used to wonder if he'd have turned out differently if Danny had been around to keep an eye on him. Would he have paid more attention to reprimands if they'd come from a father rather than a mother? Impossible to say. They might have clashed – they might have fallen out. Philip might have left home years earlier.

She could have looked for help from other men, of course,

found a father figure to stand in for Danny. She could have enlisted the support of Danny's brother Gerry, or her own father, or maybe a male parent of one of Philip's friends. She could have confided in someone, asked them to have a word with him – but she never had. Too proud – or too ashamed, maybe – to admit that there was a problem. She presented a front to everyone, pretended all was well, covered for Philip if that was what was needed – and she made sure Emily said nothing to anyone either.

The nights she'd lain awake over him though, the river of tears he'd unleashed in her. The time he'd taken a stranger's unlocked car for a spin at sixteen – God, the thought of that still brought her out in a sweat. Pure chance that he'd run out of petrol before he'd damaged it or killed someone; sheer luck that the owner, when Molly appealed to him, had agreed not to press charges.

And before that, when he was only about twelve, he was caught shoplifting at Flannery's corner shop – something stupid, a packet of chocolate biscuits. The mortification of facing Jim Flannery that time, the shame she'd felt, as if *she*'d been the one shoving the biscuits inside her coat. Jim, who'd knocked on her door with a box of groceries the day Danny died; who'd sent his daughter around to them with a bag of unsold buns every Saturday evening for ages afterwards. Weeks before she'd felt able to go back into the shop, weeks of hurrying past it on the far side of the road, praying to God nobody was looking out, her face never failing to go scarlet at the memory of what had happened.

There had always been a wildness in Philip, always a part of him that no reasoning or pleading of hers could reach. He'd be contrite when found out, when she'd smell alcohol on his breath, or discover cigarettes in his pocket, or when the school would report another misdemeanour. He'd swear every time that it had been a one-off, that it wouldn't happen again – but it always happened again. He let her down with heartbreaking regularity.

And after everything he'd put her through she still loved him with an intensity that frightened her. Still missed him as badly now as she had the day he'd left, still felt his absence every minute of every day. Still made excuses for him, let him off every charge. Still hoped against hope that he'd return. He's not dead, she'd tell herself. He's alive on the other side of the world, and maybe he's grown up at last.

'Kettle's boiled.'

'Coming.' She splashed cold water on her face to sweep away the tiny hairs that had settled on her nose and cheeks. She held a towel to her dripping skin and inhaled its cottony smell, pressing back the tears that always accompanied thoughts of her handsome darling, her cruel son.

She replaced the towel on its rail. She repositioned her smile in the mirror and left the bathroom.

* * *

She wrote *with gratitude from Emily for your kindness* on the thank-you card and put it in the envelope, along with the two lottery scratchcards she'd bought, and wrote *Martin Fitzgibbon* on the envelope. A minute later she retrieved the card and added *(working in the supermarket)* below her name. Two weeks since the episode: he might have forgotten.

She drove to the building and parked in precisely the same spot as on her last visit. She entered the lobby and climbed the stairs slowly, pausing to catch her breath on each landing.

Five flights were bad enough in normal weather: in this heat they were particularly hard going, with no air-conditioning on the stairwells. Not deemed necessary, she supposed, with most normal people opting for the lifts. She encountered nobody at all on her way up.

From a window beside the fire door on the top floor she could see the name of the supermarket where she worked spelt out in giant orange letters on the side of the building. Not far at all as the crow flew, just a few minutes away. A seven-hour shift today, and afterwards she and Mam were going to Clem's house.

The news of his father's death had saddened Mam. *I was with him only a few hours before. He was telling me about a rose garden he'd visited once with his wife. All he ever wanted, he said, was somewhere to plant a few rose bushes. He was so sweet, never a word of complaint. Poor Clem will miss him, all alone now.*

He was being laid out this evening at home. They were bringing an apple crumble they'd taken from the freezer; food to feed the grief-stricken, whether they wanted it or not.

Halfway along the corridor she came to a door with a rectangle of glass set into it, and a brass sign for Fitzgibbon Office Supplies on the wall beside it. The glass was the kind you couldn't see through – was she to walk in, or wait to be admitted? There was no bell, no intercom.

She pushed down on the door handle: it opened into a large room that contained four desks, three of which were set at various angles to one another at the far end. Two were occupied by men who tapped on computers and who ignored her beyond a brief glance; the third was vacant. The fourth was positioned just inside the door through which Emily had entered, and had a smiling dark-haired woman seated behind it.

'Good morning – can I help?'

Her face was naggingly familiar. Emily had seen her somewhere lately, probably at the supermarket. One of the people whose groceries Emily scanned, whose store cards she swiped. People she interacted briefly with every now and again, people whose faces she recognised but whose names she never learnt.

'I have a—' She rummaged in her bag and retrieved the envelope. 'This is for Martin – Mr Fitzgibbon.' A warmth sweeping into her face. 'Could I leave it with you?'

'Certainly you could – or you can give it to him yourself if you want. He's inside, and he's not with anyone at the minute.'

But she suddenly felt shy about meeting him. 'No – I mean, there's no need. If you could just pass it on . . .'

'Of course I can.'

'Thank you.'

Making her way back down the stairs, retracing her steps to the car, all the way to the supermarket she was aware of a sense of melancholy. She should have said yes: she should have gone in and handed it to him instead of scuttling away like a frightened rabbit. Locking her car outside the supermarket she imagined him opening the envelope and slipping out the card and reading her words.

Inside she went through the routine of clocking in, stowing her bag in her locker and pinning on her name badge. Taking her seat behind the cash register she pasted a smile on her face, trying to shake the feeling of despondency, but it refused to leave her.

Halfway through her shift she was released for a break and went in search of Charlotte. 'So how was the wedding?'

Her friend's beam told her all she needed to know. 'It was *great*. Sally looked amazing. Her dress was ivory – did I mention? I have piles of photos, I'll show you later. And the food was *gorgeous*, and the band was terrific. I was like the one in *My Fair Lady* who wanted to dance all night.'

She stopped, waiting for Emily to ask, so Emily asked. 'And how did it go with Ian?'

Charlotte's smile softened. 'He was kind of great too. We're going out for a meal tomorrow evening.'

'Oh, that's brilliant. I'm really happy for you, Charlotte.'

She *was* happy for her. Charlotte deserved to find someone good, and from the little Emily knew of him, Ian seemed like a decent man. There was no reason at all for the news to make her feel even more deflated.

The afternoon crawled along. At her desk she scanned and smiled and took money and made change and issued receipts. In between customers she tried to distract herself with songs from the rehearsals, but for once the music playing in her head did nothing to uplift her. So what if he had often walked down that street before? Who cared if he'd just met a girl named Maria? It was all make-believe, none of it was real.

In a couple of weeks she'd be thirty; fine lines had already begun to creep out from the corners of her eyes. She still lived at home with her mother, and it looked like her only real friend might shortly be less available to her. What did she have beyond her health, and a job that paid the bills but did nothing to inspire her, and a passable singing voice, and the ability to cook? She had a kind heart, she knew that – but what good was a heart when nobody seemed remotely interested in it?

When had she last felt truly happy?

'Hi, Emily.'

She gave a little start.

'Sorry,' he said, 'I thought you saw me.'

He was there. He was right there in the supermarket. He was standing at her checkout desk. He was holding up a scratchcard. 'I won ten euro,' he said. He grinned. 'I'm here to claim my winnings.'

His smile was warm; it sent a dart of joy shooting through her. She took the card and pressed buttons on her till. 'I'm so glad,' she said. The drawer slid open: she tucked in the card and pulled out a tenner and handed it to him. 'Congratulations.' Her face was burning. For once she didn't care.

'Thank you very much,' he said. 'There was no need.'

She drank him in. White shirt, sleeves rolled to the elbows. Green tie, grey suit trousers. He looked very smart. His rather colourless hair was thinning a bit on top. He was older than her, but maybe not by a lot. His face was . . . lovely.

'I just wanted to thank you,' she said.

'No need,' he repeated. 'I only did what anyone would have done.'

A woman approached the checkout desk, wheeling a laden trolley. 'Maybe,' he went on, 'I could buy you a coffee sometime. Just to thank you for your thank you.'

'Yes,' Emily said, 'alright.' Heart thudding so loudly he must hear it.

'Great. I'm afraid I'm tied up all day tomorrow, so how about Saturday morning?'

They settled on ten o'clock, in a café midway between his office and the supermarket. 'You never know,' he said, lifting a hand in farewell, 'I might even stretch to a muffin.'

For the rest of her shift there was a soft humming inside her.

Don't make a big thing of it, she told herself. *He's just being friendly.* But he needn't have come to the supermarket to claim his winnings: any lottery seller would have given him the tenner.

It's just coffee, just a casual thing. He feels he owes it to me, that's all. But she'd never have known about the win if he hadn't told her. He'd gone out of his way to come and tell her.

He hardly knows me. I hardly know him. We might have nothing in common. Or they might have everything in common.

Back and forth she went, between *Are you paying by cash or card?* and *Please enter your PIN* and *Would you like cashback?* and *Do you have a store card?* Back and forth, picking their short conversation to pieces, hopping from jubilation to caution.

And all the time, a tiny tentative hope sat quietly inside her. She felt a stupidly fervent desire to dance across the supermarket floor, to waltz past the cornflakes and soap and honey and yogurt, to move like Tony and Maria the night they'd met, like Eliza Doolittle when she'd begun to fall in love with Henry Higgins.

At the end of her shift she unpinned her name badge and retrieved her bag. She said goodbye to Charlotte, not off duty for another hour, and walked out to the car. She'd say nothing about him to Charlotte, not yet. Not until she saw if it was going to turn into anything.

Could it turn into something? The possibility was intoxicating.

In the car, when she pulled her phone from her bag – a quick ring to Mam to tell her she was on the way – she saw a missed call from a number she didn't recognise. It had come in about an hour earlier. No voice message had been left.

There seemed to be far too many digits in it: must be

international. Philip, she thought immediately. What if it was Philip? What if he'd finally decided to phone home? Could their upcoming birthday have prompted him to make contact? Or was there another reason? Was he in trouble again, bad enough for him to be forced to get in touch for help?

Or was he sick, or worse? Was someone else calling to give her the worst news of all?

Eleven hours. New Zealand was eleven hours ahead, wasn't it? She'd looked it up when his first postcard had arrived. She remembered thinking, *He hasn't just put miles between us, he's put time as well.* As if he couldn't get far enough away from her and Mam; as if either of them had ever done anything to deserve it.

The call had come in just after five Irish time, which would be four in the morning in New Zealand. It needn't be an emergency: he could just be up late after a few drinks, and feeling sentimental about home. Or maybe he had a job, maybe he worked a night shift. She couldn't rule it out.

She had to know. Before she could think about it for long enough to change her mind she brought up the number and pressed dial and listened to the repeated long buzz that signified an overseas ringing tone. It sounded once, twice, three times, four. The middle of the night – if it had been Philip, he was probably in bed now. She was about to hang up when she heard a click. Her heart jumped.

'Hello?' A man's voice, not his. A housemate?

'Hello,' she said. 'I'm not sure, but . . . I had a missed call from this number, about an hour ago. It might have been a mistake—'

'This is a public phone box,' he said. 'I was just passing. Where are you calling from?'

'Ireland. Er – what place, I mean, what country is that?'

'New Zealand.' Sounding amused now. 'It's gone four in the morning here. Think someone's been pulling your leg.'

'Right. Thank you. Sorry to bother you.' She disconnected and sat with the phone in her lap. A call from New Zealand, so it surely was Philip – but she couldn't respond. It was like the postcards with no return address, no way for them to answer. She'd just have to wait and see if he got in touch again.

She recalled her visit to the library, a few weeks after he'd vanished. She remembered the newspaper article she'd come across. *Man, 79, recovering after robbery*, she'd read. A widower's isolated home invaded at night, a small sum of cash taken. The man discovered on his landing the following morning by a relative, thankfully still alive but having suffered a heart attack. No evidence of physical assault. The guards appealing for information, anyone who might have noticed an unfamiliar car in the area.

The victim had lived in a farming community that Emily reckoned was an hour's drive from their town, maybe less. The robbery had occurred the night before Philip's departure.

It could have been anyone. She had absolutely no evidence to link it to her brother. But it had happened – and he'd left abruptly the day after.

If you thought you'd killed him, though – even if you hadn't laid a finger on him, even if you were only interested in taking his cash – if you'd heard him getting out of bed and seen him emerging from his room, and then collapsing at the sight of you, if you thought, *I'm after giving him a heart attack, I'll be up for murder*, wouldn't you want to get as far away as you could, as fast as you could?

It mightn't have been Philip. Philip might have had nothing

at all to do with it. It might be just a coincidence that he'd left when he had, but she didn't know, that was the thing. That was the terrible thing.

She picked up the phone again and placed the call to Mam, and waited for her to answer.

* * *

'Hi!' she said brightly. 'I feel we got off on the wrong foot last time.'

She was smiling: a dimple studded her left cheek. Her teeth were good: was it illegal to have poor dental hygiene in America? She wore a floppy white sunhat and enormous sunglasses, and a similar flowery flowing affair to the one she'd been wearing on his one and only visit to her house. Every time he saw her she was swishing around in something – didn't she have any normal clothes?

'I come in peace,' she said, offering him a brown paper bag. 'Oatmeal cookies. If I say so myself, they're damn good.'

He took the bag, his heart sinking. Sounded like she was planning on becoming his best friend. 'Thanks.'

She laughed. 'Hey, don't look so suspicious – I haven't laced them with arsenic. I'm Freddie, by the way.'

Freddie? He wasn't in the least surprised. 'Christopher,' he said. Damned if he was going to ask her in: would take a lot more than a bag of cookies.

'Can you believe this weather? I thought Irish summers were wet and cold.'

'This isn't a normal Irish summer,' he told her, wondering how he might get away, willing his phone to start ringing.

'Heard you on the guitar the other night,' she said. 'Not bad at all. You sure do like your music.'

He made a mental note to close the bedroom window next time the urge to strum a few bars of Dylan took hold. 'Thanks.'

'I play the ukulele a bit,' she said.

'Do you?'

'Laurie loves it. I play at bedtime for her.'

Yes, he could see her belting out 'By The Light Of The Silvery Moon'. The child pretending to go to sleep, just to shut her up.

'Hey, someone told me you have a choir. Sounds like fun.'

He wondered which someone she'd been talking to. 'It's just a community choir, very amateur.' He prayed she wouldn't ask to join: even if she sang like Aretha Franklin he couldn't face her every Monday night. He'd say there were no openings, which was perfectly true.

She didn't ask. 'Listen, I know Laurie still invades your garden – thank you for putting up with her.'

'Looks like I don't have a lot of choice,' he said lightly.

To his surprise, the smile slid slowly from her mother's face. She'd misunderstood his remark, hadn't realised he'd meant it in jest. 'She doesn't bother me,' he said. 'Half the time I hardly notice her, and the dog likes her.' Trying to fix it, but only succeeding in making it worse: now she was positively scowling.

She removed her sunglasses. The green eyes bored into him. 'The *dawg* likes her?'

'No – I mean I do too.' Oops, that could definitely be taken up the wrong way. 'Look, I don't mind her coming in,' he said – but she'd begun to back away from him, her mouth a tight, thin line. No sign of a dimple now.

'You know what?' she said. 'I sincerely hope those cookies choke you.'

'Come on,' he said, 'it was a joke. I was *joking*, for God's sake' – but she'd wheeled away and was striding down the path, sweeping out of the gate, her gown, or whatever it was, floating and billowing after her.

He supposed he should feel bad – she'd come around with a present, and he'd managed to offend her – but in truth he was more relieved than regretful. The last thing he wanted was for her to start dropping in with baked goods, imagining them to be friends.

Since buying the house and moving into the neighbourhood several years earlier, he'd successfully kept his distance from the inhabitants around him, managing to limit their interactions, when they occurred, to a genial nod, a 'hello' at the most. Of the dozen or so families on the road he knew only a handful of names. He felt this was probably not something he should be proud of, but it suited him. It was the way he liked it.

Now it looked as if he wasn't even going to be on those casual terms with the newest arrivals. Silly woman: her fault for being so sensitive, for not recognising a joke when she heard it. He doubted he'd be seeing much of Laurie from now on either, which was a bit of a shame. The dog would miss the attention.

In the kitchen he opened the brown bag and inhaled the contents: toasted nuttiness, no hint of arsenic. He tipped the cookies onto a plate and picked one up.

He bit into it. It was still warm. It was crumbly and chewy at the same time. It had the soft fruity burst of raisins and cranberries, and the welcome crunch of some kind of nut –

macadamia? There were little black seeds in it – poppy, he guessed – and sesame too, and he thought he detected an aftertaste of honey, or maybe it was maple syrup.

It tasted like another, and then another. Before he knew it he'd eaten four, and felt vaguely sick. He drank a glass of milk to wash them down. Milk and cookies – he was turning into an American.

He checked the time: Jane would be with him shortly. Jane, who was beginning to be a bit of a liability. Turning up without warning at the supermarket the previous week, telling his secretary she was family. Not on to invade his workplace like that, definitely outside the bounds of what he wanted. Hadn't been pleased when he'd said so either, when he'd refused to go along with her fantasy of afternoon delight in his office. A stick-in-the-mud, she'd called him. They'd got back on track after Monday's rehearsal, but all the same she might not last much longer.

He wiped crumbs from his hands and stowed the remaining cookies in the fridge and went upstairs to brush his teeth.

He looked through the landing window and saw the dog lying by the gap in the hedge. Waiting for his buddy, who surely would never show her face again.

Billy.

He could think of worse names.

* * *

'I'm so sorry,' she said. 'He was such a lovely man.'

They were in the sitting room, where Doug had done most of his living for the past few years. His bed had been moved upstairs to be replaced with his coffin, the armchairs pushed against the opposite wall to leave room for the various people who had shuffled in to sympathise with Clem, and shuffled out again to the kitchen for tea and sandwiches and the many baked offerings that cluttered the table.

Now everyone was gone but Molly and her daughter. Emily was in the kitchen; he could hear the clatter of cups and plates as she washed up.

'She doesn't have to do that,' he said. 'I can do it later.'

'Not at all. She's only looking for something to do while she's waiting for me.'

He should tell her they didn't have to stay. He should let them go home, but he didn't want to. The night would be endless enough on his own: he'd hold on to them as long as they were willing to hang around.

'Sorry,' he said. 'I wanted to let you know, so you wouldn't hear it on the radio. I rang you that day but I got no answer, and then I forgot to try you again.'

'Don't worry about that: you had enough on your mind.'

'Still, I wanted you to hear it from me.'

They sat in the two armchairs, which he'd pulled out from the wall a bit and turned towards the fireplace. He hadn't lit a fire in it since Tuesday: who else but his father would look for one in this weather? Still, it looked horribly empty this evening.

'He had lots of friends,' Molly said.

'He did. Lived in this house all his life. Everyone knew him.'

'Yes.' She tilted her head to regard the coffin, just a few feet away from them. 'He's at peace now, no more pain.'

'That's right.'

Silence fell. In the kitchen the clattering continued. His

brother Paul had flown in at lunchtime with his American wife, whom Clem barely knew. Their sons were summer-camp leaders; they hadn't come. *They hardly knew Dad*, Paul had said, as if that wasn't something he should be ashamed of. Twice he'd brought them to Ireland to meet their grandfather, in the eighteen years since the first boy was born. Two lousy trips.

'The mass is eleven tomorrow, isn't it?'

'It is, but there's no need for you to come.'

'I want to.'

'Aren't you working?'

'I've made other arrangements. My Friday person is a friend of mine. It's not a problem.'

More silence. He allowed it to drift. Tonight she wore the same orange dress she'd worn the time he'd gone to dinner, just two weeks ago. It seemed so much longer. He recalled again his text to her the following day – *my treat next time* he'd put, or words to that effect, and then he'd done nothing about it.

He should have. He should have asked anyway, even if she'd made some excuse and turned him down.

He should have given it a go.

* * *

I have a funeral, she'd said to Dervla on the phone. *A friend's father. Can I do Saturday morning instead?* Dervla had said yes. Dervla always said yes if a favour was needed.

The idea of Molly cleaning houses for a living had been Dervla's. Molly had given up her job behind the counter of a newsagent's when she'd got pregnant, and had stayed at home after the twins arrived. Money was tight with just Danny bringing home a wage but they'd managed – until he died, and she was faced with the problem of raising two children with her breadwinner gone.

She'd returned to the newsagent and asked him if he could use her in the mornings while the kids were at school. *I'm sorry, Molly,* he'd said. *I'd help you if I could, but we just don't have a vacancy right now.* Wherever she went, the story was the same. Afternoon or night shifts were occasionally available, but her afternoons and nights were already spoken for.

You could clean houses, Dervla had said, drinking tea in Molly's little kitchen. *You could set your own hours. And it's something you're good at – you could eat your dinner off the floor here.* At first the idea had felt a little offensive to Molly – was that all Dervla thought she was able for? She'd promised, a little stiffly, to give it some thought – but afterwards she'd realised that it made sense.

She *was* good at cleaning – and what was more, she enjoyed it. She got great satisfaction from a good bout of scrubbing and polishing: why not make money from it? And she'd be her own boss. She could structure her working hours around the children's day. The more she thought about it, the more sense it made. *Cop on,* she said to herself. *Don't be such a snob.*

When she told Dervla she'd decided to give it a go, Dervla immediately asked if she and Gar could be her first customers.

What? No way. You don't need a cleaner.

I most certainly do. I've just never got around to getting one.

Look, I appreciate what you're trying to do—

I'm trying to get someone to clean my house. You know I loathe all that sort of thing – you've seen the dust balls, don't pretend you haven't. I'd be delighted for someone to come and clean – and so what if I know you? At least I'd be sure you wouldn't make off with the silver. Come on – is there a law that says friends can't work for friends?

In the end, to keep her quiet, Molly agreed to clean her house once a week, *just until I get off the ground.* Twenty-six years later she was still calling to Dervla and Gar's detached four-bedroom every Friday morning for two hours, still sharing the takeaway pizza that Dervla brought along to Molly's that same evening, with her thirty euro payment.

Dervla had married well. Gar had grown up in a house three times the size of Dervla's, and had chosen a career in law; Dervla had gone straight from secondary school into a hairdressing salon. Gar's practice earned him a far bigger pay cheque than Danny's much humbler position ever had, but the difference in their respective marital situations hadn't made a whit of difference to Molly and Dervla, who'd been seated side by side on their first day of primary school, and who hadn't wandered far from one another since then. The husbands had got on fine too, until Danny's death.

Stay, Dervla had demanded, when Molly had told her, after six Fridays of cleaning, that she was off the hook. *I'm doing OK now. I have regulars for the other four days, and a few more enquiries – I'll easily manage without you.* But Dervla was having none of it. *Please stay. I've got used to a clean house. And I saw you first, not them.*

You don't have to do this.

Do what? Come on, I need you. So Molly had agreed to stay, and a few weeks had turned into months, and then years.

She stayed through all of Dervla's failed attempts to become pregnant, through the fresh sorrow that followed when Dervla and Gar had finally given up on thoughts of adoption. She stayed through her own weeks of misery after Philip's departure, when the last thing she wanted was to see another bucket and mop, when she would have given anything to go to bed and remain there until he came home.

'You want another cup of tea?'

Clem's question brought her back to the small quiet room. She shook her head. 'I've had enough tea to float a ship.' She got to her feet, needing to stretch her legs. She crossed to the coffin and stood looking down at Doug.

His face was composed. 'Peacefully', the radio announcement had said, and it did seem like he'd just drifted away. The navy pinstripe suit he wore was one she'd never seen before: every Tuesday he'd be in his cable-knit cardigan and brown trousers. He might have married in the suit; it might have been taken out afterwards over the years for other weddings, other funerals. A rosary beads twined its way around the fingers of his crossed hands; she touched the swollen knuckles, felt their waxy coolness.

'It'll be quiet for you without him,' she remarked. 'Not that he made a lot of noise when he was around.'

'No – although he had plenty to say when he wanted.'

She smiled. 'We were talking about roses, the last morning.'

'Were you?'

'He would have liked a few bushes, he said.'

'He was fond of them alright. He used to say if he won the Lotto he'd buy a house with a garden.'

'Wouldn't we all.' She came back and resumed her seat. Clem looked different too this evening. White shirt and black trousers, freshly shaven face and newly cut hair. The shoes were new too, and probably the black socks beneath them. She thought about him going to buy them on his own, and her heart constricted with pity. She wanted to reach for his hand and hold it, but the gesture might embarrass him.

'Is there anything I can do to help?' she asked instead,

and he turned his head then to look at her properly, and held her gaze for a second or two. Studying her, it felt like. Eyes between blue and green he had, like the sea on certain summery days. Flecks of darker blue in them too that she'd never noticed till now.

'Nothing,' he said, turning away. 'Thanks, Molly.'

He rarely used her name: it felt curiously intimate now. She regarded his face in profile. 'Your brother doesn't look like you.'

He didn't, a bit. He was taller and slimmer than Clem, and he had a head full of hair that was as white as Doug's. She could see no similarity at all between the brothers.

'He's more like Dad,' Clem said. 'I take after our mother's side.'

Paul, his name was. Paul and his brittle-looking American wife Callie, whose hair had had all the life long since dyed out of it, whose hand had barely touched Molly's when they'd been introduced.

So how do you know Clem? she'd asked, and Molly had told her about finding his name in the phone book when she needed a handyman. As she spoke she'd seen Callie's gaze flitting over her head to explore the rest of the room, so after a minute she'd said she needed to speak to her daughter, and moved away.

The pair had left soon after eight, when the little house was still quite full. Molly had spotted them exiting the sitting room, had watched through the window as they climbed into a waiting taxi. They'd only arrived from the States a few hours ago: they must be jet-lagged.

But it was his father's removal. What kind of person left his own father's removal before it was over, even if he was tired?

She wondered where they were staying. Would it have killed them to spend a few nights here? Couldn't they have used the empty room that had been Doug's before he'd moved downstairs? She was sure it would have been offered. Mightn't have been the Ritz, but couldn't they have put up with it for one or two nights so Clem wasn't left on his own?

She pushed away the train of thought. Not her family, not her business. 'You won't want me coming to clean any more,' she said. 'Not when it's just yourself now.'

He turned to regard her again, a small frown on his face. She was sorry then she'd brought it up; he had enough to be thinking about.

'We can talk about it later,' she said.

'No . . . I'd prefer if you kept on coming. If that's alright with you.'

'Of course it is, if that's what you want. We can take it week by week for a while if you like – as long as you promise to tell me if you find you don't need me any more.'

He said nothing, just looked at her once more in that searching way. Poor man, not thinking straight this evening.

Emily appeared just then in the doorway, pushing her sleeves back down. Molly got to her feet, plucking her bag from the floor. 'We'll go. You must be tired of talking.'

He stood too. 'Thanks,' he said to Emily. 'There was no need; I could have done all that.'

'It was no trouble,' Emily murmured.

'You'll come to dinner again,' Molly said as they stood at the front door. 'I'll give you a call when things have quietened down.'

'That would be good.'

Without thinking she leant across and kissed his cheek; for an instant she felt his hand land lightly at her waist. His skin smelt of pine trees. 'Mind yourself,' she said, drawing back. He was only an inch or so taller than her.

'I will.' He stood by the door as they got into Emily's car. He lifted a hand as they drove away and Molly raised hers in return. In the wing mirror she saw the front door closing. Going to sit up all night with his father, she suspected, while his brother slept soundly on clean hotel sheets.

She reminded herself again that it was none of her business. Maybe the two brothers had never got on. Maybe, after all, Clem was as well pleased to be left on his own.

And still the thought of him sitting alone beside the coffin left her feeling melancholy for the rest of the evening.

* * *

It had taken her a while to place the woman who'd called to the office. For the rest of the day she'd tried to remember where she'd seen her before, and it was only as she was getting ready for bed that it had come to her.

She was a checkout girl at the supermarket where Tony worked. She was the obliging one, the one who had run for the cream Paula had forgotten that time, even though people had stood waiting in her queue.

The timid smile she'd always give you, as if she didn't expect it to be returned. The way she'd entered the office yesterday too, so hesitantly, like she was waiting to be told she had no right to be there. Emily, wasn't it? Emily, her name badge said, Paula was almost sure.

She might be nice for Tony. They must know one another,

working in the same supermarket. Then again, Tony's full-volume personality would probably terrify her.

She'd brought the girl's envelope in to Martin, told him it had just been delivered – and the next time she'd entered his office, just a few minutes later, he'd been standing by the window looking out. He'd turned, and the brightness of his smile had taken her by surprise.

I won ten euro, he'd told her, showing her the lottery scratchcard – looking happier, surely, than an unexpected tenner should have made him. Still, it was nice to see him so upbeat.

Good for you, she'd said. *Make sure you spend it on something completely impractical.*

Will do.

Yes, something had definitely put pep in his step – and all day today he'd still looked pretty pleased with himself. Should do the Lotto more often, if that was the effect a win had on him.

She arrived home from work, relishing the thought that it was Friday, and only a quarter past four. Martin's idea for them to finish at four on Fridays, let the weekend begin early. Her apartment still smelt wonderfully of polish from the day before. Thursdays were when Molly came and made everything gleam. A cleaner was Paula's one extravagance, and well worth it.

Molly had been a find. She regularly emptied entire kitchen presses to scrub them out, scoured drains with washing soda, hung up clothes that Paula had left draped over chair backs. She did laundry without being asked, pegged it on the pull-out line on Paula's balcony. She ironed when the basket was full, and tidied magazines into a neat bundle, and brought

Paula's rubbish out to the communal bins. It was as if she couldn't find enough to do.

Paula had met her by complete chance, a week or so after she'd moved into the apartment. She'd been scanning the supermarket shelves for a cleaning product for the rather filthy oven that had been left behind by the previous owner. There were so many brands to choose from, all claiming to achieve the same perfect results. She'd selected one of the bottles that looked a little more environmentally friendly than the rest, and thrown it into her trolley.

You're pouring your money down the drain with that one.

She'd turned. Navy coat, brown hair, round face, good skin. Forties, at a guess. *Am I?*

You are – it's not worth tuppence. It might save the planet but it'll do nothing for your oven.

Oh dear. Sounds like you know what you're talking about.

I clean houses for a living, the woman had told her. *I've tried them all.* She'd scanned the shelves, selected a different can. *If your oven needs serious cleaning this is the only one that'll do it.*

Paula had taken in the bright orange lettering, the lightning bolt logo. Everything about it had screamed toxic chemicals. *And what about the poor planet?*

The woman had spread her hands. *I'm afraid it's save the planet or have a sparkling oven, your choice.*

You wouldn't come and clean for me, would you? Paula had asked. Purely in jest: getting a cleaner had never crossed her mind. The apartment was one bed – no way could she justify it.

But the woman had taken her seriously. *I'm afraid I'm full up right now. I only work weekday mornings and all my days are booked, but I could come and do a one-off on Saturday morning, tackle that oven if you wanted.*

Paula hadn't had the heart to say she'd been joking. *What do you charge?* she'd asked, and the woman told her twelve fifty an hour, which had seemed reasonable. A one-off: why not? She could get her to do two hours, give the whole place a good clean.

What time would suit you? she'd asked – and just like that, the arrangement had been made.

On Saturday Molly had arrived on the dot of ten. Paula had shown her around before gathering up her laptop and her handbag, the only two things of any value in the place. *I'll get out of your way*, she'd said. *I'll be back just before twelve*. She'd spent the two hours in the little café on the corner, hopping around social media and wondering what she'd find on her return.

She hadn't been disappointed. The place had undergone a transformation. The musty smell had been replaced with the crisp clean scent of polish. The wooden floors had been buffed; the bathroom was like new; windows and mirrors sparkled throughout. Rugs looked fresher, every surface shone. Even the oven was a whole lot better.

You need to leave the stuff on overnight to do it right, Molly had told her. *Do it some evening and give it a good scald with hot water the next day. Be sure to wear rubber gloves while you're using it, and wrap a towel around your face if you haven't a mask, and leave the windows wide open. It's lethal stuff, but it does the job.*

She'd indicated the two boxes of kitchenware sitting on the worktop that Paula had yet to empty. *I'd have put those away only I didn't know where you wanted things. I'm guessing you've just moved in.*

She was a marvel. Paula had thought about having this every week, coming home to a spanking clean home. On her wages she could afford it; it would be her treat to herself.

Will you put me on a waiting list? she'd asked. *Will you let me know the minute you have a space?* She'd pulled thirty euro from her purse and pressed it into Molly's hand. *You're worth every cent. Did you find the biscuit tin? I forgot to tell you where it was.*

Two months later Paula had received a phone call. *It's Molly, the cleaner. I could do Thursday mornings – do you still want me?* And that was eight years ago, and Paula's friends regularly complained that her apartment was always far too clean, and showed up their places.

Paula had heard Molly sing once, when she'd come home early with stomach cramps. As she hunted for her key on the landing she'd heard a rich melodious voice drifting from the apartment. She'd thought it was the radio until she'd walked in.

I love to sing, Molly had told her, not a bit embarrassed at being overheard. *That and cleaning are two of the things I'm good at. Why don't you head off to bed and I'll bring you in a cuppa and a hot water bottle?*

In all the time Molly had been coming, the two women had met just a handful of times. All Paula really knew about her was that she could clean and she could sing, and that she had never taken a single biscuit from the tin that lived above the fridge. Paula knew nothing about her private life, whether she was married or if she had children, and Molly was similarly clueless about hers.

She went around now opening windows, trying to banish the stifling heat of the small rooms. Never did she remember such a summer, day after day of blue skies and sunshine. Cotton dresses and shorts and melting ice-cream and oozing tar. Freckles and pink noses and peeling shoulders and people in bikinis on their lawns.

And the other by-products of the good weather were there too. Three drownings along the west coast over the past couple of weeks, the victims all in their teens. Several cases of sunstroke presenting in the busy A & E department where Paula's friend Colin worked in Dublin, and no doubt plenty more in other hospitals around the country. Crops wilting in farmers' fields amid ominous talk of water rationing, reminders on the radio not to be wasteful, not to use sprinklers, to opt for a shower rather than a bath.

She changed into shorts and a loose shirt and strolled to the nearby shopping centre. She took her place in the waiting area of the little hairdressing salon that was located between a laundrette and a toy shop.

'The usual?' the owner asked, when Paula had been gowned and shampooed and towel-dried by the young girl whose name she could never remember. Amy? Amanda?

'Yes please. Good holiday?'

'Fine. I could have stayed at home and got the sunshine for nothing, but at least in Portugal I didn't have to cut hair. Avril, will you get Paula a coffee? Milk, no sugar.'

Even though she might only see you once every six or eight weeks, Dervla always remembered your drinks order. She'd been cutting Paula's hair for as long as the salon had been open. Paula had walked in on the very first day, when Dervla was still finding homes for towels and dryers and hair products, and had made a booking for the following day. *On the house*, she was told. *My very first appointment.*

'Any developments?' Dervla asked now, combing out Paula's damp hair, sectioning it with clips. 'Have you met up?'

'. . . Not yet.'

Dervla was the only one Paula had told: even Tony knew nothing. There was something about a hairdresser that made you want to confide in them, a bit like how she imagined she'd feel towards a bartender who was measuring out her third whiskey on the rocks in the small hours. Or maybe it was just Dervla, who didn't insist on nonstop chatting as she clipped and snipped, but who left the door open for conversation if the customer felt like it. For whatever reason, Paula had found herself, during her last cut, telling her about Jenny.

The thing about Dervla was she didn't push. She didn't tell Paula off for not setting up a meeting. She didn't make any comment really, just listened and nodded and let Paula talk.

Jenny wanted them to meet. Jenny had said, more than once, *Let me know when you're free*. It was Paula who balked, Paula who kept putting it off, kept avoiding the issue. It was Paula who was terrified to come face to face with the woman she seemed to have so much in common with on paper.

It was stupid, she knew that. It made no sense to back away from the next logical step. It wasn't that she hadn't done it before: she'd been a member of the dating site for well over a year, she'd met at least half a dozen women through it – and every single occasion had ended in disappointment.

And now she'd found Jenny, who sounded so nice and so funny and so normal, who seemed exactly the kind of person Paula would get on with. For the first time she really felt like she'd clicked with someone – but that was the problem, wasn't it?

What if they met and had nothing to say? What if they knew within five minutes that they'd made a mistake? What if this thing they seemed to have, this connection they'd found that seemed so full of promise, fizzled out like all the others? Paula had such high hopes this time – could she bear them to be dashed?

'I have a friend,' Dervla said, getting to work on another section of Paula's head, 'who has a son. He's twenty-nine now, nearly thirty. Five years ago he took off. Just left, out of the blue, along with his mother's life savings. She hasn't seen him since.'

'That's awful.'

'You know what's worse? He sends postcards so she knows he's still alive, but he puts no address on them so she can't answer.'

'Why did he go?'

'God knows. He must have had a reason, but he didn't bother telling her. He was always a selfish git, it has to be said.'

Paula thought about that for a minute, tried to imagine how the mother could possibly feel, knowing her son had betrayed her. 'Did they get on well before he left?'

'Oh, they did. He was a right firecracker, always in trouble, but she was an expert at turning a blind eye to his shenanigans, thought there was nobody like him. Still thinks it. My point,' she went on, snipping and snipping, 'is that you never know what's coming. You never know when someone might just . . . disappear. You want more coffee?'

And that was the end of it. For the rest of the cut she worked in silence, leaving Paula to consider the possibility that she'd log into her account one day to discover that someone had just . . . disappeared.

* * *

'It was quite off the wall, but still very compelling. The director was a man called Todd Solondz – he's not well known over here.'

'Didn't he direct *Happiness*?'

'You've seen *Happiness*?'

'Yes, at the Dublin Film Festival last year. I went with my friend Charlotte. She's mad about the cinema – we both are. We love films that are off the beaten track a bit.'

'So what did you think of *Happiness*?'

'I loved it, so funny and so sad. I love when someone can make the dark side hilarious. And I loved that most of the cast were unknown actors.'

'Me too – I'm sick of seeing the same old faces in every movie.'

'Apart from John Goodman – I don't mind seeing him in anything.'

'He's pretty great. And Philip Seymour Hoffman. Such a waste when he died.'

'Wasn't it? Did you see him in *Capote*?'

'I did. And I loved him in *Doubt*.'

'Meryl Streep was brilliant as the nun in that.'

'Meryl Streep can do no wrong.'

The talk was running out of her, out of them. There seemed to be a million things to say, so many words suddenly there without her having to think about them. Her coffee sat going cold: she'd barely touched the apple turnover he'd bought her.

He told her about his work, the family company that his grandfather had started with a brother in the forties. 'It's not wildly exciting – we source furniture makers and commission them to kit out offices for our clients, and we also have our own plant in the industrial estate on the Galway road that manufactures office equipment – but I enjoy it. Every day is different, and I think I'm good at dealing with people.'

She told him about her job in the supermarket. 'I work different shifts, usually six or seven hours, and we get good time off, and decent holidays. Charlotte works there too – it's where we met. It's fine, just . . . I don't think my heart is really in it.'

'So where's your heart?' he asked. Seriously, not laughing at her.

Where was her heart? What a question – but her answer came without thinking.

'I'd love to work as a volunteer in a refugee camp. I see the news reports about the awful conditions the refugees are living in, the overcrowding and not enough food or medicine, and these are all people who are running from even worse places, where they were being bombed and shot, and their houses were being destroyed, and they put themselves in so much danger trying to get away – and it's so horribly unfair that they end up in those awful camps, and I really would love to be of some use if I could. I don't know if I'd be of any help, but I'd love to try.'

'Of course you'd be a help. What's stopping you?'

'Well, I'd be leaving my mother on her own.'

'Is she sick? Would she not manage?'

'Oh no, she's fine. She works and she's very independent. It's just . . . my brother.' She told him about Philip's abrupt departure, leaving out the bit about the money. 'It nearly killed her – and we can't get in touch because we have no address. And I'm all she has now.'

'But you mustn't let that stop you,' he said. 'Your going

would be entirely different. You'd keep in touch with her, and you'd get home to see her every so often. And I assume she has friends here.'

'Oh yes, she has plenty of friends.'

They talked so much she forgot the time. When she eventually checked, she got hurriedly to her feet, almost knocking over his coffee cup, which was also practically untouched.

'I have to go,' she said, 'or I'll be late. Thank you.'

'Here. Shame to waste it.' He wrapped her turnover in a serviette: their fingers touched briefly as she took it. He wore a thin gold band on his wedding finger, but there had been no mention of a wife. She refused to think about a wife.

'Thank you,' she repeated.

'I'm glad we met,' he said in a rush, his face colouring slightly. 'I enjoy your company, Emily.'

Emily. Her heart flooded.

'Listen,' he said. 'I can't – I mean, I'm not in a position to offer you—'

'It's OK,' she said quickly, not wanting to hear. 'It's alright.' *Don't say it.*

'Could we meet again,' he said, 'just as friends? Just for coffee and a chat?'

'I'd like that,' she said. Don't think about it. Don't analyse it. 'I'm on early shift next week, eight to three.'

'How about Monday, then? Say about three fifteen?'

Monday, two days from now. 'Here?'

'Why not? We'll call it afternoon tea. I'll sneak away from work, and hope the boss doesn't catch me.'

His smile was wonderful. It transformed his face and sent her heart into orbit. 'See you on Monday then,' she said.

For the rest of the day her stomach flipped every time she remembered, every time his face floated into the space behind her eyes.

Martin. All the beautiful sounds of the world in a single word.

* * *

'Molly – there you are.' Linda stepped aside to let her in. Paddy sat at the kitchen table, a Spiderman bowl of something before him, a smear of white on his cheek. He glanced in her direction and quickly lowered his gaze again.

'Hello, Paddy,' she said brightly, setting down her rucksack.

'Hello.' Stirring his breakfast with his spoon.

'This little man is on an antibiotic,' Linda said. 'I had him at the doctor yesterday with earache. I'll try to make sure he doesn't get in your way.'

'He won't bother me at all.'

He did look a little flushed. Yogurt, she thought, in the bowl, and some chopped-up banana. He wasn't making great inroads, more interested in chasing his spoon around the plate. She wanted to dab the smear from his cheek. 'He reminds me of my son at that age,' she said. Out before she knew it. 'Looks so like him.'

Linda was putting cutlery into the dishwasher. She glanced up. 'Does he? How old is your boy?' Nothing on her face but polite curiosity.

'Twenty-nine. Nearly thirty.'

'Does he have children?'

' . . . Not that I know of.' Switching on a smile. Turning it into a joke, her courage failing her.

Linda smiled back. 'Everyone says Paddy takes after my side of the family.' She straightened up and shut the dishwasher door. She turned the dial: water gushed. 'You probably noticed,' she went on lightly, reaching for a mug on the worktop, 'that his father isn't on the scene.' Her voice dipping, not reaching as far as the table.

Molly felt everything suddenly clench in her. 'Is he not?'

'We're not together.' Her voice lowered another notch. 'It was a mistake.'

'I'm sorry to hear that.' Molly darted a glance at Paddy, who was fishing banana pieces from his bowl and taking no notice of them. 'Do you have . . . any contact?'

'No.' Linda took a quick sip from her mug. Molly waited for more – but no more came.

'Look at this fellow,' Linda said, ripping kitchen paper from a roll, swooping down on Paddy with it, 'making a fine mess for himself.'

Molly turned for the door. 'I'll make a start upstairs then.'

'Thanks, Molly.'

She climbed the stairs with her bucket of sprays and bottles, unsettled by the short conversation. The possibility that Paddy was her grandson was very much alive – but the frustration of not knowing for sure was awful. Still, she'd found out a bit more today, confirmation that the father was off the scene, and maybe next week would bring her closer again to the truth. Little by little, it might come out.

Linda hadn't reacted at all though, when Molly had mentioned Paddy's resemblance to her son. Maybe she should have used his name – maybe 'Philip' would have made Linda sit up and take notice. She must bring him up again in conversation, first opportunity she got.

On the landing she plugged her ears with headphones and switched on her iPod, which she'd loaded up with the concert songs. She sang, replacing the main tunes with her alto parts, as she poured bleach into the toilet bowl and closed the lid.

In Paddy's room she folded his Gruffalo pyjamas and tucked them under the pillow. His duvet cover was a Batman one; his little blue slippers had Spiderman on them. She got down on hands and knees to peer under the bed prior to vacuuming and pulled out a plastic figurine – helmeted warrior, sword held aloft – a jigsaw piece, a single small blue sock with Thomas the Tank Engine on it. She placed everything on top of his chest of drawers, beside a stack of picture books and a little wooden train.

And as she worked she sang, but her thoughts roamed far from the songs. She imagined being accepted as part of the family, taking her place as his second grandmother, legitimately entitled to visit him, or have him come to her house. She could offer to keep him for weekends, let Linda have some time to herself.

In the main bedroom, still singing, she lifted bottles and jars from the dressing table to dust beneath them. She ran her damp cloth along the windowsill and skirting boards, and buffed the mirror until it shone. As she dusted the locker, she eyed the drawer beneath. Didn't people sometimes keep diaries in their lockers?

She threw a glance at the bedroom door, took her headphones out to listen, heard nothing. She eased the drawer open – and there it was: a maroon notebook, elastic band wrapped around its middle.

She had no right. It was a huge invasion of privacy to read

someone else's diary. Ordinarily she wouldn't dream of it. But these were no ordinary circumstances. Whatever it took, she had to know the truth.

She lifted out the notebook and yanked off the elastic band. She opened the first page with fingers that trembled slightly. *Linda Moran,* she read in blue ink, and beneath it an address and telephone number. She went to turn the page – and then she stopped.

This was wrong. She wasn't the kind of person to snoop, for whatever reason. She'd have to find the truth another way. She closed the notebook and replaced the elastic band. She returned it to the drawer, trying to position it exactly as it had been before sliding the drawer closed. She turned to leave the room – and there in the doorway stood Paddy, regarding her silently, a thumb stuck into his mouth.

'Paddy – you gave me a fright! I never heard you coming.'

Had he seen her looking at the notebook? If so, was he old enough to realise that Molly had overstepped the mark?

He removed his thumb. 'I got to do a wee.' His voice little more than a whisper, looking fixedly at the floor in front of him. 'The toilet is closed.'

'Sorry, lovey.' She steered him from the room and into the bathroom. 'I'll wait outside,' she said, lifting the seat, 'in case you need any help.'

Lord, was she in trouble? She stood on the landing, wondering if he'd tell Linda that the cleaning lady was looking in her drawers. In no time he was out, attempting as he walked to yank up the zip in his shorts.

'Want me to help you?' she asked, and he stood silently as she bent and zipped him up. 'Did you wash your hands, sweetheart?'

He shook his head.

'Come on back and I'll help, OK? It's better if you wash your hands.'

In the bathroom she flushed the toilet and ran a little water into the sink. He was barely tall enough to dip his hands in.

'You like Spiderman, don't you?'

A slight nod.

'I saw him on your bowl in the kitchen. And he's on your slippers too.'

She squeezed soap from the dispenser, thrown back to the days when she'd washed Philip and Emily's hands in just this way. The small fingers, topped with tiny nails, looked achingly familiar.

'My boy liked Spiderman too, when he was small like you. And he liked the Hulk.'

No response. She soaped the dimpled knuckles, the creases at his wrists. The velvety softness of his skin enthralled her. 'And my boy liked bananas, just like you,' she said.

He lifted his head and looked straight at her then, making her heart turn over. 'I only like *yellow* bananas, not spotty ones.'

'Ah, not the spotty ones.' She dipped his hands into the water to rinse them. 'Paddy,' she said softly, 'do you ever see your daddy?'

A shake of the head, making the curls bounce. She was taking a risk, she knew, asking the question. Like the risk she'd taken in Linda's room. Desperation was making her reckless.

She took the towel and dried each small finger gently. 'There we go, darling,' she said. 'All clean now.'

She watched him taking the stairs carefully, holding tightly to the banister. More like Emily than Philip in temperament. Philip had almost broken his neck countless times, scrambling up and down the stairs at home, ignoring her frantic attempts to slow him down.

Soon. She must find out soon.

Eventually she finished upstairs and made her way to the lower level. As she reached the final step she heard voices drifting out from behind the not-quite-closed kitchen door.

'I wish you wouldn't. It's not right.' Linda.

'Oh come on – it's just a bit of fun. It's not as if I'm going to ride off into the sunset with Christopher.'

Molly halted, a foot on the last stair. She knew the voice.

'But you're *married*. Does that mean nothing to you?'

'Linda, climb down off your high horse. What he doesn't know won't hurt him. We're being discreet.'

Jane. It was Jane from the choir, Molly would swear it.

She tiptoed into the sitting room, closing the door quietly behind her. She turned up her iPod as she worked, but the music didn't stop her brain picking apart the overheard remarks.

Jane, who was evidently a friend of Linda's. Well, the town was small enough, and they probably moved in the same circles. Both well-to-do, Jane with her expensive-looking clothes and swanky haircut, Linda clearly not short of money either.

Jane and Christopher. Of course, it might not be him at all, it might be an entirely different Christopher. All that was clear was that Jane was carrying on with someone behind her husband's back, which didn't come as a surprise to Molly.

She hoped it wasn't their Christopher. Despite his fiery temperament at the rehearsals, Molly liked him. She'd seen his other side, the polite man who'd phoned in response to her ad in the newsagent's window, who'd subsequently shown her around his house, apologising for the damp towel they'd come across on the bathroom floor. The man who always left her money in a folded note that said, *Thank you, Molly*. He came across as a decent man, and she didn't like to think of him running around with a married woman. She wanted him to be better than that. Hopefully it wasn't him.

But then she thought of Jane, doing what she could at every rehearsal to draw attention to herself. Piping up with a smart remark whenever the opportunity arose, dropping her folder with a thud in mid-song once, full of breathless apologies afterwards. Asking, just last week, for a second copy of 'Surrey with the Fringe on Top'. *I was practising in the bath and it fell in*, she said, causing a spatter of amusement.

Practising in the bath. Saying it so he'd picture it.

Of course it was their Christopher.

She cleaned the other downstairs rooms. In Linda's office, a business card she plucked from the floor revealed Paddy's mother to be an accountant. Self-employed, she must be, or on some kind of contract that allowed her to work from home at least some of the time. Again the temptation to poke about in the desk drawers was there; again she resisted it.

She delayed entering the kitchen as long as she could, hoping that Jane would have left by the time she got around to it. Not wanting them to come face to face after what she'd overheard: afraid she mightn't be able to hide the fact that she knew about Christopher.

And even though she wasn't ashamed of it, the thought of Jane discovering how she earned her living filled Molly with deep dismay. Jane with her fancy clothes, looking down her nose at Molly at every rehearsal. Ignoring her during the break, even though they'd been placed side by side in the altos section, making it plain that Molly was simply not worth bothering with. No, she certainly didn't need to know that Molly scrubbed her friend's toilet once a week.

Thankfully, the kitchen was empty when she got there, with Paddy and Linda sitting again at the patio table. Keeping out of her way. Linda turned at Molly's entrance and smiled her hello – no indication that Molly was in trouble. She set to, putting the overheard conversation, and everything else, out of her head. As she finished mopping the floor, her final task, the patio door slid open.

'Molly, I was wondering if you could help me out next week.'

'Next week?'

'I was hoping to switch you to Saturday afternoon. It's Paddy's birthday, and I'd love it if you were free to give a hand with things. It's on from two to four, but if you could come at half one you could help me get ready, and stay to tidy up till half four maybe, or five. Would that suit at all? Of course I'd pay you for the extra time.'

His birthday. Saturday week was August the sixth, the night of the concert, but Christopher had said seven o'clock at the community hall. 'I could do that,' Molly said. 'That'll be no trouble.'

'Oh great, that's super.'

Molly wiped her hands on her apron. 'Have you many coming?'

'Well, he goes to playschool three mornings a week so that's eleven if they all turn up, and his pal Archie from across the road. And his granny and his auntie and uncle will come too, of course.'

'That sounds lovely.'

She counted months as she rinsed out her bucket at the utility room sink. First week in August meant Linda had got pregnant around the beginning of November. Philip had left in the middle of March; she would have been nearly five months gone by then.

Late enough to tell him. Maybe she'd been biding her time, waiting for the right moment. Afraid of saying it too soon, afraid he might persuade her to get rid of it. Yes, that could well have been it.

It could still fit. Paddy could still be Philip's son.

And Molly would be there at his birthday. She'd get to meet the rest of his family. She'd be among his friends and their parents, mixing with people who knew him. She'd be part of his circle, even if her only purpose there was to dole out ice-cream and mop up spills. She'd still be among them, still be in a position to overhear anything that was said, or to befriend the grandmother maybe – yes, *there* was an idea. Linda's mother would be able to tell her what she needed to know, if Molly could just find the right way to ask her.

Her thoughts ran on as she wiped her hands and undid her apron. She'd get him a present. Oh, nothing big, nothing that would raise a curious eyebrow. A colouring book or a jigsaw – they had them for next to nothing in Lidl – or maybe a little bag of marbles. She'd think of something.

Back home she phoned Clem. Over a week since Doug's death: she should have picked up the phone sooner. No sign of him yesterday when she'd done her usual clean, her money waiting on the kitchen table like it always was. Doug's empty chair a sad sight, the small sitting room managing to look too big without his bed in the corner.

'How're things?' she asked.

'Alright. Doing a bit of clearing out.'

Clearing out his father's things, she guessed. Putting clothes into black plastic sacks, returning the walker to the charity he'd got it from. Boxing up keepsakes maybe: his watch, his penknife, his playing cards.

'If you need a hand let me know. I'm free after four every day.'

'I think I can manage, but thanks.'

'I was wondering if you'd like dinner on Tuesday night.'

'That would be nice.'

She wasn't so sure any more about bringing him and Emily together: maybe it hadn't been such a good idea. There was a pretty big age gap really.

In fact, Clem was probably closer to her own age than to Emily's.

She'd wear that nice blue top Paula had left out last week. A bit dressier than she normally went for, with the beading around the neckline, but she might as well get a wear out of it.

She put her phone away and spooned some of Emily's lentil and carrot salad onto a plate. They'd do something nice for him. Emily would be sure to have some ideas.

* * *

He shouldn't have answered it. He never did if the number was unknown: he let it go to voicemail and waited for a message that would reveal the caller's identity. But today he'd been distracted on his walk home from work by a parade on the street, some festival that involved people on stilts and whirling dancers in skimpy costumes, and a marching brass band whose members must be severely overheated in their jackets and striped long trousers.

When his phone rang he was idly watching a pair of female dancers as they spun in a tight circle, their skirts flying out to reveal modest cycling shorts beneath. He pulled the phone from his pocket and swiped a thumb across the screen, eyes still on the twirling couple.

'Yes.'

'Christopher, it's me – it's Robert.' All in a rush. 'Don't hang up.'

He stiffened. He should have checked. He always checked.

'Don't hang up, please. Hear me out.'

'What do you want?' Turning away from the dancing. Stepping back to lean against a railing.

'I'm coming to Dublin for a conference next week—'

'No.'

'Listen, Christopher, please. I want us to meet—'

'I have nothing to say to you.'

'Can we not put this behind us, for Mother's sake? It's killing her. Please, Christopher, just—'

'It was *your* doing that caused this, not mine. I have nothing to feel guilty about.'

'I know. I know I was to blame – and you're right, you shouldn't feel guilty – but Christopher, can you not find it in your heart—'

He jabbed at the disconnect key. He put the phone on silent and slid it back into his pocket. He strode home rapidly, ignoring the rest of the parade. In the kitchen he dumped his groceries on the table and checked his phone and deleted the two new missed calls. He tossed half a dozen ice cubes into a glass and found the bottle of Jameson. He poured a generous measure and opened the back door.

He left his sandals on the patio and stepped onto the grass. It needed a cut: his feet were half hidden by it. He walked to the centre of the lawn and lowered himself to sitting. He rattled the glass and drank, feeling the liquid burn its way down and hit his stomach. He finished it in three swallows and set down the glass and lay back. Less than a minute later, the sun too hot on his face, he flipped onto his front.

He breathed in the sweet, honest scent of grass and earth. Something tickled the back of his neck: he lifted a hand to flick it away. Something wet nudged at his knee. He moved his head and saw the dog, over to investigate.

'Hello,' he said, turning onto his side. 'How's your day going?' The animal flopped down next to him, panting. 'I'd offer you whiskey, but I drank it all. You might find some ice cubes in the grass.' The dog gave an enormous yawn and lowered his head onto his paws. Christopher laid a palm against his warm flank and felt the rapid rise and fall of the animal's breathing. Nice to be able to spend your days sleeping and eating, your only worry where your next bit of grub was coming from.

'You miss your pal?' he asked. No sign of her all week, not since Mommy Dearest had stormed off in a huff. Christopher still checked the garden when he got home from work each day, although he knew there was little point. Their small white car had passed him yesterday on his walk home: there had been no horn toot, like he'd got a couple of times before. Ah, well.

He turned onto his back again and squinted up at the miles of blue sky overhead, interrupted only by wispy clouds and the puffy stream of a jet plane's trail. Somewhere off to his left he heard high-pitched squeals, and he guessed they came from four gardens away, where a gaggle of ginger-haired children lived. He closed his eyes, threw an arm across his face.

How long? he'd asked his mother as she'd driven him home from the airport. She'd sighed and said she wasn't sure, but she didn't think it was that long, which was no help at all. So he'd waited until he got home and then he'd phoned his brother, who hadn't had the guts to tell Christopher himself, who'd left it to their mother to break the news.

How long? he'd asked Robert, safe in Dublin with his fancy suits, and his fancy job, and Christopher's girl. *How long?*

For a few seconds there had been silence on the line. Christopher had pictured him in an office with original paintings on the walls, side by side with Robert's framed degree. Was there a framed photo of him and Heather sitting on the walnut desk?

Look, Robert had said finally, *it wasn't something we planned. The last thing we wanted—*

He hadn't been able to bear the 'we'. The 'we' had made his guts churn. *How long?*

. . . March.

March. A month after she'd finished with him. He'd closed his eyes, squeezed the phone. *How?*

What do you mean?

How did you do it? Did you call her? Did you go to see her?

Christopher, I can't see why you—

Tell me, he'd said. *Tell me, or I'll come up there and hammer your door down.*

I . . . Look, it just happened. We . . . happened to meet, that's all.

It was a lie. He'd known it. He'd heard it in his brother's voice.

Tell me the truth, he'd said through gritted teeth, *or I swear to God I'll kill you.*

I gave her my number, Robert had said then. *When we met that time at Christmas. I gave her my number and said . . . anytime she was in Dublin to look me up. I swear I didn't mean—*

You gave her your number behind my back.

It wasn't behind your back—

You didn't tell me. But even as he'd said it, he'd realised that Heather hadn't told him either. She'd taken Robert's number and tucked it away, and bided her time until March, waited until she'd got rid of Christopher.

I'm sorry, she'd said. *It's not you, honestly. You're still wonderful.*

Is there someone else? he'd asked, and she'd said no, nobody else. But she'd lied, because there had been. There had been someone else, and he was called Robert, and he was everything Christopher wasn't.

So she rang you?

She did, yes.

And there it was, the ugly truth. He'd introduced her to Robert at Christmas, and she'd seen something in him that she'd never seen in his brother, and Robert had given her his number.

And Christopher, planning his college application, planning his proposal, looking forward to their life together, poor, stupid Christopher had had no idea, no idea at all. He'd returned to Lanzarote in March, he'd been there when she'd picked up the phone and dialled Robert's number and arranged to meet him.

And now Robert wanted them all to be friends again.

'Never going to happen,' he said aloud, making the dog

cock an ear. 'Not if Hell freezes over.' He debated getting more whiskey, but thought better of it. Not yet seven o'clock, bit early to be looking for oblivion. He'd have a few belts later on, enough to make sure the happy couple didn't plague his dreams.

He lay there, half dozing, as bees hummed about the shrubs, and another plane droned overhead, and neighbourhood children yelped and shouted in the sunshine. At some stage he was dimly aware of the dog rising to his feet and shuffling off, presumably to find a shadier spot.

Eventually he woke, his head heavy, his mouth dry. He sat up. Something had woken him. He looked around and saw the dog sitting by the gap in the hedge – and as he watched, a small hand emerged and fed it something.

He got to his feet and walked across. 'Hi there.'

No response. The hand withdrew. He crouched and peered in. She sat cross-legged on her side of the hedge, a half-eaten bagel topped with what looked like cream cheese on her lap. 'What's up?'

'Nothing.' Sulky – or maybe defensive. 'I was just giving Billy some bagel.'

'Want to come in?'

'Mommy says I can't.'

'Oh.'

'Mommy says you don't want me in your garden. Mommy says you don't like me.'

He felt a stab of anger. Ridiculous woman, skewing what he'd said to poison her child's mind against him.

'Mommy got that wrong,' he said lightly. 'You can come and play with Billy any time you like.'

'Can I come now?'

'Yes.'

She scrambled through the hedge, dropping the bagel in transit. 'It's a bit icky,' she said when she emerged. Bits of hedge and earth were stuck to the white stuff.

'Billy won't mind.' He rose to his feet. 'I'll be back in a minute. Try not to wreck the place.'

As he made his way next door he determined not to lose his cool. He wasn't going for a showdown, just a reasoned discussion. To be on the safe side he took a couple of deep breaths as he walked up her driveway. He would be the essence of patience. He would explain, quietly and calmly, that he had no objection to Laurie visiting his garden, and stress again that he'd been joking when he'd insinuated otherwise. Clearly it was a cultural misunderstanding that could easily be straightened out.

He rang the bell and waited, feeling the sun hot on the back of his neck. Even without sun protection cream his skin never burned: in Lanzarote he'd become as coffee-brown as the natives within a week. Robert, to his secret satisfaction, had inherited Mother's pale skin – he only had to think about the sun for his nose to turn pink. Robert and calamine lotion were made for one another.

The door was opened. For once she was dressed normally: denim cut-offs, white T-shirt with Bob Dylan's face on it in black and grey. Her legs were skinny and pale, her feet bare. Her dark red hair was caught up on her head with what appeared to be an enormous butterfly. She looked mildly surprised to see him.

And for whatever reason, his good resolutions immediately went cartwheeling away, and he felt once more the irritation her presence always seemed to provoke. 'I can't believe you told your daughter I didn't like her,' he said sharply. 'What's *wrong* with you? You know I never said such a thing.'

She seemed to study him for a second. 'Have you been drinking?' she asked mildly.

'*What?*'

She lifted a shoulder. 'All I know is you arrive on my doorstep all het up in the middle of the day, smelling of booze. What am I to think?'

Infernal woman. 'For starters, it's not the middle of the day, it's early evening, and if you must know – not that it's any of your business – I had *one* small drink, with good reason. Stop trying to change the subject. Why did you tell Laurie I didn't like her?'

Another shrug. 'Because I thought you didn't.'

'I was joking,' he said tightly. 'How could you not see that? You said thanks for putting up with her, I said I didn't have much choice. It was a *joke*, for Christ's sake.'

'No call to take the Lord's name. If my memory serves me right, you also said your *dawg* liked her.'

'Well, he *does*. What's wrong with that?'

And then, incredibly, she smiled. 'Relax, Christopher – I'm just pushing your buttons.' She shook her head. 'Boy, you sure operate on a short fuse.'

He glared at her. '*Me? Me* on a short fuse? I'm not the one who hit the roof over nothing. I'm not the one who made me out to be a monster to her child.'

She spread her hands. 'What can I say? I guess I'm a little sensitive where my baby is concerned. Look, I'm sorry – but I did think she really might be bothering you.'

'Well, she's not – and you had no call to say I didn't like her.'

She nodded slowly. 'I guess you're right. I'm sorry about that . . . So she's in your place now, huh?'

'She is. I caught her feeding the dog a bagel through the hole in the hedge. I told her to come through.'

He waited for her to blow up again – contravening her orders! – but instead she laughed. Out came the dimple. 'That's my girl. I have yet to get her to finish a full bagel.'

A beat passed. 'Well, I'll be—'

'You want some coffee?' Cawfee. 'Now that we've achieved a truce, I mean.'

No coffee. Coffee was a bridge too far. Coffee was what friends did, and they were a long way from friends. 'No thanks – I'm expecting company.'

She lifted an eyebrow. 'Your girlfriend with the fancy red car?'

His girlfriend? Was she spying on him now?

Seeing his expression, she raised a palm. 'OK, OK, enough with the evil eye, Christopher – I've seen her coming to visit a few times, that's all. You want some more cookies? You could tell her you made them yourself – she'd be real impressed.'

'No, thank you.' He could imagine Jane's face if he presented her with a plate of cookies.

'So Laurie can come and go, right?'

'Within reason,' he said. 'I don't need her living in my garden.' There: another opportunity for her to slam the door in his face, making theirs the shortest truce in history.

She didn't. She tipped her head to one side, causing the butterfly hair thing to wobble precariously. 'So – what are we saying here? Five-minute visits? Ten? We need to get the boundaries clear so you don't come over and launch another attack.'

'What? I'm not going to *time*—'

'Gotcha,' she said. 'So easy. See you around, Christopher.' Waggling fingers at him.

He turned to go, prickling with irritation. What was it about her that caused him to lose the rag so easily? He shouldn't rise to it, he should laugh her off, treat her like the silly woman she was. But she was so . . . What? Argumentative. Confrontational. Blunt. From now on he'd keep his distance.

'Easy on the booze,' she called. 'Stick to the cawfee, Christopher.'

He pretended not to hear. It felt like the wisest course of action.

* * *

'So he's coming again on Tuesday. You'll be around, won't you?'

'I will.'

'Oh good. I thought you might do chicken this time, with that nice lemon sauce. What do you think?'

'I could do that if you want.'

When I was about five, I got lost in the shopping centre by the hospital. I wandered off when my mother was trying shoes on Philip. I probably wasn't missing very long, just a few minutes, but when she found me she slapped me. I remember how shocking that was: I was so happy to see her again, and she was so angry.

'And I don't know if you need to bother with dessert. I don't think Clem is pushed really.'

'Fine.'

'Or maybe you could just do a small fruit salad.'

'OK, I'll do that.'

When I was eight or nine, I rode a bike that was too big for me. It belonged to a neighbour. I couldn't control it: I sped down a hill and went flying straight onto a main road. I just missed being hit by a car – I think the driver got more of a fright than I did.

Were you hurt?

Not really. Some cuts and bruises when I crashed into a hedge on the other side of the road. My father had words with the neighbour: I think it was the only time I ever saw him really angry.

'Poor Clem. He sounded a bit lonesome on the phone.'

'Did he?'

'I wonder would he think about getting someone in to share the house. He'd have a bit of company, and rent coming in too.'

'Right.'

My father died when I was three. I barely remember him.

I was twenty-two when my father died.

Is your mother still alive?

Yes.

'This salmon is lovely. What did you put in that topping?'

'Parsley, lemon rind and a shallot.'

'Very tasty.'

I hate spinach. It's the only vegetable I don't like.

With me it's celery. I don't mind it raw in a salad but I can't abide it cooked. Oh, and I'm not gone on Brussels sprouts either.

I love Brussels sprouts! The trick is to slice them thinly and fry them in butter with chopped-up bacon.

Now that I could probably eat.

'Wasn't that an awful accident out on the Galway road last night? Two killed in one car, one in the other. Did you hear?'

'I did. Terrible.'

I enjoy cooking. I learnt it at school – well, I started to learn there, and then I got a few books. My mother can do lots of things, but cooking isn't one of them. I make practically all the meals in our house now.

My mother was always a great cook. Her Sunday lunches were legendary.

'What do you want to do for your birthday, love? You could invite Charlotte around for dinner, and I could ask Dervla. We could get a takeaway so you wouldn't have to cook. Or you might prefer to do your own thing with Charlotte.'

'I hadn't really thought about it.'

'It's less than two weeks away.'

'I know . . . I'll have a think.'

I'm Leo.

I'm Capricorn.

'Won't feel it now to the concert, a week on Saturday.'

' . . . I know.'

I can't swim.

Neither can I – well, I can do a doggy paddle that runs out of steam after about two minutes.

Mam was always nervous of water, after Dad having drowned. Philip and I weren't brought to the beach as kids, or to a pool. The first time I saw the sea was on a school tour when I was about sixteen.

And on and on and on. They would never run out of words. She talked to him like she'd never talked before, like she'd never wanted to talk before, even to Charlotte. In the café on Monday the manager had come down to tell them that he was closing up: she couldn't believe it was half past five, that they'd been there for over two hours.

Friends, that was what they were. That was all they could be, because a wife existed: she hovered silently in his background. *It was a mistake*, he'd said, and that was all she'd let him say, all she could listen to. It might have been a mistake, but it had happened, he had married her. Emily would make do with his friendship because she had to – but the unfairness of meeting someone so in tune with her only to be denied any kind of closeness with him was sickening. The cruelty of it was terrible.

She wouldn't dwell on it, she would focus on the positive. They were meeting again tomorrow, Friday; she could hardly wait. She'd take what she could get, enjoy it for however long it lasted, make do with the segment of him that was allowed to her.

After dinner she watched a TV programme that she instantly and thoroughly forgot as soon as it ended. She attempted to read her book but the words and paragraphs might as well have been hieroglyphs. Eventually she went to bed and fell into a fitful sleep.

The following morning the insistent buzz of her phone woke her. She put out a hand, still half asleep, and felt about on the locker until she located it.

'Yes?' Her voice slurry with sleep.

'Em, it's me. Are you alone?'

Her eyes snapped open. She scrambled into a sitting position, saw six forty-two on her clock radio. Rubbed her eyes with her free hand.

'Philip?'

'Yeah. Are you on your own?'

His voice, so clear. So close he sounded, he could have been in the next room. 'Yes, I've just— Is that really you, Philip?'

'Yeah, course it's me. How're things?'

It was him. It was her brother. He was on the phone. 'Where *are* you?' So many questions, and she asked the most useless one.

'I'm in New Zealand – you know that.'

'Why did you go there? Why didn't you tell us? Why have we no address for you?'

'I move around. I don't stay in one place. I keep in touch, don't I?'

But he'd answered the wrong question. 'Philip,' she said, closing her eyes, 'did you – was it because of the old man, was that why you left?'

'What old man?'

'Did you – break into his house? Was it you?'

'What are you *talking* about? I didn't break into anyone's house – why would you think that? *Jesus!*'

Relief poured through her. He used to lie so effortlessly, but this sounded like the truth to her. 'Well, why did you go, then?'

A second's silence. Two seconds. 'If you must know,' he said, 'I got myself into a . . . sticky situation.'

'What situation?'

'Look, I – got involved with someone I shouldn't have.'

'What do you mean?'

'A woman. She was married – I didn't know at the start. We had a— I got involved with her, and her husband found out, and he – well, he made it plain that he'd hurt me if I didn't make myself scarce.'

A woman. A married woman was why he'd run away. He'd fled from her threatening husband, he'd gone all the way to New Zealand because of a sordid little affair.

'He has contacts, he's into drugs, bad stuff. He could have had me killed, Em. He could still do it, if I came home.'

A drug dealer. He'd had an affair with a drug dealer's wife. The possibility was there, she thought, that he'd got involved with drugs himself. It was likely that there was more to the story, but she didn't ask.

'Did anyone come looking for me?'

'No. Nobody came looking for you.' You weren't worth it. They didn't waste the time. 'You took Mam's money,' she said. 'You stole it. How could you?'

'I had to. I'll pay it back.'

'When?' she demanded.

'When I can.' As evasive as ever.

'You broke her heart,' she said. 'What you did nearly killed her. It took her months to get over it. Every time your postcards arrive she gets upset again. Don't you care at all about her?'

'Of course I do.' But he didn't. He couldn't. 'I had to go the way I did,' he said. 'I couldn't tell her – I was protecting her, and you. That's why I never put my address.'

'Not because you move about.'

'. . . No.'

Protecting them. She let it go, let him go on believing that he was more important than he was. 'Are you working? Do you have a job?'

'I do bits and pieces. I get by.'

Bits and pieces. Five years later he was the same Philip, the same ducker and diver, the same useless charmer he'd always been. She didn't ask if he was coming home because she knew the answer. He'd never be home to them again because he'd have to have the price of the air ticket, and without a mother to steal it from over there, he didn't have a hope. He'd never stay in a job long enough to earn it – or if he did, he'd spend it as quickly as he made it.

'Write to her,' she said. 'Write her a proper letter. Clean yourself up and send her a photo. Give her an address, get a post-office box if you have to. Nobody is looking for you, we'll be quite safe. And send her money, even if it's a fiver. Do that much for her.'

'I will, Em,' he said. 'Honest, I'll do that.'

He might. You could never depend on him. 'Why did you ring me?' she asked.

'I just . . . I wanted to check in. See if ye were OK.'

It had only taken him five years. 'We're OK, but she's lonely. She misses you every day. I can see it.'

'Don't tell her why I went,' he said. 'Will you not tell her, Em? Don't say I phoned, even. I . . . can't talk to her. I *will* write, I promise. OK? OK, Emily? I'll do it tomorrow, I swear.'

'OK,' she said, because what else could she say? 'But if you don't write, I'll tell her.'

'Deal. Look after yourself. I'll ring again sometime.' And he was gone.

It was only afterwards, as she sat in bed cradling the phone, that she thought of all the questions she should have asked: *Are you eating enough? Do you have a place to stay, and a bed to sleep in? Did you make friends? Are you happy? Do you miss us at all?*

Do you miss Mam even a fraction of how much she misses you?

She'd wait and see if he wrote. She wouldn't hold out much hope, but she'd wait and see all the same. He might surprise her.

Her alarm began to beep. She reached out and turned it off.

* * *

Hi Jenny

Happy Friday! It's a few minutes after six and I'm home from work and relaxing on the balcony with a mini Magnum, my weakness! Today my boss came back from lunch with iced coffees for everyone – he must have had that Friday feeling . . . but in fairness he's decent all the time. He seems in particular good form these last few weeks, though, whatever the cause.

She reread it, deleted the last bit. Jenny wouldn't be interested in what form her boss was in, good or otherwise.

Any plans for the weekend? I'm expecting my brother and his wife to visit tomorrow from Galway – they turn up every so often to take poor saddo Paula out to dinner.

She reread it, deleted it.

What are you up to for the weekend? I'm going out to dinner tomorrow night with my brother and his wife. They live in Galway, they're great fun. She's pregnant with their first, due in November. I'll be Auntie Paula, can't wait!

She sat back and folded her arms and thought for a bit. She began to type again.

Don't faint: I think I might be ready for a face-to-face meeting!

No. Too flippant.

Maybe we should grab a coffee sometime. Or a drink, or dinner.

No. Too indecisive. Like she had no mind of her own.

I think I'm finally brave enough to meet you!

No. Sounded like she was dreading it.

I know I've been dragging my feet a bit about meeting up, not because I don't want to but because I do, very much . . . and I'm scared because of that, if it makes any sense. But let's just do it, and hope for the best. Where and when is good for you?

She signed it *P*, added an *x*. She pressed *send* before she could change her mind. She watched it vanishing from her screen, imagined it popping up in Jenny's inbox. Pictured her finding it on her computer, or tablet, or phone.

After a shower and a cheese-on-toast dinner – having been unable to summon the energy to do anything more ambitious – she called Tony. 'What are you up to?'

'Watching rubbish TV. You?'

'Nothing. Have you eaten?'

'I have. Pork chop, apple sauce, green beans.'

'Are you in for the night?'

'I am.'

'Can I come around?'

'You can. Bring booze and we'll have a picnic on the lawn.'

'See you in five.'

She took a four-pack of cider cans from the fridge and walked the three blocks to the house he shared with Bomber, the abused golden retriever he'd brought home three years earlier from the animal shelter, the dog he'd rebuilt in every way.

The slanting sun lit up the windows of the houses she passed, bathing gardens in honey. She loved this time of the day, when the light was softening and night hadn't yet taken hold. A swarm of midges floated out from a hedge to bob around her face; she batted them away. A tempting scent of cooking meat suggested a nearby barbecue. Jazzy music drifted through an open window: Dave Brubeck, Miles Davis, someone like that. Perfect for this balmy evening.

Tony met her at the open back door with Bomber. He handed her a folded throw. 'Give me two of those for the fridge.'

She spread the throw on the lawn beneath the overhanging branches of a neighbour's horse chestnut tree. She sat down and opened her can and took a sip. 'Come on,' she said, patting the ground, and Bomber settled beside her.

Tony returned with a little dish of peanuts.

'You know I hate nuts.'

'They're not for you, they're for me and Bomber. You want popcorn?'

'No thanks.'

'A glass?'

'No. Sit down. I have news,' she told him, scratching the warm space between Bomber's ears.

'Let me guess.' He dropped to the ground with the dog between them and popped the tab on his can. 'You won the Lotto, and you're here to share it with your closest friend.'

'Nearly right.' She told him about her online encounter with Jenny, about their emails since then, and her feeling that they were compatible. 'I've just suggested meeting up. I'm waiting for her to respond.'

'Good for you,' he said, dipping into the nuts, scattering them over the edge of the bowl. 'Let me know how it goes.'

She felt deflated. Was that it? 'What's wrong?'

'Nothing,' he said. 'Nothing at all is wrong.' He threw a nut into the air: it missed his open mouth by a mile and landed by Bomber, who sniffed at it before snapping it up. 'Nothing in the wide world is wrong,' he said, his eyes on the dog.

It didn't sound like it. 'Are you OK? Did something happen?'

He looked up. 'Sorry,' he said. 'Take no notice of me. This heat has me floored, that's all.' He reached for her hand and squeezed, his skin cool from the can. 'I'm happy for you, sweetheart. I am really. I hope it goes well. Hope it all goes well for you. Keep me posted.'

But he wasn't happy, not really. There was no smile in his eyes. She wished again that he'd meet someone. He was lonely, it was patently obvious to her – not that he'd admit it in a million years. He preferred to shove it away, hide it behind jokey chatter where nobody but his closest friend could see it.

'There's a concert coming up in the community hall,' she said. 'Will you come?'

'A concert? Who's playing?'

'Just a local choir – my cleaning lady's in it.'

He gave a bark of laughter. 'Your *cleaning* lady?'

She thumped his arm. 'Don't be such a snob. I've heard her sing – she's great. She left me a leaflet about the concert. They're doing all the hits from the old musicals, *Oklahoma!* and *My Fair Lady*, all the big ones.'

He raised an eyebrow. 'The old musicals? What age are you – ninety?'

'Come on, some of those songs are lovely. It'll be a bit of fun – and it's only down the road. And I'd like to support Molly. Come on, I'll treat you.'

'When's it on?'

'Tomorrow night week.'

'Saturday night? You want me to go to hear cleaning ladies singing songs from *Oklahoma!* on a Saturday night?'

'They're not all cleaning ladies, just Molly – and had you other plans?' He never did: his male friends, all of whom were married, went out with their wives on Saturday nights.

He threw another nut into the air, missed its downward descent again. 'Something might come up. I might get an offer I can't refuse.'

'Something *has* come up. Come on, I want to go, and I don't want to go on my own.'

He sighed. 'Go on then – as long as you promise not to sing along.' He yawned noisily, stretching his arms above his head, causing his white T-shirt to ride up and expose a substantial slice of golden fuzzy abdomen. At least he'd drawn the line at tattooing after the arms were done. 'Tired,' he said. He took a long swallow from his can and lay back. He closed his eyes, belched loudly. 'Begging your pardon. Jesus, how long is this heat going to go on for?'

Paula drank cider and tilted her head to look at the branches above her, and found tiny bits of darkening sky in the gaps between the leaves. Why did love happen so easily for some people while others had to wait and hope for so much longer? What was that all about?

They finished the cans one by one, letting the silences between their chatter lengthen as warm darkness fell.

Towards midnight he walked her home, Bomber padding along contentedly between them.

* * *

She wore a top that picked out the blue of her eyes, and a pair of loose grey pants whose ends she'd rolled up to just below her knee. Her feet were bare, her toenails painted the creamy pink of the tall fragrant lilies his mother had loved. She looked nice.

'You look nice,' he said.

'You look nice yourself.'

He'd worn the trousers of his new suit, and the shoes. The shoes pinched a bit and made his feet too hot but he'd wanted to make an effort. He wished he was barefoot like her. His shirt felt a bit looser than it had at the funeral, probably because he hadn't eaten very much in the past dozen days. He hadn't felt like proper meals, just picked at stuff.

'Thank you,' she said, dipping her head into the bunch of mixed flowers he'd bought that morning in a proper flower shop. 'You shouldn't have.'

He'd forgotten the wine. He'd meant to get wine and then he'd forgotten. He opened his mouth to tell her this, and closed it again.

'How are you?' she asked, as they settled with glasses of lemonade on the patio. 'How have you been?' The questions sounded like real ones, not ones she felt obliged to ask.

'I've been OK,' he told her. 'I'm keeping busy. It's helping.'

He didn't mention the horrible emptiness of the house, the hollow feeling in it that his father's death had brought into being, the awful silence he felt compelled to kill with the radio or the television. Any kind of noise at all, just to fill up the air so there was no room in it for the silence.

He didn't tell her that waking up each morning, as he moved slowly from oblivion to consciousness, he would experience a fresh swipe of sadness when he remembered that he was now fatherless.

He said nothing about the reminders that kept ambushing him: a half-empty tin of shoe polish under the sink, a pack of dog-eared playing cards on a shelf by the back door, a packet of lemon puff biscuits with just one or two gone out of it in the press. He kept quiet about the long-handled shoehorn propped against the sitting-room wall that never failed to bring a lump to his throat when he glimpsed it but that he couldn't face parting with.

'It's just you and me this evening, I'm afraid,' Molly said. 'Emily was asked at the last minute to do a few extra hours at the supermarket: they're short-staffed with people off sick, or on holidays or something. She should have finished at three but now she's staying on till they close at nine.'

She sounded a bit put out about it – she would have been counting on her daughter to do the cooking. He didn't mind: after his self-imposed banishment of proper mealtimes he was looking forward to any kind of a home-produced dinner.

'Roast chicken,' she said. 'Even I can manage that – I hope. And Emily told me how to make the lemon sauce she does with it, so I'll give that a go in a while.'

'I'll help,' he said. 'Two chefs are better than one.'

She laughed. 'I'm not so sure about two chefs – I think it'll be more a case of the blind leading the blind. So when did Paul and Callie go back?'

For twenty minutes or so they talked, as the scent of cooking meat began to drift into the air. He told her about his one and only trip to America with his parents for Paul's wedding more than thirty years earlier, the dead heat of Minnesota in August that had nearly killed them, and the nephews who'd come along since, and who were near-strangers to him.

She told him about the choir rehearsals, and Christopher's increasing tetchiness with them as the date of the concert approached, despite her own belief that really they were doing fine. 'You might like to come,' she said. 'It's this Saturday. I could get you a ticket' – and he found himself saying yes, he'd like that, even though he'd never been much of a one for musicals, or concerts of any kind.

'I'll buy my ticket though,' he said – and then felt his face becoming hot as he realised she might not have been offering him a free one.

If she noticed his discomfiture she didn't let on. 'You can get one on the door on the night so, if you want. I'm sure they'll be available.' She checked the watch on her wrist, rose to her feet. 'Time to get that sauce sorted.'

In the kitchen he weighed out butter and flour, and poured boiling water onto a stock cube while she grated the skin from a lemon and squeezed out its juice. 'Now,' she said, 'comes the fun bit.'

She set the chunk of butter in a pot over a flame; in seconds it had started to sizzle. 'Shake in the flour,' she ordered, and Clem obeyed while she stirred. 'Now pour the stock in slowly – I'm supposed to whisk it to stop it getting lumpy.'

Famous last words. The more liquid he added, the more it clumped together. 'Here,' he said, 'give me that,' handing her the remaining stock and claiming the whisk – but his efforts, while more enthusiastic, proved as fruitless as hers. They ended up with an elasticky gloop that stuck to the pot when Clem turned it upside down.

'Maybe we should add the lemon skin and the juice,' he said, so they did – but this only caused the gloop to take on the consistency of loosely scrambled eggs.

'We're wasting our time,' she said, and turned off the flame.

Clem looked at her.

She looked at him.

'If you had any cracks in the walls,' he said, 'I could fill them in now while you carved the chicken.'

Her mouth twitched. 'We're a disaster.'

He grinned. 'We have other talents.'

'I hope so.'

'I never cared much for sauce anyway,' he said.

'You're just saying that.'

'I am not.'

'You'd like it if Emily made it.'

'Maybe so – but I'm happy without it.'

The sauce was disposed of; the chicken, which was pleasingly tender, served up. He let a wedge of butter melt into the baked potato that accompanied it.

'I forgot the peas,' she said, but it didn't matter. Sitting across the table from her, eating the meal she'd prepared, passing salt and pepper back and forth, he felt a letting-go in him, a sense of easement for the first time since he'd walked into the backyard and found his father's body.

She didn't produce wine. Instead they stuck to Emily's lemonade, which had a sharper, more refreshing taste than the shop-bought stuff. 'She puts a bit of ginger in,' Molly told him. 'That's what gives it the kick.' Would be nice, he thought, to have that skill, to be able to turn ingredients into tasty dishes and drinks. Then again, good company could make a feast of beans on toast.

'Another bit of chicken,' she said when he had cleared his plate, and he accepted more, and a second potato.

And then, over the fruit salad that followed, without having planned it – maybe because of her kindness, maybe because of his father's death, maybe because she'd confided in him about her son – he found himself telling her about Mary, and about Lucy.

'I was married,' he said. 'Long time ago. She was English. I met her when I moved to London in my early twenties. Her father owned the building company where I worked. He and his wife never thought I was good enough, but it didn't stop us. Two years after we married, we had a daughter.'

He broke off, passed a hand across his mouth. This was the hard bit. He waited until the lump in his throat had moved on. 'Lucy, we called her. She was just the best little—' Another pause while he clamped his mouth closed and studied the halved strawberries and chunks of melon and pineapple in his bowl. 'Well, anyway, I lost them both. Mary was driving Lucy to a friend's birthday party. They were unlucky enough to meet a man who was hell-bent on killing himself, and who saw nothing wrong in taking them both with him while he was at it. Drove straight into them.'

'How old was she? Lucy?' Her voice soft and heavy with sorrow for him.

'Four, a week off it.' He cleared his throat, drew in a few breaths. 'I took to the bottle after that, made it my best friend. I liked a jar before, Mary and I both did, but I let it take hold of me. My in-laws tried to help, I'll grant them that much, but I didn't want help, and in the end they gave up. I lost my job – well, I left more than lost it, left before he had to kick me out. Lost my friends too, one by one. Pushed them all away.

'And then my father showed up, and he made me come home with him. It took some effort – I was nearly beyond help at that stage – but he stayed on until I gave in. He saved me, went along with me to AA, kept me on the right road until I was able to manage by myself.'

He shook his head. 'The funny thing was, not funny, just . . . the thing was, we'd never been that close when I was growing up, you know? It was nothing to do with him, it was just the way things were. My mother raised us, me and my brother, and my father went out to work. We always got on OK, we didn't fight, but I never really felt I *knew* him. We didn't have any kind of real conversations, you know?'

He stopped. There was silence. He took another mouthful of fruit salad, already regretting his outpouring. Why had he inflicted all that on her, burdened her with his tale of woe? He hadn't shared it with anyone else since he'd come home, hadn't planned to tell her either. But there was a relief in him now, a feeling of having dumped a load.

He laid down his spoon. 'Sorry,' he said. 'I don't know where all that came from.'

'Such a terrible thing,' she said. 'I had no idea.'

'Sorry, I shouldn't have—'

'No, no.' She blinked a few times. He saw the skin had become pink around her eyes, and he realised that he'd brought her perilously close to tears. 'It's just, I never knew. You never mentioned them, and neither did Doug. Poor you.' She reached across the table and took one of his hands between both of hers. He couldn't remember when a woman had last held his hand. 'You don't forget,' she said quietly, 'do you? You never forget.'

'No.'

Maybe it was her husband she was thinking of: his account would have reminded her of her own cross. Seconds ticked by. It felt good, sitting there with her. It felt right.

'Clem,' she said eventually, 'can I let you into a secret?'

He was grateful for the change of subject. 'You can.'

'This will probably sound daft,' she said, letting go of his hand, drawing hers back. Her gaze shifting slightly to his left, her eyes taking on a different look. 'I . . . came into contact with this little boy lately. I started to clean for his mother, four or five weeks ago.' She paused. 'And the minute I saw him' – her eyes coming back to find his – 'the thing is, Clem, he's the image of Philip. My son.'

The son who'd left, the son who'd gone to New Zealand. He could see straight away where this was heading.

'I got such a shock,' she said. 'And I could be all wrong – but Linda, his mother, has told me that her relationship with the father didn't work out. And he's the right age – he'll be five on Saturday, and Philip went five years ago, in March. It all fits.'

It might fit time-wise, but to assume what she was clearly assuming was a bit of an outlandish leap. Look at the hope in her face though. Look how much she wanted it to be true. 'You think he might be your grandson,' he said.

'He might be. It's not impossible, is it?'

'Not impossible, no,' he agreed. He hunted about for the kindest response. 'It would just be . . . a bit of a coincidence though, wouldn't it? You going to clean for her, I mean.'

'Oh, I know it would, I know that. But he's so like him – I'm not imagining that, I know I'm not.'

'The thing is,' he said, 'even if he resembles your son, it needn't follow that he's his father. Maybe you shouldn't get your hopes up, that's all I'm saying.'

'I know. You're right.' But any fool could see her hopes were already up, just about as high up as she could get them.

'How can you find out though?' he asked. She needed to know, one way or the other.

She shook her head slowly. 'I have no idea. I'm going to be helping out at his birthday party – I might get talking to his mother's mother, who'll be there, but it's all very . . . I'll just have to bide my time, and maybe it'll come out eventually. Or maybe Philip will come home, and I can ask him.'

She didn't sound hopeful. He wondered what the son had been like. The impression he was getting was that he was very different from his sister.

'I haven't told Emily,' Molly said. 'She'd think I was daft. Don't mention it if you meet her.'

'I won't.'

The possibility that she was the boy's grandmother was there, but the odds, he felt, were low. Maybe she just needed something to hang on to after losing her son, in the same way that he couldn't let go of the shoehorn, or the photo album he'd brought home from London. Still couldn't open it, but the day would come.

She rose and gathered up the dessert bowls. 'Enough of this foolish talk,' she said. 'Will you have some coffee?'

'Please.' He got to his feet. 'Let me do it.'

'Put on the kettle so.' She stowed the bowls on the draining board with the rest of the crockery. No dishwasher, like himself.

He filled the kettle and plugged it in. Now, he told himself.

Do it now. 'You must let me pay you back for this,' he said. Quickly, before he lost his courage. 'A meal out sometime.'

'Ah no,' she said, taking mugs from hooks. 'You don't need to do that, Clem.'

'I'd like to, though.'

'Isn't that sweet of you?' She opened a press and took out a glass jug. 'I have to tell you something else,' she said, 'a kind of confession really.' She turned to him, the corners of her mouth beginning to twitch now, paving the way for a smile. 'Something I was trying to do – but I can see the funny side of it now.'

He wondered what confession she could possibly have to offer. He stood by the sink and folded his arms, his own smile ready to break out.

'When I asked you to come to dinner that first time,' she went on, pulling out a drawer, taking a spoon from it, 'I told you it was to say thanks for helping out when I came off the bike, remember?' She twisted open the instant coffee jar, added spoonfuls to the jug. 'And it *was* why I asked you. But once you said you'd come, I thought of another reason.'

'Oh?' His cheeks reddening, the light in the room suddenly too bright. This was moving in an unexpected direction: he wasn't sure he wanted it to.

'I decided,' she said, 'to try and fix you up with Emily.' She gave a small laugh. 'I thought you might suit one another.'

Something went cold inside him. Emily?

'Emily,' he said.

The kettle began to sing; she rested a hand on the handle. 'Imagine – me, trying to be a matchmaker.' Another laugh. 'The idea of it.'

Emily. She thought he might suit Emily.

He wished heartily he hadn't spilt his guts to her. He could see her waiting for him to make some kind of response, but there was nothing to say.

'I don't know what I was thinking, Clem.' Her smile beginning to dim. 'It was a daft notion, I can see that now. I hope you're not . . . put out.'

The room felt different. He lifted a hand to run it along his jaw, just for something to do. 'No harm done,' he said. But a new awkward thing had moved into the space between them, and he knew it and she knew it.

'I shouldn't have tried to—' She broke off, started again. 'It's just . . . Emily is so shy, and she deserves to meet someone lovely. She's the best in the world, she really is. So kind, so generous.'

He wished she'd stop talking. 'I get it,' he said. 'You meant well, it's alright.' But it wasn't alright. None of it was alright.

Just then, to his vast relief, he heard the scrape of a key in the front door lock. 'Emily didn't know about this,' Molly said quickly. 'I said nothing to her.'

The kitchen door opened. 'Hello,' Emily said. She looked from one to the other. 'I'm home.'

'There you are,' her mother said. 'You must be tired. Your dinner's in the oven, just needs heating up. We failed with the sauce, I'm afraid – it went all thick and lumpy on us so we had to throw it out.'

Talking for the sake of it, it sounded like. As relieved as he was that Emily had come home, glad of an interruption.

'Actually I might skip the coffee,' he said. 'I have an early start I forgot about.'

They both looked at him.

'You're not going,' Molly said.

'Don't go on my account,' Emily said at the same time.

There was a change about her this evening, a sort of animation he hadn't seen before. Pink stains blooming in her cheeks.

He pulled the van keys from his pocket. 'No, I'd best be off really. Thank you for the meal,' he said to Molly. 'No need to see me out.'

But she walked to the front door with him. 'I'm sorry,' she said. 'I feel I've put my foot in it. Take no notice of me, I can be very foolish. I shouldn't have done it.'

'You've done nothing wrong,' he told her, and it was the truth. Her motives were good: she was trying to do her best by her daughter. 'I had a very nice time tonight, thank you.'

He opened the door and stepped into the warm night. 'Thank you,' he repeated, opening the van and climbing in. Not giving her a chance to shake his hand, or kiss his cheek again like she'd done on the night of his father's laying out.

'We could go out, if you like,' she said. 'Out for a meal, I mean. Like you said.'

'Sure, I'll give a shout sometime,' he replied. 'Be seeing you,' he said, and slammed the door.

He drove off without looking at her again.

She'd thought he'd suit her daughter, who deserved to meet someone lovely. She'd looked at him and all she'd seen was a man who might suit someone else.

That was that then.

* * *

'I ate at work,' she said. 'I got stuff from the deli counter.' More lies, on top of the earlier one.

'I hope they didn't make you pay for it, and you doing them a favour by staying on.'

'They didn't. Had you a nice dinner?'

'We had. It was fine, apart from the sauce.'

There was something muted about her. Maybe conversation had been tricky over dinner, with Clem still down after his father's death. Maybe she was still a bit miffed that she'd had to do the cooking.

'I think I'll have a shower,' Emily said, moving towards the door.

'Do, love – you've had a long day.'

In her room she sat at her dressing table and regarded her face. She pressed the backs of her hands to her cheeks, felt the heat in them. The heat he'd put there.

What time are you finished on Tuesday? he'd asked. *I'm calling to a supplier in Galway – I'd be leaving here around four – but I won't be long with him. I was thinking you might like to sit in, and we could get a bite to eat on the way home afterwards. I'd be glad of the company, if you'd fancy it.*

And Emily had thought of Clem coming to dinner on Tuesday and the roast chicken with lemon sauce she'd promised to make for him. And then she'd imagined travelling to Galway – forty-five minutes there, forty-five back – and having dinner someplace small and quiet where nobody who knew him was likely to be. Three hours in his company, more or less. Three hours of him all to herself.

I'd like that, she'd said, *I finish at three*, so they'd arranged to meet at the café, where Emily would leave her car.

She hated lying to Mam. She didn't remember ever having done it before. She'd made stuffing for the chicken before leaving for work. She'd assembled the fruit salad; she'd halved strawberries and cut melon and pineapple into cubes, and tossed them in orange juice, and left them in a bowl in the fridge.

I'll see you for dinner, Mam had said as she was leaving, and Emily had felt horrible, knowing she wouldn't.

She'd driven to work, her stomach flipping every time she thought of what lay ahead. At one she'd phoned home and told Mam she'd been asked to stay on till closing time.

The news hadn't been well received. *Didn't you tell them you had plans? They can't just expect you to be at their beck and call.*

I didn't like to, she'd said. *They don't often ask. Everything is done except the sauce. I can tell you how to do that – it's very easy. Have you a pen?*

Hard to believe it was just over five weeks since their first encounter, when he'd turned up at her checkout desk without his wallet. Since then they'd met a handful of times, no more than half a dozen – and yet she felt like they'd known one another forever. They were kindred spirits, made to be together, born to find one another. And he felt the same, she knew he did.

She stood under the shower, reliving the events of the past few hours. The drive to Galway, much too short, where she'd told him about the woman who'd dropped a jar of pasta sauce as she was transferring it from her trolley to Emily's conveyor belt, and who was now threatening to sue the supermarket for the cost of laundering her spattered white jeans; and about the small child who'd gone missing for a terrifying three minutes, everyone searching the aisles until he was found playing with his toy car behind the trolleys in the bay; and about the argument that had broken out over a dented bumper between two customers in the car park.

The shopping centre he'd dropped her at for the half hour it had taken him to attend to his business, where she'd picked out the presents she'd buy for him if they were married – a coloured glass paperweight, an olive green shirt, a painting of a lighthouse, an art-deco lamp with a brass base – and where in the end she'd got him the only thing she could: a bag of the peppermint creams he'd been buying the first time they met.

The little country hotel they'd stopped at on the way home afterwards, where she'd eaten sea bass and he'd had fish pie as he'd told her about the childhood summers he'd spent with cousins who lived in England. *They had a big dairy farm in Devon, miles from anywhere. I loved it. I had freedom like I never had at home. Mum was strict, I suppose a bit over-protective of her only child – so when they sent me off to Devon every summer it was a bit like escaping from prison.*

His mother was blind, he'd told her, the legacy of a stroke some years earlier – and it hadn't taken more than a question or two to discover that his mother was none other than Kathleen, the woman *her* mother read the paper for every weekday afternoon.

Kathleen, who Mam said was cranky and impossible to please. Kathleen, whose husband had run the company Emily's father had worked for before his death, the company Martin had inherited.

I remember your father, he'd said, when they'd figured out the connection. *He always had a bag of liquorice allsorts in his desk drawer – he'd let me dip in when I called around after school. And he could do that thing where he found a coin behind your ear. I remember when he died: it was the first funeral I was at. I was about eight at the time.*

Her father had worked for his father. He'd attended her father's funeral. They'd been in the same surroundings, she a child of three, he an older boy of eight. Even all those years ago there'd been a common thread linking them. No degree of separation.

They'd shared a slice of lemon cheesecake for dessert. They'd drunk coffee, he'd offered her the little complimentary chocolate that sat on his saucer: *never eat the stuff*. She'd felt her spirits sinking lower on the journey home, every signpost reminding her that they would soon have to part. The sight of her car waiting outside the café, signalling the end of their stolen time together, was not welcome.

And then, after she'd thanked him for the meal and was on the point of opening the door, he'd reached out and taken her wrist and said *Emily, would you let me kiss you?*

Would you let me kiss you? A question he had no right to ask, a question she should have given a different answer to. Standing under the shower she closed her eyes and relived it. Her whispered *Yes*, his hand tilting up her chin, his head bending, his lips finding hers – and the kiss, oh, his kiss, oh, the completely unexpected delight of it, the delicious thrill of it, their opened mouths pressed together, oh, oh, every dormant thing in her waking up, everything uncurling and opening and flaring into life at the taste of him, her eyes closed to savour it as they kissed, as they found one another, his arm wrapped around her, holding her close, his other hand now caressing her cheek, now moving to cradle her head, the scent of him so close, cotton and sweat and spice, she could scarcely believe the wonder of what was happening . . . and when at last he'd drawn back she couldn't bear it, and without thinking she'd reached up and cupped the back of his head and claimed him again, she'd wanted more, and she could feel his smile in their second kiss, she could feel that he liked being pulled back to her, and on and on it went as every part of her had responded to the kiss that she'd wanted never to end.

But of course it had ended, and he'd murmured *Emily* as he'd run the back of his fingers from her temple to her chin, their faces still close, still just inches apart, and the wonder of her name on his lips had made her want to cry as she'd finally slid away from him and opened her door, and he'd said *Saturday? Are you working Saturday?* and she'd told him no, and they'd arranged to meet at the café for lunch at one.

She turned off the water, reached for a towel. She buried her face in it, trying to drown the voice that had begun in her car on the way home – but the voice refused to be silenced. The voice insisted on being heard.

You can't do this, the voice said. *It can't go on, you know that. You can't just be friends with him. You've gone beyond that now. He's married. He has a wife, and maybe children. You can't do this to another woman.*

And the voice, of course, spoke the truth.

She didn't blame him. What had happened wasn't his fault or hers. It was down to both of them, unable to resist the pull towards one another – but it had to stop. She had to stop it, if he couldn't. She must give him up now, while she still could.

She would stay away on Saturday. The thought of seeing him again, just to put an end to it, was too painful. He'd understand when she didn't show up, and she felt sure he'd respect her feelings and wouldn't try to change them.

And hopefully, he'd find somewhere else to shop in future.

And maybe, just maybe, he'd take steps to end his marriage, if he truly felt about her the way she felt about him. But she couldn't think about that, couldn't live her life waiting and hoping for something that might never happen.

She put on her dressing gown and tied it around her waist

and went downstairs to drink tea with her mother. Life would go on, because that was what it did.

* * *

'He wants a divorce,' she said, buttoning her skirt.

Christopher took his damp head out of the towel to look at her. 'He does?'

'He's met someone else. Can you believe it? I've told him he'll get a divorce over my dead body.'

It was Friday evening, a day before the concert. She'd appeared at Christopher's house an hour or so earlier, and they'd done what they always did when she called around.

'Why not give him what he wants?' he asked, regarding his unruly head in the mirror. He could do with a haircut: get one tomorrow afternoon.

'Because I have no interest in being divorced,' she replied, stepping into her shoes. 'Because it suits me to stay married.'

'How can you say that? You've told me you don't love him.'

She looked amused. 'Darling, what's love got to do with it? I'm having my cake and eating it, aren't I? Why on earth would I want to change that?' She met his eye coolly, waiting for his reaction.

She was a monster. It wasn't a big revelation, it wasn't a sudden case of the scales falling from his eyes. He'd known all along, right from the start – he just hadn't allowed the knowledge to float to the surface. She was the worst kind of person, one who didn't give a damn about anyone but herself, one who wasn't concerned about anyone's happiness but her own. What was more, it didn't bother her who knew it.

He finger-combed his hair into some sort of shape. He was

nobody to judge; in his own way he was no better than her. Shutting everyone out, letting nobody come close. Using women, married or not, for what brief physical pleasure they could give him. The only thing in his favour was that he was a free agent, and not deceiving anyone, but the fact remained that he was his own kind of monster, unable to move beyond a broken romance of almost two decades ago.

He accompanied her downstairs. In the hall she lifted the handbag he suspected had cost in the region of his weekly salary, if not his monthly. She moved towards him for their usual goodbye kiss.

He stepped back. 'This has to stop,' he said. 'It's run its course.'

She tilted her head, raised her eyebrows. 'Really? You're suddenly developing a conscience?'

'It's run its course,' he repeated, moving past her to the door, opening it. 'I'm sorry, but it stops now.'

She stayed where she was, her expression hardening. 'You knew I was married. I never made a secret of it.'

'That's true.'

'And now – what? I tell you he's looking for a divorce, and you're afraid it's all your fault?'

He shook his head. 'I don't flatter myself that what we did made any difference to your marriage.'

'Too right. You weren't the first and you won't be the last.' She slung her bag onto her shoulder. 'But why stop now? Weren't we having fun?'

He shrugged. 'We did have fun. It's just time to stop now, that's all.'

'So that's it?'

'That's it.'

Their eyes locked. He wondered if she was going to hit him.

She probably wasn't used to being the one who got dumped. 'No hard feelings,' he said.

'No feelings at all,' she answered tightly, and strode past him out of the house. His timing, he realised, was a bit off: he should have waited till after the concert. Tomorrow night might be awkward.

To hell with it. To hell with her. At least she hadn't given him a black eye. He closed the door and retreated to the kitchen, where he took down the bottle of whiskey. Friday night, he'd be having it anyway. He was reaching for a glass when the doorbell rang. His heart sank. She was back: she'd thought better of letting him go without at least a torrent of abuse.

It wasn't Jane. It was Freddie, wearing some sort of all-in-one shorts and top affair, and Laurie, looking fretful.

'Christopher, we're locked out – I can't find my keys, and Laurie needs to pee. Can she please use your bathroom?'

After Jane, the sight of them came almost as a relief. He stepped aside and let them in. 'Top of the stairs,' he said, and Laurie scampered up.

'Thanks. I was afraid she'd have to go in a flowerpot.' She blew hair out of her eyes. Not pinned up today, tousled and damp looking.

'How are you planning to get in?' He could hardly send them away without attempting some kind of help.

'There's an upstairs window open: all I need is a ladder. You don't have one, do you?'

'No – but I know someone who does. Hang on.'

On the crowded kitchen noticeboard he eventually found the number of the man who'd replaced roof slates for him in winter. After several rings his call was answered. He reminded the man of his existence and explained the situation.

He hung up and returned to the hall. 'He'll be over in twenty minutes.'

'See, this is what I love about Ireland,' she said. 'In the States no repair guy will come out after hours, unless it's a life or death emergency – and then you gotta take out a second mortgage to pay them. Thanks, Christopher.'

'No bother.'

A beat passed. Could he leave them standing on their doorstep for twenty minutes? He thought of the whiskey bottle sitting on the kitchen table and remembered their previous encounter, just after he'd had a belt of it. *Have you been drinking?* she'd asked. What would she think if she saw him at it again?

Let her think what she wanted: he'd do as he pleased in his own house. 'Can I offer you something to drink? I was just about to have a shot myself.'

She regarded him dubiously. 'You sure? You don't have to, we can wait outside.'

'I think I can cope,' he told her, as the bathroom door was flung open and Laurie thumped down the stairs.

'Did you flush and wash your hands?'

'I forgot.'

'Back up you go, missy. And use soap – I'm gonna smell them.'

He led the way into the kitchen. He saw her regarding the bottle and waited for a sarcastic comment that never came. He raised it enquiringly but she shook her head. 'I'm not much of a drinker, thanks. Goes straight to my brain, makes me even more of a klutz. But don't let me stop you.'

'You want coffee? I only have instant.'

'Sure.'

He put the kettle on and spooned granules into a mug. He filled his glass with ice and sloshed in a generous wallop of whiskey – more, probably, than he would have taken if he were alone. Daring her, childishly, to comment. Still she remained silent. Not like her.

'You got a nice place here,' she remarked, looking around his uncluttered kitchen – and he remembered Laurie exclaiming *Your house is clean!* the first time she'd been inside it. What expression of her mother's had she followed it with? Ah yes: *Messy houses are happy houses*.

He indicated a chair. 'You want to sit down?'

She sat facing the window: he remained standing, arms folded, as he waited for the kettle to boil.

'So,' she said, 'how's your week been?'

'Same as all the others,' he told her. 'Go to work, come home, eat dinner.'

She smiled. 'You sure do lead an exciting life, Christopher. How's your choir coming along?'

'Fine.'

'Keeps you outta trouble, huh?'

'Something like that.'

He was unsure whether to mention the concert, not wanting it to seem like an invitation. Then again, if she heard about it by chance, or saw a poster, she might wonder why he hadn't told her.

While he was still debating, Laurie reappeared. 'Can I go see Billy?'

'Hands,' her mother said, and she held them out for inspection. 'OK – if Christopher says you can.'

He crossed to the back door and opened it: the dog was sitting by the shed. 'He's waiting for you,' he said, and Laurie bounded out. Only the first week of August but already he could notice a shortening of the days: at just after eight the colour was beginning to wash out of the sky.

The kettle boiled. His guest said yes to sugar and no to milk. He lifted his glass, searching about for a harmless topic of conversation. 'So what made you move to Ireland?'

She didn't answer right away. He watched as she stirred sugar into her coffee. Already he regretted the question, which clearly didn't have a straightforward answer. Maybe she was running away from something, or someone. Was she going to call him a nosy parker, fling the coffee at him and stalk out?

'Look, forget I asked. It's none of my business.'

'No, no – I'm just wondering where to start.'

Where to start? Dear God, all he wanted was a bit of small talk. Was he going to get her life story?

She sipped the coffee, added more sugar, stirred again. 'I got Laurie through a sperm donor clinic in the US,' she said then, 'and my family didn't like it, so I relocated. That's the short version.'

The short version was fine. The short version was all he wanted, more than he wanted.

'The long version is a bit more complicated.'

'You don't have to tell me.'

'I don't mind. It's not a secret.' She paused, oblivious to his discomfort – or maybe, he suddenly thought, relishing it. 'When I was fourteen,' she said, looking directly up at him, 'my stepfather tried it on. I broke his nose.'

He took a mouthful of whiskey, felt the heat slithering down. Through the half-open door Laurie's voice, with its light musical lilt, floated in – 'When I say *paw,* it means you gotta lift your paw, like this . . . '

'After that I moved out, went to live with my grandma. Mom guessed what had happened – she must have. She never asked me why I was going. Grandma didn't really want me, but I gave her no choice. My first boyfriend – I mean my first serious one, at seventeen – shared photos of me with his friends. Intimate photos that he'd taken.'

Intimate photos. He did not want to know about intimate photos. He raised his glass again, willing Laurie to come back in, or a furious Jane to reappear. Any interruption at all would do. Why hadn't he asked about the weather in her part of the States?

'When I left school I got a job with a big ad agency in Boston, thirty miles from the small town where I grew up. I worked as a junior copywriter. I wrote the copy, the words, for store leaflets and press releases and so forth. The salary was crap – I could just afford to share a crummy apartment – but I didn't care. After I'd been there a few months my boss suggested I sleep with him in return for a pay rise. I told him I didn't operate that way. Not long after that, he fired me. I coulda sued for wrongful dismissal but I figured he could afford better lawyers than I could. He must've had some kinda conscience though, because I got a pretty great reference.'

She lifted her mug and drank. Twilight was taking hold, the light in the room dimming. It was becoming difficult to pick out her features clearly.

'I got a job with another agency. A bigger one, with a better salary. I started going out with one of the art directors, and I married him within a year. I think I was still running from my stepfather, or something. I thought if I was married I'd be safe, you know? A week after our honeymoon, my husband slapped me because I burnt his toast. He was sorry, I forgave him, blah blah. Couple months after that he slapped me again, this time because I forgot to pick up his dry-cleaning.' Another pause. 'I didn't forgive him the second time.'

A stepfather who hit on her, a grandmother who didn't want her, a boyfriend who betrayed her, a boss who tried to take advantage, a husband who was physically abusive. If it was true – and he had no reason to disbelieve her – she'd had her share of knocks.

'So we got a divorce – I was twenty-four when it came through – and I got another new job, and when guys asked me out I pretended I had a boyfriend in the military who was posted overseas. Oh, and I wrote a book for children, and it got turned down by every literary agent I contacted.'

She raised the mug again to her lips. A siren sounded distantly. He supposed he should turn on the light, but he made no move. Her story seemed better suited to this half-light.

'And then,' she said, her pace slowing, a new note in her voice, 'when I was twenty-seven I found Karl, or maybe he found me. He was forty-two, we met in the gym, and had the usual banter across the machines, and after a few weeks he asked me out. I said yes, because I fancied him like hell, and I was tired of being alone, and I felt he was a decent man who wouldn't mess me around. We dated for almost a year, and I thought I had met the love of my life, and he told me he felt the same.'

She stopped talking, her face tilted towards her coffee cup. Christopher raised his glass and waited.

'And then,' she said eventually, her voice lowered so he had to strain to hear it, 'I was at work one day when a call came through and I saw Karl's name on my phone, and when

I picked it up it was his wife. She'd found a bunch of texts he'd probably forgotten to wipe. Or maybe he'd gotten tired of me, and that was his way of putting an end to it.'

She pushed the mug aside and planted her palms on the table and turned her face up to find his. 'So I stayed away from men after that. I figured I'd given them a fair crack of the whip, and they'd disappointed me every chance they got. But I'd always wanted kids, so when I turned thirty I decided to go the sperm donor route. It took a while to negotiate the red tape: by the time I had Laurie I was thirty-three. My mom and my grandma were horrified – and my second stepfather wasn't too impressed either.'

With her index finger she traced a circle on the table, round and round. 'Nobody came to be with me at the birth, nobody even sent a friggin' card to say congratulations. I sent them photos of her: nobody answered. So rather than have Laurie go through that crap I gave up my apartment last fall and moved with her to Ireland because I'd seen it in a movie and thought it looked like a good place to bring up a kid. We started off in Dublin, but it was expensive so we came here.'

Silence fell. Laurie's chatter drifted in again: 'No, you gotta *jump*, you can't just *walk* over it, you gotta jump like *this*.'

Freddie cocked her head at him. 'Bet you didn't bargain for all that lot, huh?'

'Not really.'

'Kinda long answer to your question.'

He smiled. 'You could say that.'

'And hey – that book I wrote for kids? I finally struck lucky and found the best agent. She worked with me until it was good enough to show to publishers, and I was offered a two-book deal with a pretty good advance. I kept on my job for a few years – I needed the cash for the donor clinic, and then for Laurie's expenses – but by the time I decided to move to Ireland I'd become a fulltime children's writer. I'm on my eighth book now, my second series, and I've been translated into about a dozen languages, and there are two movie deals in the offing.'

'Well done,' he said. That explained the working-from-home bit. He wouldn't have pegged her as a writer. Then again, he'd never met a writer. He wondered if he should have heard of her, and realised he didn't even know her last name.

'I'm not filthy rich, if that's what you're wondering –'

'The thought never crossed my mind.'

'– but I'm doing OK, and we're happy here. And I've promised Laurie a little brother or sister, so I'm making plans for another trip to the clinic, in the fall or maybe after Christmas.' She gave a soft laugh. 'No offence, Christopher, but sperm donations apart, men are pretty much surplus to requirements as far as I'm concerned.'

And a second afterwards, as he was debating the wisdom of attempting a response to that, the doorbell rang.

She pushed back her chair. 'Thanks for the coffee,' she said, 'although I have to say it was pretty crap. Remind me to make you a decent cup sometime.' She moved to the back door and called Laurie, and Christopher switched on the light and went out to help Clem with his ladder.

All in all, a fairly eventful Friday evening.

* * *

And later that night, as Laurie slept the sound sleep of innocent four-year-olds and her mother lay unblinking in the neighbouring room, her mind disturbed with newly awakened memories; as Christopher twitched and muttered in his bed, conducting a subconscious concert during which every possible sort of musical disaster occurred; as Molly drifted in and out of sleep, thoughts of the following day's birthday party combined with the heat keeping her from sound slumber; as Emily lay curled in a forlorn ball, searching for hope in the desolate situation in which she found herself; as Clem looked at his bedroom ceiling and made plans; as Tony listened to Bomber's soft snores at the bottom of his bed and closed his eyes and saw the face he always saw when he stopped looking at anything else; as Paula smiled in her sleep, dreaming of the encounter that was to come; as Jane slept serenely, having taken her usual pill; as Martin paced his kitchen floor, having abandoned all hope of sleep; as his mother tossed irritably, now throwing off her sheet, now fumbling for it again; as each character passed the hours of darkness in their disparate ways, the drought that had endured for over six weeks finally ended, and fat drops began to tumble from the sky and spatter onto the parched ground.

Saturday, 6 August

It hadn't stopped raining all morning. After so many days of sunshine it was a startling change. The steady downpour and accompanying drop in temperature sluiced away the mugginess, but the low, smudge-grey sky lent the day a kind of dull dreariness that had pedestrians huddling under umbrellas and wrapping reclaimed raincoats more tightly about them.

Emily spent the morning in her room. She culled her wardrobe, filling a black bin bag with clothes unworn in the past year. She went through her underwear, throwing out anything discoloured or tired. She folded and refolded the contents of her scarf and sweater drawers. She sifted through her few pieces of jewellery, teasing the knots from a thin gold chain, polishing a silver charm bracelet and a couple of rings, dumping a dented bangle, a few single earrings, a brooch without a back.

She cleared the surface of her dressing table – hairbrush, comb, tissues, nail file and clippers, moisturiser, tin of petroleum jelly, perfume, hair clips. She dusted it and polished it, and replaced everything in a new arrangement. She did the same with her bedside locker – hand cream, magazines, lamp, clock-radio – and the top of her chest of drawers: photographs, CDs, her candle collection.

She vacuumed the carpet. She cleaned the window. She changed the sheets on her bed. She added a pair of threadbare slippers to the black bag, and took them out again.

She replaced the head on her electric toothbrush.

She sewed a button onto a jacket.

She rearranged the remaining clothes in her wardrobe according to colour.

When she could find nothing more to do she looked at her watch and saw it was a few minutes to noon. She tied the top of the black bag and brought it downstairs. She found her mother in the kitchen, wrapping a child's jigsaw in brightly coloured paper.

'I was wondering where you'd got to. Aren't they unlucky with the weather for the party?'

'When is it starting?'

'Two o'clock, but she wants me there for half one. Hope it clears up in time for the concert, or people won't come out.'

The concert, just a few hours from now. Emily couldn't think about it: her head was too full.

Her mother bit off a length of Sellotape. 'I should be home around five. Will I pick up a pizza on the way, save you cooking?'

'Do so.'

'Ham and mushroom?'

'Grand.' She let a beat pass. 'I'm going to walk into town.'

Her mother lifted her head. 'You're not, are you? In this rain?'

'I just need to get some fresh air. I've done a bit of a clear-out and I've got stuff for the charity shop so I'm going to drop it off.'

'Are you feeling OK, love?'

'I am, I'm fine. See you later. Enjoy the party.'

Outside she lifted her face and let the drops fall onto it, a novelty after the weeks of sun. She thought of him arriving at the café in about an hour. She wondered how long he would wait for her – ten minutes? Fifteen? Longer? She pulled up the hood of her raincoat and set off in the direction of town. Her sandals were wrong – within minutes her feet were wet, but she kept going.

She delivered her donation to the charity shop and stayed around to check out the rails. She bought a pink top for her mother and an unopened bar of almond soap for Charlotte. She crossed the street to the newsagent's and leafed through the magazines for ten minutes, taking in nothing.

A youth sat behind the counter, flicking through a book. The clock on the wall above him read twenty to one.

She couldn't do it. She couldn't leave him sitting and wondering. She had to meet him, had to tell him face to face.

She caught a bus across town, her mood bleak. A woman with hair plastered to her head took the adjoining seat: Emily ignored her, staring fixedly at the window all the way, watching drops tumble and roll down the glass. Willing herself not to break down in his presence as she said what had to be said.

By the time she reached the café it was ten past one. She scanned the cars outside and didn't see his.

He wasn't here. He must be here. Could he have walked? She pushed open the door and went in.

The overheated, cloggy air rushed to meet her. She smelt coffee, and fresh-baked bread, and damp clothing. The place was crowded, most of the tables already occupied, a few heads turning at her entrance. She scanned the room quickly: no sign of him.

She threaded her way across the floor to one of the remaining tables, a small round one set for three. She deposited her carrier bag on a chair, draped her sodden raincoat over the back. Waitresses passed her bearing plates of food, leaving savoury wafts in their wake. She should be hungry – breakfast had been a cup of tea and a slice of toast that she'd played with more than eaten – but the food didn't tempt.

He was late, that was all. Something had delayed him. Any minute now he'd rush in, full of apologies. Her anticipation at the thought of seeing him battled with the dread she felt at having to say goodbye. How would she bear it? Maybe she should just leave now, stick to her original plan of not meeting him again – but the embarrassment of having to gather her things and walk back through the room kept her where she was.

From the corner of her vision she became aware of a woman at a nearby table staring fixedly in her direction: after enduring it for several seconds she forced herself to turn and look directly at her, and the woman's gaze slid away.

She placed her hands on the table, moved a knife an inch to the left. They'd never sat at this side of the room, always the other. She could see the table they'd taken on their first visit, occupied now by a woman and a child.

She shifted her hands to her lap. The café's wooden floor was patched with damp footprints. Her feet felt chilly now in their wet sandals. Her heart jumped every time the door opened.

A waitress approached: Emily asked for a pot of tea. 'I'm waiting for a friend,' she said, though no enquiry had been made. Her watch told her it was approaching twenty past one. Where was he?

The chatter flowed around her; she was impervious to it. A chair scraped across the floor, making her start. A fork or a knife landed with a clatter on someone's plate. Despite her cold feet, she felt the room too warm. Her palms were damp; her forehead itched with sweat. Rain continued to fall outside: in conversation lulls she could hear it pattering against the plate-glass window to her left. Making up for its long absence.

The tea arrived. She poured milk, glad of something to do. She stirred, watching the door. Why wasn't he here? Had she got it wrong, the time, the place? But she hadn't, she knew she hadn't. This was their place, one o'clock the allotted time.

She sipped. The tea was too hot; it burnt her tongue. She added more milk, sipped again, everything in her wound so tightly that she had to concentrate on breathing. She felt a desperate and growing need now to see him again, even if it was only to bid him farewell. *Please,* she said silently. *Please come. Please appear, breathless and full of apologies.*

People left. People came. She sat on. She waited until two o'clock, and then she asked for her bill. She paid, and pulled on her raincoat, and walked out into the rain that hadn't stopped for a single minute.

In the end, he'd come to the same conclusion that she had. He'd stayed away, as she'd intended to do, unable or unwilling to face her and say goodbye.

It was over. She tried to feel anger towards him, but couldn't. He wouldn't have wanted to hurt her, she was sure of it.

She walked the entire way home. In the rain, nobody at all noticed her tears.

* * *

Such a shame: one day earlier and he'd have had his party in the sunshine. Now he and his little friends would be stuck inside. She hoped Linda hadn't booked a bouncy castle. She might well have though, all the rage these days.

The jigsaw might be a bit hard for him – she couldn't remember if the twins had been able for thirty pieces as five-year-olds. No matter, he'd grow into it. She stowed it in a plastic bag and clipped it to the bike's carrier.

Her green waxed jacket was stiff with disuse. She shook it out and put it on, and yanked up the hood. Overwhelming as the heat had been at times, she didn't relish being back to the rain. Travelling by bicycle was a challenge in wet weather, roads slick with moisture, passing car tyres sending out sprays of water – she'd swear some people drove through puddles on purpose. In the rain, pedestrians and motorists alike were grumpier, less inclined to be nice to cyclists.

And if this weather continued, it didn't bode well for the concert tonight – who'd bother going out unless it was to something a lot more exciting than a musical medley, sung by an enthusiastic but amateur choir? They could find themselves performing for a handful of family members and friends who felt duty-bound to show up: no fun at all.

She'd done her best to drum up support. She'd said it to all the neighbours, and Dervla and Gar were coming, and Paula had left her a very nice note on Thursday promising to be there, and to bring a friend.

Clem had said he'd come too, but she doubted she'd see him there. What was she to do about Clem? Clearly she'd upset him the other night – he'd nearly run out of the house as soon as Emily had appeared, couldn't get away fast enough. There had been no thank-you text the following day either, like he'd sent after the first time, and no repeat of his offer to take her out in return.

She felt bad for having offended him – the last thing she wanted was for them to fall out – but really, wasn't he being just a bit touchy? All she'd done was try to bring him and Emily together: what was so wrong with that? She'd thought he'd be amused, even a bit flattered, but clearly he wasn't pleased.

She thought back to his revelation of the life he'd had in England, the woman he'd married, the daughter they'd had – and the horrific way they'd both been taken from him. How little she'd known about him. He'd been in love; he'd been a husband and a father. He'd been robbed of his spouse far too young, just like her.

His talk of going to pieces after their deaths resonated too. She knew all about that, knew how happiness could suddenly be snatched away, leaving nothing but a terrifying void in its wake that made it hard to see any kind of future ahead. She knew all about sleeping for months with the light on because the dark without Danny had become intolerable. If she hadn't had the twins to look after, if she hadn't had to confine her anguish until they were asleep, to keep afloat because of them, who knew where she'd be now? She might well have taken to the bottle too, might have lost everything.

Clem had been doubly shattered, robbed so cruelly of his wife and little child, the two people dearest to him. Left with nothing, nobody to be responsible for, nobody to keep him from falling headlong into the abyss until the father he'd never felt close to had come and pulled him back from the brink and brought him home, and helped to mend him.

And now Doug was gone, and Clem was alone again – and

Molly had managed to upset him while he was still grieving for his father. What could she do? How could she make it up to him?

She'd pay him a visit, she decided, tomorrow morning. Bring him an apple tart or something, apologise for putting her foot in it. They'd be fine again; he wasn't the type, she was sure, to hold on to a grudge. And there'd be other concerts he could come to – only last Monday Christopher had mentioned a harvest festival that he was planning to put them forward for.

Christopher probably didn't think they were ready for tonight's performance – he never did. Concerts, or the run-up to them, always had him on edge. On Monday he'd railed against the altos for coming in too late during 'Anything Goes', and the sopranos for their pacing in 'Surrey With The Fringe On Top'. He'd practically shouted at Ultan for whispering to his neighbour, and when Dorothy had dared to question his running order he hadn't been long letting her know who was boss. Poor Dorothy, only trying to help. Poor Christopher, taking it all so seriously when really he should have been enjoying it.

The concert didn't worry Molly in the least. They wouldn't be perfect but they'd be fine: they'd rise to the occasion like they always did, and Christopher would forgive them everything. They'd present him with the usual bouquet – Harriet had collected their contributions on Monday – and everyone would go home smiling.

She wondered if he was still involved with Jane. She'd watched him at rehearsal, trying to find evidence of their affair, but he hadn't given any indication that Jane was in any way special to him – on the contrary, he'd snapped at her last week for arriving late again. If only he'd picked one of the unattached singers, or preferably someone entirely unconnected with the choir, to have a fling with. She knew it was none of her business, but still she felt disappointed in him.

She cycled through an intersection, her tyres shooting up little jets of water. Despite the inclement weather, she was looking forward to the afternoon. The twins' parties, up until their teens, had been low key, due in part to lack of money and in part to the inevitable sense of loss the day would bring. Another year older, another landmark Danny was missing. She'd paint on a smile and let them invite two friends each, and cobble together what party food she could for the six of them: cocktail sausages, jelly and ice-cream, chocolate cake. Today's party, she knew, would be an entirely different business – and of course she'd see Paddy again, and meet his family, and see what connections she could make.

The traffic was heavy. She pedalled carefully, head bent against the driving rain. She hoped Emily wasn't getting too wet – what in God's name had brought her out in this? It wasn't as if the charity shop was desperate for her cast-offs. Then again, the poor girl was probably looking for diversions to take her mind off the show tonight. Shame today was her day off, really – work would have made the hours pass quicker for her.

The first things she saw as she approached Linda's house were a clutch of brightly coloured helium balloons, bobbing above the gate on intertwined silver ribbons. She wheeled her bicycle down the side passage and propped it where she always did – and there was the bouncy castle, taking up a good half of the garden. She could hear the soft *pock* of the raindrops as they landed on the inflated plastic. Such a shame.

She tapped on the patio door, shaking rain from her coat.

She'd forgotten the jigsaw: she scuttled back and released it from the carrier. She returned to the door, gave another rap. She could see things piled on the table – multipacks of crisps and popcorn, bags of marshmallows, cartons of juice. A tower of pastel-coloured bowls, a stack of serviettes. The fridge full of stuff too, probably.

A minute passed, with no sign of anyone coming to let her in. The television in the living area was off, the floor in front of it free of its usual jumble of bricks and toy cars. She checked her watch: twenty-five to two. Twenty-five minutes before the little visitors would begin to arrive.

Maybe they were upstairs getting ready. She left the bicycle where it was and made her way back up the side passage to the front of the house, and rang the doorbell. Several seconds passed, and still nobody appeared: how peculiar. She pressed her face to the bevelled-glass panel beside the door and saw no movement, heard no sound from within.

What was she to do? She glanced around – and noticed for the first time that Linda's car was absent from the driveway. No car meant no Linda, and presumably no Paddy either. Where on earth would they have gone, with the party due to start shortly?

Maybe Linda had thought of something she'd forgotten to get, and had done a mad dash to the supermarket. Maybe Paddy had been taken ill and they were on their way to a doctor, or a hospital. There was no note pinned to either door, nothing to tell her what was going on.

She opened her bag, rummaged around for her phone. She'd ring Linda, see what the story was. *Missed call*, her screen told her. It was from Linda, and it had come through fifteen minutes earlier or so, when Molly had been pedalling through the rain. There was no voicemail message.

She pressed the key to return the call and listened to the rings that went unanswered. 'It's me,' she said, after the beep. 'It's Molly, just wondering if there's anything wrong. I'm at the house.' She couldn't think of anything else to say so she disconnected.

What now? Should she wait around, and hope they showed up? As she stood there uncertainly, she heard her name being called. She turned and saw a woman beckoning to her from the doorstep of the neighbouring house. She drew up the hood of her coat and crossed to the low wall that divided the properties.

'You're Molly?' Young, around mid-twenties. Brown hair twisted into a knot on top of her head. What looked like a man's striped shirt belted at the waist, narrow black pants beneath. A baby was lodged on her hip, eyeing Molly impassively.

'Yes, I'm Molly. Is anything wrong?'

'All I know is that Linda left about ten minutes ago with Paddy – she said there was a family crisis, and that she'd tried to ring you—'

'I saw the missed call. She didn't say what it was?'

'No, just that the party was cancelled, and if I saw you I was to tell you. She said she'll be in touch.'

Molly thanked her and went to collect the bike. A family crisis, whatever that meant. How awful, and for it to happen today of all days – but at least she and Paddy were OK.

No point in hanging around here. She tried to post her present through the letterbox but it was too big, so she clipped it to the carrier again – she'd bring it back with her next Wednesday. She wheeled the bike down the path and pushed open the little gate – and as she did so, one of the helium balloons came free of its moorings and began to drift away.

'Oh no!' She propped the bike against the wall and raced off in pursuit, just managing to leap and grab the end of the ribbon before it escaped. She retied it firmly to the gate, and then checked the ties on the others and tightened them too. Even though his party had been cancelled, he might be glad to see the balloons still in place on his return.

She stepped back – and it was then that the message on one of the balloons in bright bubble letters caught her eye. *4 today*, it said.

She frowned. She looked at the others. The message on all of them was the same.

Four, not five. And there were four balloons. She stood in the rain, trying to take in this new knowledge, trying to follow it all the way to the end.

Today was his fourth birthday, not his fifth. He was a year younger than she'd assumed.

And suddenly, standing there in the continuing rain, she saw it all clearly.

She'd told herself he was five because five would fit, and she'd wanted it so much to fit. She'd wanted him to be her grandson so she could have another chance. She'd made a mess with Philip, but maybe she could get it right with his son.

She'd hoped and hoped that he was her grandson, but he wasn't. Philip had left Ireland well over a year before this child was born. He looked like Philip, but he wasn't Philip's son: he couldn't be.

And even though there had never been a shred of evidence

to back up her conviction – apart from the boy's physical resemblance to Philip, which maybe, after all, only she might have seen – she was conscious as she stood there of a feeling of utter loss.

She felt like Philip had left her all over again.

* * *

He'd spent the morning in the supermarket, although he generally gave it a wide berth at the weekend. On the day of the concert he needed a distraction, or he'd wear out the kitchen floor with his pacing. He caught up on emails, drafted letters for his secretary to type up on Monday, signed forms that waited in his inbox, did a bit more work on a report for head office.

At one o'clock he pulled on his raincoat and left, nodding at staff members he encountered on the way. No sign of Emily. She'd be nervous, he knew, in advance of the performance. Not one for the limelight, unlike Molly who had no problem with it. But Emily wouldn't let him down: she'd obey his cues and get on with it, and midway through the first song he'd see her let the music take over, and she'd be fine.

On the way home he dropped into the shopping centre and ate a mediocre Caesar salad – too much iceberg, not enough croutons – and drank a good cappuccino in a small café. He was reminded of Freddie in his kitchen the night before, giving him her potted history as she endured his instant coffee. How long since she'd moved in – a month? Longer? How many times had they clashed since then? He couldn't remember the last time someone had irritated him so much.

She probably made decent coffee, though. And he couldn't fault the cookies.

After lunch he dropped into a little hairdressing salon a few doors up from the café. It wasn't where he normally went, but that was too far away to trek to in the rain today.

'I don't have an appointment,' he told the dark-haired woman who approached, 'but I just need a tidy-up.'

'For the concert,' she said.

He looked at her in surprise. He was sure he didn't know her.

'You're the conductor of Molly's choir. My husband and I go to all the concerts – she's my best friend.'

'Ah. Yes.'

'Your name?'

'Christopher.'

'Dervla. Can you give me about twenty minutes?'

He could. He leafed through her selection of magazines and read an article about an up-and-coming band from Carlow that he'd never heard of, and looked at fashions for men that he wouldn't be seen dead in. He could see Freddie in some of the female garb, though: she seemed partial to the weird and wonderful.

In due course his hair was washed by a young girl and trimmed fairly competently by Dervla, who thankfully didn't ask him about planned holidays. Didn't talk much at all, once she'd taken his order for tea with nothing added – but when he was paying afterwards, paying less than his usual barber asked for, she wished him luck.

'I always enjoy the concerts,' she said.

'Good to know.' He left her a generous tip, and phoned his mother on the way home.

'I'll be setting off in a few minutes,' she told him. 'I'll bring dinner. Is it raining there too?'

'Pouring. Pack your umbrella.'

'Oh dear. I hope it doesn't put people off coming tonight.'

'We'll have to wait and see. Safe trip.'

As he approached his house he saw Freddie's white car outside hers. He wondered how she'd be when they met again, if her disclosure of the previous night would change things between them. They'd parted on cordial terms – she'd gone off happily with Clem and his ladder, and hadn't reappeared – but would she regret having shared so much with Christopher?

Half past three. In a few hours he'd be heading to the community hall; his gut gave a small leap at the thought. He let himself into the house and hung up his damp coat. In the kitchen he glanced through the window and saw no sign of Laurie in the back garden. Too wet, the rain still coming down. No sign of the dog either, must be taking refuge in the shed. He slotted Sinatra into the CD player and opened the newspaper that had been delivered earlier, after he'd left for the supermarket.

He turned to the crossword page. Nothing like Sinatra and a crossword to chill you out before the spotlight blinked on.

* * *

Her gloom increased as she cycled home. Today was turning into something pretty horrible – and the weather wasn't helping. No sign of respite in the sky, no lighter patch evident in the low, dense cloud cover, the rain falling from it as steadily as ever. As she negotiated the puddles she thought of the concert, just a few hours away. For once, she didn't feel in the least like singing.

She got home and wheeled the bike into the hall. 'Emily?'

No answer. She stood still and listened, and heard a distant splash from upstairs. She peeled off her raincoat and stepped out of her wet shoes. Could do with a bath herself.

She left the jigsaw on the hallstand and trailed up. The landing smelt of Badedas. 'Emily, it's me.'

'Mam – what are you doing home?'

'Party was cancelled, some family trouble. I'll talk to you when you're out.'

In her room she climbed onto a stool and took down a cream canvas bag from the top of the wardrobe. She sat on the bed and upended it. Folded pages tumbled into her lap and spilt across the duvet.

She picked one up at random and unfolded it.

My dear Philip,

Our second Christmas without you – hard to believe it's coming on for two years since you left. I hope you're with friends for Christmas. Emily did the turkey crown again, no point in

She dropped it and chose another.

My dear Philip,

I wish you'd let us have an address for you, so we could send you the news, not that there's a lot happening around here. James Clohessy got engaged, Carol was over the

And another.

My dear Philip,

Your latest postcard arrived this morning. A wet week here, everyone is like a drowned rat. I hope you're getting better weather in New Zealand. I looked it up and

And another.

My dear Philip,

It's been three months since you left, and I miss you every day.

I do hope

She scanned more of the letters, eyes skimming over the words, some of which were blotched and misshapen with her tears. As she read, she felt her despondency harden into something else.

He'd walked out on them without a word, without leaving even a note of explanation. He'd stolen from her, his mother, who'd only ever wanted good for him, who'd always made sure he had everything he needed, who'd held her tongue when he disappointed her, who'd given him the benefit of every doubt, who'd made the world of excuses for him.

He'd taken all that and thrown it back in her face. There'd never been a word of apology in his postcards for helping himself to her savings – and still she wouldn't hear a word said against him. Still she'd been delighted when she'd met a little boy she'd thought might be his, ready to clutch at anything, anyone with a connection to him. Even in these letters, ones he'd never read, ones that allowed her to say whatever the hell she liked, she didn't chastise him, or rail against what he'd done.

She was a fool.

She pushed the letters aside and found her writing pad. She took up a pen and began to write, the words spilling out.

Philip,

I love you. I loved you from the moment they put you and Emily in my arms in hospital. I remember crying with happiness, the only time I think I ever did that, except maybe on my wedding day. I watched you both grow up and I thought myself the luckiest woman in the world to be your mother – and after your father died, you became even more precious. You were my reminders of him, you and Emily.

I don't remember when it started, when you began to go wrong. Maybe it was when Mrs O'Neill in second class called me in because you were tormenting Sean Reilly. Maybe it was before that. I do know that you were still young enough for me to make allowances for you, to call it childish foolishness that you'd grow out of. But you got older, and it continued, and still I tried to pretend it wasn't serious.

And slowly it got worse. You stole from our local shop, you took a car that didn't belong to you, you were suspended from school for cheating in an exam. I could go on, there was plenty more, and every single time I forgave you, and I begged you to change, and every single time you promised you would. I fell for your lies every time, not wanting to believe you could be so uncaring, but you were. You probably still are.

And then, out of the blue, you disappeared without a word to me or to Emily, and you took every cent I'd been saving with you. You left us without a clue as to where you were for over a month, and then we got a postcard with no return address. And since then I've been writing you silly letters about Emily's rise in salary and my new haircut and Aunt Maura's hip replacement. I've been writing the kind of letters I'd write if you'd gone in the normal way to live somewhere else, because I didn't want to face up to the way things had really happened – until now.

You send cards that tell me nothing, other than that you're still alive. I've gone through five Christmases without you. Next week you'll turn thirty, and you won't be here, and I won't know if you're even celebrating your birthday – and for all you know, Emily and I could both be dead and buried.

Why did you do it, Philip? Why did you leave without any goodbye, with no explanation? Why didn't you ask for money if you needed it, instead of taking it like a common thief? Why haven't you once picked up the phone in five years to check if I'm alright? Are you punishing me for something you imagine I've done to you? It's cruel and it's unfair, and I don't deserve it. I gave you everything I could, and still you broke my heart.

Six weeks ago I met a little boy who looked just like you at that age. I convinced myself you were his father. I thought I had found someone to connect me to you, and I clung to him, like someone drowning. Today I discovered I was wrong, you couldn't be his father, and it was like losing you all over again.

And the thing is, the stupid thing is, you are still and will always be my precious son. I hate what you've done, but I don't hate you. I still love you as much as I always did, which probably makes me the biggest fool on earth. I will love you until the day I die, and I'll never stop hoping that you'll come back to me.

I hope you know all that. I think, somewhere inside, you probably do.

Love Mam xx

She didn't reread it. She set down her pen and stretched her cramped fingers. She folded the pages in two, and tore and tore and tore until she'd made scraps of it. She gathered up the scraps and balled them together in her fist and dropped the ball into the bin beside the wardrobe.

It helped a bit, but not all that much.

* * *

Paula,
Greetings from Mayo! Murphy's law: you finally ask to meet up, and my poor mother slips getting out of the shower and breaks her ankle. She's fine, more annoyed than injured – she had to pull out of a trip to the Lake District with her walking club – so I've taken a week off to pamper her. I'll be back for work on Monday, so maybe we could get a bite to eat that evening? Let me know if you're free.

J x

Jenny,
Your poor mum, hope she's on the mend. I broke a finger once; that was enough. I'd love dinner on Monday – how about Indian, or Thai? Or anything really! I finish work at five; we could meet up anytime after that.

P xx

Indian it is. The Curry Palace at six?

J x

I love The Curry Palace – I'm always tempted to lick my plate after their lamb korma (but I promise I won't on Monday). Maybe a drink beforehand in O'Malley's at half five? I swear I'm not a lush, but I thought it might take the nerves away!

P xx

Nerves? You have nothing to fear from me. Even if we don't head into the sunset together we'll definitely be friends – but I'm happy to go for a drink (not a lush either, but partial to a cold crisp white). See you in O'Malley's.

J xx

PS I'll wear a red carnation in my lapel, just for the laugh.

And that last one was yesterday, and today was Saturday, and Monday was two days away, and for the past week she'd been skipping lunch and doing ten sit-ups three times a day, like it would make an ounce of difference. She'd decided what to wear for the occasion, new skirt, green top, and promptly changed her mind, white trousers, blue top, then changed it back. She'd made a Monday lunchtime appointment with Dervla for a wash and blow-dry; yesterday she'd had her legs waxed and her nails shellacked.

You have nothing to fear from me. The logical side of her knew she had nothing to fear: she was a grown woman, not some lovestruck teenager. They'd either click or they wouldn't; either way, she'd survive. The illogical side was filled with nervous anticipation at the thought of walking into O'Malley's on Monday night for what was in essence a blind date.

She took a jacket from the hook inside her front door. She lifted her umbrella from its stand. She left the apartment as an ambulance raced by, siren blaring. She made the sign of the cross like she always did, although whether she was offering it in mute appeal for the occupant, or in gratitude that it wasn't her, she could never decide.

She began to walk. Thank God for the change in the weather. The wall-to-wall sunshine they'd been having was pleasant, but walking in the rain had always appealed to her; whenever she was feeling under pressure she found the steady fall of it soothing. She did a lot of her best thinking in the rain: it seemed to loosen her mind, allowing her access to ideas and solutions she might previously have missed.

She passed the cinema where she and Tony went roughly once a week. They didn't always agree on films but they shared a love of French cinema and Woody Allen and the Coen brothers, and anything with Harvey Keitel or Javier Bardem in it.

She stopped at the fruit and vegetable shop and bought parsnips because Tony was coming to dinner.

'Is the rain down for the day?' Angela behind the counter asked.

'Looks like it.'

'Doing anything nice for the weekend?'

'Going to a concert tonight, down at the community hall. It's a choir called Lift Up Your Voices.'

'Never heard of them,' Angela said, bagging the parsnips. 'I'd be more into heavy metal myself – Disturbed, Five Finger Death Punch, that sort of thing. That'll be one forty, pet.'

Back home she fried onions and browned cubes of meat and chopped parsnips and made stock, and tumbled everything into a casserole dish. She wasn't a cook, had never been interested enough to get the hang of it, despite Tony's repeated offers to teach her. Her solo meals ranged from cheese on toast to microwaved jacket potatoes to pasta with a jar of pesto stirred in. When she was feeding Tony she rose to a casserole – casseroles were very forgiving – or a shepherd's pie that a child could put together.

She loaded the washing machine. Awful to have to go back to trying to dry them inside, barely enough space to set up the clothes horse in the bathroom, but she hated it anywhere else. She hauled her sewing machine from the bedroom and took up the hem of a skirt she'd bought on sale. As she sewed she listened to the news items on local radio: ongoing forest fires in America, talks to avert strike action among teachers, a fatal road accident that morning just outside the town.

She checked the casserole, gave everything a bit of a stir. She emptied the washing machine and hung the clothes on the horse. She showered and dressed in her new skirt, and decided that the green top didn't suit it after all, and found a black one that did. Back in the kitchen she set out cutlery and slipped two plates under the grill to catch the heat of the oven beneath. While she waited for Tony she checked emails, and found one from her mother, telling her about her cousin Doreen's new baby – she could almost hear the wistful tone – and one from a dating website she'd long since abandoned that kept trying to woo her back.

We have hundreds of people waiting to meet you! it told her, which was so clearly a lie she wondered how they got away with it. She replied to her mother – *delighted to hear, must drop her a line* – and switched off her computer. She gave the casserole another poke and looked out at rain that was definitely beginning to outstay its welcome.

'Do you like my new skirt?' she asked when Tony arrived.

'Do a twirl. Very smart.'

He never noticed what she wore. She could cut armholes in a pillowcase and he'd be none the wiser. She ladled the casserole into bowls.

'Do we have to go to this thing?' he asked, jabbing at a chunk of carrot.

'Yes, we do. I've bought the tickets.'

'I could refund you the money, and we could just go to the pub. Or we could stay in and do Netflix.'

'We are going to the concert. We can have a drink after. We can do Netflix anytime.'

'You're a hard nut to crack.'

'So you like to tell me.'

Silence fell as they ate. In between the clink of cutlery on plates she heard the soft pit-pat of rain on the window.

'You all set for Monday then?' he asked.

'As set as I'll ever be.'

'You'll wear the new skirt, I suppose.' A grin all ready to erupt on his face.

'Probably.'

He drank the wine she'd poured. 'So how long's this concert going to go on for?'

'Not that long, I'd say. An hour and a bit at the most.'

'I get to pick the next film.'

'Only if it's not too gory – and you pay for it.'

'Deal.'

They finished the casserole, and the mango sorbet she'd bought to follow it. He washed up, she dried. They opened umbrellas and walked out into the rain, and made their way on foot to the community hall.

* * *

'Who took my lip balm? I left it right here. Right *here*. Ultan, did you take it?'

'I most certainly did *not*. I wouldn't *dream* of using someone else's lip balm. *God*.'

'Have we a full house, did anyone see?'

'Rita, your lip balm is on the floor, over there. No, there, under that chair.'

'Has someone got a comb I could borrow?'

'There's no paper in the loo, just letting everyone know.'

'I'm going to be sick.'

'You're not. Deep breaths, you'll be fine.'

'George, your shirt tail is sticking out.'

'Who's got the right time?'

'I've lost my phone. Has anyone seen my phone?'

' . . . Are you alright?'

'I'm fine.'

But Emily didn't look fine. She looked far from fine. She was paler than usual, and blinking too rapidly, and worrying at her bottom lip with her teeth. She looked, Molly thought, as if she was just waiting for the nod from someone to burst into tears, to fall apart completely.

In the tiny gaps between the chatter in the dressing room, rain could be heard pelting against the windows. Molly caught her daughter's hand and squeezed it. 'It'll be OK, love. You always get this way before a performance. You'll be grand as soon as we start, wait and see.'

The door opened and Christopher appeared. You could almost smell the tension from him. Dark hair rumpled, jaw clenched tight, red dicky bow askew. 'Anyone seen Jane? Anyone heard from her?'

No one had seen Jane. No one had heard from her.

It was ten minutes to performance.

* * *

Bitch.

This was her way of getting back at him, his punishment for finishing with her. He tried her mobile again, and again heard her telling him to leave a message, and again resisted the urge to leave her the message she deserved.

The altos would have to manage without her. Molly Griffin's

was the strongest voice in the section; he'd adjust her position and they'd cope. He scanned the room and found her next to Emily, who looked as tense as he felt.

'Molly.'

She looked up; he beckoned and she approached. She nodded calmly in response to his instruction, and he was heartened. You could depend on Molly.

'Five minutes,' he told them. The room seemed to give a collective shudder. 'Remember what you've been taught. Breathe. Stand tall. Come in strongly, don't wait for someone else. Have yourselves lined up when I get back.'

He made his way to the hall, peered out at the auditorium from the side of the stage. Over half full, others still coming in. More than he'd hoped for, given the weather.

He caught his mother's eye in the centre of the front row. She gave him a small wave; he nodded back, reluctant to draw attention to himself. She'd arrived in the afternoon, bringing salmon she'd already poached. She always brought food when she came to stay; he chose not to take it as a criticism of his culinary efforts.

I met your neighbour on the way in, she'd said, doling the fish onto plates. *Freddie, charming woman. You never told me they were American.*

Didn't I?

I said I was here for the concert: she knew nothing about it.

He'd presented his most innocent face. *Did she not? Could have sworn I mentioned it.*

And such a sweet little girl.

He'd been strongly tempted to tell her that the sweet little girl's father had come from a test tube. *I don't see much of them really.*

She told me she plays with your dog.

Amazing how much information she could extract in a relatively short space of time. *She comes through the hedge now and again. I'm usually at work.*

Did you know Freddie is a children's book author?

She did tell me that, yes.

He'd waited for more, but that seemed to be the extent of it.

Any romance? his mother had asked while he was clearing the table, and he'd told her truthfully no, not at the moment, and he'd seen her trying to swallow her disappointment.

Robert was home during the week. He had a conference – he stayed a couple of nights. Because when she thought of Christopher and romance, she thought of Robert. It was a natural progression.

He didn't tell her he knew about the conference; he made no mention of Robert's phone call, over a week ago now. There'd been no call since, no repeat of his brother's invitation to meet up and bury the hatchet.

He let his eyes roam around the assembled crowd. There was Ian Redden, a recent arrival among his crew of junior managers – and wasn't that the girl who worked in the bakery section in the seat beside him? For the life of him Christopher couldn't think of her name, but he was pretty sure it was her.

He was surprised to spot Tony Shaw a few rows behind the others. Couldn't forget *his* name – he made sure you remembered it. Cheery fellow, always called out a hello if Christopher passed by the meat counter. Gave the impression he enjoyed what he did. Christopher wouldn't have pegged him as a fan of choral music, but you never knew.

'Christopher!'

A sudden shout from the back of the room, causing heads to swivel. Causing him to cringe.

'We're down here!' And there she was, just inside the door. There the two of them were, waving up at him, beaming. Clad in identical yellow raincoats that were splashed with giant blue and red flowers, and matching wide-brimmed hats. Impervious, it seemed, to the glances and nudges their colourful presence was attracting. Wonderful: thanks, Mother. He lifted a cautious hand in response and made a swift exit.

Two minutes. He collected the choir – still no Jane – and shepherded them to the side of the stage, where they remained hidden from the waiting audience. He straightened his dicky bow and ran a hand through his hair and turned off the main lights, leaving only the stage illuminated. He stood waiting while the chatter died down and turned into an expectant hush. When all was silent he walked onstage and laid his list of songs on the waiting podium. He gave his usual few opening words – all very welcome, delighted with turnout, hope you enjoy, blah blah – while the choir members filed into place silently behind him.

He finished speaking. There was a polite spatter of applause. He turned to face his choir. He took his tuning fork from his breast pocket and tapped it against the podium, and hummed the opening notes for each section. They echoed him, and fell silent once more.

He counted to three in his head. He raised his arms.

They began to sing.

* * *

She sang to him. He wasn't there but she saw him reaching for her in his car, heard him murmuring her name, felt him wrapping his arms around her. Every word was for him. He was the lover in every love song.

And as she sang, as she heard the communion of their voices rising and falling, now soft, now strong, now whisper-quiet, now thunderous, despite her immense heartache and stage fright she became aware of the mounting euphoria their perfect harmonies always called into being, the sensation of floating, the lightness of spirit the music they made never failed to create for her.

Tomorrow she would cry more tears for him. In the coming days and weeks she'd mourn the passing of the far too brief time they'd had together. The loss of him would ambush her for months, maybe even years – but tonight she was singing. Tonight she was flying.

* * *

They were doing well, she could hear it. She could see it in the faces of the people in the front row, the only ones visible from the stage. There was Christopher's mother as usual: she hadn't missed a single one of their performances. Molly had met her in his house once, not long after she'd begun cleaning for Christopher. Dignified was how you'd describe her. Not unfriendly, but not one you could imagine having a good old natter with.

She wondered if Clem was somewhere in the audience, and thought he probably wasn't. Every time he entered her head she had a sense of things being out of kilter, like a foot going into the wrong slipper. She resolved again to cycle by his house in the morning with a peace offering. If he wasn't there she'd leave it with a neighbour; that was all she could do.

She hoped she hadn't lost him as a friend: she didn't want their uncomfortable parting the other night to be her last encounter with him. She'd got used to him being there if she needed him, that was the thing. You could say she'd grown accustomed to his face.

She kept her eyes on Christopher as she sang, but her mind continued to wander. Where on earth was Jane? She hoped nothing bad had happened – but what else would have kept her away from the concert? It would have been her first performance with the choir, and Jane definitely relished the limelight – she surely wouldn't have stayed away unless something serious had prevented her from coming.

Unless she and Christopher had had a row, of course. That was the trouble with mixing business and pleasure, wasn't it? If things went wrong on the pleasure side, the business suffered too.

Her thoughts drifted to Paddy, and the message on the balloons that had told her what she needed to know. How would it be, she wondered, when she saw him again on Wednesday, knowing he wasn't the boy she'd fancied him to be? In the few hours since her discovery, she thought she'd become a little easier in her mind. Maybe, after all, the letter she'd dashed off and then turned into confetti had helped; maybe it had purged what needed to be purged. Paddy would still be the same shy curly-headed little child he was before; she would smile brightly and say hello, just like she had on all the other Wednesdays.

The song ended. During the applause she stole a glimpse at Emily, off to her left. Poor thing looked more composed now, over the worst of the nerves. Maybe after this Molly could persuade her to take a few days off. The two of them could head to Dervla and Gar's mobile home in Connemara for a little break – why not? Dervla was always at her to use it, lying idle most of the time since they'd bought the apartment in Portugal.

Two songs to go, an encore after that if the audience looked for more, and they were done. Might go for a drink with Dervla and Gar after, if Emily didn't mind going home alone. Had the rain stopped yet? There'd be floods if it kept up much longer. There'd been something about a crash a few miles out of town earlier; she'd got only the tail end of the news, but she gathered someone had been killed. Imagine that news coming to your door.

Like the day Danny had died. The frightened-looking faces of the two uniformed young guards on the doorstep, her hands floury from the dough she'd been kneading, Philip yelling in the kitchen over a broken car. *Have you a friend you can call?* the female had asked, and for a minute Molly hadn't been able to remember Dervla's name.

A few weeks off for the choir after this, back in mid-September. Much as she enjoyed the Monday evening sessions, the thought of a break wasn't wholly unwelcome. Yes, a week in Connemara, if she could persuade Emily, might be just what they both needed. Fill their lungs with sea air, recharge the batteries with a few long walks, bundle up in the raincoats if summer decided not to come back. And Kathleen would just have to make do without her.

She brought her attention back to the concert, and to Christopher, and to the final song of the programme.

* * *

The audience rose to its feet, demanding more. The choir sang a prepared medley of the night's offerings, and once again gave their bows. The applause was loud and sustained, rising in volume when Harriet scuttled offstage and returned with a large bouquet and presented it, blushing, to Christopher, who accepted it with his usual good grace.

The crowd and the choir members dispersed slowly, emerging in chattering clusters from the hall into a late evening that was calm and cool and finally dry. People got into cars and moved off; others travelled on foot to adjacent hostelries, or to the nearest bus stop.

Molly accompanied Dervla and Gar to their local pub for a nightcap: Emily was persuaded by Charlotte and Ian to follow them in her car to another pub.

Christopher drove his mother home, after a brief ambush in the car park by Freddie, who was bundling a sleepy Laurie into her car seat: *Hey, you guys were amazing – I'm gonna be singing all the way home!*

Paula and Tony walked to the nearest bar. 'Admit it: you enjoyed it.'

'I did, actually. Wasn't bad at all.' He hummed an out-of-tune snatch of something she didn't recognise. 'Still can't believe my boss is in charge of it.'

'Good-looking man. Looks a bit like Kevin Costner.'

'Does he? . . . Saw someone else from work too, didn't realise she was in a choir.'

'Are you talking about Emily?'

He looked at her in surprise. 'You know her?'

'Only from going in and out of the shop – and she called to my work a couple of weeks ago, dropped something in for Martin. Nice girl, very obliging.'

They darted across the street, hopping over puddles that had formed on the potholed surface.

'I could murder a cider,' Paula said. 'Where's that pub?'

'She's actually quite sweet.'

She looked up at him. 'Who?'

'Emily. I've seen her packing bags for the old dears. None of the others do it.'

Emily, who would be so good for him, who'd ground him and give him back his confidence. 'You like her?'

'I do.'

'You should tell her you were at the concert,' she said, 'next time you see her.'

'Yeah.' He started to say something, then stopped. Then started again. 'She's a bit afraid of me. I think I'm too full-on.'

'Dial yourself down a bit then. Be like you are now.'

'Mmm.'

'Get her on her own if you can. Tell her you enjoyed it. Or give her a congratulations card – leave it in her pigeon hole, or whatever ye have.'

'We have lockers. Maybe I'll do that.' He pulled open the pub door; the hot air met them.

The evening passed. Emily reached home shortly after ten and found the house empty. She flicked through television channels and found nothing of interest. She made a pot of tea and poured it over a bowl of dried fruit in preparation for a brack she wanted to bake in the morning. She cleaned her face of its unaccustomed make-up and made her way to bed, shutting out thoughts of Martin when they surfaced.

An hour later, Molly was dropped off by Gar and Dervla. She stepped out of her shoes in the hall and padded upstairs to change into pyjamas and brush her teeth. No sound from

Emily's room, but her car was in the driveway. Good that she'd gone off with Charlotte and that boy instead of coming straight home.

Funny she'd said nothing about Charlotte having a boyfriend. Maybe he was the reason for her being in a bit of a mood lately . . . Maybe she was afraid she'd be left on her own now.

On the other hand, he might have a friend to suit her.

She should go to bed, but she felt wide awake: she was always on a bit of a high after a concert – and tomorrow was Sunday, she could stay in bed as long as she liked. She'd slept like a log the night before, once the rain had come and washed the heat away.

She slipped back downstairs. In the kitchen she lifted a tea towel that was draped over a bowl, and dipped her head to smell the plump fruit that was steeping, and smiled at the thought of warm tea brack for elevenses. She put the kettle on, humming a few lines from 'Anything Goes' – stuck in her head now. She switched on the radio to banish it and dropped a teabag into a mug.

Sunday tomorrow. She was reminded of her intention to call to Clem's. She rummaged in the freezer and found a batch of Emily's almond fingers: they'd do. She tore a page from her shopping-list notebook and wrote, *Clem, I'm sorry that I upset you, I really didn't mean to. I hope you'll accept this as a peace offering, and forgive me – Molly*. She folded it and sat it on the bag of cookies.

The kettle boiled. She made tea and brought it to the table as the pips for the midnight news came on. She listened to reports of flooding in Cork after the day's rain, and an earthquake in Japan that had levelled an entire village, and a new initiative announced by the government to reduce hospital trolleys: good luck to that.

And then, just before the weather report, she heard the name of the person who'd been killed in that morning's road crash, causing her hands to fly of their own accord to her mouth, almost tumbling her mug to the floor.

The day after

Sunday dawned fresh and bright, the rain gone, the sun coming and going as it moved across a pale blue sky striated with white. A stiffish breeze nudged at hanging baskets and dried up the last of the previous day's puddles.

For once Molly cycled slowly, her thoughts sombre after the previous night's discovery. So suddenly it could happen: alive and well one day, in the funeral parlour the next. She'd go to the removal later; Emily had already offered to drive her. Not long since she'd said goodbye to Doug; now she was about to stand beside another coffin.

There was no sign of the yellow van outside Clem's house, no response to the buzz of his doorbell. He wasn't working on Sunday, was he? As she was wondering where to leave the almond fingers a window in the neighbouring house was pushed open, and a man in a vest poked his head out. 'He's gone to London, went a couple of days ago.'

'Oh . . . thank you.' His face looked familiar. Maybe she'd seen him at Doug's funeral. 'Do you know when he'll be back?'

'Didn't say.' The head disappeared. The window was closed.

London, out of the blue. Surely it had nothing to do with their conversation on Tuesday night – he couldn't possibly have been so annoyed that he'd pack his bags, could he?

Could he?

And when was he coming back?

And what if he wasn't? With his father gone, there was nothing to hold him here – and London, even with its sad associations, would surely offer more work possibilities.

If he'd moved back there for good she had no way of contacting him, other than a call to a mobile phone he could choose to answer or ignore. She'd have to find another handyman, one who might not be as obliging, and whose prices might well be higher.

And what about Tuesday mornings? Had he left her high and dry, not even bothering to tell her that she was out of a job? Replacing him wouldn't be a problem – always someone looking for a cleaner – but it wasn't right, if that was what he had done. It was cruel of him, if that was how he was treating her.

She cycled home full of gloom, the bag of almond fingers swinging from the handlebars.

* * *

Christopher stood on the path, bidding goodbye to his mother. She'd stayed long enough to go to mass with him – he'd had to check the times online – but they were skipping their usual Sunday lunch together: she was anxious to get back to Barney, the portly ginger cat she'd left to fend for himself in the house. The fact that Barney would live quite well for at least a week on his own body fat didn't seem to have occurred to her.

'You should be nice to Freddie,' she said. 'She's new to the neighbourhood – she could do with a friend.'

'I *am* nice to her.'

'And she came to the concert,' she went on, as if he hadn't spoken. 'She came to support you.' She reached up and touched his cheek. 'It's you I'm thinking of, Chris.'

'I know.'

'I hate to see you alone.'

'Don't worry about me.' He moved to open her car door. 'I'm fine.'

'Mothers always worry. It's part of the job description.' She leant on his arm as she lowered herself into the seat. Moving a little more carefully each time they met: wear and tear, she called it. 'Well done again on a wonderful performance. I'll give a ring.'

'Drive carefully.'

'I always do. If I'm killed on the road it'll be someone else's fault. Goodbye, dear.'

Back in the house he tipped the leftover croissant into the dog's bowl and washed and dried the breakfast dishes. No sign of Laurie in the garden this morning; still asleep, more than likely, after her late night. Nice of them to come and support the choir though. He should be more gracious.

On the whole he was pleased with how the concert had gone, and relieved that Jane's act of defiance hadn't sabotaged it, like she'd probably hoped it would. Her absence really hadn't had much of an impact on the altos: they'd coped well without her. There had been a few minor pacing blips – he must work on the tenors in September – but apart from that he was happy. They were coming on, they were evolving as a unit. It was rewarding to see.

He made fresh coffee and read the paper, which was full of the usual Sunday mix of news, reviews and celebrity nonsense. He solved all but two of the crossword clues, and failed miserably with the sudoku like he always did. He ate an apple and some cheese for lunch. He watered the houseplants and ironed his work shirts, listening to Lyric FM gone all jazzy. Still only mid-afternoon, and the day felt like it had gone on forever: without the trip to Dublin to fill the middle bit of Sunday he felt discombobulated.

'Come on,' he said, taking the dog's lead from its hook. Might be a match on in the park, pass an hour or two, give him an appetite for dinner.

He paused on the doorstep – an umbrella, just in case? Back to typical Irish weather, hard to know what the day was going to do. He decided to live dangerously and chance it. They headed off at their usual leisurely pace, the dog sniffing at every gatepost, cocking his leg at frequent intervals.

The streets were quiet. A few kids kicking a ball around a garden, a few adults out like himself for a Sunday afternoon stroll. First week of August, families decamped to mobile homes, or gone further afield. His own holidays over the years had been sporadic: the last one was to Croatia, three or four years ago. A couple of days exploring Dubrovnik's old town with its stepped alleyways and giant cobbled squares and massive ancient walls, followed by a week of driving up the rocky coast to Split, dipping into harbours to find freshly caught fish dinners, swimming whenever the urge took him in the cool, clean waters of the Adriatic.

A few years before Croatia it had been the Austrian Tyrol, where he'd tramped along mountain paths and chased thick slices of roast pork with pints of glorious beer. Rome a couple of years before that, to walk among the ruins and throw his loose change into the Trevi Fountain and marvel at how small the *Pietà* was and explore the narrow, earthy-smelling corridors of the catacombs.

He always holidayed alone. For some reason, his mother thought it terribly sad. For him, it was the only way to travel.

They'd almost reached the park when it happened. He was idly watching a thrush, or was it a sparrow, hopping along the top of a hedge, when he heard a high-pitched '*Billy!*' from the opposite side of the street.

He turned and saw Laurie running across the road towards them, beaming, arms outstretched – right into the path of an approaching car.

'*Laurie!*'

Her mother came racing up the path, too far behind to catch her. Christopher didn't think – he dropped the lead and ran onto the road and dived in front of the car to push the child backwards, out of the way. A shriek of brakes, a wild barking, a scream – and then repeated jolts of pain as he was sent rolling and tumbling along the tarred surface—

And then the lights went out, and the music stopped.

* * *

The funeral parlour smelt of the big creamy lilies that stood in white vases in the exact centre of every windowsill. Emily and her mother joined the end of the queue that snaked along the corridor, and shuffled slowly towards the room where the body was laid out.

'Good crowd,' Mam murmured. 'The family would be well known, of course.'

The woman ahead of them turned. A hand on the strap of her bag, every finger with a ring on it. Dark red lipstick straying into the creases around her mouth. A ladybird brooch pinned to the lapel of her beige jacket. 'An awful thing, wasn't it?'

'Shocking,' Mam said. 'I couldn't believe it when I heard.'

'Here today, gone tomorrow. We know not the day nor the hour, do we?'

'We do not, very true.'

Emily stopped listening. They were fifteen or so people away from the door. In a matter of minutes, three or four at the most, she would see him. Her hands were cold, even though the day wasn't. A headache pulsed gently in her temples, the same twist in her gut that she'd felt while she waited for him in the coffee shop.

He hadn't stood her up, hadn't decided against meeting her again. His car had aquaplaned, had slid across the surface of the wet road before slamming into a wall – or so they'd heard from Joan Flahavan three doors down, whose paramedic nephew had attended the scene of the accident.

Car written off, she told Mam. *The whole side of it gone in, Cathal said.*

The queue inched on. The crash had occurred shortly after noon. Emily had been in the charity shop at noon, trying to distract herself, trying take her mind off him. She'd been flicking through rails of clothes while he was spinning out of control towards a wall. She rubbed her cold hands together, trying to warm them.

'I'm a neighbour,' the woman was saying to Mam. 'I live a few doors down from Kathleen. Are you the lady I've seen coming on the bike to her?'

'I am. I read the paper to her every afternoon, two to four.'

Emily switched off again and focused on the wallpaper. Dark wine in colour, wide stripes that ran from floor to ceiling in alternating smooth and knobbly textures. Its thick, heavy quality, too much for the narrow corridor, gave a closed-in feel to the place. She was reminded of a lift that had stalled, a hand reaching for hers. Anchoring her to him.

They approached the room. She could hear murmurs coming from within, see the soft flicker of candlelight on the patch of wall that was visible to her. She drew a mass card from her bag, steeling herself for the sight of him.

They reached the doorway and turned in. The first thing she saw was the closed coffin, flanked at either end by a fat white candle on a stand. A small wicker basket sat on a spindly-legged table by the head of the coffin, overflowing with envelopes: she dropped in hers as she passed.

And there he was, standing at the top of a line of mourners, one sleeve of his dark jacket empty, his left arm trussed in a sling beneath, his face unmarked apart from a graze under one eye. The survivor of the crash that had taken the life of his passenger.

Emily stood silently as her mother embraced him, heard her low words of condolence, his murmured thanks. 'My daughter Emily,' Mam whispered then before moving on, and he turned and looked at her.

She could feel a pulse pounding in her head. His lost expression broke her heart. She held out her hand, not having the courage to hug him. Aching to hug him. 'I'm sorry for your loss.' The words coming out with difficulty, her mouth dry, her breath having deserted her.

He gave her a smile that was terrible in its bleakness. 'Thank you.' His hand was warm in hers, their eyes locked on one another. 'You're cold,' he murmured. She felt a squeeze of his fingers that caused a corresponding clench in her chest. 'Thank you for coming, Emily.'

No, not her name. Don't say her name. Her eyes filled with sudden, stupid tears. She blinked hard and drew her hand from his, and went to move on.

'My wife,' he murmured – and Emily found herself face to face with Jane from the choir.

Jane, in a grey summer coat, her hair newly cut, her make-up immaculate.

Jane, who hadn't shown up at the concert. Jane, who was his wife.

Her hand was extended: Emily shook it wordlessly.

'Thank you for coming,' Jane said, no sign of recognition in her face. Jane, the newest choir member, only interested in getting to know people like Ultan, whose family owned a string of hotels, and Harriet, with her chic little boutique on the main street, and Barbara, whose son had a part in *Fair City*. Jane didn't bother with people like Emily, who checked out other people's groceries for a living.

She moved down the line, shaking hands with strangers, telling them she was sorry about the death of a person she'd never met. When she ran out of mourners she spotted her mother in conversation with a blonde-haired woman who sat in a corner with a little curly-headed child on her lap.

She stood waiting nearby, trying to process what she had just discovered.

He had married Jane, who was pretty and confident. He had stood in a church, or in a register office, and promised to be faithful to Jane, who was self-centred and snobbish, for the rest of his days. He had taken Jane for his wife, his life partner, for better or worse.

He had fallen for her looks, or her sex appeal. For whatever reason, he had picked Jane. Of all people, he had picked Jane, who now had the right to stand next to him at funerals, and everywhere else. Jane, who presumably loved him.

'There you are.' Mam tucked her arm into Emily's and they left the funeral parlour. 'That was Linda – she's my new person on Wednesdays. Turns out she's Jane's sister; small world. And Martin and Jane – can you credit it? There's a pair I would never in a million years have put together.'

They reached Emily's car and got in. As they drove off, a few drops spattered the windscreen. She thought of him going home afterwards with her, when everyone had finished shaking his hand.

Martin and Jane. Husband and wife. A mistake, he'd said, but still together.

'Did you notice the little boy sitting on her lap?' Mam asked.

They drew up at a red traffic light. 'Whose lap?'

'Linda's.'

A woman crossed the street in front of them, unfurling an umbrella. Emily tried to remember a child. 'Curly hair?'

'Yes, that was Paddy. It was his party that was cancelled.'

'Oh. Yes.' The lights went green: they moved off.

' . . . Did he remind you of anyone?'

Emily glanced at her. 'I didn't really see his face.' She'd barely noticed him; only the curls had registered.

'No . . . I thought he looked like Philip. Same eyes. Same chin.'

Philip. She recalled her brother's phone call, over a week ago now.

'Gave me a bit of a land,' Mam said, 'the first time I saw him.'

Emily shot her another glance. 'Did it?'

She gave a little laugh that sounded forced. 'I actually got it into my head that Philip was his father. I thought that was why he left. I know it's ridiculous.'

Not ridiculous. By his own admission, Philip had been having an affair with a married woman. Another thought struck her: was Mam working for the wife of a drug dealer – or was that part even true? 'Is there a husband on the scene?'

'No – she told me it hadn't worked out with Paddy's father. That was why I thought Philip might— But then I discovered that Paddy was turning four yesterday, not five. So I was wrong, he couldn't be . . . who I thought he was.'

Something, a new note in her voice, made Emily look at her again. She was facing straight ahead, her expression composed – but a single tear rolled slowly down her cheek. 'Your mother can be a very foolish woman sometimes,' she said, dashing the tear away.

She'd thought she'd found a grandchild. She'd thought she'd found Philip's child. Emily reached for her hand and squeezed it. 'You are not foolish.'

'Thanks, love.' Returning the squeeze before she released Emily's hand to find a tissue and blow her nose. 'All over now. End of story.'

The rest of the trip passed in silence. The rain became a heavy drizzle, swished away by the wipers. People walked with upturned coat collars or raised umbrellas. A soft day, damp and gentle. As good a day as any for goodbyes.

At length they arrived. Emily pulled up in front of the house and switched off the engine.

'I'm just remembering something,' Mam said, unbuckling her seatbelt. 'I was cleaning in Linda's house a few weeks ago, and Jane called in. I didn't meet her, I heard her, and I recognised her voice. I thought they were just friends.'

Emily waited, watching drops running down the windshield.

'She was telling Linda about – an affair she was having.'

An affair. She turned to regard her mother.

'Oh, I shouldn't even be saying it—'

'Jane was having an affair?'

'Yes – but the thing is, she called him Christopher. *Our* Christopher. At least, I'm assuming it was our Christopher. You know the way she was at rehearsals.'

Yes, Emily knew the way she was. *Christopher, do we really have to have all the words off by next week? Christopher, will you go over that bit again please? I keep getting stuck in the middle. Christopher, I left my house in plenty of time, but the traffic was really bad.*

'Anyway,' Mam said, opening her door, 'it's poor Martin I feel sorry for.' She got out. 'Are you coming?'

'Yes, coming.'

They walked into the house together, where the scent of roasting chicken waited to greet them.

* * *

Poor Martin. He'd been lucky to get off so lightly himself – a broken arm, cuts and bruises – but to lose his mother like that was awful. Paula's heart went out to him when she saw him at the funeral parlour, so thrown down and miserable he looked. He should have been at home in bed, instead of having to endure hours of this mournful carry-on.

Crotchety old Kathleen. She knew she shouldn't speak ill of the dead but honestly, the woman wouldn't know a smile if it bit her in the rear end; face on her like vinegar anytime Paula had encountered her. Of course she hadn't had it easy – but did she have to be so grouchy all the time? Couldn't she have tried to make the best of it, appreciate all she did have?

Everyone knew her though, or knew of her. The company had been around for so long, an institution in the town. People respected that, the home-grown family business employing the locals, contributing to the community.

And of course people were fond of Martin. Paula had seen customers and suppliers alike at the removal, people he dealt with honestly, people who'd shown up for his sake, not for his mother's.

She hugged him when her turn came, being careful to avoid his injured arm. 'I'm so sorry, Martin.'

'Thanks, Paula. Good of you to come.'

'Why don't you take a few days off, when this is over?' she suggested. 'We can manage.'

'I might. I'll see how I feel.'

She moved on to the wife. Look at her, not even bothering to pretend she was upset. Wondering how soon she could get away, more likely. 'Thank you for coming,' she said coolly to Paula, and it was all Paula could do to remain civil, to sympathise when clearly the woman wasn't in need of sympathy.

Outside she spotted Molly Griffin getting into the passenger side of a small blue car. She wondered what connection she had with Kathleen, or maybe it was with Martin. Must get her a card to say well done for the concert, leave it out with her money on Thursday.

Back home she removed the dress she'd put on for the funeral parlour and changed into T-shirt and sweat pants. She checked emails and found nothing. She mooched about the apartment, flicking on the television, surfing through the channels, flicking it off again. She buttered crackers and ate them standing at the window, looking out at the rain that had decided to come back.

She'd never been a fan of Sundays. What was that song . . . something about Sunday making a body feel alone? Without a family, without a partner, the day felt too empty, too hollow. And today she didn't even have Tony, who was gone to his newest nephew's christening. He'd invited her along, but since the broken engagement his mother had been a bit funny with Paula. Best not to draw that on her.

She licked butter from her fingers, brushed crumbs from her T-shirt. Enough of this: she'd walk to the cinema, see what was on. She took her umbrella from its plastic bucket inside the door and headed for the stairs.

As she reached the lobby her phone beeped. She pulled it from her pocket: a new email. She clicked on her inbox and saw Jenny's name.

Paula
I'm so sorry but I have to cancel tomorrow: I've been asked to help out with something that I can't really say no to, and I'm not sure how long it will take. What about Tuesday, same time, same place?
Jenny x

Another delay: someone clearly didn't want them to meet. *No problem*, she typed. *See you Tuesday*. She added an *x* and sent it off, and left the building.

The paths were shiny with water, and busy with people emerging from the nearby cinema. She threaded her way through them, thinking about the following day. If she switched her lunchtime hair appointment with Dervla to Tuesday she might as well attend the funeral she'd been planning to skip. She'd like to be there, for Martin.

She reached the cinema. Her choices were bleak: nothing French, no charming period drama, none of her preferred actors.

Sod it. She bought a ticket for a thriller that had just started, and a Diet Coke. She fumbled her way up the aisle of the darkened auditorium, praying she wouldn't sit on anyone's lap.

The day after that 

The nice nurse was Annie. Annie plumped his pillows without being asked, and offered him chocolates from the box she'd just got from a grateful departing patient. Annie found him a toothbrush and paste, and came to say goodbye when she was going off duty. *See you in the morning, Christopher*, she said. *No wild parties now when my back is turned.*

The other nurse was Sadie. Sadie crimped her mouth when he looked for water, and left him waiting fifteen minutes for it, and told him not to be a baby when he winced as she'd cleaned and dressed his various wounds.

The lady who'd brought him a dinner tray at some hour the night before, whose name wasn't displayed on a lapel badge, was lovely. *I've given you an extra spoon of mash*, she'd told him in a stage whisper, *to keep your strength up*. After the meal – of which the mash had been the only edible component – she'd reappeared with a giant teapot.

Goldgrain or Ginger Nut with your tea, pet? He'd asked for Goldgrain and she'd returned with Ginger Nut, but she was so cheery and smiling he'd said nothing – and to tell the truth he couldn't have cared less.

What did biscuits matter when you'd seen your life flashing before you – or you would have, if you'd had the time? Laurie's cry, her advance onto the road, his headlong unthinking dash to save her: all had happened in less time than a blink. Nothing flashing before him, no chance for memories, or regrets.

He might have died. It might all have been over in an instant, in the middle of an ordinary Sunday afternoon. His whole life, such as it was – his childhood and adolescence, his early dreams of making it as a musician, his time with Heather, his university years, the career he'd wandered into, the choir he'd founded – all of that might have been wiped out in the second or two it had taken for him to leap to Laurie's rescue.

He might have died. Every time it hit him – and it kept hitting him – the realisation was astonishing. The fact that he hadn't died, that he'd escaped relatively unscathed, was equally astounding. True, his hip and thigh sported a darkening bruise the size of a small country from where the car had struck him, and he was cut and grazed and stiff and sore from head to toe after the subsequent thumps and jolts he'd endured – but all things considered, he'd been unbelievably lucky.

He hadn't broken or fractured a single bone, not even a tiny one in a finger. The tests and X-rays he'd undergone in the hours that followed the accident showed his spine intact, his skull undamaged. Thanks to the lightning reflexes of the driver, who'd swerved in the right direction at the right instant, Christopher had been hit by the car's wing rather than head-on: the blow had certainly been hard enough to bruise, but hadn't done any lasting damage.

The driver's name was Eamon. He and his wife Judith, also

in the car at the time, had been on their way home from the brunch they always treated themselves to after Sunday mass. He had dim memories of someone holding his hand as he came round, of something soft being eased under his head, of a voice telling him an ambulance was on the way.

That was us, they'd told him later. They'd followed the ambulance to hospital and sat in the waiting room until a doctor, some hours later, had allowed them to look in on Christopher, who was groggy by then from painkillers.

I thought I'd killed you, Eamon had said.

He did – and I did too. We got the fright of our lives. How are you feeling?

They'd looked to be in their sixties. They'd been so apologetic and anxious that Christopher had found himself taking on the role of comforter.

They're letting me home tomorrow – they're only keeping me in for observation, because of the concussion. Really, I'm fine. It wasn't your fault, you did everything you could.

They'd left, still apologising, when Sadie had thrown them out, and Christopher had fallen asleep almost immediately afterwards. And now it was morning, and everything hurt when he moved. He felt like he'd been run over by a series of steamrollers, but he was still alive, he was still here.

After a breakfast of thick lukewarm porridge and warm, limp toast, Annie reappeared, back on duty. She carried a copy of the local newspaper, and she was beaming.

'Guess who's made the front page.'

'What?' His jaw complained when he moved it.

She handed him the paper. 'You should be very proud, Christopher.'

Hero was splashed across the page, above the head-and-shoulders photo of him that featured in the supermarket's company brochure. With growing dismay he read: *37-year-old businessman Christopher Jackson is today being hailed as a hero after risking his life to rescue a young neighbour yesterday afternoon.*

Dear God. He skimmed the rest of it. It was all there: Laurie's dash, his reaction, the arrival of the paramedics, all couched in mortifyingly dramatic phrases. How had the paper learnt of it?

Towards the end of the piece he got his answer.

The mother of the child, children's author Freddie Lobowitz, said her little daughter was shaken but physically unhurt after the incident. 'It all happened so fast: Laurie just took off when she saw Christopher's dog, and I wasn't quick enough to stop her. I'm so thankful to Christopher for the brave thing he did.'

'By the way,' Annie said, 'your wife phoned just now. She'll be here as soon as she can – she's coming straight from the airport.'

Wife? Airport? He lowered the newspaper and stared at the nurse.

'One of your neighbours phoned her with the news last night. She must have got such a shock: she took the first flight home she could get. You should have said, when we asked if there was anyone you wanted us to contact.'

He understood the words, but they made no sense. He wondered if maybe they'd missed a brain injury after all, if the fact that he was married had somehow fallen out of his head.

'She's been trying your phone all night: I told her you must have lost it in the accident. Hang on to that paper, she'll be delighted to see it' – and off she whisked, not giving him time to admit that he couldn't quite recall who his wife was.

He reached, wincing, into the drawer of the locker by his bed and drew out his phone, which he hadn't lost, which was still working despite its shake-about in his pocket. Battery half full, no missed calls. None of this made sense. Who had claimed to be trying to reach him, who was flying in from God knows where to see him?

He thought of Heather in London – and dismissed the idea as soon as it occurred. She couldn't possibly have come across this news article; he was pretty sure the local paper didn't stretch to an online edition. And of all people, Heather was the last woman in the world to pretend to be married to him, or to rush to his bedside even if he was dying, which he most certainly wasn't.

Could it be Jane? She might have seen the article, might have been stricken by a qualm of conscience after missing the concert – but again he discounted it. Jane wasn't the compassionate type – and even if she was, she wouldn't invent some off-the-wall story to see him, she'd just barge in. Nothing for it but to wait and see.

He wasn't waiting long.

'Christopher!'

He turned. So did the other five patients in the room. She stood in the doorway, dressed in a long, shimmery green dress and clutching a brown paper bag. She hurried towards him, her dress billowing out behind.

'Christopher – God, look at your poor face.'

He hadn't seen his face. Just as well, by the sound of it. He took in her bloodshot eyes, the dark smudges beneath, her ghost-white cheeks, the messy bunch of her hair. She looked small and terrified and hollow, as if someone had scooped the life out of her; so utterly unlike her usual cocky self he was astonished that he'd recognised her.

She stood by his bedside. 'Christopher, do you know who I am?'

'What? Of course I do.'

'Oh, thank God.' Searching the outline of his prone form. 'Can you walk? What have you broken?'

A turquoise pointed thing was sticking out of her hair; he decided to assume it was deliberate. 'Nothing's broken, just cuts and bruises. Did you tell them you were my wife?'

'Christopher, I had to – I figured it was the only way I could get them to let me in at this hour.' The words rattled out of her: he could hardly keep up. 'I phoned a bunch of times yesterday but I could get no information when I said I was a neighbour – this bitch of a nurse, pardon my French, kept telling me you were having tests and stuff. I thought you were brain-damaged – I thought I'd find a vegetable lying here. You knew it was me, right, when they told you?'

'How would I know it was you? And why did you say you were flying in?'

'I figured I'd better tell them I was on business overseas, or they'd wonder why I hadn't shown up yesterday. I said I was in France; I figured I'd better not make it too far away. I told them I'd been trying your cell phone – I would've if I'd known your number.'

He had to admire her ingenuity. He should have guessed it was her: who else would have dreamt up that cock-eyed story?

'I wanted to come in yesterday,' she went on, words still almost knocking one another over in their hurry to get out, 'but I couldn't leave Laurie – thanks to you she wasn't badly hurt, just some cuts and scratches where she fell on the road, but she was real shook up. I had to bring her home right away – I couldn't hang around to see how you were. She thought you were dead. I told her you weren't, even though I didn't know till I called the hospital.

'She took an age to fall asleep when I put her to bed – I had to sing her a million songs. And then when I went to bed myself I couldn't sleep – kept thinking you still might die. Jeez, I'm so glad you're not seriously hurt, Christopher.'

She sank onto the side of his bed, coming into contact with his bruised hip and causing him to yelp in pain. 'Oh my God, I'm so sorry—' She leapt to her feet, almost dropping the brown bag. 'Are you OK? What did I do? Do you need me to call a nurse?'

'No, I'm fine – just a little tender. You can sit, but try not to touch me.'

'Oh, Jeez.' She stayed standing. She drew in another shaky breath, let it out again. She seemed as tightly wound as a clockwork toy all set to launch. 'Christopher,' she began, and stopped, pressing her lips together. A little pink washed into her face. She seemed unable to continue.

'How's Laurie today?' he asked, feeling that some effort on his part was called for.

'She's fine. I dropped her to playschool. I wanted to keep her at home but she said no, she was dying to show off her scratches.' She blinked rapidly several times, took a few deep breaths. 'Christopher, you have no idea—' She broke off, shaking her head – and then to his alarm she burst into sudden loud tears. She dropped the bag onto his locker and gave herself up to sobbing. 'Christopher,' she wept, her hands fluttering about him, looking as if they were searching for a place that was safe to land. 'Christopher,' she cried, his name apparently the only word she could manage.

She wailed without embarrassment, noisily and messily, mouth gaping, nose running. He was taken aback by the intensity of her outburst, and mystified as to its cause. Despite her revelations of the other night, they hardly knew one another. Six weeks ago they hadn't even met – surely the sight of him a bit roughed up shouldn't have brought her to the edge of hysteria.

'Hey—' He hoisted himself slowly upwards, conscious of their rapt audience, afraid that Sadie might reappear at any minute and tell her not to be a baby. 'Hey, ssh, please don't cry, look, it's OK, everything's OK. I'm going to be fine.'

But she bawled on, face crumpled and red. 'Sorry,' she sobbed, 'I'm – suh-sorry, Chris-Christopher, it was – just so – so – so—' She broke off, overcome by a fresh onslaught of tears. He wanted to pull the curtains, let her cry without the benefit of an audience, but they were frustratingly out of his reach, so all he could do was sit and wait helplessly for the situation to resolve itself while she cried and cried.

To his relief Annie arrived at length with a box of tissues, presumably having heard the commotion. 'Now, Mrs Jackson,' she said, pressing the box into Freddie's hands, 'he's fine. I know you got an awful fright but he'll be grand. Didn't I tell you we're letting him home today? You'll be able to look after him yourself.'

Freddie nodded, tears still streaming. She yanked out a fistful of tissues and blew her nose forcefully.

'Cup of tea?' Annie asked. 'I'm sure I could organise one.'

'Thank you,' she managed to say, blotting her face with more tissues. When they were alone again she drew in a tremulous breath and attempted a very small, very damp smile. 'I hadn't the heart to tell her I can't abide tea, Christopher – you'll have to drink it when she's not looking.'

'I'll see what I can do,' he promised, vastly relieved that she'd regained control.

She lowered herself carefully onto the edge of the bed. She took several more ragged breaths, looking down at her hands – and then she lifted her head and met his eyes. 'Listen to me, Christopher,' she said, in a voice that was low and still a little wobbly. 'Listen to me, because I have got to say this to you. As long as you live, you will never know what you have done for me. Never.'

Her cheeks were blotched, her eyelids puffy and raw-looking, the tip of her nose bright red. And oddly, there was something . . . arresting about this version of her, something softened and real about her.

So intensely green her eyes were, with chips of blue, or turquoise.

'I might have lost her,' she went on, ignoring the single new tear that spilt out and rolled down a cheek. 'That terrifies me so much—' She inhaled sharply, the remnants of a sob, and reached out to the hand that was closest to her, and touched it, light as a butterfly, with the tips of her fingers. 'You saved the most precious thing in the world to me, Christopher, and for that, you have my undying gratitude, whether you want it or not.'

He felt uncomfortable in the face of her intensity. 'I did what had to be done, that's all.'

'Oh shush, Christopher,' she replied, almost crossly. 'You did a wonderful thing and I won't let you say otherwise. You are a brave and wonderful man.'

She hadn't been crying on his behalf. Her tears had been for herself: they'd been a release, a washing-away of the shock and the terror that Laurie's brush with death had caused, the might-have-been horror that must have kept her awake all night. She was calmer now, she'd let it all go.

'Tea?'

He hadn't even heard her approach, the cheerful lady he'd met yesterday. She carried a tray with a pot and two cups. 'I was told you might need some,' she said, addressing Freddie as she set it on the locker. 'I hope he showed you the paper. We all had a read.'

He'd forgotten about the paper. The tea lady indicated it, folded on the bed. 'You should be very proud of your husband.'

Freddie took it up and unfolded it. 'Oh my,' she said, eyes widening. 'Christopher, you never said anything about this. I knew nothing about it.'

She deserved an Oscar. He watched as she scanned it. 'I know it was you who told them.'

She looked up at him, the picture of innocence. 'Me? I was in France, remember, darling? It must have been the mother of the child you saved – look, they have a quote from her here. Thank you so much,' she added to the tea lady. 'I'm so glad to see this. He's always far too modest.'

She was beginning to enjoy herself, he could see it.

'Such a shock you must have got, poor thing.'

'Oh, I really did, you have no idea.'

'Bet you can't wait to get him home.'

'I certainly can't. My hero.' Looking at him fondly. 'We're gonna have a big party when he's all better.'

'Good idea.'

Time to call a halt. 'Maybe we could pour the tea,' he said. 'I'm sure you're dying for a cup.' Their eyes met again: a mischievous flash in hers. Hadn't taken the old Freddie long to reappear.

'Of course, darling.' She lifted the pot, and the tea lady withdrew – no doubt to tell everyone what a wonderfully supportive wife he had.

'I'm guessing your mother doesn't know about any of this,' Freddie went on, filling one cup, ignoring the other. 'She was gone home, right, before it happened?'

'She was, yes.'

'You gotta call her, Christopher, before someone else does. Someone's gonna tell her, and it should be you.'

She was right. Ireland being the tiny place that it was, it was surely a matter of time before his mother heard about it. Better for her to get the true version from him.

'And you gotta show her this' – tapping the paper – 'next time you meet.'

'Maybe.' No way.

She regarded him sternly. 'Show it to her, Christopher. Believe me, this is something a mother would love to see.'

'Maybe, I said.'

'I'll take that as a yes – but just in case you forget, I'll hang on to my copy.'

She was impossible. He wanted to be annoyed – but for some reason it was more mild amusement he felt. Must be the painkillers, taking the edge off him.

She got to her feet. 'I'm gonna come back and give you a ride home when you're all set. I'm gonna ask that nice nurse to give me a call.'

'What? There's no need for that – I can get a taxi.'

'Are you kidding me? In your delicate condition? No way. Anyway, Laurie's dying to see you. We've been looking after Billy, by the way. He slept in our kitchen last night – and he didn't poop, mercifully.'

'Thanks.' He was slightly wary of this new devotion. Was she going to become his best friend? Was he going to have her dropping in at all hours, eager to show him some more of her undying gratitude?

'Don't worry, Christopher,' she said, as if he'd spoken aloud. 'I'm not gonna invade your territory – I know how much you value your privacy – but you will get regular cookie deliveries. Here's the first.' She presented the brown bag. 'They're yesterday's, made before . . . everything happened, but they'll still be good. And I'll be happy to help you into the bath until you're well enough to manage yourself.'

God almighty. 'What? No – I don't need your help.'

She smiled. 'Gotcha. Your face. So easy.'

After she'd left he opened the bag and drew out one of her offerings, and had it with his tea. He tasted nuts again, and nuggets of dark chocolate, and cranberries. Regular cookie deliveries he could probably live with – and Laurie in his garden, and occasionally in the kitchen, wasn't something he objected to either.

And he supposed it wouldn't kill him to have coffee with her mother once in a while. He liked a decent cup of coffee when he could get it.

Cawfee.

He took a second cookie and left it by his cup. He manoeuvred himself out of his bed and offered the bag to his neighbour.

'Pass them around,' he said. 'Home-baked. Pretty good.'

He took his phone from the locker and called his mother and filled her in. He assured her that he was fine, and that Laurie was fine, and that everything was fine. 'I'm only telling you because I didn't want you hearing it from anyone else.'

'But you must be injured – you're in hospital.'

'Nothing's broken. I'm just a bit battered and bruised, and I'm going home today, as soon as the doctor signs me out.'

'How are you getting home?'

' . . . A neighbour is collecting me.' He might get away with it.

He didn't. 'Freddie?'

'Yes. She's insisting.'

'I'm coming down. I can stay as long as I'm needed.'

'Mother, there's really no—'

'I'm coming down, Christopher. I'll be there in a few hours. I'll bring dinner.'

He gave in. When she called him Christopher, argument was futile. 'There's a bit in the paper,' he said. As long as she was coming, she was going to see it.

'About you? What paper?'

'The local. You can read it when you come.' She'd enjoy it: how could he deny her that?

After he hung up he sat with the phone in his hand.

He could have died. It kept swinging back at him, like a ball on a length of elastic that's attached to the bat in your hand. He could have died without doing the one thing that would make his mother truly happy, far happier than a few lines in a local paper ever could.

He went into his contacts.

He pressed his brother's name. He listened to a phone ringing in London.

* * *

The envelope had been stuck to her locker door with masking tape. *Emily*, it read, in handwriting she didn't recognise. She glanced around: nobody was nearby. She pulled off the tape and ripped open the envelope and slid out the card that was inside.

Congratulations, she read. It was written in gold lettering above a wildly applauding cartoon crowd. She opened it.

Well done to you – I was at the concert on Saturday night. You were fantastic.

And underneath, *Tony (the butcher)*

Tony.

She turned it over: no sarcastic PS on the back. Nothing at all that would suggest it was another of his jokes – but it had to be a joke.

He'd been at the concert: she couldn't believe it. Charlotte mustn't have spotted him, or Ian. They'd surely have mentioned it.

She slipped the card back into the envelope and stowed it in her locker. She pinned her name badge to her blouse and went out onto the shop floor, where the only topic of conversation was Mr Jackson's heroic act, which had landed him in hospital.

She walked towards the meat counter, stopping some distance away. Joke or not, she had to thank him. She watched him serving a woman, saying something that had her in peals of laughter. Always the comedian – but they all seemed to enjoy it. Who wouldn't like to meet someone who made them laugh?

She waited until he was free. He looked up at her approach, and she braced herself. He smiled, brows lifting, as if she was the surprise he'd been promised. 'Emily.'

Emily, not Emmy. Today she wasn't an award. 'Thank you for the card,' she murmured, feeling her face getting warm. Hoping to God Charlotte wouldn't suddenly appear.

'Not at all.' He gave a small laugh. 'I have to admit I was dragged there by a pal, but I really did enjoy it. You been in the choir for long?'

'Since it started, about eighteen months.'

'Wish I could sing – I'm like a bag of cats.'

She smiled. 'I'm sure you're not.'

'I'm sure I am. And Mr Jackson is in charge of it – that was another surprise. You heard about what happened him.'

'Yes, awful.'

'So I suppose the choir will be on a break now for a while?'

A beat passed. 'Actually, I'm quitting it,' she said.

Eyebrows shot up again. 'Yeah? Leaving the choir? Why so?'

'Just . . . I think it's time to move on.' A customer approached, wheeling a trolley. 'I'd better get to work.'

'See you later then,' he said, lifting a hand.

It was the longest conversation they'd had. He hadn't poked fun at her once, hadn't begged her to go for a drink with him.

Nice of him to send the card. Surprisingly nice.

She collected her float and made her way to her usual spot. She logged on to her register, and shoppers immediately began drifting towards her.

She smiled hello to the first and began scanning the groceries that floated towards her on the conveyor belt.

It was over. Whatever they'd found, or thought they'd found, was over now. Meeting his wife, realising it was someone she knew, had been shocking. It wasn't the fact that he was married, because she'd known that. It was coming face to face with Jane. It was shaking hands with the wife of a man she'd met in secret, a man she'd kissed, and realising it was someone she knew. It brought it out into the open: it shone a light on it and showed it up for the pathetic thing that it was.

The news of Jane's affair had been another revelation – but in a way it was almost beside the point. The point was, Emily had been right to decide to put a stop to her encounters with Martin, and wrong to go to the café to tell him in person. The accident, dreadful as it was, had achieved some good in preventing him from turning up – for who was to say she wouldn't have weakened if he'd begged her not to stop seeing him? Who was to say how quickly after that she might have become his mistress?

She'd fallen for a married man, like so many before her. Whatever the state of his marriage, and however he might feel towards Emily, he and Jane were still man and wife, and Emily deserved better than someone else's husband. She was worth more than that.

Telling herself that, believing it, made it easier to let him go. He would still invade her head from time to time, but she would wave him on. He was behind her now, part of her past.

She was finished with the choir too. There was no room for it in the future she was planning, the future she'd already begun to put in place with the email she'd sent off the other evening, after coming home from the concert and the pub. If the response turned out to be what she hoped for, if she passed through the subsequent steps, immense changes would follow, changes that exhilarated and terrified her – but she was determined. She was resolute.

It was time. It felt right. All that remained was to tell Mam.

At one o'clock, she and Charlotte left the supermarket and sat on a bench out the front with their sandwiches. The day was grey but dry, a small breeze bringing with it the possibility of a shower.

'What about our hero?' Charlotte peeled the cellophane from her ham and tomato on wholewheat. 'Wouldn't have thought he had it in him.'

Charlotte didn't have a high opinion of Christopher: she considered him distant and stuck-up. Emily wondered what she'd say if she knew about him and Jane. 'It was a brave thing to do,' she said.

'You'd find something nice to say about Hitler,' Charlotte said, lifting the top slice of bread to peer inside. 'You'd like how tidy he kept his moustache.'

'I would not. I hate moustaches.'

She'd say nothing of her plan to Charlotte for the moment, not until she was sure how it was going to go. As she ate, Emily watched a woman manoeuvring a squirming child into a trolley seat. 'Charlotte,' she said, 'I met someone.'

In the act of taking a bite, Charlotte halted. 'You what? A man?'

'Yes. I . . . really fell for him, but—'

'Emily, that's wonderful! I'm so—'

'Charlotte, he was married – he *is* married.' She paused. 'It's over now. It never got off the ground, to be honest. But there was . . . feeling on both sides.'

'Oh, Emily, why didn't you tell me?' Charlotte set aside her sandwich and wrapped an arm around her shoulders. 'Oh sweetheart, I'm so sorry.'

'Don't be. I'm alright now. I will be alright.'

'Now you listen to me.' Charlotte tilted her head so it touched Emily's. 'There's someone waiting for you out there,

I know there is. I thought there was nobody for me, and then Ian came along. I *know* you'll meet someone, I just know it.'

Someone waiting for her. She wanted so much to believe it. Someone waking up each morning wondering if today was the day they'd meet. It was a lovely thought, and she wished it could be true, but she knew it might not be.

On Thursday she would turn thirty. All the more reason to make changes, to take a step in a new direction at this numerical landmark.

'Let's go out tonight,' Charlotte said. 'Let's eat out – we never do that. We can go straight from work, have a drink somewhere and then choose a place.'

She thought about it. Why not? She could ring Mam, tell her to pick up a takeaway. 'Thanks. That would be lovely.'

They finished their lunch. They returned inside as the first shower of the day began.

* * *

Christopher had been a shock. Dervla had rung earlier, just as Molly was finishing up in his house, assuming him to be gone to work as usual.

Have you seen the paper?

No.

Your choir director was knocked down, saving a little girl. At death's door, it sounds like.

What? I'm in his house right now, he's my Monday person – so of course Molly had immediately rung Christopher, to be informed that not only was he nowhere in the vicinity of death's door, but being sent home from hospital that very afternoon. *I'm a bit stiff and sore but nothing serious. A few days in bed will sort me out.*

That's a relief. Actually, I've just finished cleaning your house.

Oh God – today is Monday. I forgot. Will you call later in the week for your money?

Not at all – next week will be fine. I'm heading to a funeral now, but would you like me to drop anything in on the way back, any food or whatever?

No need, thanks. My mother's insisting on coming to stay. She'd heard a small laugh. *You know what mothers are like.*

She did indeed.

After hanging up she'd changed into the navy trousers she'd brought along with her, and set off for Kathleen's funeral. On her way she'd stopped at a shop and picked up a copy of the local paper, and read all about Christopher's heroic act, and decided to forgive him his affair with Jane. Nobody was perfect.

In the church she'd sat beside distant cousins of Kathleen's and told them, when they'd enquired, of her connection with the dead woman. *She wasn't the friendliest*, one of them had remarked, and Molly had replied that she'd had her challenges, and said no more. Whatever about speaking ill of someone when they were alive – and God knows she'd done her share of that where poor Kathleen was concerned – once they died you left them alone.

And now the mass was over and she was at the graveside, waiting for the prayers to begin. The crowd was substantial, another good turnout. She thought back to Doug's funeral just a few weeks before, the neighbours he'd known all his life who'd turned up to bid him goodbye – and inevitably Clem's face slid into her head. Clem, whom she might never see again.

Martin looked disconsolate, shoulders hunched, arms

folded, as he waited to put his mother into the ground. She eyed Jane standing next to him. Red jacket over black trousers, heels not designed for graveyards, looking just as bored as she had the day before. It occurred to her that she'd never once encountered Jane at Kathleen's house, and had no memory of Kathleen ever mentioning her daughter-in-law's name. A fairly safe bet, she thought, that the two hadn't got on.

'Molly.'

She turned. 'Paula – what has you here? You knew Kathleen?'

'I did. I work for Martin – I'm his secretary. I met Kathleen the odd time when she came into the office, but I'm really here for him. What's your connection?'

They chatted until the prayers started. Afterwards, they walked to the cemetery gates together.

'Are you going back to the house?' Paula asked. 'I hope you are – I told Martin I would, but I won't know anyone if you're not there, and I'm not great at small talk with strangers.'

Martin had issued a general invitation at the church – *a bite to eat at my mother's house* – but Molly didn't relish the thought of going back to the place she'd approached with dread so many times.

'Please come,' Paula said. 'It'll only be for a few minutes – I just want to show my face. Unless you're rushing off.'

'Not really – but I have my bike.'

'We can throw it in my boot,' Paula said, so they did.

The house looked the same. Hard to believe Molly had been there just three days before, reading the paper as she always did. Kathleen had been the same as ever, giving out about new shoes that had skinned her heels, little imagining that she had less than a day to live.

According to the distant cousins, mother and son had been returning to town from a hotel on the outskirts when the accident had occurred. *He took her out for brunch every Saturday morning,* the cousins told Molly. *He was very good to her*. In all the time Molly had been calling to her, Kathleen had never once mentioned the Saturday excursions.

The front door was open: this was Molly's first time to enter the house through it. As they made their way past the people in the hall, Paula said, 'I need the loo,' and Molly directed her to the one beneath the stairs, and told her to follow her to the kitchen.

Platters of food filled every worktop. The air was heavy with the scent of coffee. Molly spotted Jenny, Kathleen's main carer, washing cups at the sink as people milled around her. 'I've been drafted in to help,' she told Molly. 'I couldn't say no to Martin when he asked.'

Jenny had done her penance with Kathleen. She'd been there as long as Molly, a month longer. 'What will you do now?' Molly asked, finding a tea towel.

'Oh, the agency will find me another place easily enough. Molly, you don't have to do that – get yourself something to eat. The kettle's nearly boiled again, or there are drinks in the sitting room, if you'd prefer.'

'I'll give you a hand for a few minutes. How's your mum?' A broken ankle that had meant a week off work for Jenny, much to Kathleen's annoyance.

'Much better, thanks. Back to her old self. Little did I think when I headed to Mayo that I'd never lay eyes on Kathleen again.'

Molly dried a cup, placed it on the worktop with the others. 'Never know what's around the corner.'

'Indeed we don't.'

'Hello.'

Paula had found them. Molly made the introductions. 'Jenny looked after Kathleen. Paula is Martin's secretary. Maybe you've met already.'

Neither of them responded. No handshake, no word, just stood staring at one another. Odd. They might have met and not hit it off. Molly wasn't sure what to do with the silence, so she picked up another cup and began to dry it. Stay out of it, whatever it was.

'Your surname wouldn't be O'Brien, would it?' Jenny asked eventually.

'It would,' Paula replied. 'Where's your red carnation?' – and for some reason they both began to laugh. For the life of her Molly couldn't see the joke.

'We were due to meet,' Jenny explained. 'It's complicated.' The kettle came to the boil: she drew her hands from the sink. 'Martin and Jane are in the sitting room, if you want to meet them.'

'I'd rather help out here for a bit,' Paula said. 'Want me to make tea?'

'Do so – teabags in that caddy.'

'We weren't staying,' Molly said, looking at Paula. 'We were just going to show our faces.'

'You go ahead, Molly – I'll be fine here.' Paula pushed the lid onto the pot. 'Thanks for coming with me.'

'No problem.' She was missing something, definitely. Paula, who'd professed to being no good at small talk with strangers, looked to be settling in for the afternoon with someone who'd been a stranger up to two minutes ago. 'Right so, I'll be off then.'

'Here.' Jenny rummaged in a drawer, pulled out a roll of freezer bags. 'At least take home a few sausage rolls. I had one a minute ago – they're delicious.'

Molly took the sausage rolls and stowed them in her bag. She fought her way into the sitting room and said hello and goodbye to Martin, who looked like he could sleep for a week, poor creature. 'Thank you for all your help with Mum,' he said, clasping her hand in his. 'She really appreciated it, even if she didn't show it.'

'Not at all. I was happy to do it.' A white lie she'd surely be forgiven.

'And . . . say hello to Emily for me.'

'I will.' Nice of him to remember her name. She left the house without looking for Jane. She wiped rain from the saddle of her bike and set off in the direction of Clem's house.

She wasn't going to beg him to forgive her – far from it. She was calling only to find out if he was back from London, to see if she still had a job as his cleaner. That was all.

She'd come prepared. She'd written him a stiff little note last evening, in case there was still no sign of him.

Clem

Your neighbour says you're in London. I wish you'd told me you were planning to go. Since I don't know if you're coming back I'll take it you don't need me any more on Tuesdays, unless I hear otherwise from you. You have my number.

If you are gone for good, I'm disappointed that you left without saying goodbye. I thought we were friends. I understand that you were upset by what I was trying to do, and I suppose I should have minded my own business and not tried to be a matchmaker. But you should be flattered that I thought you might suit Emily, not offended. In any case, I've decided you'd be all wrong for her now.

Yours sincerely

Molly

She wasn't a writer. It was the best she could do. If nobody was at home she'd put it through his letterbox and forget about him.

The yellow van wasn't there: no point in ringing the bell then. She posted the note and turned her bike around and climbed up, and pushed off.

'Molly!'

The call startled her, made her wobble as she jammed on the brakes. She planted her feet on the ground and looked back, and saw him emerging from the house, her note in his hand. 'You nearly made me fall off.'

'Sorry.'

Blue jeans, bagging at the knees. A grey T-shirt she'd seen a million times – didn't he ever get anything new? 'I was told you were in London.'

'I was,' he said. 'I'm back. Will you come in?'

She didn't move. 'Where's your van?'

'Gone to the van graveyard. It finally gave up on me.'

Hadn't shaved in a day or two, a mix of brown and grey stubble darkening his jaw. 'I phoned you,' she said, 'lots of times.' She could hear the sharp edge to the words: he must too.

'Did you?'

'You know I did. You must have seen my missed calls.'

'Actually,' he said mildly, 'I didn't. I dropped my phone into a bucket of wet cement last week.'

' . . . Oh.' Not ignoring her then. Not aware of her calls.

She switched tack. 'You said you'd come to the concert. Why didn't you come? Why did you just up and go to London? I thought you were gone for good. You might have told me.'

A beat passed. He seemed to be studying her. 'To be honest,' he said, 'I didn't think you'd be that bothered if I didn't show up.'

'So you went to London just to spite me, because you were sulking about Emily. Was that it?'

'I went to London,' he said then, in the same mild tone, 'for the anniversary. I go every year. It didn't click, when you mentioned the concert.'

The anniversary. His wife and child he must mean, that anniversary. She'd been thinking the worst of him when he'd been remembering his dead family.

'Come in,' he repeated. 'I'll make tea. Or coffee.'

She couldn't, not after laying into him like that. 'I'm on my way home,' she said. 'From a funeral. I should—'

'Who died?'

'Nobody you know. The woman I went to in the afternoons.'

'The one you read the paper to?'

'Yes.'

'Was that the car crash outside the town?'

'Yes.' Pause. 'So you still want me to come on Tuesdays?'

Another pause. 'Will you not come in, Molly?'

But some stubbornness made her stay put. 'Do you or don't you want me to keep coming? It's a simple question. I need to know, otherwise I'll have to find someone new.'

He looked down at his navy sneakers, ran a hand across his stubbly jaw. She could hear the rasp of it. 'Well?'

He looked up again. 'Molly, I'd prefer to do this inside—'

'Just say what you have to say.'

'I'm leaving,' he said. 'I've decided to move back to England.'

She stared at him, her anger setting in again.

'Look,' he said, 'it's got nothing—'

'I can't believe you're being so – so – *childish*.'

He frowned. 'What?'

'Just because I tried, in my innocence, in an attempt to help my daughter, just because I thought you and she might – I thought you'd appreciate me trying to— Look, I was just trying to help, and maybe I should have kept my nose out, but I don't deserve to be – I don't deserve for you to act like I've ruined your *life*.'

'Molly, it wasn't—'

She swept on: 'I can't believe you're packing up and *moving* over such a tiny thing – were you even going to *tell* me, or let me turn up here in the morning and find the place locked up and me without a job? *Were* you?' There was no stopping her now. 'I thought we were *friends*, but clearly all I am to you is your cleaning lady.'

'Of course you're not – and I was expecting you tomorrow. I'm not going for another while. I *was* going to let you know.'

She felt spatters of a fresh shower: she ignored them. A couple approached on the path, the man wheeling a buggy. 'Friends tell one another what they're doing – they don't sneak off like thieves in the night.' Belatedly she remembered the reason for his trip to London. 'I mean, obviously you had good cause to go when you did, but to *move*, to up sticks and just *go* because you're annoyed with me—'

'Molly, would you ever listen to me?'

She wouldn't. She was past reasonable discussion, way past it. She grabbed the handlebars and hoisted herself up on the saddle, throwing a glare at the passing couple, who quickly looked away. 'You can just bugger off to London then,' she hissed. 'See if I care. Good riddance to you.' She pushed off, managing another precarious wobble before pedalling off furiously.

The worst of it was, she thought, flying past lampposts and parked cars, narrowly missing a pedestrian who darted out between two vans and then had the gall to shout at *her*, the really ridiculous part of it was that she couldn't quite figure out why she was so angry with him. So he was moving back to London: so what? It wasn't as if they were joined at the hip, it wasn't as if she didn't have other friends. Yes, she was annoyed that his decision to move seemed to have been prompted by her matchmaking – but she shouldn't be *this* cross, should she? She shouldn't want to thump him as hard as she did right now, should she?

The rain continued. By the time she got home she was wet through. She plucked an envelope from the hall floor and dropped it onto the phone table without a glance. She slammed doors, banged things around in the kitchen. She stomped upstairs and changed, towel-dried her hair but didn't bother looking for her comb. Let him go to London – let him go to Timbuktu if he wanted: she'd manage fine. Dropped his phone into cement, my foot – did he think she'd come down in the last shower?

And why did he *always* have to look like someone you'd throw a coin to? Would it kill him to buy a few decent things to wear? They were as well off without him, better off. Emily had had a lucky escape – much more sensible not to marry at all than be saddled with such a contrary old bugger.

She sat glumly at the table, looking out at the rain. Ate

half a sausage roll without enthusiasm, sipped tea she didn't want. A few minutes after three: the rest of the afternoon and evening stretched ahead of her, no rehearsal to look forward to.

Her phone rang. She saw Emily's name.

'Hello there.'

'Mam, Charlotte asked me to go out to dinner. There's a pizza in the freezer, or you could get yourself something from Mario's.'

Great – on her own for several hours. Still, Emily could do with a nice meal out. 'That's fine, love – enjoy yourself. See you later.'

As she was dragging the vacuum cleaner from its home under the stairs – might as well freshen up the place – the doorbell rang. What now? She attempted to pat her tangled hair into some kind of order as she went to answer it.

'Hear me out,' he said, as soon as she opened the door.

He was soaked. T-shirt stuck to him, hair plastered to his head, water dripping from him onto the mat.

'What are you doing here?'

'You didn't give me a chance,' he said, 'so I had to come after you. Will you hear me out?'

Didn't look like she had much of a choice. Tempting as the notion was, she couldn't very well slam the door in his face. She stood back and he stepped in. He bent and undid his shoelaces. 'My socks are clean,' he said, stepping out of the sneakers.

They might be clean but they were also as wet as the rest of him. 'Did you walk here?' she asked.

'I did. Quicker than waiting for a bus.'

'Haven't you a raincoat?'

'I couldn't find it. I think I might have left it on the plane.'

He was a disaster. 'Stay there,' she ordered. Upstairs she took two bath towels from the hotpress and threw them over the banisters to him. In Philip's room – untouched since his departure – she rummaged in the wardrobe and found an old pair of slippers and some socks. Forget anything else – Clem was half Philip's height and twice his width.

He just about squeezed into the slippers. She draped his socks over the back of a chair and stuffed his sneakers with last week's *RTÉ Guide*.

After a vigorous towelling his hair stood upright on his head. She handed him her comb. 'I suppose you want tea.'

'I don't. I'm sick of tea.'

'Coffee then?'

'Nothing,' he said, standing in the middle of the kitchen, holding her second best towel. 'I just want to explain things.'

She looked at him, torn between exasperation and curiosity. Hadn't they said all that they needed to say – more than they needed? What could possibly be so important that he'd had to trudge through the rain to explain? Serve him right if he caught his death.

'You'd better sit down,' she said, but he made no move.

'The thing is,' he began, 'I wasn't mad at you for trying to . . . put me and Emily together. Not mad, more – disappointed.'

'Why?' she demanded. 'You didn't think she'd be good enough for you?'

He shook his head. 'It wasn't like that at all, Molly. There isn't a thing in the world wrong with Emily. The man who gets her will be lucky – but it won't be me. I'm all wrong for her.'

He stopped. Kept looking right at her, so she felt obliged to look right back.

'You're cross with me,' he said.

'I am. I'm cross that you're moving to London over this.'

He smiled. She didn't. 'Molly, I'm not moving because of this – at least, not in the way you think.'

What was he talking about? What other way was there?

'See,' he went on, 'it seems to me that you wouldn't be cross if you didn't care whether I went or stayed. It looks to me that you might be a bit bothered if I wasn't around any more.'

'What? Well, of *course* I'd be bothered – I mean, I've got used to— Look, you can't just up and leave when you're— It's not fair to people who—' She seemed to have forgotten how to finish a sentence. She could get the first part fine, but then they ran away from her.

'Hang on,' he said. 'Just let me have my say here. For . . . a long time after I lost my wife I thought that part of my life was over. I let myself go, I stopped caring what I looked like – and of course I drank. The thing was, I didn't expect to meet someone again, I thought there was only one woman for me, and I'd already met her.'

He stopped. She started to say something, but he raised a hand to silence her.

'And then I did,' he said. 'I met someone who was really . . . good. A proper good decent person. And I knew she didn't see me the way I saw her. I knew she just saw me as a friend, someone she could call when she was in trouble. I should have said something maybe, or asked her out, but I was too long out of the habit, and I didn't have the courage. So I bided my time, to see if she might change her mind about me – and for a while there, I began to think there might be hope.' Another small smile. 'And then,' he said, 'she told me she was trying to match me up with her daughter.'

Molly's mouth fell open.

'You can see,' he said, 'how that might have come as a bit of a blow. I decided then that with my father gone there was nothing to keep me here anymore, and I could work just as well in London as here. I met up with a few of my old buddies when I was over at the weekend: I think they'd have me back.'

'Clem.'

'But then, when you turned up at my house today, and got so cross when I told you I was going away, it got me thinking. It made me wonder if maybe I'd got hold of the wrong end of the stick or something – if maybe you *did* like me, and just didn't know it.'

'Clem.'

'So I decided I had nothing to lose if I followed you home and said what I maybe should have said a while back, and then at least there'd be no more wondering. And if I'm wrong about this, and you're just cross because you're losing a handyman, or because I didn't tell you or something, or because you think I'm just going off in a huff, well, at least I'll know I gave it my best shot. If I'm wrong I'll just keep going with my plan and move back to London.'

'Clem.'

'The thing is,' he said, 'you've got under my skin. I can't seem to do anything without thinking about you while I'm doing it. I was always delighted when you rang up – it made my day, even if you were only looking for me to put a new lock on a door, or fix a loose floorboard. And when you started cleaning for us, I used to like the thought of you in my house, going from room to room, leaving your mark for when I got home.'

His face, gone all pink.

'And the day you called me when you came off the bike, I was happy that I was the one you turned to. And being invited here for dinner, sitting across the table from you, it made me imagine what it would be like if . . . and that time we were making the sauce, or making a bags of it more like, it felt *right* between us, it just seemed like the way it should be . . . and then, later on that same night, you said about wanting me and Emily to get together, and I thought that was that.'

He ran a hand across his head, mussed up the hair he'd just combed. 'Anyway,' he said, 'that's how it is. So now you know.'

Now she knew. While she'd been imagining him with Emily, he'd been picturing a whole different scenario. Was he right? Did she like him that way, and not realise it? She was older than him, maybe a whole decade older, but that didn't seem to worry him. Imagine him gone, she told herself. Imagine not having him at the end of a phone. Imagine never laying eyes on him again.

She couldn't. She couldn't imagine life without him in it.

It made her angry to think of it.

'I've started walking,' he said. 'Believe it or not, I used to run. I ran a lot, I did a few marathons, but I couldn't run to the end of the road now, so I'll try walking for a while and take it from there. And I'm watching what I eat – well, I'm trying to be a bit more sensible. I know I've a long way to go, but I've made a start. I don't know if it's making any difference – I don't have a weighing scales – but I think it is.'

He was walking, and watching what he ate. He was doing it for her.

A second passed, and another few. He looked down at the towel, or maybe at Philip's slippers on his feet. He was waiting for her to say something. She had to say something.

'It's true I don't want you to go,' she said. 'I don't like the thought of you moving away, and it's not because I'd have to find a new handyman, it's not that. It's that I like the thought that you're *there*, a mile and a bit down the road. I like the thought of you just being there. You, not the handyman. You. It would just be . . . weird if you weren't nearby.'

He looked like he was considering this.

'Maybe you could put off going to London,' she said. 'Maybe give it a few months.'

'I could do that,' he said, 'if you felt it was worth a try.'

'You might take me out to dinner. We could start there, see how that went.'

'We could try that.'

'You'd have to shave, and wear something decent.'

He smiled then. 'Yes, ma'am.'

'And if you got another van you'd have to keep it fairly clean, if you expected me to sit in it.'

'I might rise to a taxi for a night out.'

'That would be good. But in the meantime you need to get home and change out of those clothes before you get pneumonia. Hang on to the socks. Philip won't be needing them anytime soon.'

'I'll be fifty,' he said, 'in a few weeks. Just so you know.'

Fifty. Only seven years younger than her. Seven years wasn't much at all.

On the other hand, he was twenty years older than Emily. Twenty years was a ridiculous gap.

At the door she put her arms around him, and pressed. He was a bit damp, but he felt solid. He felt like someone who'd still be there tomorrow. He wasn't much taller than her, only an inch or so; they fitted in well. She took her time about letting him go.

'Do you still want to come and clean?' he asked.

She thought about it. 'It might feel a bit funny. What do you think?'

'Come tomorrow,' he said. 'We can play it by ear.'

Play it by ear. It didn't sound like a bad plan.

She closed the door behind him. On her way back to the kitchen she spotted the envelope lying face down on the hall table, the one she'd thrown there earlier without looking at it. She picked it up and turned it over and saw a New Zealand stamp, and her name and address in Philip's writing. She tore it open and found two photographs, and a ten-dollar note, and a letter saying sorry, and a return address.

* * *

'He wrote,' she said, her face alight. 'Philip wrote, he sent a proper letter. And we have an address for him now.'

Rushing out to the hall as soon as she'd heard Emily's key in the lock. Not even giving her a chance to take off her jacket, not asking her how the dinner with Charlotte had gone. Waving a page at her, looking happier than she had in a long, long time.

'And he sent money,' she said, 'and photos. And he's sorry – well, you can read it yourself. Isn't it wonderful?'

Emily hung her jacket on its hook. She took the letter, a single sheet, and skimmed over her brother's words silently.

'I wanted to ring you and tell you, I was dying to tell you, but I said I'd wait till you got home, so you could read it for yourself.'

He'd written, against all her expectations. He'd kept his

word, maybe for the first time in his life. Certainly for the first time that she could remember.

'Isn't it great? We have an address now. We can write to him.'

She looked up, regarded her mother's happy, happy face. 'He sent money?'

'Ten dollars – but it's a start. And photos, come in till you see the photos. He's too thin.'

He did look a little thinner in the photos. His hair was shorter too, his skin darker. He wore a black T-shirt and loose cream shorts that came to his knee, and flip-flops. The snap had been taken from too far away to make out his expression properly but it looked to her like he was smiling. That, or squinting at the sun.

'And this one,' Mam said, thrusting it at her.

A close-up, a better view of his face. More weather-beaten, lines spidering out from the corners of his eyes. On Thursday he'd be thirty, like her, but she thought he looked older. His looks, at twenty-nine, had started to fade. He wasn't going to age well.

'Aren't you pleased?'

She lowered the photos, regarded her mother again. 'Yes, I'm pleased.'

'You don't look it. I thought you'd be happier.' Her wide smile dimming. 'It's what we've been waiting for, isn't it?'

In the end, that was all it took. A few lines of nothing, no mention of work, or his living situation, a feeble apology for having cleaned her out – *sorry about the money, I just needed to get away* – and a promise to pay her back, which if he did it ten measly dollars at a time would take a decade or more. Throw in two photos, and just like that he was the golden boy again.

The injustice of it stung her, like it had stung all through her growing-up years.

'You'd forgive him anything, wouldn't you?' she asked.

Her mother's smile vanished completely, like Emily had wiped it off. 'What? Ah, Emily, don't be like—'

'You never saw any bad in him.' A quiver in her voice but she kept going. 'You always gave him another chance, you let him away with everything. It wasn't *fair*.'

'Now that's not—'

'And now he writes a letter, and he finally gives us an address after five years of *nothing* – and he sends you ten dollars, and you wipe the slate clean.'

'Emily—'

'You always preferred him.'

There.

It was out.

It sat between them in the kitchen, ugly and real. Emily swallowed hard, trying to push down the lump in her throat. Trying to stop the tears that were making her eyes burn, demanding release.

'Emily,' Mam said gently, putting a tentative hand on her arm. 'Emily, pet, I can't believe you thought that.'

Emily looked mutely at her, still trying hard to keep from breaking down.

'I did let him off,' Mam said. Slowly, as if she was thinking it through. 'You're right. I was far too soft on him. I suppose I didn't want to admit that he was . . . the way he was, and I was too foolish, or too proud, to let anyone help. But whatever he did he's still my son, and I still love him. No matter what he does, that won't change. It'll never change.'

She shook her head, her eyes never leaving Emily's. 'But,

love,' she said, in the same soft, deliberate voice, 'I never preferred him to you, not for a single second. I love you differently, it's true, because you *are* different – for twins, you could hardly be less alike. Philip broke my heart nearly every single week. You never gave me a moment's worry.'

She gave a small smile. 'He took more of my attention, that's all it was. You were so good, so little trouble, I suppose I didn't feel you needed me as much – but I promise you were just as precious to me, you *are* just as precious to me, and I'm so sorry you didn't see that. I should have made it plainer. I should have given you more time.'

A beat passed. They stood close together, searching one another's faces.

'Do you believe me?' Mam asked.

'Would you have been as upset if I'd left the way he did?' Emily asked in return – but instead of the answer she was expecting, Mam gave another shake of her head.

'Emily, love, it would never have happened. You'd never have gone off the way Philip did, you'd never have hurt me like he did. You'd have told me – and even though I'd know that I'd miss you terribly, I'd have sent you with my blessing if it was what you wanted. I only ever wanted the two of you to be happy.'

Now was the time, she realised. She'd been going to wait but now was the perfect moment. 'I have to tell you something,' she said. 'I have to tell you what I'm thinking of doing.'

She sat Mam down at the table. They talked.

* * *

Lying in bed, he couldn't keep the smile off his face.

Play it by ear, that's what they were going to do. It sounded good to him.

The way she'd hugged him, really tightly.

You might take me out to dinner, she'd said.

He should have shaved. He should have had a wash and changed his clothes and scraped the stubble off his face – but he couldn't stop to do any of that, or he'd have lost his nerve. He'd had to just follow her home, walk after her in the rain. He'd had to get it off his chest, say it out and see what happened.

Nothing might come of it. He knew that, he wasn't stupid. She might decide after all that she wasn't interested. He might be back in London this time next month, or in six months' time, trying to forget all about her.

The way she'd hugged him though. So tightly.

He fell asleep sometime after two, still smiling.

Four months later

'Will we have a whiskey?'

Paula put her shocked face on. 'It's seven in the morning.'

'But it's Christmas Eve.'

'You'll turn me into an alcoholic.'

'Christmas Eve.'

In the end they compromised, and ordered two coffees and two Jamesons from the air hostess, and they drank Irish coffee with UHT milk instead of softly whipped cream, thirty-two thousand feet up, at a few minutes past seven in the morning.

They were going to Gran Canaria for ten days, to lie in the sun and make up life stories about their fellow tourists. They were running away from Jenny's mother and Paula's parents, who preferred not to have their Christmases upset by things they'd rather not dwell on.

They were planning to eat pizza for Christmas dinner, or maybe pasta. Something Italian anyway – they both felt Italian suited Christmas. And they were going to ring in the New Year in a hot tub if they could find one, with cocktails if they could swing it. And Paula was going to teach Jenny how to swim, or at least how to put her face in the water without thinking she was going to drown.

And when they got home, Jenny was going to move her things into Paula's apartment, and as soon as they could organise it they were going to invite Molly Griffin around for dinner, because Molly was claiming all the credit for bringing them together, and they hadn't the heart to tell her she hadn't really.

Paula had had dinner in Tony's house the night before. They'd exchanged presents, and she'd made him swear not to open his till Christmas Day.

I'm glad you're happy, he'd said, and she'd thought back to the time they'd been engaged to one another, and she'd been trying to convince herself she was happy, and feeling nothing like she felt now.

You will be too, she'd promised. *I'm sure of it. Keep me posted.*

Five minutes after she'd got home he'd phoned her to thank her for the sweater: brat. His present to her was still wrapped at the bottom of her suitcase. She knew what it was – she'd admired some earrings, knowing he needed a bit of help – but she was waiting till tomorrow to open it. She could keep her word, even if he couldn't.

'To us,' Jenny said, lifting her paper cup. 'Our first Christmas.'

Their first Christmas. Paula tipped her cup against Jenny's, imagining all the Christmases yet to come, all the happiness ahead of them.

* * *

By eight o'clock she and Frances had rinsed and cooked ten kilos of lentils for the dhal, and peeled and grated enough carrots to fill three waiting plastic containers for the salad.

'Let's take ten minutes,' Frances said, so Emily got to her feet, stretching the life back into her cramped limbs. She pulled on the old waxed jacket that nobody owned and everyone used, pulled it on over her three sweaters. Layers were the thing, lots of layers to keep the bitter French winter at bay.

Outside, the morning sky was still edged with darkness, and pocked with a few leftover stars. She balled her hands into fists and shoved them deep down into the coat's pockets. She'd mislaid her umpteenth pair of gloves the day before yesterday. Easy to lose things here, put them down for five minutes and someone else claimed them. No matter: another pair would turn up, like they always did. People, she'd discovered, were very generous.

She walked rapidly across the frozen bumpy ground, her breath coming out in white puffs. She did her usual circuit, past the rows of waterproof tents, round the seven born-again shipping containers that now served as communal spaces for those residents who wished to come and cook on wood-burning stoves rather than take the handout meals that Emily and the other volunteers provided daily. Past the blocks of latrines, and the free shops filled with donated foods, and the women-only area, and the straggle of ramshackle huts that were rudimentary classrooms and health clinics, past the wooden structure where she and the other live-in volunteers slept.

So many lost souls here, so many stories she'd heard since her arrival in September. People fleeing war or persecution or hunger or other danger. Everyone looking for a better life, many risking everything to find it. She'd met people from Syria and Yemen, Iraq and Afghanistan, Somalia and Ukraine and Eritrea, all desperate for help from anywhere they could get it.

She was needed here, that was the thing. She was making a difference each day as she chopped and sliced and grated and cooked, as she handed out plates of steaming food, as she scrubbed worktops and cauldrons and serving dishes. They needed her. That was what she loved about it.

And the little children, with their huge dark eyes and beautiful unbroken smiles, who would clamour around her when she distributed baskets of peeled oranges to the classrooms. The little children, too small, too thin, wearing someone else's clothes that didn't fit, the tiny hands that would tug on her sweater to get her attention. They melted her heart every single day, those innocents born in the wrong place at the wrong time, not knowing that their lives could be, should be, so much better, so much more joyful. They were why she'd come; they were why she stayed.

Fourteen weeks she'd been here, arriving two days after she'd walked into the locker room at the end of her final shift at the supermarket. Ambushed there by a crowd of her co-workers, waiting for her to blow out the candles on a giant cake that said *Good Luck Emily*.

You shouldn't have, she'd said to Charlotte.

I didn't.

Turned out the impromptu party was the work of Mr Jackson, whom Emily hadn't even told about the refugee camp. *Personal reasons*, she'd written in her letter of resignation, not wanting to draw attention to the real one – yet somehow he'd found out.

You must let me know how I can help, he'd said, when the cake was eaten and she was finally leaving. *When you get a chance, send me a list of foods they need and I'll organise something*, and he had. Within a week of him receiving her email, a loaded truck bearing the supermarket logo had arrived at the refugee camp, and had returned once a month since then.

It was kind of him. It was a new side to him that she hadn't seen, either at work or at the Monday-night practices. *The choir will miss you,* he'd said. *You might come back to us sometime,* and she'd promised him she would, realising that she'd miss it too. She'd call to the supermarket when she was home, bring him a present to thank him for his contributions.

Everyone had been so nice to her.

All the best, Tony had said, when she was leaving. *Drop us a line, let us know how you're getting on. We're all proud of you.*

A week after her arrival in the camp, when she got a few free minutes, she'd written to Charlotte. *Tell everyone I said hello. Give them my love. Pass my address on to anyone who wants it.* Knowing that it would be offered to him, leaving it up to him to get in touch if he wanted.

And he had. *Got your news from Charlotte, sounds like you have your hands full. Sending a small bit to help out.* A folded twenty-euro note tucked into the page. *It's not much, but it might do something. Write back when you get a chance, would be good to hear how you're getting on. Let me know if I can do anything else at this end.*

So she'd written back, just a few lines, to thank him for the money. *It was kind of you. I've donated it to the school fund – they're always running out of supplies. It'll be put to good use.*

A fortnight later he'd written again, this time with two fifty-euro notes that he told her had come from a few friends. *I passed the hat around in the pub on Friday night. Sometimes all you have to do is ask, especially after a few pints. I've got another pal on the case too, she knows people in high places. Fingers crossed.*

Funny how people could change. Or maybe he hadn't

changed at all: maybe this was the real him, hidden up to now behind his jokes and his banter.

Are you coming home for Christmas? he'd asked, in his last letter. *I could meet you at the airport if you wanted,* and she'd told him yes, and given him her plane's arrival time, grateful that she wouldn't be depending on a bus on Christmas Eve.

Other money had come too, a large bank draft from a woman she'd never met who said she was a neighbour of Christopher's. *He's told me what you're doing,* she'd written, *and I think it's just wonderful. I got in touch with friends back home in the US, and they all wanted to help.*

Freddie, her name was. *We must meet up when you come home,* she said. *I bake a mean cookie. Christopher is a big fan – he must have gained ten pounds since I moved in next door*. Sounded like they got on well. Maybe he'd moved on from Jane.

Paula had written too. *You might not remember me,* she said. *I'm a friend of Tony's; he told me about you going off to work in the camp, good for you. And we've actually met too – you called to my workplace a while back. You were dropping something off for my boss, Martin Fitzgibbon.*

His name, out of the blue like that, had caused a small constriction of her heart. Martin.

I mentioned you to him, told him where you were, and he insisted on making a very generous contribution on behalf of the company, which I'm enclosing here. He said to say hello.

Emily passed the money on, sent her thanks back via Paula. *We were very grateful to get it,* she wrote, *very generous of your boss. Please pass on our thanks*. Best to leave it at that.

At one she came off duty. She hugged the other volunteers and was driven to the airport by Sam from Australia in the rusty three-wheeled jalopy that someone had donated to the camp.

'I feel guilty,' she said, 'abandoning everyone at Christmas.'

'Don't be daft, we'll hold the fort. You're due a bit of R & R.' Sam worked as the camp's chief gardener, overseeing a group of refugees who coaxed all manner of vegetables from the soil, but if called upon he could turn his hand to most other tasks too. He claimed to be fifty-two but looked forty, and had visited every country in the world, and had a story from each one of them. 'How long you gone for?'

'Five days.'

Mam had wanted her to stay longer, but five days was as long as she could bear being away from here. Anyway, by the sound of it, Mam wasn't exactly on her own these days. Amazing how many times she could drop Clem's name into a conversation when Emily phoned.

She and Mam had grown closer, which made little sense. They lived in different countries, they spoke once a week at the most – but something had shifted between them after Philip's letter had come, after Emily had finally asked the question she'd always avoided, and Mam had answered it.

'You got someone meeting you at the other end?' Sam asked as they approached the airport.

'I have, yes.' And she was quite surprised at the happy little lurch her insides gave at the thought of it.

* * *

'So how was Santa?'

'Good. Mrs Claus is making him shepherd's pie for dinner. She always makes him that on Christmas Eve cos it's his favourite. He's gotta leave here soon so he can get back to the North Pole in time.'

'Is that right?' Sounded like Tony, who'd been replaced temporarily behind the meat counter so he could do duty in Santa's grotto, was taking the job very seriously. 'What did he give you?'

She showed him the doll with the curly black hair. 'You gotta feed her water, and then she pees her diaper. Her name is Emily.'

'Is it? Who told you?'

'Santa.'

It was Tony who'd told him where Emily was heading, back in August when she'd handed in her notice. It was Tony who'd suggested casually that it might be nice for the supermarket to give her a bit of a send-off. It was Tony who'd asked to be released from his Santa duties half an hour early this afternoon so he could collect Emily from the airport.

And now he was naming dolls after her. Didn't take a rocket scientist to figure out what was going on there.

Christopher took off his jacket and draped it over the chair back in the supermarket's recently opened coffee dock. 'What's everyone eating?'

'Cheeseburgers,' Freddie replied. 'We ordered one for you, and some coffee.' Cawfee. 'That OK?'

'That's fine,' he said. 'That's just dandy.'

Things were fine all round. Things had been just dandy for some time now. Ever since the Thing We Don't Talk About, which was what Freddie called it whenever she talked about it, life in general had taken a distinct turn for the better.

Last month he'd met Robert for lunch, when business had called his brother back to Dublin again. He'd said nothing to their mother in advance, not knowing how the encounter would go. He had no idea if Robert had told her they were meeting, but he guessed not. They'd eaten steaks and drunk red wine, and Robert had shown him photos of the newest arrival, Chloë, who'd been born the week before, and of George and Lucy, the earlier arrivals.

As conversations went, theirs had been a faltering affair, not without its awkward silences. They'd stuck to safe topics – their mother, the children, the supermarket, Robert's business and Heather's job – and managed to avoid the serious stuff. There'd been no apologies, no attempts to revisit their fractured history, no emotional embrace on meeting or parting – but it was a start. It was the first step, and the second was to be taken tomorrow, when Christopher travelled to his mother's house to eat turkey and ham with her and Robert's family.

The look on her face when he'd eventually told her about his lunch with Robert – clearly, she'd known nothing of it – and asked if he could join them for Christmas dinner. The look on her face, the softening of it, her eyes swimming as she'd put her arms around him, was worth it. *Thank you,* she'd breathed, but he didn't deserve her thanks for the years of sorrow he'd put her through.

Tomorrow would be interesting, and not a little daunting. It wasn't so much the thought of meeting Heather again, although of course that was part of it. It was all of them: it was sitting around a table for the first time with Robert and Heather, everyone under unspoken pressure to have a good time, to let the past stay in the past. They'd manage it too, if they all wanted it enough.

Uncle Christopher. He could live with that.

He thought Lucy had his mother's smile.

Freddie had helped with presents. *I've never met them,* he'd said. *I have no idea what to get for them* – and instead of asking why he'd never met the relatives who only lived across the Irish Sea she'd taken his money and gone to a department store that had a branch in Dublin, and brought him back three outfits and matching gift receipts.

Everyone wears clothes, she said. *I had to guess the sizes, but if they're not right they can be exchanged.*

Somewhere along the line, somewhere between their first encounter, when he'd literally fallen flat on his face at her feet, and the first time he'd spent the night, or most of it, in her house – almost a month ago now, sneaking out before daybreak, before Laurie woke – she'd become important to him. Who would have thought it? Certainly not him – and yet here they were.

He wasn't entirely sure where 'here' was, or how they'd go in the future. The word 'love' hadn't been mentioned by either of them. She could still drive him to distraction when she put her mind to it; he could still send her stomping home from a visit to his house.

But they made one another laugh, a lot. And they could talk about anything, or sit comfortably in silence. And they could coax one another out of a mood, and hold on to one another in the dark.

No more talk had been made of her plan to revisit the sperm-donor clinic: to date, it hadn't happened. For now, he was content to leave it at that.

And he was making music again. It was coming back to him. He wrote songs about trust and betrayal, about hope and new beginnings and surprises and slow-dawning love. He wrote about how life could pick you up and give you a shake, and make you see all the things you'd been blind to. All the good things you'd forgotten were there. He thought some of the songs were fairly decent. Freddie thought all of them were wonderful, but that was Freddie. She had a pleasant gutsy voice herself, not unlike Dolly Parton's. She could belt out a mean 'Jolene' to the ukulele when the humour was on her.

He wondered how Billy would take to the new puppy that was already installed in Christopher's kitchen, prior to being transferred next door after Laurie was safely asleep. These days, Billy tended to divide his time between the two homes, in much the same way as the human occupants did.

Hopefully they'd all get along. Hopefully they'd figure out a way to make it work.

* * *

It was all his fault.

'It's all your fault,' she said.

'What?'

'It was your idea to get a goose.'

'I just said it might be nice. You didn't have to agree with me.'

'Well, I did agree, so it's your fault. I don't know what possessed me. A *goose*.'

He laughed. He always did that, he always laughed. '*Stop* it. It's not funny.'

He caught her around the waist, swung her off her feet. 'It's hilarious,' he said. 'How can you not see how funny it is?'

'Put me down, Clem Murphy.' The smirk of him: she wanted to slap it off his face – but for some unknown reason she kissed him instead, which took quite a while.

'Listen,' he said eventually, 'we don't have to cook it, we can leave it to Emily. She'll know what to do with it.'

'We are *not* leaving it to Emily. Emily has been cooking for hundreds since she left here: tackling a goose is the last thing she'll want to do on Christmas morning.'

'Well, we'll do it then. How hard can it be?'

They'd found a recipe in a book from the library. The book wasn't modern, far from it – but the recipe sounded simple enough, if you ignored instructions like 'gut the goose and singe off the pin feathers and down'. Potato stuffing was called for, which turned out to be mashed potato with stewed apples and onions and a few other things added in.

The goose had to be boiled first, in a stock that had about fifteen ingredients in it – unless they used a couple of the stock cubes that were still in the press from Emily's time – and then filled with the stuffing and roasted. They could surely manage that between them, while Emily caught up with the sleep that she was bound to be in need of.

And if they got it wrong, if they messed up and burnt the damn bird, or if it came out as tough as a leather shoe, they'd open a can of beans and chuck a few fish fingers on the pan, and the world would go right on spinning, and they'd still have the happiest of Christmases.

'I'll be off then,' Clem said, wrapping the scarf she'd knitted for him a month ago around his neck. Every time he wore it she saw a new dropped stitch. 'I'll give a ring later on to say hello to Emily.'

She hadn't asked him to make himself scarce when Emily was due. She hadn't needed to: he'd sensed that Molly would want her daughter to herself, at least this first night. It was one of the countless things she loved about him, the way he knew without having to be told.

She loved him. It had occurred to her out of the blue, in

the middle of wiping a damp cloth across the windowsill in Linda's bedroom. *I love him,* she'd thought, she'd suddenly *known,* in the middle of a chilly September morning, not long after Emily's departure for France, and about a week before his fiftieth birthday. *I really love him.*

By then they'd had a handful of meals together, a few trips to the cinema, the odd brisk walk in the evening after he'd finished work. There had been no big declaration on either part, nothing more than a hug on meeting and leaving. She hadn't said anything to Dervla, not knowing what exactly to tell her, how to describe what was going on. For some reason, 'dating' sounded a bit ridiculous to her. And before she left, Emily hadn't seemed to notice that her mother had a – what? A *boyfriend*? – so caught up was she in planning her new adventure.

How had it come about, Molly wondered, this feeling of togetherness she was aware of now, this sensation, this conviction, of having found what she'd hardly known she was seeking? When exactly had Clem gone from being a friend to something more?

In many ways he was so different from her husband. Physically they were nothing alike, Danny so tall and gangly, Clem short, and still on the tubby side, despite losing a little weight over the past while. Clem was more forgetful and less impulsive than Danny had been, and more prone to bouts of melancholy. Not in the least musical. More stubborn.

So many differences – but in all the ways that mattered, he and Danny were kindred spirits. He was so good to her, so thoughtful, so generous. He complimented her, brought her little gifts when he called – a roll of the toffees she liked, a pot of cyclamen for the windowsill, a purple biro because she'd mentioned that it was her favourite colour. He phoned her every day, even if they were due to meet later on.

And since then, since her realisation of her feelings towards him, with a little encouragement from her they'd gone a little further than hugs. And since the middle of November, every couple of nights he stayed at hers, or she stayed at his.

There was no talk of moving, him to her house, or her to his. She liked it this way, even though the house seemed so big, so quiet sometimes, without Emily in it. Maybe in time they'd come to a decision about moving in together, but for now this was fine, this was enough.

Dervla approved, when Molly had finally come clean. *He's good for you,* she said. *You've got a twinkle in your eye again.* Emily would approve too, once Molly told her how it was. She'd dropped hints when Emily phoned, scattered his name into her sentences, let it be known that he was about the place – but she hadn't come out and said they were together. News like that needed a face-to-face conversation.

She'd heard other news lately, not that Emily would be interested. Martin and his wife, Martin and Jane, were splitting up. Paula it was who'd told her, when they'd met by chance in the supermarket. *They're getting divorced,* Paula had said. *He's given her his mother's house, and a half-share of the company's profits.* Everyone, it would seem, had their price.

She spotted something yellow poking from under the fridge and bent to retrieve it. Paddy was always leaving pieces of Lego behind him: she found at least one after each of his visits. Tuesday and Thursday afternoons she walked to his school and brought him back here on the bus, and looked after him till Linda collected him.

He called her Molly. His hand found hers as they walked

together, and he sat in her lap while she read to him from the Ladybird books the twins had had as children. His favourite was Rumpelstiltskin, which Philip had loved too.

His father, she'd eventually been told, was French, and had moved back to France when his relationship with Linda had failed, soon after Paddy's first birthday. Reading between the lines of Linda's carefully worded sentences, Molly thought that violence might have been a factor. There had been no contact since then.

The curls had been cut off, to Linda's public and Molly's private dismay. Oddly, the resemblance to Philip didn't strike her half as much when they were gone: now she looked at him and just saw someone else's sweet little boy.

Funny how things worked out.

What time was it? Half five. Emily had called from the airport, a little after four. *Just landed*, she'd said. *Queues everywhere, will take a while to get out. See you soon*, she'd said, sounding happy.

A friend had driven to pick her up, a man who worked in the supermarket. That was all Molly had been told.

Maybe Emily had some news of her own.

She opened her bag and drew out Philip's latest letter, his fourth. Once a month he wrote, just like the postcards, but now she could write back. Twenty dollars he'd sent her the last time, twice what the other three had contained. Slowly he was repaying her, slowly he was making amends. *You don't have to pay me back*, she'd written, thankful that Emily wasn't looking over her shoulder. *I'd much rather you saved it up and came home to see us* – but the money continued to arrive, and she understood that he wasn't planning to come home.

Not just yet. Maybe next Christmas.

He was working, he told her. Shifts at a local bar, some casual work with a furniture removal company. He'd done a few weeks on a building site, but he hadn't liked it. *It wasn't me*, he'd written. He'd also worked briefly with a painting and decorating company, but they'd had to let him go when business slowed down. It didn't sound to her like he was all that gainfully employed, but he was apparently keeping body and soul together so she said nothing.

He hadn't sent any more photos, so she contented herself with the two from his first letter. He looked happy, she thought. Fairly happy. There was no mention of a girlfriend, but that wasn't to say one didn't exist. Maybe he had lots, maybe he hadn't settled for someone special yet.

She'd hoped he'd ring home for Christmas, but she hadn't suggested it. Phone calls would be expensive from New Zealand: he'd have better uses for his money. If she had a number for him she'd use it and bugger the expense – she'd tried his old mobile number countless times in the past – but again some instinct had stopped her asking.

He might surprise her though. He might ring tomorrow, when they were in the middle of trying not to ruin the goose.

She heard a car pull up outside, heard doors opening and slamming. She tucked away the letter and went out to welcome her other child home.

Acknowledgements

Here we go again – another new arrival skidding onto the bookshelves, actual and virtual, another opportunity to thank the many wonderful people who helped it along the way:

Thanks to Gretta O'Shea and her marvellous Unity Gospel Choir Limerick who raised the roof at my last book launch and inspired me to put a choir into this story. (Having said that, any resemblance in Christopher's choir to any UGCL member is entirely accidental!)

Thanks to the ever-friendly Paul, Carolina, Carl and Julie of The Terrace Bar, Playa Blanca, Lanzarote – my home from home when I'm writing in the sunshine. They never fail to have one of my books sitting on the counter when I walk in: bless.

Thanks as always to Ciara Doorley, Joanna Smyth and all at Hachette Books Ireland for their invaluable support and encouragement every step of the way, and to my ever-helpful agent Sallyanne Sweeney of MMB Creative.

Thanks to Hazel and Aonghus for their usual thorough copy-editing and proofreading: nothing gets past them.

Thanks to booksellers in Limerick and beyond whose passion for books gladdens my heart, and who work tirelessly on behalf of us writers. Particular thanks to Colette and team in O'Mahony's Booksellers, and Nora and team in Eason Ireland for their various launches over the years, and to Vickie in NCW Books, Newcastle West who never fails to organise an event to celebrate each new arrival.

Thanks to Frances at O'Mahony's who paves the way for library events and festival appearances, to Julie and all at Limerick's main library for their staunch and continuing support, and to Barry and Chelle in Gallagher's Seafood Restaurant at Bunratty West for their delightful book-related events.

Thanks to Joe and Annemarie at Limerick's Live 95FM, to Mike, Louise, Dominic, Donal and Patrick at Limerick City Community Radio, and to Sharon at West Limerick 102FM for their willingness to have me sit across the desk from them whenever I come looking for a slice of airtime.

Thanks to my family for their constant encouragement: Mam and Dad, down the road from me in Limerick, my sister Treasa in Brussels, my brothers Tomás in Clare, Colm in the Philippines, Ciaran in California and Aonghus here in Limerick.

Thanks to my Facebook and Twitter friends, far too many to mention, who are always there with messages of friendly encouragement, and who share and retweet faithfully when I post book news.

Thanks to Fred and Ginger, my feline housemates, who provide company and amusement (and the odd dead mouse) as I tap at the laptop.

Thanks above all to you, dear readers. Where would I be without you?

Roisin xx

@roisinmeaney

www.facebook.com/roisinmeaneywriter

Author's Note

I've always loved music. I grew up listening to Radio Luxembourg, and I never missed an episode of *Top of the Pops* on telly. My first single was 'Killer Queen', and my first LP was Supertramp's *Crisis, What Crisis?* (Yes, I'm that old.) But my musical tastes extended further than pop: like Molly, I devoured the old musicals, from *Oliver* to *The Sound of Music* to *Thoroughly Modern Millie*, and to this day I know all the words from all the hits. I also love a bit of jazz (especially on a mellow Sunday afternoon) and I'm partial to American country, blues, light rock and bluegrass – and when I'm writing I like classical in the background (can't listen to words; they're too distracting).

I love to sing, and thankfully I can carry a decent enough tune – also like Molly, I'm an alto. Being Irish, I love nothing better than a good old singsong – particularly if the vocal chords have been lubricated with a drop of Guinness. I favour the American songbook when my turn comes around – 'Someone to Watch Over Me' was one of my party pieces for years – and I'm a huge fan of Ella, Nat, Billie, Sarah and everyone who did those wonderful songs such justice.

To my chagrin, I can't play an instrument. I was sent to piano lessons when I was eight or nine, much against my will. I did as little practice as I could get away with, and not surprisingly, I learnt precisely nothing: after six weeks or so, the music teacher (sorry, Mrs O'Regan) advised my parents to stop wasting their money. In my teens I decided I'd like to play the guitar (probably thanks to Janis Ian) but again I lasted only a few weeks: I simply couldn't get the hang of the chords (and probably didn't practise enough either). Now, at my advanced age, I would give anything to be able to sit at a piano and belt out the tunes, but given my congenital laziness, I doubt that I'm going to do anything about it.

I was in a choir once for a few months. I really enjoyed it, but sadly I had to give it up when rehearsals intensified before a performance and took up too much time – I was chasing a writing deadline, and every hour counted. I'm not sure that I'd last a week in Christopher's choir – I think he'd terrify me far too much! My secret ambition, along with having one of the books turned into an Oscar winner and writing a play that makes it to Broadway, is to compose a smash hit song. (I don't ask for a lot really.) Maybe I'll actually sit down some fine day, when I'm in between books, and give it a go . . .

Roisin Meaney

One Summer

Nell Mulcahy grew up on the island – playing in the shallows and fishing with her father in his old red boat in the harbour. So when the stone cottage by the edge of the sea comes up for sale, the decision to move back from Dublin is easy. And where better to hold her upcoming wedding to Tim than on the island, surrounded by family and friends?

But when Nell decides to rent out her cottage for the summer to help finance the wedding, she sets in motion an unexpected series of events.

As deeply buried feelings rise to the surface, Nell's carefully laid plans for her wedding start to go awry and she is forced to make some tough decisions.

One thing's for sure, it's a summer on the island that nobody will ever forget.

Revisit the island of Roone in *After the Wedding* and *I'll Be Home for Christmas*

Also available as an ebook

Roisin Meaney

The Reunion

It's their twenty-year school reunion but the Plunkett sisters have their own reasons for not wanting to attend . . .

Caroline, now a successful knitwear designer, spends her time flying between her business in England and her lover in Italy. As far as she's concerned, her school days, and what happened to her the year she left, should stay in the past.

Eleanor, meanwhile, is unrecognisable from the fun-loving girl she was in school. With a son who is barely speaking to her, and a husband keeping a secret from her, revisiting the past is the last thing on her mind.

But when an unexpected letter arrives for Caroline in the weeks before the reunion, memories are stirred. Will the sisters find the courage to return to the town where they grew up and face what they've been running from all these years?

***The Reunion* is a moving story about secrets, sisters and finding a way to open your heart.**

Also available as an ebook

Roisin Meaney

Two Fridays in April

It's Una Darling's seventeenth birthday, but nobody feels much like celebrating. It's been exactly a year since the tragic death of her father Finn, and the people he left behind have been doing their best to get on with things. But it hasn't been easy.

Daphne is tired of sadness, of mourning the long life she and her husband were meant to share, but doesn't quite know how to get past it. And she can't seem to get through to her stepdaughter – they barely speak any more, so Daphne knows nothing of the unexpected solace Una has found, or of the risk she's about to take.

When Una fails to appear for birthday tea with her family, Daphne suddenly realises how large the distance between them has grown. Will she be given the chance to make things right?

Also available as an ebook

Roisin Meaney

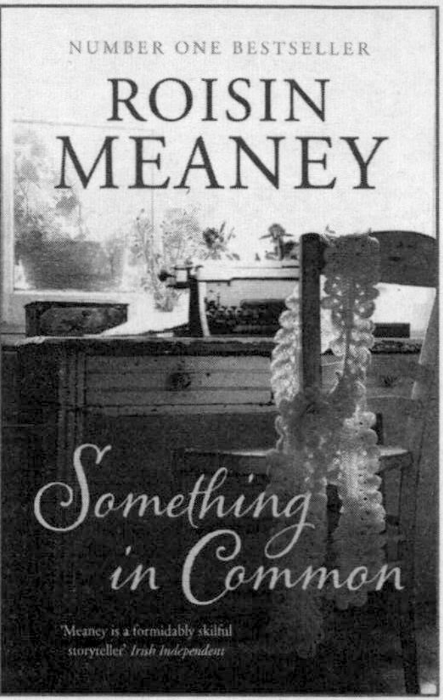

Something in Common

The friendship starts with a letter . . . from aspiring writer Sarah to blunt but witty journalist Helen, complaining about Helen's most recent book review. And there begins a correspondence that blossoms into a friendship which spans over two decades.

As the years pass, the women exchange details of loves lost and found, of family joys and upheavals. Sarah's letters filled with thoughts on her outwardly perfect marriage and her aching desire for children, and Helen's on the struggle of raising her young daughter alone.

But little do they realise that their story began long before Sarah penned that first letter – on one unforgettable afternoon where, during a distraught conversation on a bridge, Sarah changed the course of Helen's life forever.

This is the story of Helen and Sarah, and the friendship that was part of their destiny.

Also available as an ebook

Roisin Meaney

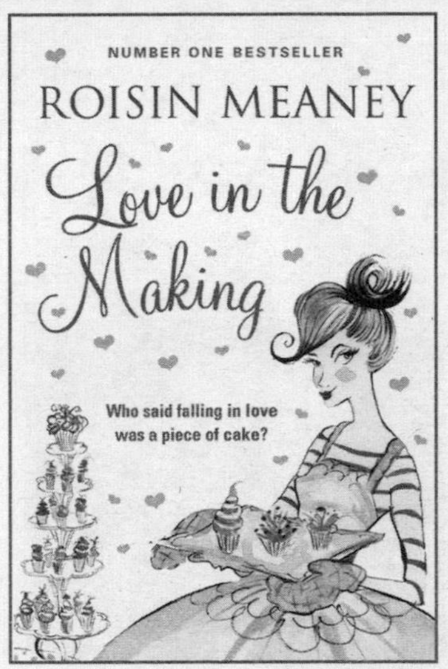

Love in the Making

Hannah Robinson is just about to open the doors to her new shop Cupcakes on the Corner when out of the blue her boyfriend Patrick announces that he's leaving her for another woman. Faced with starting a business on her own, Hannah begins to wonder if her life-long dream has just turned into a nightmare.

So her best friend Adam sets his birthday as a deadline – seven months to make her shop a success, or walk away from it all. And as Hannah immerses herself in early-morning icing, she soon discovers that she's too busy to think about Patrick and his now pregnant girlfriend . . . or to notice an increasingly regular customer who has recently developed a sweet tooth for all things cupcake . . .

But while Hannah is slowly piecing her life back together, family friend Alice's is falling apart. Her husband Tom's drinking is getting out of control and things are about to get a whole lot worse.

As the seven-month milestone approaches, Hannah must decide her future. And while she's figuring out what's really important, it becomes clear to everyone that happiness in life, and in love, is all in the making.

Also available as an ebook